FRANC

THE BOOK GAME

A group of old friends reunite in the simmering heat of August for an idyllic week-long retreat.

There is reading by the pool and writing in the shady corners of the garden that surrounds a spectacular eighteenth-century home. In the evenings there are communal drinks, dinners outdoors, midnight swims, games.

But someone is playing a game the others don't understand, meddling with their work and appearing to lurk on the edges of the retreat. As tensions rise, desire and deceit bubble to the surface. By the end of the week, their friendships will never be the same again…

COMING 13 MARCH 2025

For publicity requests please contact
nicola.webb@harpercollins.co.uk

Hardback | 9780008679255 | £16.99

Trade Paperback | 9780008679262 | £14.99

THE BOOK GAME

FRANCES WISE

4th ESTATE • *London*

4th Estate
An imprint of HarperCollins*Publishers*
1 London Bridge Street
London SE1 9GF

www.4thestate.co.uk

HarperCollins*Publishers*
Macken House
39/40 Mayor Street Upper
Dublin 1
D01 C9W8, Ireland

First published in Great Britain in 2025 by 4th Estate

1

ISBN 978-0-00-867925-5 (hardback)
ISBN 978-0-00-867926-2 (trade paperback)

This book is set in Adobe Garamond Pro at HarperCollins*Publishers* India

Printed and Bound in the UK using 100% Renewable
Electricity at CPI Group (UK) Ltd

This book is produced from independently certified FSC paper to ensure
responsible forest management.

For more information visit: www.harpercollins.co.uk/green

Dedication [TK]

'from morn
To noon he fell, from noon to dewy eve,
A summer's day'
John Milton, *Paradise Lost*, Book 4

'We can't behave like people in novels, though, can we?'
Edith Wharton, *The Age of Innocence*

Prologue

Claudia is bleeding, two bright streaks running from wrist to elbow. Ash has an arm around her. They are walking steadily, determinedly, across the courtyard, away from the garden and towards the house. Through the bedroom window, himself unseen, Lawrence watches: dead still, gripped by the panicky lightness of adrenaline, and with a nauseating sense of a transgression that cannot be reversed.

Beyond the courtyard the lawn stretches down to the large pond and the tall poplars that mark the edge of the estate. The window frames the view as a series of rectangles, divided from one another. In the late sunset, each of these scenes looks unnaturally still, as though the garden contains no movement of any kind, as though the living have been expelled, cast out, leaving behind only abandoned objects which, separated from people, are returned to quiescence, frozen in their last moment of drama: a wrought-iron bench, tipped over at the far end of the lawn; a book splayed on the grass by a deckchair; six metal croquet hoops leaning against a stump; broken pieces of a bowl on a white table.

As if in reaction to Lawrence's thoughts, Claudia and Ash stop moving directly below the window. Lawrence leans forward as though he might hear them talking, but no sound permeates the thick glass. He watches as his wife draws her injured arm towards her body and raises her other hand to Ash's face, her fingers just touching his hair. For a moment they stand motionless, and then Claudia lifts her head and kisses Ash's cheek, her hand clasping his face.

Lawrence makes no sound but he covers his mouth with his hand. He sees Claudia turn away from Ash towards the house, for a moment keeping hold of Ash's hand. Until this past week, Lawrence would have called Ash his best, his oldest friend, the person he trusted most, after his wife. He steps back from the window to keep out of sight. As he takes his hand away from his mouth, he notices blood across his own palm, still wet.

Chapter One

Lawrence's office is the largest in College, and he reminds himself of this several times a day. The largest, that is, by volume. By sheer floor footage, Clarke's is slightly bigger – Lawrence has paced it out, taking the keys from the porters' lodge on a Sunday – but he's convinced himself that volume is the fitter measure. The space is extravagantly, pointlessly grand. The previous occupant had owned a harpsichord (although he hadn't played); Lawrence himself has a mobile stepladder for the higher shelves; and the sofa, three armchairs and low desk which sit marooned in the centre have the effect, in their drawn-together isolation, of making the room feel like an outdoor space, a section of a garden. There is a pre-modern unevenness to the wooden floorboards and the limestone window frames. The two large casement windows on the right-hand wall, as one looks from the door, gaze from this second floor across the rounded tops of Cambridge's buildings. The wooden boards are partly covered with a single huge rug, a gift from Claudia on Lawrence's appointment twenty-two years ago. Its edges are fraying, and there are a number of red wine stains, but Lawrence likes the visible decay. He calls it 'historical texture', rubbing his fingertips to his thumb, and hasn't asked for the thing to be cleaned. Two of the walls are lined with tiers of bookshelves that stretch the full length: every space is crammed with books, neat verticals augmented with volumes squeezed on top and these are supplemented with several piles of stacked books on the floor. There are nine or ten books on the chair by the door: this is Lawrence's 'return to the library' spot. Running all the way around the perimeter of the room, snaking across the shelves and under the windows and over the desk, are cards emblazoned with 'Thank you!' or 'Congrats!' or images of famous authors or old libraries or manuscripts or abstract art. Five or six printed invitations to dinners at various colleges are grouped in a cluster beneath a print of medieval Cambridge. Under the casement windows, and so below the view over the rooftops, is a large old wooden desk with a laptop, a mess of papers, jars with pens and pencils, a framed photo of a middle-aged woman standing on a bridge in Venice, another of a teenage boy leaping into a swimming pool with raised arms, and an asparagus fern, thin green shoots tumbling down the side of the desk. A tall glass vase holds three peacock feathers that arc towards the ceiling. Beside it stands a metal trophy, ugly but given its prominence clearly prized, with gold lettering spelling out 'Cambridge University Student Union Teaching Initiative Award 2016–17'.

But the most striking feature of the room is the far wall, opposite the door. The top half of the stone wall has a series of eight leaded glass portals, each the size of a football, cut into the stone, through which Lawrence – or his earlier, fifteenth- or sixteenth- or seventeenth- or eighteenth- or nineteenth- or

4

twentieth-century incarnations – might look down directly into the interior of the college chapel. Lawrence's room was built for the chaplain and the little round windows meant Angell Robert or Thomas Arderne or Aston James (Lawrence had transcribed the names under the heading 'Staircase 11, room 1: 1442–present', sitting snug in the college archives in the first term of the job) could time their dash to the service with the filling of the pews. Lawrence is looking at the rebus cut into the fourth portal, an ash tree and a well for George Ashwell, and imagining his own name represented in glass: notes swelling up from a violin, perhaps. Right now, the chapel, and in fact the whole college, is deserted. It's a Monday morning in the second week of August.

Lawrence is standing with no clothes on.

'You know this is probably the most architecturally complete fifteenth-century room in Cambridge.'

He seems to address the comment to an empty room – that wouldn't be out of character – but a reply comes sharply from the sofa in its centre.

'Jesus, Lawrence.'

American.

'This isn't a tour.'

East coast.

'Will you come back over here?'

The Danby Visiting Fellow in Medieval Studies.

'I have less than twenty minutes.'

Professor Angela V. Olson (University of Pennsylvania).

As Lawrence moves towards the sofa, he catches his reflection in the mirror above the sink in the corner of the room. He stops for a second; turns a fraction.

'Do you know that if I stand *here*' – Lawrence shifts his position a bit, lining things up – 'and look in the mirror, I can see my own buttocks, and also the Wren Library?'

'Sir Christopher's masterpiece.'

'I've been called worse.'

Lawrence is wrapping a used condom inside a tissue which he places in an old envelope he pulled from a desk drawer, the envelope labelled 'Earl of Surrey – images'. He drops it in the bin in the corner of the room.

Angela is lying on her stomach, her elbows propped on a cushion and her chin resting on one hand. The light streaming through the windows falls so that the shadow traces a curve across her back, the lower half of her naked body luminous in the sunshine.

Lawrence stands and looks at her with satisfaction. For the rest of the day, Angela will be outside of this room, walking around the city, working in the library, in meetings, and she will elicit, Lawrence reflects, intense desire from other men; but right now, the object of this desire is here in his room, on his sofa, behind his locked door, belonging to him alone. This triumph gives Lawrence pleasure.

'You look like a goddess. The *Rokeby Venus*.'

Angela rolls her eyes at him and raises herself a little on her elbows.

Clothes are scattered around the room: his shorts, her denim skirt, his checked shirt, her white T-shirt and sunglasses. Angela's bra is draped across *The Intellectual Origins of the English Revolution*.

Lawrence looks at his watch, which he never takes off.

'Lawrence?'

Lawrence smiles, but the smile has nothing to do with anything. It is a placeholder. His head is now elsewhere: specifically, three miles east in Hawton Manor. He had said to Claudia he'd be back by mid-morning with aubergines and mint. He's yet to go to the shops. The guests are meant to arrive by two. He's been insistent enough in his emails about punctuality that he can't be late himself.

Angela can feel his growing distance without looking at him. She shifts her position on the sofa and folds her arms.

And the pool needs cleaning. Skimming and filter. Claudia can do the beds of course. But he has some emails to get through. Then the seating plans with his special quill. He says it out loud: 'Oh God, the seating plans!'

'Jesus Christ, Lawrence, can you just be present? Here and now.'

He steps towards her; sits down on the edge of the sofa; rests a hand on her thigh. 'I'm sorry. Of course. I am here. You look absolutely beautiful.'

'Fuck you.'

Angela pulls herself into a sitting position, sliding away from Lawrence's touch, and picks up her T-shirt and bra.

'Where's my underwear?'

Lawrence looks round, ineffectually. 'I'm not sure. Maybe by the printer?' He's thinking about whether there are enough of the good wine glasses.

'I should just leave it for a student to find. Would that work for you? I bet it would, actually.' Angela fishes behind the printer under Lawrence's desk. 'Narcissus.'

'Angela. *Mon ange.* Don't go.' Lawrence takes the clothes from her and drops them to the floor. One hand traces the length of her spine. 'Of course we have time. I'm sorry. I was being an idiot. Forgive me.'

Ten minutes later, Angela retrieves the rest of her clothes and gets dressed quickly. Lawrence, now lying on the sofa, watches her pick up her bag, unfold her sunglasses and put them on.

Angela says, 'Next time, a hotel.'

'Of course. I'll book us somewhere special.'

'You always say that and you never do. Maybe I'll book us somewhere.'

Panic flickers inside Lawrence. 'But I can't get away this week. I'm hosting.'

'You could come say hello.'

Angela bends down to pull the straps of her sandals over her heels.

Lawrence says, 'I'll see what I can do.'

He pauses for a moment, as if waiting. Then: 'Aren't you forgetting something?'

Angela's hand goes to check the back pocket of her skirt for her phone. 'What?'

'My chapter?'

'Fuck, of course.' She pulls a stack of papers from her bag and puts it on the coffee table. 'I read it on the flight over. In between *Elvis* and *Death on the Nile*. I'll leave my notes to reveal which I thought best. Sorry they're a bit of a scrawl.'

'Super,' says Lawrence, grasping the pile of papers a little too urgently, almost snatching them, reaching for his glasses in a donnish manner, holding the first page close, and forgetting, in his absorption with his own reception, that he is a 53-year-old professor reclining naked before the 55-year-old Danby

Visiting Fellow, forgetting his wife making beds in the spare rooms three miles away, forgetting his son in France, forgetting his friends travelling right now across the country towards Hawton for a week-long writing retreat.

'I can't wait to see what you made of it.'

In the sealed capsule of his train carriage, Ash is dislocated from the world below and around him. The train sweeps past a series of long gardens, back fences flush with the railings guarding the track, which runs along a stretch of higher ground, so that the traveller looks down into the green patches below. Garden after garden flashes by, each empty of people but filled with the paraphernalia of lives: a vegetable patch; a trampoline; a child's bike; a swing. As the houses give way to fields, Ash sees a smudge of smoke on the horizon, which reveals itself to be a bonfire on the edge of a scrap of land, the kind of space that has become the resting-place of unwanted objects, too large to be removed: farm machinery, an iron bedstead, and a caravan. For a moment, Ash can smell its thick smoke, and then the field and the bonfire are gone, along with the familiar scent, surely the product of his memory and not the real fire.

Ash shifts in his seat. Even at this time of day the train is unbearably hot and airless, the windows locked shut and the air conditioning not functioning. Ash tries to adjust his legs into a more comfortable position and opens his laptop on the fold-down table. It's very cramped. The train WiFi isn't working so he connects online via his phone and clicks on the shortcut to *The Guardian* Comment section. His piece on the attainment gap in A-level results between white and ethnic minority students already has eighty-seven comments. Ash has a policy of never looking below the line but he keeps an eye on the numbers: his academic publications seem to be met with silence on a cathedral-like scale so he likes the sense of readers. His editor uses the word 'traction'. He closes Safari and clicks open a desktop folder labelled 'Et in Arcadia Ego' and then a document titled 'Case Studies – Current Draft'. He scrolls through the document until he gets to the last section, which has the heading 'LNA: Plagiarism/ Power abuse'. These paragraphs Ash reads through, until he realises that his gaze has fixed on the screen and he has stopped paying attention to the text: he is looking at pixels, not letters. He runs a hand over his face and checks the time: twenty more minutes till Cambridge.

Claudia pushes through the iron gate in the orchard wall and places her cup on the rickety picnic table beyond it. In front of her lies the swimming pool, shaded at this time of the morning, its surface quiet and still. Claudia unbuttons her dress and folds it over the wooden bench. She walks slowly to the deep end, where she raises her arms above her head and grips the stone edge of the pool with her toes before diving into the water. Its cold bite is all-encompassing, taking her briefly and painfully beyond thought and entirely into the realm of feeling. As she surfaces, heart thumping, Claudia pushes her wet hair from her face and begins a slow breaststroke to the pool's shallow steps, touching the edge with her fingers before turning back towards the deep end and repeating the action, settling into the rhythm of her swim. The cold water, its chill lasting through the heat of the morning, the solitude and the calm green of the trees beyond: these are the things, Claudia tells herself, which keep her sane.

'I'm not saying you're being selfish, I'm just saying it's bad timing.'

Josh, tucking in his shirt, says nothing. He fastens his watch and turns to the mirror, running a hand through his hair until it falls forward to just the right amount. He knows he just has to endure this for a few minutes, and then he's free for the week: it's the price he has to pay.

'It's really bad timing that you're going on this "writing retreat"' – Gemma mimes scare quotes and says the words with sarcastic emphasis – 'now, this week, and it was bad timing last month when you had Mike's stag do, and it's going to be bad timing next month when something else happens, and at some point, at some point, Josh, you're going to have to start putting this ahead of whatever else is happening in your life.'

Josh straightens his collar.

'So, you *are* saying I'm being selfish.'

'No, but it's starting to feel as though it's not actually a priority for you, right now, making a baby together.'

Josh flinches internally at that phrase. Is it the word 'making', or the word 'baby'? He glances at Gemma, who is lying on the bed wearing only a T-shirt with 'PARADISED' printed across the front. A pillow is wedged under her buttocks and her legs are resting up the wall, toes pointing at the ceiling. Her face, looking back at him, is disturbing, its upside-down position lending it a comical, clownish air, forehead rutted and eyes slightly bulging.

'Gem, it is a priority, of course it is. And, at the risk of stating the obvious, we have just had sex. We could be . . .' – he swallows – 'making a baby together right now.'

'I'm not ovulating until Thursday at least. It's highly unlikely that an egg released then could be fertilised by ejaculate more than seventy-two hours old.' Gemma adjusts the pillow and looks at the ceiling. There could be nothing less erotic, Josh thinks, than that sentence. Trying to conceive involved more and better sex, in which Gemma's need for him was urgent and satisfying; the accompanying conversations were not.

'But, sweetheart, the retreat is this week – not next. And it's Lawrence.'

Josh only calls Gemma 'sweetheart' when he's pleading a case.

'I honestly can't see why Lawrence still exerts such an influence. It's like he has you in a spell. You finished the PhD ten years ago.'

'Twelve.'

'And he didn't get you a job.'

'Supervisors don't get their students jobs,' says Josh, putting his wireless headphone case, a phone charger and a power cord into his bag. 'That's not how it works.' Gemma's distance from academia had been one of her attractions when they met at a teaching conference five years ago, and Josh's dissertation on 'T. S. Eliot and the invention of the seventeenth century' (the title had been Lawrence's), and his hopes for an academic career, were long behind him.

'I still don't understand how you can have a system where you write for four years—'

'Five.'

'– for *five years* producing a three hundred-page dissertation which eight people read and then there's no job at the end of it.'

'Eight's actually rather optimistic.'

'I mean: how can that be? Why do people put themselves through that? Masochism?'

'There are jobs. There were jobs. There will be jobs.' Josh zips up the bag like he's concluding an argument. 'Just not for me.'

Gemma's devotion to Josh is such, and her reverence for his intellect is so great, that she can only understand Josh's academic failure in terms of some higher negligence, and her aim falls, commonsensically enough, on Josh's teacher. Why else would Josh, with all his brilliant capacities, not get what he wanted?

Josh had stuck it for three years after the viva, eking out a living on sessional teaching where he was paid £32 for a lecture which took him ten hours to write, and doing increasing volumes of better-paid but demoralising private tutoring for the children of affluent parents preparing for the eleven-plus. He saw his peers get jobs or jump ship to law conversion courses or journalism, or the civil service. He started to see people younger than him get the posts he was applying for. The only ones who held on, waiting for the job which may or may not arrive, were those with family money or an employed spouse, who were able to endure three years on £6k. Josh knew he couldn't wait that long. In job interviews, Josh began to feel a worse version of himself unfolding within as he sat in the waiting room: he was resentful at his failure even before he started the interview, and he began to give answers with the intention of confirming that foreboding. He was in a downwards spiral. On the morning of his 32nd birthday, Josh emailed Lawrence at 3 a.m. and told him he couldn't hang on any more: the money from his mum was gone. 'I feel I've let you down,' Josh wrote, 'but this is no way to live.' Josh had a panicked sense of months spooling past, of time as reels of film falling rapidly to the floor as a wheel turns and turns. This year, when Gemma talked about being thirty-six and wanting a baby, the terms she used brought those images flooding back.

'It's nice of Lawrence to ask me after all this time,' says Josh, 'and there will be a ton of networking opportunities for the film. You know Lawrence's wife, Claudia? She's absolutely loaded. It's her family's place, that massive house they live in. If I can persuade her and Lawrence to put some funding into *Canterbury*, then that's a week well spent.'

'You really think they'll go for it?'

'Perfectly possible. Lawrence has already agreed to be a consultant. He said so. He's not exactly a Chaucer expert but close enough, and the pitch will read better with his name attached. Once this draft of the script is finished, I'm going to ask him to have another look. And that's another thing: if I can do a full week concentrating on the rewrites, it will be done before term starts.'

Lawrence hasn't actually agreed to anything, and Josh knows this, but when talking about the film with Gemma, he's prone to turning things-that-might-be into things-that-definitely-are. He doesn't want to worry her.

'You're obsessed with that bloody film.' Gemma removes the pillow and hugs her knees into her chest.

'Well, we both have our obsessions.' The comment comes out sharper than Josh intends. 'And the retreat is really going to help me get somewhere.'

The switch from academia to teaching had been a natural step for Josh, the rhythms of one academic year sliding into those of another. His attempts at moving into scriptwriting alongside his post at a minor public school in north London have been more disjointed and ever more time-consuming. This increasingly intense work on what even Josh admits can only be a massive long-shot has come at the same time as Gemma's desire for children has grown. The alignment is not a coincidence.

'You're not going to fall in love with some glamorous poet, are you?'

Josh leans over and kisses Gemma on her inverted forehead. 'I wouldn't find anyone I'd swap you for.' The response isn't quite right, he thinks, suggesting a failed search, rather than a desire not to look, but the moment passes.

'And, sweetheart,' says Josh, 'I'm not going anywhere next month. It's September. Back to school. The little cherubs.' He picks up his bag and leaves the room, feeling his pockets for his car keys. 'The little shits.'

'Maybe I could come and visit? Josh?' Gemma's voice follows him into the hallway.

'Visit? No, I don't think so. I don't think it works like that. It's just for writers.'

'I know, but I could come just for the evening, maybe Wednesday, and come straight back here on Thursday morning. Or Thursday night. No one would even have to see me.'

'Gem, no, it just wouldn't work. It would be breaking the . . .' Josh reaches for the right word, 'the atmosphere. The agreement. Believe me, I would love to see you, and I know it's bad timing, but it just wouldn't work. Anyway, I'll have the car.'

'I could get the train? Their house is, what, fifteen minutes from Cambridge station. You could pick me up?'

Josh collects the door keys from the hallway table and sticks his head back around the bedroom door.

'Goodbye, my darling. Have a good week.' Then he adds, bluntly, 'It's all going to be all right, I promise.'

But before Gemma can ask 'What is?' Josh crosses the room to kiss her again. Gemma pats the side of his face at an awkward angle.

Josh says, 'You know I love you. See you when I get back.'

A peacock stalks across the courtyard, its feet picking out a beat to which its head keeps time. For no apparent reason it stops, raising itself erect and cocking its head to one side, as though in response to a sudden sound. All that can be heard is the familiar church clock striking eleven and the distant noise of traffic on the main road. After a moment, the bird resumes its stately progress, following the curve of the cobbles around the wall of the house, its tail feathers trailing behind it over the warm stones.

'You're late.' Lucy watches Neil unhook the rope latch of the front gate and then, as he pushes it open, looks down at her feet, bare and dusty on the bottom step of the stone stairs which lead to her front door. She flexes her toes, delaying the moment of eye contact.

'I think you'll find I'm on time.' Neil checks his watch. 'Yes. Eleven-thirty on the dot. To the minute. Christ, it's hot.' He stops on the path and takes a bottle of water out of his bag, loosening its cap with a click. 'So you see I'm not late.' Lucy's position on the step puts their heads, as Neil straightens up, at exactly the same height. Neil raises his wrist towards her so that the face of his watch is at her eye level and a fraction too close for comfort. Lucy notices the tan line where the watch slips on his arm, the trace of blue veins on the taut skin of his fist. She leans backwards, just a little.

'Neil, we agreed nine-thirty. You're two hours late. Two hours. You can't keep doing this.'

'Doing what? I'm not "doing" anything.' Neil lowers his arm and takes a drink from the bottle before putting it back in his bag. 'And you certainly told me eleven at the very earliest. I made a note of it.' He moves closer to Lucy. At an earlier point in their relationship, he might have reached his hand out to gently tuck her hair behind her ear. But he doesn't, and his closeness has the quality of resistance: a physical threat. He says, 'You must be very tired.'

'I'm fine.'

'You look exhausted.'

'I'm sleeping fine.'

'Washed out.'

'I don't want to talk about this with the kids inside. You should have called.'

Neil holds up his hands in a don't-shoot gesture. 'Let's go into the house and you can take me through whatever comprehensive documentation you've no doubt prepared.'

'I haven't prepared anything. You've got my number. I'll only be at Lawrence and Claudia's. It's ten minutes away if anything happens. I've left the GP's number on the fridge.'

'This is progress,' says Neil. 'One day soon I might even be allowed to tie my own shoelaces.' Lucy hates Neil's continually sarcastic mode. Early on, when they'd just met and in the first year or two of marriage, she'd thought of it as a kind of dry charm. Now it's just a ceaseless undermining of everything. He never stops; there is no moment when the mask falls and the real person behind emerges. Neil follows Lucy up the stone steps and into the hallway of the house he used to live in. 'The last time you went away for a week, you left a fucking manual.'

'Neil!' Lucy admonishes in a whisper. 'The children are in the sitting room. They can hear you.'

'A veritable tome,' Neil says, at the same volume, 'with sectional instructions for each day.' He smiles, amused at his formulation. 'But you always did infantilise me.'

'Why do you talk like this?'

'I'm surprised you didn't include an index.'

'We're not married any more, Neil.'

'We actually *are*,' Neil says. 'Even your quickie divorce is going to take longer than four months.'

'It's not . . .' Lucy begins, then stops. 'Come and say hi to the kids and then I'll get going.'

'You can go now,' Neil says.

'It's good for them to see us together,' Lucy replies, still quietly, 'being amicable.'

'Our children can take reality. We shouldn't lie to them.'

'Neil, they are ten years old.'

'How can you expect me to be amicable when you are literally forcing me out of my own home?'

'For fuck's sake,' Lucy hisses, and watches immediate satisfaction spread across her husband's face like a blush. 'It

18

was you who had the affair, you who said you needed space – not me. I didn't make those things happen. *You* left *me*.'

'No, I left because you made me leave. I didn't want to.'

Lucy continues as though he hasn't spoken, 'And now I am just trying to be an adult and make the best of it, for the kids' sake.'

'As am I. You're not the only one who thinks about the kids.'

'Right.' Lucy steadies herself. 'Do you want to take your bag up before you come through? I made up the bed in the spare room upstairs.'

'I know where the spare room is,' says Neil, pushing open the hallway door so that it bangs on the radiator. 'It's my fucking house.' Raising his voice, he calls: 'Where are my beauties? Daddy's home!' and Lucy hears her children squeal with excitement as she follows their father into the room.

Claudia is standing in the middle of the kitchen. Lawrence is listening, or half-listening, his eyes glancing down at his phone. Claudia says, 'So, Deborah and Lucy are in the annexe bedrooms, and I'm putting the artist woman, Inês, in the spare room, and Miles upstairs, so that leaves Ash in your study, and I guess Josh in Tristan's room? Does that work?'

'It does as long as I'm not sleeping in my study too.' Claudia looks up quickly, but Lawrence is smiling and his tone amicable; she smiles back.

'I will enjoy having you in with me.'

'Me too,' he says. 'And I promise not to snore. Mind you, Ash would probably rather be in the annexe next to Lucy. You could swap him and Deborah.'

'No, Deborah will want more space than she'll get in your study. And Lucy's been through so much, it's not a good time for her to be with someone new. Even Ash.'

'He'd be great for her. Loosen her up a bit. He's always had a bit of a thing for her.'

'He's not over Kate.'

Lawrence looks up from the screen. 'How do you know? Did he tell you that?'

'No, just a feeling. I did talk to him about it a bit, a while ago.'

'You did?' Lawrence's tone is still affable but there is now a texture to it which Claudia recognises. Lawrence doesn't get jealous, exactly, but he resents not knowing things first: wanting always to be the origin point, he finds discussion of Claudia's life before they met, including her friendship with Ash, difficult. 'I haven't seen Ash since May. At the Michaels' party.'

'Me neither. It was before then.'

'He's probably feeling quite differently now, in that case.'

'Maybe. Anyway, Lucy doesn't need the stress of a new relationship right now. She needs some time alone.'

Lawrence is about to say 'You seem very keen to keep them apart' but his phone pings and he glances down to swipe it open.

'Lucy's vulnerable, that's all, and Ash . . .' Claudia lets the sentence drift.

'Best thing for her, as far as I can see.' But Lawrence is losing interest, his eyes on the screen.

'Did you have a shower when you got home?'

'What?' Lawrence doesn't look up.

'Your hair's wet. And you've changed your shirt.'

'Hmm? Yes, it was extraordinarily hot,' Lawrence says, starting to type. 'Christ, another Master's student panicking about their dissertation. I don't think a single one of them is going to finish on time at this rate. The anxiety levels are absolutely through the roof this year.' Lawrence is silent for a moment as he concentrates on wording his reply.

'Well, that's everyone,' Claudia concludes. 'All the beds are done, and I asked people to bring their own towels, so I think that's it. Just dinner for tonight to get ready and I'm doing that. Did you manage to do the seating plans?'

'Not yet, darling. And please don't badger. The shopping took longer than I thought. It's on my list.' He pauses for a moment, then adds, 'Your dinner will be sensational. The best of the week.'

'Miles is an excellent cook.'

'Not as good as you.' Lawrence finishes checking his emails and puts his phone face down on the table. 'Okay, finished, and that's my out-of-office done. I am officially on retreat. What are we making?'

'*Melanzane parmigiana*, now that I have enough aubergines.'

'I got good ones, didn't I?'

'I've asked everyone to do veggie because Miles is and I don't know about the artist woman.'

'She's Portuguese. She won't be vegetarian.'

'She could be. Which reminds me, Deborah doesn't keep kosher, does she?'

'No, no,' says Lawrence, getting up and going to the fridge.

'Okay,' Claudia says, 'well, it's just salad for lunch. It's too hot to want anything else.'

'I think we should start as we mean to go on.' Lawrence opens the fridge and selects a bottle of wine, uncorking it and pouring her a half glass, himself a full one.

'It's a bit early, isn't it?'

'Nonsense. Cheers, darling. Here's to our retreat.' He clinks his glass against hers.

'To our retreat.'

There is a pause as Lawrence assesses the wine. 'Delicious. Almost as delicious as you.' He leans over and kisses his wife's cheek. 'You look absolutely beautiful.'

As Claudia puts down her glass, she registers Lawrence glance at her wrist – a tattoo of a horizon and clouds – and then quickly look away.

Lawrence hates his wife's tattoos. She'd had this first one done two years ago, on her 47th birthday, and Lawrence had hit the roof in a manner she hadn't foreseen and found astonishing. He'd said it was inappropriate, 'particularly for someone of your age', and that it 'puts you on display like you're in the mosh pit at Glastonbury'.

Claudia had said, 'I don't think you want me to have a body at all,' and Lawrence had cycled off to sit in his office all evening.

Claudia turns her arm so that the tattoo is hidden against the table. She takes another sip and then opens the paper bag of aubergines. She had asked for five, and Lawrence has bought three, but her frustration registers only in a little shake of her head which is over in a second and certainly before Lawrence can notice. She takes her favourite sharp blade from the knife rack.

'I'm going to go and clean the pool before anyone gets here.'

Lawrence walks to the back door, carrying his glass. 'I'll be in the garden if you need me. Thank you, darling, for doing it all, as always.'

Once alone, Claudia reaches for her phone and selects a playlist. Puccini streams into the kitchen as she picks up an aubergine and cuts into it smoothly, the long slices falling one by one onto the chopping board. Claudia finishes the first and starts on another. Through the open window she catches sight of Lawrence heading towards the orchard, putting on his favourite cap, an old khaki one that he bought at an army and navy surplus store in Connecticut. He swerves a little to avoid a peacock standing on the path. The bird doesn't move, seemingly oblivious to Lawrence's proximity. Claudia's knife pauses and she suddenly and vividly imagines – the thought comes in an instant, unbidden: how it would feel to slice the blade down the peacock's long narrow neck, to feel its slender throat open up. As she watches, Lawrence raises his wine glass to his lips with one hand and with the other adjusts the cap over his eyes before slipping his phone from his shorts pocket.

Chapter Two

Monday afternoon

In the back seat of the cab, Miles reaches into his bag for his phone, opens Twitter, scrolls down his timeline. *The Telegraph* has footage of floods in Pakistan. A man he once met at a conference has got tenure. *Another History Podcast!* (Miles was on this last month) has a new episode on gender nonconformity in the long eighteenth century. His former colleague from King's has baked a savoury galette. Miles gives this last post a like, and posts a note of congratulations and a champagne emoji to the newly tenured professor. He switches from Twitter to emails, quickly deleting a series of new messages in bold without opening them, then back to Twitter. *The Guardian* offers a long read on energy citizenship and the low-carbon future. Jane Fonda has been diagnosed with non-Hodgkin's lymphoma. Miles puts down his phone and looks out of the window. The brick and stone of Cambridge have given way to fields, high green hedgerows flanking the taxi as it swings onto a single-track road. He swipes his phone on again and checks Google Maps. Five minutes to go. He closes his eyes.

When he opens them, the taxi is pulling up alongside a stone wall topped with grey railings; the driver cuts the engine and checks his meter.

'That'll be twenty-two pounds, please, mate.' Miles hands over three ten-pound notes and tells him to keep the change. The driver says, 'You know you gave me three tens?' and Miles says, 'Yes, that's right.' As the car pulls away, Miles feels a sudden urge to run into the road after it, to wave his arms and make it stop and take him back to the station. He checks himself, takes a breath. This is normal, he tells himself. Just a natural feeling of apprehension about seeing old friends, revisiting old haunts. A difficulty getting over the threshold, but he will soon be over it. And what would he rather be doing on a Monday afternoon? Sitting at his habitual third-floor desk in the London Library, facing the mid-afternoon slump? Or arriving at the country house of old friends for a week's writing retreat, during which he will, knowing Lawrence and Claudia, enjoy some decent food and wine, and get some work done on his book in good company? And if there is one person there whom he'd rather not have to see: no matter, he can face it. Miles squares his shoulders, adjusts the strap of his bag, and opens the gate.

At the bottom of the back staircase in Hawton Manor is a row of sprung bells, each with its painted label to indicate where a servant is required: Drawing Room, Dining Room, Bedroom 1, Bedroom 2, Bedroom 3, Side Door. The bells are made of brass, each about two inches in diameter, with a small pendulum hanging beneath, designed to swing after the bell has been rung and the sound can no longer be heard. Originally, each bell was attached to an intricate system of coiled springs and wires, which ran inside the walls of the house like veins from the rooms to this hallway. The bells have not been used since the house was wired for electricity in the early twentieth century and are no longer functional. In the still air, the faintest breeze drifts through the open back door, and the pendulum of the side-door bell moves very softly in the draught.

Lucy hears the car door slam and looks out of the window. Her room, one of a pair fitted into the eaves of what she guesses was once a stable block, has windows on three sides, overlooking the main entrance to the house, the narrow road on which it stands, and the garden and woodland beyond. The house is shaped like a sideways E with its central stroke missing; the main entrance lies in the middle of its longest side, where that stroke would begin. From Lucy's vantage point, the front of the house is obscured from view by one of its extending wings, but she can see the high double front gates with their neat metal twists and next to them a smaller entrance, cut into the long wall and railings which encircle what is left of the estate.

Standing at the gates is Miles Palmer, Lawrence's friend, whom Lucy has met at a number of Lawrence and Claudia's parties over the years. It's a particular kind of relationship: the friend of your friends whom you meet regularly at parties and dinners, but who never becomes a friend. Locked in a dance that remains eternally and respectfully mid-range. He must be the same age as Lawrence, early fifties, because Lawrence mentioned that he, Miles and Ash were all in the same year at Cambridge. Despite this and, as Lucy can see from this angle, a receding hairline, camouflaged by the close crop of his hair, Miles seems younger. He looks good, Lucy thinks, like he works out, which he likely does: no kids, handsome younger husband, probably he's in the gym every day. Lucy can feel the flickerings of resentment which she tries to suppress. She recognises her tendency to see other people's lives as simpler than her own, a tendency compounded during the separation from Neil. Miles must feel pressure to keep in shape now he's got a public profile: popular historians have a shelf life, especially ones like Miles who enter the game already in their mid-forties. Miles is looking over his shoulder, his torso twisted and muscular beneath the fabric of his striped shirt.

Lucy catches sight of her reflection in the mirror on her bedroom wall and straightens her posture. Muscle mass decreases approximately 3–8 per cent per decade after the age of thirty. Does this mean that now, at forty-two, she is 8 per cent physically weaker than when she married Neil? She can believe it. The past decade, and motherhood, have depleted her; this body that she inhabits is a less vital version of its younger self, as if a gradual weakening has taken place inside her, consuming her strength like sucking marrow slowly from a bone.

Lucy takes a step closer to the mirror. Lifting her fringe away from her face, she raises her eyebrows and then drops them, watching the ridges in her forehead gradually fade into lines. If she no longer bears the complete exhaustion of early motherhood, when she could have lain down and slept at any given moment of the day, on the bus, in the park, on the pavement, she is nonetheless very tired. She remembers Neil's phrase this morning: 'washed out'. The eyes which hold their own gaze are the same familiar pattern of brown and green, but now that she takes the time to look at the rest of her face, it seems curiously unrecognisable, the lines around her eyes deeper than she remembers, the pale skin underneath them purple with fatigue.

Lucy sits on the bed and smooths the checked quilt under her hand. In this bed, tonight, she will sleep, alone, for as long as she likes. She is going to put on some lipstick, go downstairs, and have an adult conversation with other adults, and then she is going to do some work, and then, delicious prospect, she is going to get into this bed and go to sleep.

It is dark in the passageway and when the phone's screen lights up it seems sudden and out of place. Lawrence shifts the stack of paperbacks he is carrying so that he can better see the screen.

Lawrence its Phoebe, I really need to see you, can we meet up? At yours or in town I dont mind. Its important. Pls reply asap

Lawrence slides the phone back into his pocket and leans over to deposit the books on top of Claudia's piano, which stands in the hallway. He straightens up and turns his head to one side to relieve a slight pain in his neck. The movement allows him to process the message. It's a habit he has, stretching like this, when he's thinking. Lawrence stands still for a moment, and then makes an almost inaudible 'Huh', in the way one might in receipt of a fact, or news, that doesn't quite fit. Then he continues down the passage, carrying the books in front of him.

Deborah has two large cases and they rattle loudly across the cobbles.

'I'm not first, am I? Or last? I'm usually one of those.'

Her voice echoes across the courtyard and Lawrence, Claudia and Lucy, sitting round the old wooden kitchen table drinking tea, hear her before they see her.

'Perfect timing,' Lawrence calls, standing up.

Deborah enters the hall as she does everything: decisively, loudly, without hesitation or self-doubt, and swearing.

'Fuck me, this is posh.' Deborah stands in the middle of the kitchen looking round. 'Isn't it? Thank God Claudia has money, Lawrence: you don't get a place like this writing books about medieval clerks.' Classical music – opera, of some kind – is playing in another room.

'Welcome, welcome, welcome,' says Lawrence, leaning down to give Deborah a hug. Deborah is wearing a bright green linen shift and spiky green earrings which pinch against Lawrence's cheek as she pulls him in for a kiss.

'It's really lovely to see you, Lawrence. God, you're a handsome devil,' she says, standing back to look at him properly. 'You look . . . like things are going very well. Are they?' But before Lawrence can answer, she says, 'But where is everyone else? Floored by the heat already?'

'Ash is in a taxi somewhere between the station and here,' says Lawrence. 'Imminent.'

'And my protégé?'

'Miles has arrived already. Upstairs. Miles!' Lawrence calls loudly. 'Your very powerful and somewhat intimidating literary agent is here!'

Deborah sticks out her tongue.

Miles is unpacking in the self-contained room above the kitchen Lawrence and Claudia sometimes rent out to lodgers. There's a muffled cry – something like 'Oh, lovely!' – and the sound of feet moving across the ceiling and then quickly descending the stairs.

'Deborah, love!'

'Miles. You've lost weight.'

'Stop it. I adore the hair.'

They perform a version of this routine every time they meet.

'Thank you. I'm fifty-six and the rest has gone but *thank God* for my hair.' Deborah puts a hand to her head, which is peroxide blonde, cut short up the sides and tightly curled on top. 'Now listen.' She holds Miles's hands as one might when dispensing advice very earnestly to a nephew. 'I don't want to do business right away but we need to talk properly at some point in the next day or two. There is *serious chatter* about the new one. *Serious serious.* And potentially even more exciting news, fingers crossed. And toes. And whatever else you can.'

Lawrence forces a smile and Deborah, who sees most things, notices his discomfort.

'But that's for later,' she says. 'Can we drink? Something that isn't tea?'

'Of course,' says Lawrence. He's used to being the person who sets the agenda and he finds Deborah, three years his senior, with her surging energy, a little disorientating. He is aware of the beginnings of this discomfort, so he smiles and says, 'Lovely,' and collects glasses from the drying rack and the bottle of Touraine from the fridge. As he pours he says, 'What's the title, then, Miles?'

'Of what?'

'Of bestseller number three.'

'There was an eight-way auction,' Deborah says, sipping the wine.

'Don't hate me, Lawrence. "*A History of Marriage in 12 Divorces*". I've got a conservatory to pay for.'

'Oh, I like that,' says Lucy, taking a glass for herself and another for Claudia. 'Can mine be chapter five? After Catherine of Aragon but before Gwyneth Paltrow.'

'You're in,' says Miles, raising his glass to Lucy and taking a long swallow of his wine.

Deborah turns to Lucy. 'You've left Neil?'

'Four months.'

Deborah nods slowly, weighing the news. Lucy can see her doing what all her friends do when she tells them that she has left her husband of over a decade: Deborah is considering whether to say what she thought of Neil – which will be that he was some variety of appalling. A narcissist (her mother used the word about Neil last week) whose fragile self-esteem (her friend Rosie said it yesterday) depends on diminishing those closest to him. Neil is a type Lucy has started, in the four months since she's left, to see everywhere among successful male academics: the intellectual with impeccable and very public leftist credentials, who – once the front door has shut – treats his wife like a servant.

But for now Deborah just says: 'We can talk later, darling, if you want. I know what it's like – or a version of it.'

The phone rings.

'You have a landline!' says Miles.

Claudia answers. She mouths to Lawrence *It's Ash*, and

then turns back to the phone, covering her ear to drown out the excited chatter and the sound of Radio 3, giving detailed instructions – past the church, six hundred yards, the large old brick manor building on the left, pull in at the second metal gate – which Ash is relaying to a taxi driver unused to these little villages outside Cambridge with roads with no names.

Ash arrived in Cambridge mid-morning but rather than heading straight for Hawton he has spent the subsequent five hours in the Rare Books Room of the University Library. He has five small wooden boxes on his desk. Each box has a label with a handwritten description – '60 & 48 pt Romans'; 'Italics: Nonpareil, Brevier, Long Primer, Pica Small' – and a lid which opens to reveal rows of what look like metal bullets, each about two inches long with the shape of an inverted letter cut into the top. The boxes are lined with green felt, cushioning and displaying the bullets as if they were ammunition destined for an elite assassination. But these are not bullets: they are type punches, hand-cut in York in the 1750s, made of hard metal. Their function is – or was, before they became historical artefacts to be consulted in a library – to be driven into soft copper to create matrices in the shape of a letter which in turn, locked into a mould, would be used to make letters from hardened liquid metal. The punches are heavy and cool to touch.

For the last nine months, Ash has been engrossed in the world of the eighteenth-century printer and type-designer John Eaves. Ash hopes, some time soon, to have written a chapter on Eaves, which will form part of his book on the long history of typography, a series of vaulting chapters from 1440s Germany to digital publishing today. But Ash has a tendency to wander off, or rather to climb down deep, and the book, only one third written, is already six months overdue. The university press haven't said anything yet, and Ash doesn't panic. He draws comfort from the knowledge of his friend Ralph in the History department, who handed in his book on the social history of death fifteen years after his deadline.

The metal punches on his desk in the hushed and largely empty reading room (the undergraduates all back home, the faculty at conferences or nosing round Tuscan backstreets) come from Eaves's own press in York, passed down after his death in 1775, first to his wife Sarah, and then through a series of printers in England and France – disappearing for much of the nineteenth century – until they were bought by Cambridge University Library in 1953. As Ash turns the punches, noting the shape of each inverse 'a' and 'e' and 't' and 'r', he is transported away from Cambridge and today: he is lost in that stretch of time connecting the past to the present. These are the punches Eaves held in his fingers in 1758 when he made the letters with which he printed his miraculous edition of *Paradise Lost*, the book Ash inched through in York Central Library last week, three hundred yards from where Eaves lived. Ash takes a photo of each punch but for much of the time he simply sits, holding and turning these pieces from the past.

Ash is thinking about them still as he sits in his taxi, the driver shaking his head.

'No numbers,' the man says, gesturing at the road.

'Pardon?'

'Houses too posh for numbers, round here.'

'Oh I see. I think . . . oh, there's the church.'

'You want to stop here?'

'No, a bit on. One minute more.' Claudia had said six hundred yards and then the brick manor building on the left. While Claudia was speaking, spelling out the directions, Ash could hear Mozart playing in the background and this had created a sense of a little world that was running without him, that he was about to enter from off-stage.

The taxi pulls up by the second gate.

'I can't believe they've actually got a blue plaque to him.'

'You what, boss?'

'Nothing. Talking to myself. Here's twenty-five. Keep the change.'

The blue plaque above the main door records the names and dates of the early twentieth century author Horatio Russell, an author Ash had written about, almost thirty years ago, in his undergraduate dissertation. Russell was a pillar of the colonial establishment who churned out (Ash purposefully risked that verb in his introduction) hugely popular thrillers that combined – so Ash's argument went – middle-brow taste with deadly imperial ideology. 'Russell persuaded his readers of the good of Empire without them realising they were doing more than passing their time with a page-turner.' Ash remembers that sentence, and now he's coming for a writing retreat in the manor where Russell lived. Lawrence had mentioned the link to this famous literary past with a performance of head-shaking ('*awful* man') – undermined, more than a little, by the growing collection of Russell first editions Lawrence keeps in the lower living room, on the low shelf behind what Lawrence and Claudia call 'the stage'. Ash thinks about Lawrence's casual hypocrisy; about Lawrence's first-year seminars on post-colonial theory prepared in the grounds of Hawton Manor; about how the world still, today, after all the chatter of change, simply opens up, offering itself, to white men of Lawrence's background. But conscious that he is arriving for a week as Lawrence and Claudia's guest – and also that he profoundly needs a rest, which means in part a rest from the critique of the world that runs continually in his head – Ash pushes these thoughts to one side. The critique morphs into a different kind of thought. Ash thinks of his grandmother's house in Sri Lanka, which he visited only once, when he was a small boy, the country which Russell – his dates would have overlapped with Ama's – would have called British Ceylon.

Ash stands for a moment before the gate as the taxi heads off back into Cambridge, his suitcase by his side, his rucksack on his back. He stands stock still and closes his eyes. The long journey and the heat have developed his earlier discomfort into an entrenched headache, now pulsing across his temples. Ash had a very bad lockdown. Kate called off their engagement two months in but couldn't move out until summer. His department at the university is haemorrhaging students, and he's in charge of admissions. Ash breathes in and out. Through the open kitchen door he can hear voices: shouts, laughter, a woman calling. The world outside it feels paused, hushed. There are no cars: the narrow, unmarked road stretches right and left in still silence. Ash stands motionless for a minute, trying to feel what it is like to be here right now, and then he opens the gate.

❊

A couple of hours later, Josh lifts the worn door-knocker and then lets it fall back for a second time. He takes a step backwards and assesses the door: no discernible bell. He never visited Lawrence at his home when Lawrence was his supervisor, and their occasional meetings over the last ten years have all been in London. As he smooths his hair into place, Josh is surprised at how nervous he feels: his fingers are actually shaking and his shirt is uncomfortably damp against his back.

Josh looks around, then rests a thumb on the edge of the letterbox and slowly pushes it open, crouching to bring his mouth close to the gap.

'Hello? Can I help you?'

Josh jumps and as he straightens up, the letterbox closes sharply on his hand. He turns around, bringing the sore side of his thumb to his mouth.

Approaching him from the left wing of the house is a woman whom at first Josh sees as a stranger. Barefoot, she's a little shorter than he is, and a little older, her fair hair drawn back from her face, her smile welcoming. She's attractive, Josh thinks, for her age, nice body, although swamped in some sort of awful denim pinafore. For a moment he imagines reaching out to touch her, to kiss her mouth, to pull her close. She would be shocked, would resist him, what a dreadful mistake it would be, but what if he were to do it, right this second? And then he realises with a sudden sense of being caught out, of having his private thoughts exposed, that this is Claudia, Lawrence's wife, whom he met once at a college fundraising event when he was just starting the PhD.

'It's Josh, isn't it? I'm Claudia.' She shifts her basket to her other arm and puts out a hand.

'Claudia, yes, of course, it's a pleasure to meet you again. It's been . . .'

'An age,' says Claudia. 'Lawrence will be so pleased you're here.'

They shake hands. 'I'm sorry, I did knock, but—'

'Oh, we never use that door.' Claudia gestures behind her in a manner that suggests *how funny to think we would use that door!* 'We mostly use this one' – the kitchen door stands ajar – 'but I was in the veg patch.' She lifts up the basket to show a clutch of onions. 'Do come in.'

Josh follows his hostess through the kitchen door and puts his bag down on the floor.

'Wow. What a beautiful kitchen.'

Late afternoon light floods through the large window above the sink. The room is dominated by a long, old, wooden table, marked with wine glass rings and patches of dried candle wax and with ten similarly aged chairs around it. Josh has a sudden, vertiginous sense of family meals, conversations, of decades passing, of the door to the garden flinging open and children charging in. Dried herbs hang in bunches from the old wooden beams. A large calendar, with photographs of Lawrence and Claudia and what must be their son, is pinned to a central wooden pillar: August shows them on a beach that might be Italy, the three of them standing at the edge of the sea. Classical music, a solo piano, is playing quietly from an old Roberts radio on a shelf by the cooker.

'Thank you,' Claudia smiles. 'You've not been before?'

'No. Sadly. But, you know, I wouldn't expect it. It's lovely to be asked now. Thank you.'

How jumpy he is, thinks Claudia.

'Well, the kitchen is my domain. And Lawrence's too, of course, but cooking is my thing.'

'And . . . singing, I recall?'

Claudia puts the onions in a wooden bowl. 'Used to be. But, you know. Time. Life.'

'I remember opera performances in the hall on West Road. I remember Lawrence saying.'

'Did he?' Claudia smiles. 'A thing of the past, I fear.' There is a little pause and, briefly, an awkward sense of a difficult intimacy too quickly reached.

Claudia says, 'But what can I get you? Tea? A cold drink? The others are mostly working, I think. I was just getting dinner started. I'm not sure where Lawrence is, exactly, but he'll be along in a bit. Or would you like to see your room?'

'Yes, please, great, I mean if that won't delay your cooking?'

'Oh, not at all,' Claudia says, 'a welcome distraction.' She wipes her hands on the sides of her dress. 'Come through this way.' Josh picks up his bag and follows. 'You're actually in Tristan's room, our son. He's in France with his grandparents for the week. Back on Saturday.' Claudia leads Josh down a corridor, through a hallway, up some stairs, another corridor, more stairs. Josh thinks, this place is endless.

'This is you.' Claudia opens a door. 'I'm sorry about the size of the bed. And I have had a tidy up, but apologies for any residual mess. You know what teenagers are like!'

As she says this, Claudia thinks, I'm sure you don't, I'm sure you've no idea, and as she thinks this, she registers a sudden spike of envy for a childless life, for the freedom to do what she wants, for the possibility of turning up at a beautiful house she doesn't know with no family and one bag and being shown to a room by a friendly woman and letting the future present itself.

'Right. Well, I'll leave you to it. It's a little stuffy in here in this heat – you might want to prop that window open. Come down to the kitchen when you've settled in. Lawrence is making drinks in an hour or so. Cocktails. You know how he is: everything planned. Let me know if you need anything.' Josh steps further into the room and Claudia closes the door behind her.

'Will do. Thank you. It's a wonderful room,' he calls after her. He opens his bag and puts his laptop on the desk, next to an Arsenal pencil-case and a money bank shaped like the night bus from Harry Potter.

Wow, Josh thinks. A house this huge and I'm sleeping in a fucking child's bed.

Lucy stands facing the swimming pool and steps slowly into it, inching her feet into the water. Although it is late in the day, the temperature is climbing, as if the heat means to keep rising into the night. Lucy takes a further step, and another, enjoying the contrast between her chilled legs and the dusty heat of the rest of her body. Crouching forwards, she takes a few delicious strokes before diving under the water, feeling it encase her head and pull back her hair with its weight. She surfaces and turns onto her back, floating, closing her eyes against the sky, sensing something inside her release its hold.

What Ash sees, for that first moment, is a corpse, splayed in the water, dark hair drifting outwards, hands upturned at its sides. He stops immediately on the steps, as still as the dead thing before him, neither of them breathing. He takes a step closer, and another. He thinks of Millais's *Ophelia*, although this woman, unidentifiable at this distance, is not weighed down by clothing but almost naked in a bikini, and absolutely without motion. The body is slender to the point of thinness; as he approaches, Ash notices the hip-bones slightly protruding above the black fabric of the bikini, and higher, the gentle trace of the ribcage. After the first shock, he realises two things: this is not a dead body, because its hands have started slowly sculling the water, causing the surface to break and ripple, and also, this is Lucy, Lawrence's former PhD student, whom Ash has met several times.

The last time he saw her was at a party for a literary magazine in London, a publication to which Ash occasionally, and Lawrence more frequently, contributes. He'd been there with Kate and Lucy with her dreadful husband, whose name Ash can't recall. He had thought then, he now remembers, that theirs was an inexplicable marriage, one that could only be made possible by some flaw in them both, for what else could draw this apparently intelligent and certainly beautiful woman to a man like that?

To encounter Lucy suddenly in this way, when she is unaware of his presence and her own exposure, is to Ash both erotic and deeply awkward. He considers, wildly, whether he can reverse up the steps in silence, then go around the other way to the house, or perhaps walk back down from the terrace and signal his approach loudly. Is there any other form of escape? He has almost convinced himself that it would be wise to drop to the floor and crawl sideways, out of sight of the pool, when Lucy, suddenly and in one fluid motion, stands up, taking a loud breath, pushing her hair off her face and then opening her eyes, blinking. Ash for a split second has the image of a child on the brink of death, long ago, suddenly gasping back to life.

'Hi! Ash! What a surprise!' Lucy walks forward through the water and climbs the steps out of the pool. She collects her towel from the grass and begins drying herself. Ash is saying hello when she continues, 'I mean, it's not really a surprise, I saw your name on the email, not to mention Lawrence's helpful list, of course.' They share a smile. 'I like the beard. Did you just get here?'

'Thank you.' Ash's hand goes to his face. 'Yes. I stopped at the UL on the way.'

'Lawrence was twitching. He wanted everyone present and correct by two on the dot but I think only half of us were. I've only seen Miles and Deborah, so far, and Lawrence and Claudia, of course.' Lucy wraps the towel around herself and tucks in the loose end. 'How are you?'

'I'm fine, thanks. I'm very well. You?'

'I'm okay.' Lucy slips her feet into her Birkenstocks, collects the pile of her clothes, then looks up at him. 'That's the headline. The real answer is much longer. But I'm okay.' A pause. 'We'd better get back. It's drinks at six and I sense that the timetable is not to be disobeyed.'

They walk slowly together back up to the house, not talking. Ash feels physically aware of the proximity of Lucy's body, of the strangeness of walking next to her like this, in a much more intimate way than their acquaintance would usually allow. He imagines he can actually feel the warmth coming from her skin. Lucy seems unaware of any awkwardness; she moves easily, pushing aside the branches of the trees which encroach

41

on the path through the long grass, unsticking their leaves from her damp arms. Together they cross the lawn towards the back door, which is open; Ash stands aside to allow Lucy to go first, then steps after her into the darkness of the house.

Lawrence, standing at the dining-room window, watches their approach and disappearance. Briefly he feels like a voyeur, as though he is spying on a moment of intimacy, although of course, he says to himself, this can be nothing of the sort. Lucy has been swimming and Ash must have been here less than an hour. Nonetheless there is an ease between them which sparks in Lawrence a brief but intense irritation. Without realising it, he clenches his right fist shut. What is it about Ash that women like Lucy, like Claudia for that matter, seem to like so much? He has seen his wife smile in pleasure when Ash enters a room. To watch him and Lucy together now, himself unseen, feels uncomfortable, even intrusive. Lawrence turns back to the table, which he has been laying for the evening meal, takes a breath and sighs. He relaxes his hand. He straightens a knife against the edge of the cloth, adjusts a glass, stands back to take it all in.

Chapter Three

Monday evening

Lawrence is alone in the kitchen when Deborah enters. He is very carefully pouring a pale red liquid from a large preserving jar into seven glass tumblers. He does all seven to precisely the same level halfway up, and then goes round again until the liquid is evenly distributed. Then he spoons one small, dark, oval fruit from the jar into each glass.

Deborah, leaning against the door frame, watches Lawrence for a moment, noting his cautious precision, thinking how this meticulous preparation for his friends' enjoyment is both endearing and tyrannical.

'Darling, that looks like something that would alarm my urologist.'

Lawrence places the jar in the sink.

'Damson gin.'

'Oh, how divine.' Deborah looks reflexively towards the wine rack. The champagne she gave Lawrence earlier is resting in the top row of bottles. If she refrigerates it, will he consider this an overstepping of her status as guest? Deborah decides that the prospect of chilled champagne is worth the risk, but on opening the fridge finds it already crammed full. While Lawrence's back is turned, Deborah removes a large jar of olives and slots the champagne bottle into its place.

'I made it last September.'

'Of course you did.' Deborah slides the olives beside the bread bin.

'The tree *there* . . .' – he points through the window – 'was bursting with them. The year before it had nothing, so it was loaded last autumn. Hugh F-W says you need to leave it to sit for two years but I'm risking it at a hasty ten months. Will you join me on this wild ride of chance?'

'I'm in.' Deborah takes a seat at the kitchen table.

Lawrence turns around to collect two glasses.

Deborah says, 'Who's Bill Shankly?'

'Pardon?'

'On the back of your shirt.'

'Oh. A football player, I think. England's best ever. Masses of goals. Here you go.' Lawrence hands Deborah a glass.

'And what does it say on the front?'

He pulls the front of his T-shirt taut so Deborah can read it.

'"The socialism I believe in is everyone working for each other, everyone having a share of the rewards. It's the way I see football, the way I see life." Damson gin socialism, is it?'

'Very funny. I made chutney, too.' Lawrence nods in the direction of the high shelf, with a row of identical dark brown jars with labels.

Deborah counts ten of them. The labels have been hand-printed. Deborah remembers the agency Christmas drinks the previous year when Lawrence had presented both herself and her young assistant with a large Kilner jar filled with pickled quinces, which had sat all evening on the mantelpiece like incongruous bookends, conspicuously on display.

'Ben used to make chutney. Little jars just like that. That's how I knew he was fucking his research assistant.'

'Oh.'

'*Gabriella.*' Deborah says the name in an exaggerated posh accent. 'He suddenly became very enthusiastic about chores around the house which was far more suspicious than the affair itself. He did the steps down to the cellar that had been broken for years. He did the fence. He even did the sundial! It's like he wanted me to find out.'

Lawrence raises his glass. 'Well, if you can accept that this version of domesticity isn't a mark of mid-life crisis . . .'

'Of course I can't do that.'

Lawrence nods his head and closes his eyes as if to indicate, with equanimity, *fair enough.*

Miles comes down the stairs with his phone in his hand. 'Lawrence, I've never met a straight man who so vividly embodies the phrase "pre-dinner drinks".'

'*Bien sûr.*' Lawrence hands Miles a glass.

Miles looks round the kitchen, his smile suggesting appreciation but also an undercutting irony. 'Presumably the *Cambridge Companion to Middle-Class Cultural Capital* is nearly finished?'

Lawrence pulls a face.

Deborah says, 'We were just talking about chutney-making as a sublimation of illicit desire.'

'Literally what else is there?' Miles looks at Lawrence. 'I adore the little evening timetables you sent.'

'Sorry if it seemed OTT.'

'Of course it did but I love it.'

Miles and Deborah clink glasses. Lawrence says, 'Oh, let's wait for everyone to come before we drink. Start off together. I said six prompt.'

Miles gives Deborah the tiniest roll of the eyes but also a grin: he has a long-held appreciation for Lawrence's attempts to curate life and the goodwill that is entangled with his vanity. Deborah puts her glass back down on the table.

The door from the garden opens and Claudia comes in with a bunch of herbs which she spreads out on the chopping board.

Lawrence says, 'Is that the wonderful rosemary, darling?'

'We don't have any rosemary.' Claudia takes a small knife from a drawer.

Deborah says, 'Oh dear, has Lawrence been putting dog fennel in the soup again?'

Lawrence says, 'I'm sure – by the pool.' He hands Claudia a glass. 'Have one of these, anyway. You're working so hard.'

Claudia thinks how that 'anyway' spreads Lawrence's ignorance between the two of them. She takes a sip as if to wash away the irritation.

Lawrence says, 'Darling, please, let's wait for the others.'

'I have to say,' Miles says, 'I do find the whole idea of a cooking *rota* rather intimidating.' As Lawrence turns away, Miles takes a quick sip from his glass.

'When are you "*on*"?' Deborah turns her own glass slowly on the table and moves it so that the red liquid catches the light. She feels a craving to drink it that is hard to ignore: she shifts her position in an attempt to suppress it.

'Tuesday – right Lawrence?' Miles says.

'That's right. We're doing tonight.'

'Given that we have more people than dinners to cook,' says Deborah, pushing the glass away and crossing her arms, 'I'm grateful to be left out of it. But I can be your sous chef, Miles.'

'I plan to get up at 4 a.m. to start foraging,' says Miles. 'That will give me an edge. Do a sweep of the woods first. Then expand out, across the county. I assume, Lawrence, we're talking covert competition veiled beneath an appearance of no-pressure fun?'

Lawrence smiles and shakes his head and says, 'It's just a chance to share some lovely food, Miles.'

'What I'm actually going to do,' says Miles, 'is pop to M&S and buy lots of things in trays.'

Lawrence flashes an immediate shocked look at Miles and then, realising he is being mocked, relaxes his face.

Deborah says, 'We're not supposed to leave Hawton, isn't that right, Lawrence?'

'That makes it sound rather more official than I'd intended,' says Lawrence.

Miles says, 'A perimeter of steel.'

'Not at all. But yes, I think it's best if we keep to the estate for the week, don't you? Other than for walks and so on. Otherwise, what's the point of a retreat?'

There is a pause while this sense of the week sinks in: an idyllic house-and-garden set apart; but also a confinement.

Miles says, 'So what are you two cooking?' He looks at Lawrence who looks to Claudia.

'Aubergine parmigiana,' she says.

Lawrence nods, 'That's right.'

Claudia says, 'Nothing fancy.'

Lawrence pats her hand. 'Should be lovely.'

There are salted sliced aubergines sitting between paper towels. A pan of tomato sauce. A large brown bowl with a green salad. A huge chunk of Parmesan. The oven is buzzing.

'What a pleasant scene.' This is Ash, who comes in with Lucy. He has a sweater tied round his shoulders and wears a blue shirt over white linen trousers and flip-flops. Lucy's hair is tied up but hasn't dried yet from her swim.

'How beautiful you both are,' says Deborah. 'Ash, you look like a Merchant Ivory hero. It's 1992. It's eternally sunny. Is that a cricket sweater?'

'No, I'm afraid not,' Ash replies. 'I'm sure Lawrence has got one I can borrow, for the full effect.'

Lawrence says nothing to this, but hands out glasses.

Deborah says, 'Lawrence, can we please be allowed to consume this alcohol before the drink evaporates in the heat and the evening ends?'

'Just Josh to come. And here he is.'

'Thank God you're here, Josh,' says Deborah.

Josh looks surprised at Deborah's urgent welcome. 'Sorry, all. Am I late?' Josh runs a finger under his collar; he is, despite the heat and the informality of the others, wearing a pressed shirt and a tie emblazoned with an institutional insignia.

Deborah leans forward as if in conspiracy and fake-whispers, 'Lawrence says we're not allowed to experience pleasure until everyone has arrived.'

'Not in the slightest,' says Lawrence. 'We're all very relaxed here. No hard rules!'

Miles winks at Deborah. Lucy sees, and suppresses a smile.

Lawrence says, 'Cheers, everyone', and they clink glasses.

Ash finds himself looking at the back of Lucy's neck.

Josh is grinning and methodically making eye contact with each person as he raises his glass. Deborah glances at Miles, who is looking at Josh with an expression she can't quite read: not hostility, exactly, but a certain distaste. She makes a mental note to ask Miles about this young man with his tie and his grin and his laboured eagerness to become part of the group.

Claudia puts her glass down and goes to check if the grill is hot enough. She starts to transfer the aubergines to the baking tray then slides the tray into the oven. She does the timings in her head, closing her eyes as if this will mute the chattering around her. Lawrence's booming laugh at something distracts her and she counts again. The grilling takes ten, then put the whole thing together, breadcrumbs, oregano, parmesan, another ten, bake for thirty then stand for fifteen. Where is the vinegar? She opens the cupboard.

'Lawrence, did you get extra balsamic?'

Lawrence turns to her. 'Sorry, what? Oh, no I didn't. I thought we had a bottle already. The one that came back from camping.'

'But I asked you to,' says Claudia. 'I wrote it down.'

'Sorry, darling,' Lawrence says, and then adds, uselessly, 'do you want me to pop out and get some?'

'Of course not *now*,' Claudia begins, and then stops. She takes a breath. 'So: eating at . . . seven, I think,' she finishes.

'Oh, I thought . . . that's fine.' Lawrence pauses, and then addresses the group. 'Shall we all take a turn in the garden?'

Miles says, 'So Edwardian.'

'Bring your drinks, of course.'

'I'll have a quick refill, in that case,' says Miles, and then, as Lawrence gestures towards the supply of damson gin on the shelf, 'from a jar, how rustic, and you seem to have pints of it.'

'It's homemade.' Deborah watches as Miles carefully releases the metal clasp on a jar and ladles himself a second measure. She opens the packed fridge, resting her fingers against the champagne to test its temperature.

Gradually the group filters out of the kitchen door and follows the path on the right to the back of the house. The French windows are open and music is playing to the empty garden. Early solo Paul McCartney on the playlist Lawrence had created yesterday.

Josh, following Lawrence closely, says 'Jesus Christ' under his breath. The lawn slopes slightly from the back of the house down to an orchard and, to the left, through an archway in a brick wall which is clearly centuries old, to an elegant pool that looks like it was built in the 1930s. The edge of the pool is framed with elaborate mosaic tiles. Beyond the pool is a line of fir trees and then, opening suddenly out, a long lawn which culminates in a large pond. Beyond and above the pool and the lawn are high poplars, marking the limits of the estate, and dead still in the heat. There is a sense of deep calm – of the garden standing as it has done for three hundred years – and of a large space that is nonetheless confined.

Josh thinks of his cramped two-bedroom flat in Tufnell Park. 'What's the little building by the water?'

Claudia says, 'Oh, that's Lawrence's project.'

Lawrence says, 'Francis Sharp's project, darling. The original owner of this place was a librarian at the university. Funny figure. Seems to have spent a career not quite getting the plum job but, good eighteenth-century antiquarian that he was, he built a folly by the pond. A sort of fake ancient Roman ruin.'

Lawrence is walking briskly in the direction of the folly

now, gesturing with a sweep of his arm, and Josh has to move quickly to keep up. As Josh walk-trots – an awkward mode which must (Josh thinks) look as ridiculous as it feels – he reflects how he will never escape the position of student in relation to Lawrence. He could be eighty-three and he'd still scuttle after a nonagenarian Lawrence like a spaniel.

'Sharp was a fairly disastrous librarian.' Lawrence is speaking the words out into the air with a sense of indirection – flinging them over his shoulder in the knowledge that a following Josh will gather them up. 'Just about the only thing he did was catalogue the coins in the Fitzwilliam. So I think he had a lot of time.'

They are in front of the folly now: a narrow building with an open front and stone walls tiled in slate, under which sit a wooden bench and a small writing desk. The building clings to the bank which runs down to the large pond.

Josh says, 'And what's it for?'

Lawrence says, '*For?*', his tone acquiring a sharp edge which turns Josh into a student again. 'It's quite like Pope's grotto on the Thames at Twickenham, which was 1720 of course. Or so. Ours is 1740. Slightly larger.'

Josh remembers Lawrence from supervisions, when his enthusiasm got going and he'd spring up and pull down book after book from his shelves.

'We redid the roof a couple of years ago. It was in a terrible state, even for a folly. A folly's folly, I used to say. The thing's listed, of course, like everything here, and we had to get the council's permission.'

Josh thinks it looks absurd: pointless and pompous and without purpose. 'I love it,' he says. 'So elegant.'

'It takes you back in time, doesn't it?' replies Lawrence. 'Which is what I like.'

'Me too,' says Josh. 'Absolutely agree.'

Deborah is walking next to Lucy. Lucy brushes her hair out of her eyes and Deborah looks over at her. 'You okay? You good?'

'I think so. I mean everything is chaos. But I'm feeling better than I was.'

'You seem better.'

'I suppose so.' Lucy registers, with a moment's unease, the implication that she had previously seemed to be doing badly.

'Unburdened and gorgeous.'

'Hardly. But yes, unburdened.'

They walk a few steps in silence. Then Lucy says, 'I've not thought of the kids for hours. I can't remember the last time that was the case. I swam on my back before dinner and looked at the sky.'

Deborah clasps her hand for a moment. Lucy squeezes it back.

Lawrence is at the front, nearing the pond. 'Good session in the library, Ash?'

Ash pauses for a second, recognising the slight edge in his old friend's question. For a second he searches for a cause, and then realises – of course! – the timetable.

'Very good, thank you.'

They are standing at the edge of the water. The folly is to their left. The pond is thick with algae and purple-headed plants growing straight up out of the water. It is wild and overgrown, maybe a bit artfully so, but beautiful. Ash can see a plaque on the inside wall of the folly: 'Built by Francis Sharp, 1740. Restored by Lawrence Napier Ayres, 2021.'

'Got much done?'

'You know they have Eaves's printing type? Two full fonts. 1757. That's why I went.'

'I didn't. How wonderful. Two full fonts?' Lawrence looks out at the pond. 'Every book you can imagine, latent in those little pieces of lead.'

Ash considers that comment – its easy reach for universality. 'Not every book. It's the Latin alphabet. So not Arabic books or Hebrew books. Not books in Sinhala.'

There's a pause, then Ash adds, 'From Sri Lanka.'

Lawrence forces a smile. 'Yes, but you know what I mean.' He moves nearer the folly so he can read the plaque with his own name on it. 'It's a philosophical point. Shame you missed a couple of hours of day one. That was the idea behind the arrival email.'

Claudia, catching them up, says, 'Are you actually telling Ash off?'

Lawrence smiles, although his wife's defence of Ash (which is how Lawrence interprets her question) irks him a little. He often finds it awkward when it's just the three of them, but he tries to bury his sense of a disturbance – he knows he finds laughing at himself difficult – and says, 'I'm sorry. You know me and planning.'

Lawrence notices that Claudia, now standing just behind Ash, has placed a hand on his back. As they both turn a little towards him, their bodies close together, Lawrence has a sudden impression of Ash and Claudia as a unit, as though they were the married couple and he the outsider. He reaches out for Claudia's hand and grasps it.

Ash finds Lawrence maddening when he is covertly hypocritical – when his selfishness is concealed beneath goodwill.

53

But in Lawrence's comical attempts at control – like this, now, and like the emailed timetable and the seating plans and the damson gin – Ash finds him endearing. He forgives him, for the moment, his ignorance of books from other places in the world. Ash raises his glass and intones, 'Before all things: punctuality.'

'Of course, we hardly ever eat in here,' Lawrence opens the door, 'but we thought, as it's our first night, it might be fun to enjoy a sense of occasion.'

Lawrence crosses the room to open the French windows on its far side. To enter the dining room is to step back in time, Ash thinks, or perhaps up in social register. The bohemian tenor of the more lived-in parts of the house here gives way to a quieter formality: pale green walls hung with muted watercolours, a walnut cabinet displaying delicate porcelain figures. The last time Ash had been in this room, the table was crowded with candles, the chandelier lit, curtains drawn against the night. Now, even at seven o'clock, rich golden light streams across the table, catching the glass and silver, flaming little vases of flowers into vivid torches of colour. This table, thinks Ash, must have been what Lawrence was doing all afternoon, for all he was griping about Ash's short hours in the library. But the general expressions of surprise and pleasure as his guests catch sight of it show that Lawrence's efforts have not been wasted.

'Come in, come in,' Lawrence beckons from across the room, 'and do sit.' His tone is a brushing aside of formality, even as the room displays his meticulous planning.

'Do you mind who goes where?' Miles approaches the table. 'Oh I see, there's a placement. What fun.' He scans the table.

'Look, here's me, and here's you, Debs, come on.' They take their places, closest to the window, and the others gradually find their seats. Lawrence circles the table, pouring wine into outstretched glasses, then takes his place at its head, silhouetted against the bright garden.

'What's this?' Lucy, on Lawrence's left, picks up the leather notebook lying between her knife and fork. Opening it, she exclaims at the richly marbled inside cover, bright blues and greens swirling across the paper. 'Oh, what a nice thing.'

'There's one for everyone,' Lawrence smiles. 'I hope you like them.' He grips his hands tightly under the table as his guests exclaim over the books, each with endpapers marbled in different inks, opulent shades of cobalt, violet, ochre, crimson. 'I had them put together by a bespoke stationer near the Fitzwilliam.' He pauses. 'I made the endpapers myself, actually.'

'No, really?' Miles runs his fingers over the thick paper, its surface granular and uneven, its edges glued onto the soft leather inside the cover.

'Well, it's just a little spin-off from the printing press. I started making my own paper, a very messy process, and then once I got competent at that I tried my hand at marbling. It's not difficult actually. A child can do it. Child *did*. Dye everywhere.'

'What a wonderful gift. Thank you, darling.' Deborah raises her glass to him and one by one the group join her, holding up their glasses, thanking him, a circle of smiling faces, and Lawrence is suffused with pleasure.

'You are very welcome, and you are very welcome here. In fact, I'd like to drink a toast, to all of you, to welcome—'

'Wait a minute!' says Lucy, 'Claudia's not here. She should be here,' and at that moment Claudia shoulders open the door, carrying a heavy tray with both hands and so unable to brush aside the hair that has fallen over her face. Ash, sitting nearest to the door, jumps up and holds the door open for her.

'Thank you.' Claudia gives him a grateful smile, and looks around at the group, 'What did I miss?'

'Nothing at all, darling, perfect timing.' Lawrence takes the tray from Claudia, then passes plates – he says, 'Let me do this' – while she puts platters of antipasti among the settings on the table. He circles to pour her wine. 'I was about to make a toast. Thank you so much, everyone, for joining us, and for creating what I know is going to be a really splendid occasion. I am so glad you could all come. Hawton Manor, as you know – I think everyone's been before, except perhaps you, Josh? – well, this house has a rich literary history, back through Russell and his gatherings, not to mention some other poetic forebears of Claudia's, to the great Samuel Johnson and dear old Francis Sharp in the 1700s, and I am really delighted to add to that history in what I hope will be the first of many such occasions. I foresee an annual event that I hope will run for many years. You are the first. This week we will eat and drink together, enjoy one another's company, talk, swim, enjoy the gardens, and perhaps even get a little work done.' He pauses for them to laugh. 'Here's to all of you, and – to the retreat!'

'The retreat!' they echo, and the guests lean forward to help themselves to food.

'"To add to that rich history",' Miles misquotes softly to Deborah as he passes her a plate, 'my goodness. He's at his most pompous.'

'Hush now.' Deborah helps herself to prosciutto, and nods towards Lawrence on her left, turned away as he serves Lucy.

'He's in his element. He really loves all this, and he does it very well. Now, fill this up, please,' she gestures with her glass, 'and let's get on with the eating and drinking bit. I'm good at that.'

'What was here before Francis Sharp, Lawrence?' Josh's question comes from genuine interest, but also a desire to make an impression and establish his standing in the group. He senses the history of the building is a rich seam.

'It's fascinating, and more than a little uncertain.' Lawrence leans forward. Josh feels satisfied that he's the source of this well-received conversational development. 'It looks like this place was the site of some kind of religious house, before the Reformation. A small monastery, perhaps. The building got destroyed during the 1530s by Cromwell and his henchmen, like the abbey did, down the road, in 1538, and after that it stood as remains until 1726, when Sharp trotted up the hill, became the village curate, and built the manor we're in now.' Lawrence takes a sip of wine. 'There's a map of Cambridgeshire from the 1640s printed in Amsterdam that has a little sketch that looks like it might be ruins, pretty much on this spot. And another in 1659. Actually, there's a framed facsimile of that one in the lower living room.'

'Oh, I'll take a look after dinner. Are there any remains now of the original material fabric?' Josh is pleased with 'material fabric'.

'Sadly not. Or at least not visible. Everything that you can see that's old is Sharp's work.'

'Below the ground?'

'Possibly. And maybe one day we'll have a dig.'

'That would be fabulous. Do please keep me posted.'

Lawrence nods but doesn't say anything in reply.

Deborah watches Josh, wondering at these eager questions:

there is something cunning in him, she thinks, a sense of a cause being incrementally advanced. She suspects he will prove, in the long run, either unstoppable or destructive.

'Well, I must say librarians were better paid in the eighteenth century,' says Miles. 'Which I suppose is a very good thing. Imagine a university librarian today building this pile. My friend Jacqueline at UCL can hardly pay her studio rent.'

'Let me guess,' says Deborah, tapping her finger on the table with each word. 'Seventeen hundreds. Cambridge man. Wealth beyond what we'd expect from his job. I'm sensing colonial entanglements?'

'Well done.' Lawrence's smile becomes a little fixed. 'Spot on. Good. Sharp was a librarian and he seems never to have travelled further than London but his family had links to sugar plantations in the Caribbean. His brother-in-law William, who died at forty-one in Barbados, was a pretty high-ranking administrator. Knee deep in colonialism and some of the money must have come to Sharp.'

'Did Russell know all this?' asks Ash, who hadn't heard about this past.

'Not clear.' Lawrence rubs the bridge of his nose. 'But possibly. Probably.'

'That is . . . interesting,' says Ash.

There is a pause. Claudia has begun to collect up the starter plates. Lucy stands to help but Claudia ushers her back down. Lawrence wants to steer the conversation elsewhere. Of course, there's a time for these important discussions. Lawrence after all teaches a course on 'constructing whiteness in pre-modern literature' which was nominated for a Student Union teaching initiative award. But the first night of the retreat isn't that time.

The light outside is fading now and the room feels dimmer, more intimate.

'But the other thing you should know,' he begins, trying another path, 'is that Claudia's grandmother was certain there were ghosts here.'

'Oh, how delicious.' Deborah clasps her hands together. 'Details. All.'

'Well, *a* ghost. She was called Mabel,' says Claudia, stacking the plates. 'My grandmother, I mean. Keep your knives and forks. It's not especially exciting, I'm afraid. The usual thing: a woman in black, just standing in her bedroom, and sometimes walking in the garden I think, late at night. The family story is that whenever she was seen, a tragedy would follow. Her husband saw it too, once, at the foot of their bed.'

'There's a painting of Mabel in the hall,' Lawrence puts in. 'Odd portrait. Big arms.'

'But *here*?' says Miles. 'She saw a ghost here, in this house?'

'In this house,' Claudia repeats.

There is a pause.

Claudia says, 'Mabel didn't have an imaginative bone in her body so perhaps it's true.'

Lawrence can't quite read the atmosphere. He was hoping for a sort of pantomime it's-behind-you, but he hasn't got that. Deborah looks fascinated, Ash is smiling at least, but Miles actually seems tense.

Miles says, 'Well, I'm afraid you need to tell us which room Granny Mabel slept in.'

Deborah says, 'Oh, Miles, are you worried? Do you believe in ghosts?' She laughs and says, 'I'm sorry, that's an absurd thing for one adult to ask another.'

Miles, dead serious, says, 'I actually do.'

'Really?'

'Absolutely.'

Deborah looks at Miles for a moment, weighing him up. 'Well, that's a Catholic upbringing for you.'

'Don't joke, Debs. They're real. I know people think that sounds mad in this day and age, but I'm sure of it.'

Deborah says, 'How unexpected.'

'There's no need for panic,' says Claudia. 'She was in our room. And we've never seen anything.'

Miles says, 'But do you . . .'

Claudia lifts the tray.

'Do I think this ancient house is haunted?'

Miles nods.

At exactly the same time, Lawrence says, 'Of course we don't', and Claudia says, 'Maybe.'

A momentary pause, and then everyone laughs.

'I'm not sure,' says Claudia, 'Lawrence is sure', and she carries the tray out to the kitchen.

'And how about the extra seat?' Deborah indicates the end of the table, where an extra place is set, notebook included. 'Is someone missing or do you always set a place for poor old Mabel?'

Lawrence pushes his chair back a little. 'Ha, no – someone *is* missing, actually. The final member of our retreat. Inês Coval Moreno. She's a Portuguese artist. Portuguese, but . . .' he pauses for a fraction of a second, his lips pursing, 'of Mozambican heritage, I believe. She is really extraordinarily talented, and she's starting a fellowship at Caius next term. I thought she was already in London but perhaps not. She did say she'd be here today. I tried calling her earlier but couldn't get through.'

'What kind of artist is she?'

'She works with glass. She makes these fabulous sorts of . . . sculptures,' Lawrence gestures with his hands, 'and she's installing a new piece in the college. A window. She was delighted to be asked to the retreat. I can't think what the problem is.'

'Has she been here before?'

'No, no, she's been to Cambridge a couple of times, I think, but I've only met her once myself, in London, then I invited her here.'

Claudia sticks her head around the door. 'Darling, can you give me a hand bringing in the plates?'

'What? Sorry, yes, of course.'

After the door has closed behind them, Miles looks around the room, aware that for the first time the guests are gathered together without their hosts, like children without the grown-ups. He's about to remark on it when Lawrence returns, balancing a stack of plates, a loaf of bread, and a salad bowl, leaning on the door to hold it open for Claudia, who is carrying an enormous baking dish, which she places in the centre of the table to general exclamation.

'Oh, it's nothing,' says Claudia, but she is pleased with how the dish has turned out, and with the silence that falls as everyone starts to eat.

In the conversation that follows, people chat in smaller groups of two or three, so Claudia can sit quietly and look around the table. Aside from the non-appearance of Inês, it is all going well. Everyone is apparently enjoying themselves, and Lawrence seems to be unwinding as a result. Claudia tries to catch his eye, but he is deep in conversation with Lucy, setting up the salt cellar and his glass to recreate the objects in some story he is telling, Lucy smiling, leaning in. Lawrence's face is vivid, animated; Ash and Josh are listening too, now, starting to laugh as Lawrence reaches the punchline.

Miles breaks a crust of bread in half. He leans over a little from the table and rests an arm across the back of Deborah's chair as she reaches for the wine and refills both their glasses.

In a low voice, Miles says, 'You're right, Lawrence is in his element, isn't he? Holding court.'

Deborah glances towards the other end of the table. 'Ash seems a bit quiet.'

'Yes, I thought that.' Miles takes a large swallow of his wine. 'Taking a while to warm up, maybe. He had a total shocker in lockdown, did you hear?' Deborah shakes her head. 'His fiancée found out he'd been having an affair – it had been going on for months beforehand, a colleague at the university – and then he met up with this other woman actually during lockdown. Layered moral transgressions. He and the fiancée had this horrible drawn-out break-up – Ash said it was like being inside the worst ever fight, but in slow motion. Eventually she left him, called off the wedding, but they had to carry on living together for months before she could move out. He was all over the place afterwards.'

'I didn't know.'

'I'm quite surprised he's here at all. I got the impression he was rather off Lawrence these days.'

Deborah watches Ash smile at Claudia and address a comment to her, drawing her into the group.

'Perhaps he's here for our hostess?' she says quietly to Miles,

62

raising her eyebrows when he looks at her with a pantomime expression of shock. 'Stranger things have happened. Stranger things *will* happen. It's just a question of timing.'

'Ash hasn't dated a woman his own age in years.'

'Maybe not. But they are old friends and Claudia is . . . exceptional.'

'Actually,' Miles replies, 'I don't think Lawrence has ever got over the fact that Ash knew Claudia before he did, way back when.'

'Knew her or *knew* her?'

'Oh, just knew her, I'm sure. Or at least that's what I'd assumed. I think Ash introduced her to Lawrence. But who knows if anything happened between Ash and Claudia. Maybe even Lawrence doesn't. I don't think he likes it, anyway, that sense of a history before Lawrence. I suppose it's because it's something he can't control.' Miles notices Lawrence looking in his direction and so pulls his chair closer to the table to signal his participation, or at least his non-apartness. Miles tops up his own glass again and leans across to offer the bottle to Josh, who smiles and nods enthusiastically, reaching forward with his glass, mouthing 'thank you' and holding Miles's gaze a fraction longer than necessary, before returning his attention to Lawrence.

Deborah says quietly, 'And what's his game?'

'What? Whose game?'

Deborah looks meaningfully at Josh.

'Don't ask. I can't tell you about it now. I'm surprised Lawrence has asked him here, I will say that much.'

'He's so pretty.'

Miles shakes his head.

Deborah looks away before her interest in Josh becomes obvious. 'Later, then.'

When everyone has finished eating, Lawrence pushes back his chair and taps his glass with the side of his fork.

'So, you'll all have seen from the notes I sent . . .'

'The *rules*,' Miles begins, and Deborah shushes him.

'From the *notes*,' Lawrence says and looks at Miles over his glasses in a mock schoolmaster manner, 'that I'd like us to take turns to say a little about the work we are doing here. Perhaps two of us each evening? There's no rota as such but perhaps someone would like to volunteer?'

Lawrence's guests all suddenly have something else to look at.

'Miles, won't you start us off?'

Miles puts his hands in the air and shakes his head. 'No, absolutely not, Lawrence. I'm far too drunk. If we are going to do this, it should really be before dinner and with sufficient warning.' There are murmurs of assent.

'Well, tomorrow we can do it before dinner, but if we don't start tonight, we won't all get a go,' Lawrence points out. 'Come on, Miles, tell us about one of your divorces. Or is it all under embargo on pain of returning your massive advance?'

Something shifts in Miles and he raises his head to meet Lawrence's eye.

'Not tonight, Lawrence, all right?'

'All right, but I don't see why—'

Josh breaks in. 'I'll do it, if you like. I can tell you a bit about what I'm working on. About the film. I think you all might be interested. And then Miles can do another night.'

'All right,' Lawrence says evenly. 'Let's do that. Thank you, Josh.' He gives the tiniest little nod to Miles.

Josh straightens his collar and makes to stand, but before he can speak again, the phone rings in the hallway. Claudia goes to answer it. The room is quiet as they listen.

'Hello? Yes . . . yes, of course, just a minute.'

Claudia's head appears around the door. 'Lucy? It's for you.' Josh resumes his seat.

'Me? Who is it? Is it one of the children?'

As Lucy pushes her chair away from the table, Josh interlocks his fingers and pulls his palms tightly together. How typical, how inevitable, that Lucy should divert the group's attention from him just as he was about to claim it.

'No, a man – I think it's Neil? He didn't say. The phone's just here.' Claudia shepherds Lucy into the hallway and then comes back to the table, shutting the door behind her.

'I guess I'll wait till she's back.' Josh looks over to Lawrence, who shakes his head, but Claudia starts piling plates and cutlery, and says, 'I may as well go and get the pudding now, while Lucy's on the phone. Won't take a minute.'

'I'll give you a hand,' Josh rises from his seat, 'and actually I wouldn't mind a quick cigarette, before we get going. Anyone care to join me? Deborah?'

'I'd love to, but I'm not allowed,' says Deborah. 'Have one for me, won't you?'

Josh says, 'Miles?'

'Not for me.'

Josh pauses for a fraction of a second, registering these rejections, then gives a little salute as he leaves the room with Claudia.

'We'll never get started at this rate!' says Lawrence, his mock-exasperated tone doing little to mask his actual exasperation.

He busies himself by going round the table lighting the candles, although it's not quite dark enough for them yet. But being productive is Lawrence's response to frustration. 'The weather's been so hot, half of these had melted in the box,' he says. 'I wanted to keep the electricity out of this room when we had the house rewired, so that it would only be lit by candles. But Claudia wasn't having any of it.'

Ash, sipping his wine, observes how Lawrence's comments often position Claudia as a source of denial or negation.

As Lawrence completes his circuit, Claudia comes back in, her tray this time holding a large cake, studded with purple fruit, which she places carefully on the table.

'Oh, Claudia, that is lovely,' says Miles.

'I'm afraid it's more damsons. But cake, this time. Everyone?'

Claudia starts cutting slices. There is cream in an old-fashioned jug. Lawrence tops up the wine.

After a moment, the door opens and Lucy comes in, to Lawrence's relief – but then he realises that she is clearly upset. Yet another delay to the presentations! Lawrence sighs, internally. Lucy's eyes are red and she is avoiding people's gazes. Claudia stops cutting. Lawrence has to check himself from shaking his head.

Deborah stands and stretches her hands out to Lucy. 'Darling, what's the matter?'

Lawrence says, 'Shall we carry on?'

Lucy takes Deborah's hand and then slumps in her chair. The slice of cake looks incongruous.

'It was Neil. He only calls when he needs help. John had an asthma attack, a worse one than usual. Neil freaked out. He didn't know where the spare inhalers were. He didn't know what to do. I've always been there, before. Neil told me I was selfish for going away and this kind of thing was always going to happen.'

Deborah says, 'Says the man who spent two semesters solo in Barcelona when his twins were two.'

'I think I should go home.'

A chorus of 'No's.

Claudia says, 'How is John now?'

'I talked him back to calm. He gets nervous without me there. Isobel was so sweet.'

Deborah thinks, *Neil made this up*. Or he caused it, made it worse.

Lucy stabs a fork into her cake. 'Neil was fucking hopeless. He has this uncanny gift in a crisis for becoming another crisis himself. He's forty-eight but when I need him, he's eighteen. Not even eighteen. Eight. By the end of the call, I was calming *him* down.'

'He's an adult,' Claudia says, 'and he's their father. You shouldn't have to give up your one week away. That's not fair. Also, it's not good for the twins seeing you junking what you want to come and sort things out every time their father can't cope.'

Lucy thinks, eyes straight ahead. She says, 'You know he actually didn't know what year they were in at school? How is that possible?'

Deborah says, 'Men who don't take responsibility. I could write an opera.'

Ash had stood up when Lucy returned and he hasn't resumed his seat. He wants to say or do something to be of help to Lucy. But he doesn't know what that could be. So he just stands still, his hands clasped behind him, awkward. Claudia, with a contrasting naturalness, crouches next to Lucy's chair and places a hand on her arm.

'Lucy, it's all right. John's had an asthma attack but he's fine, he's safe and he's with his father. He'll be going to sleep now and you can call in the morning to see how he's doing. If he's not well, or even just if you want to, you can go home and see him tomorrow. I'll drive you.'

Lawrence shifts in his chair and lets out a small sigh.

'But don't go now,' says Claudia, 'not because of this. Have some pudding, and then you can go to bed and get an early night. You'll feel better in the morning.'

Lucy has turned to face Claudia. Ash watches her take a breath and lift her shoulders. Something passes between the two women. 'Thank you. You're right, I know you're right. Except about the early night. If I'm here, then I'm definitely going to enjoy myself.' She flourishes her empty glass. 'Could somebody top me up?'

Ash upends the remains of the white wine into her glass. 'The night is young,' he says.

Lucy looks over her shoulder and gives Ash a wide smile, then turns back to the table and lifts the glass to take a long swallow of her drink.

'Josh, I'm so sorry I interrupted you. Please do tell us what you're working on. Your film.'

Josh finds that tone – that magnanimity – maddening. He watches Lucy as she turns to him and shifts in a stroke away from her anxiety about Neil and the asthma attack. Visibly straightening her back, Lucy looks at Josh with an expectant confidence which, for Josh, instantly recalls her attitude in

68

a seminar room and, later, the manner in which she would ask questions at conferences. The assurance with which she takes her place in a group of her seniors, and the unaffected certainty with which she expects her voice to be heard and listened to, are undiminished in Lucy. Some people might find Lucy inspiring, but Josh, positioned too tightly in his own mind as rival, feels his confidence slip in the face of her poise. Her presence reduces him, and with all her vaunted acuity she must know this. And if she knows this, how else can Josh understand Lucy's preternatural authority, except as a kind of hostility, to him, in particular? There is a pause as Ash and Claudia return to their seats and the group shifts its attention to him. Josh can feel expectation becoming a weight: the room is suddenly filled with a series of faces all turned towards him. When he's suddenly nervous he sometimes stutters, and he does this now. For this moment, Deborah finds him deeply attractive.

'Well, o-o-okay,' Josh begins, trying to recall the opening of his practised pitch for his film project which, in these different circumstances, is eluding him. He smooths his hair with his hand. He turns a fraction so he can't see Lucy. 'For the past two years I've been doing a screenwriting MA, part-time because of work, and I've just finished it.'

'Gosh, that's impressive. Where do you work?' Deborah asks.

'Fern House,' Josh replies. 'I don't know if you know it?'

'In north London?' says Deborah. Josh nods and she goes on, 'Yes, I had a colleague whose son went there. It's doing rather well, isn't it?'

'Not bad,' Josh nods again. 'Anyway, I've just finished the MA and I'm developing a script which I really think has potential, so this week I need to get to grips with what I hope are the final rewrites.'

'A film!' Lucy exclaims. 'That's so exciting, Josh. I couldn't be more ignorant about film production. What happens when you finish the script?'

Josh feels a wave of irritation at Lucy's happy admission of ignorance.

'I've got a director who's interested, so basically once I finish this draft I'll be looking for an agent to help me sell it.' Josh carefully avoids Deborah's eye at this point; he knows Deborah doesn't do films herself, but there is a woman at her agency called Rebecca (Josh googled it last night) who does. 'But also I am hopeful we can put it into production ourselves if we can find the backing.'

'Backing?' says Lucy.

'Money.'

There is a pause and then Claudia, reaching across the table for another bottle, says, 'Tell us what the script's about.'

'It's a modern retelling of "The Knight's Tale" from *The Canterbury Tales*,' Josh replies, 'interspersed with a sort of biopic of Chaucer himself.'

'I'm afraid I can never remember which tale is which,' says Deborah. 'Is that the arse-kissing one?'

'Not exactly. I mean no. "The Knight's Tale" is this story of two cousins who fall in love with the same woman and compete for her and they end up fighting a tournament. My version is set in an inner-city estate, so that becomes gang violence.'

Lawrence thinks: Christ, this sounds even worse than the first time I heard it.

'Lawrence has kindly agreed to be a script consultant.'

'Well,' Lawrence interjects, 'I said I'd read it through, but with some fairly major caveats. It's not my field and I know next to nothing about film, really.'

Miles says, 'And how are you on inner-city gang violence?'

'We don't get much of that in the village,' says Lawrence, shifting the position of the central candleholder. 'But happy to help out if I can, of course.'

'Wasn't there a film about "The Knight's Tale" twenty years ago?' says Deborah. 'With Heath Ledger in it? I'm sure there was.'

'Well, it was called "*A Knight's Tale*" and it had a character called Chaucer in it,' Josh replies. 'But really that's all they have in common. Mine's a quite different film.'

'Is yours not a comedy, then?' Deborah asks.

'No,' Josh says, more firmly than he meant to. 'No. It's a love story, but at the heart there's an ethical dilemma.'

'About Chaucer?'

'Well, no, about . . . masculinity, really.'

Josh smiles stiffly. He thinks, God that sounds trite. He has looked forward to telling everyone about his script, but the conversation has not developed as he'd hoped. He is conscious that his film seems terrible.

'Well, that sounds wonderful, darling,' says Deborah. 'I can't wait to see it and tell all my friends I know the writer. Now, Lawrence,' she continues, turning to their host, 'does that satisfy you, or do you want another volunteer?'

Josh starts to say, 'There's more that I . . .' but Deborah carries on, the drink increasing her volume, and he fades away.

'Because I spent most of the day working on my emails,

and I don't think anyone wants a précis of those.' As Lawrence opens his mouth to object, Deborah continues, 'It's all right, I'll be doing proper creative work for the rest of the week, I promise. And Miles . . .' Deborah places a proprietorial hand on his arm, 'I need you to myself for a few minutes. Let's get a breath of air, and then I'm going to collapse on a sofa and drink expensive whisky. Thank you, Claudia, that was divine.' Deborah gets up from the table. Miles follows.

'Sofas and whisky it is,' says Lucy, rising a little unsteadily to her feet. 'Ha! That would be a good name for a bar: Whisky and Sofa. Do you get it? I'm going to open a bar on Mill Road and call it that.' She and Ash and then gradually the others follow Deborah and Miles from the room.

As Claudia places the cutlery in the dishwasher, Lawrence sits in his chair, surveying the table, turning a cork slowly but methodically over and over in his right hand. Abandoned glasses. Plates empty of food. Chairs pushed back at stumbled departures. By most accounts, the trappings of a successful evening. But Lawrence has a nagging sense of dissatisfaction. He sees that Miles has left his notebook. He thinks about Josh's rather sub-par presentation, not helped by all that fuss Lucy made. He reflects on Ash's . . . distance. He considers how he can pull things back on schedule.

Ash sits up in bed. He has a large biography of Joseph Roth in his lap but his eyes focus above the book at the small square window on the facing wall which doesn't have a curtain and through which he can see the moon. It is a beautifully clear night. In his mind, as is his habit, he starts to proceed methodically through the events of the day, a kind of mental diary-keeping he has done since he was a child. But his thoughts fall on Lucy. He thinks of her asleep in her bed, or reading, or lying looking at the moon. He knows it's unlikely anything will happen, but the prospect of her in the same house lends the week ahead a lovely shimmering excitement. He tries to remember the line from *Mrs Dalloway*. He has an excellent memory for quotations, even for those memorised for Finals thirty years ago. 'Clarissa . . . standing' – was that it? – 'standing in her bedroom' – yes! – 'standing in her bedroom at the top of the house holding the hot-water can in her hands and saying aloud, "She is beneath this roof . . . She is beneath this roof!"'

Miles is finding it hard to focus, and he can hardly read the characters on the screen. He is considerably drunker than even he realised, but he still tries to scroll through Twitter. 'Notifications' is encircled in blue. Twenty-two new followers. A message from a reading group in Bath who are enjoying his last book. Another he can no longer read. The room starts to sway. Miles drops the phone and closes his eyes and slumps asleep fully dressed, with one shoe on.

'Darling, have you seen my Snore Wizard?' Lawrence is on all fours, stretching an arm under the bed.

'On top of your book.'

'What? Oh. Thanks.' Lawrence puts the rubber guard in his mouth and gets into bed. He says, 'Good night, love – and thanks for cooking that wonderful meal', but with the Snore

Wizard in, his words are indistinct. He puts on his eye mask and inserts one headphone into his right ear.

'Poor Lucy,' says Claudia. 'What an arsehole Neil is.'

'Can't hear you. Headphone in.'

Lawrence is listening to the closing headlines of *The World Tonight*.

Claudia turns out her bedside light.

'. . . In Ukraine, President Zelensky calls for strict sanctions against Russia for "nuclear blackmail" . . .'

Three minutes later Lawrence is snoring.

Josh is typing a text. 'Good night squirrel! Miss you. All fine here. Working hard, lots of interest in the film! Will try to call but there's no internet out here – nightmare! xxx'

After he clicks send, Josh leans forward so that he can read the Wifi password scrawled on the back of his notebook, and enters it into his phone.

The windows of Deborah's room are all open, and she is lying on top of the bedclothes, fanning herself with the *London Review of Books*. Her thoughts are spooling through the day, moving associatively across the people and the things said as she drifts towards sleep. She thinks about Josh and his plotting, and Neil's (she feels sure) fictional asthma crisis, and Ash's clear (but he thinks covert) attraction to Lucy, and Lawrence and his rules that aren't rules (but are rules), and Claudia's service which Claudia has just about but not quite convinced herself is her own choice and contentment. How funny Miles says he actually believes in ghosts. Can this be right? And not for the first time Deborah reflects how it is inconsistencies that she likes in people, much more than pattern. Deborah finds her thoughts looping round Claudia and her duty and her singing. Deborah lets the paper drop to the floor. What does Claudia want? Deborah makes a mental note to find that out, and to help Claudia achieve it, and, although she is falling asleep as she makes it, she is Deborah and so she knows she will do it.

Lucy is sitting up in bed with her phone. The screen casts a white glow on her face, like a Renaissance painting of a woman reading a Bible. She is smiling, and is entirely fixated on the screen, as she scrolls through picture after picture of John and Isobel. Here they are in Norfolk, at the campsite standing together arm in arm next to the pizza oven. Here is John in his Everton top. Here is Isobel in her drama club's *Tempest* when she had one line – 'Lead, monster; we'll follow' – rehearsed over and over hundreds of times.

Chapter Four

Tuesday morning

Claudia hovers on the step that leads down into the kitchen, balancing on the balls of her feet. The room is a scene of moderate devastation. When the children were small, tidying up after dinner had been Lawrence's job; she would go up to bed to the sound of him humming to the radio and loading the dishwasher, and she would come downstairs in the morning to a clean kitchen. Officially, they share the cooking, with Lawrence delivering spectacular Sunday roasts and thumbing through Nigel Slater for weeknight suppers, but the kitchen-tidying, like all of the cooking that is not spectacular, has gradually slipped into Claudia's orbit. A hundred years ago, Claudia reflects, putting on the kettle, this house had two live-in maids as well as a cook and a woman who came in to do the rough work. She and Lawrence have a weekly cleaner; during one lean winter when the roof needed repairing and the oil tank replacing, Lawrence had suggested that a saving could be made on her wages, but Claudia had refused to listen. During lockdown, with everyone at home all the time, Tristan requiring constant snacks and Lawrence baking his own bread most mornings and then disappearing to his 'research' for most of the day (how she came to despise that word which seemed to mean simply 'reading'), Claudia had found herself filled with disbelief and then unspoken fury at the relentless energy the house required of her, an endless repetition of tasks that seemed to make no progress at all, developing a secret loathing for the building itself, or rather for its insides, which has only recently begun to dissipate.

Now she must choose between achieving a sense of calm from cleaning the kitchen or from her solitary swim. No one last night mentioned a desire to swim early, but it's quite possible that someone might, and she is a little later than usual. Claudia picks up her mug and towel and very gently opens the back door.

Miles has a pounding headache and is sitting alone at the kitchen table. Someone had been in before him – the kettle was warm – but he hasn't seen anyone. The kitchen is quiet. He has just swallowed three paracetamol and is now drinking a second large mug of coffee. Miles rests his head on his arms and closes his eyes and remains like this for five minutes, on the edge of sleep. In the courtyard a peacock lets out a loud squawk. Miles takes this as a kind of prompt from the natural world and gets up and begins the washing-up. Even hungover, which he certainly is, and which in fact he increasingly is these days, with a frequency that is beginning to concern his husband, Miles is carried forward on a deeply felt sense of happiness which gets him through any amount of exhaustion. After years of frustration, Miles's life has recently become better, radically better, and even domestic chores fill him with a low hum of pleasure at the sense of things being put in their right place. He empties the dishwasher. He fixes the rollers on the pull-out rack. Miles is loving writing *A History of Marriage in 12 Divorces*. Last month he finished Nicolas and Cécilia Sarkozy. Miles puts in rinse aid, finds some dishwasher salt under the sink and adds that too. He reloads the washer with most of the dishes. In the spring he did Charlemagne and Desiderata ('The Divorce that Built the Holy Roman Empire'). He puts the machine on eco setting, and washes the remaining dirty plates, glasses and cutlery by hand. His argument, roughly, is that it is divorce, not marriage, that cements society and leads to social and political progress. That in fact divorce is not marriage's failure but its promise, and its proper fulfilment. This week he's tackling Henry VIII and Catherine of Aragon ('Divorce and the birth of Protestantism'). Miles likes the irony that he married Craig the week before signing the contract for this book. They treated the £300,000 advance as a wedding present from Clio and bought a new house.

For Miles to be happy represents a profound transformation. From his late twenties to his early forties, Miles's experience of work was a profitless toil and this discontent spread across all his life. He couldn't unlock himself to anyone and so he kept everyone at bay. He hated teaching, and the history students at Bangor University hated his seminars. His course feedback was dreadful. And yet in his twenties Miles had been a compassionate, empathetic, dynamic person. By the time he was thirty, he was fifty-five; by thirty-five, he felt seventy. What had happened? 'Seems entirely uninterested in student views', read one feedback slip, and this was undeniably true. His stock in the department, high on entry almost twenty years ago, had descended slowly but consistently until he was, at forty-three, seen universally, and undeniably, as dead wood. He had failed to convert his PhD into a first book and the three articles he dragged out of himself dropped into the vast waters of academic publishing with no perceptible ripple. Three articles, dreadful teaching reviews and no book is not two decades' good work. But then on a day in March 2016, sitting at his laptop at his study table at home, he suddenly found a different writing voice. It came to him all at once and the effect was immediate, like Augustine hearing a child chanting 'Take up and read!', opening his Bible, and converting to Christianity.

The voice was sparky and funny and gossipy and cocky and smart and quick and untroubled: it was Miles at his best, the fullest expression of himself, the Miles who had been buried and repressed for twenty years by constraint and worry and doubt, hemmed in by pedantic footnotes. And as soon as he had a voice, he had an idea for what would become his first book, dumping the joyless rewriting of his hateful PhD, 'Protocols of Documentation at the Inns of Court, 1603–1660', and starting suddenly on 'A Queer History of Stuart Kings'. Two days later he asked his journalist friend Liam for the name of a literary agent: Deborah Nicholls wrote back the day he emailed her an outline and the sample chapter he had written in two delirious non-stop days. She 'loved it' and invited him to lunch.

A week later, feeling a strength he had never felt – a strength which he gradually began to realise was conviction – he resigned his academic job. His head of department, a specialist in medieval coinage who replied 'Not really my period' to most questions, said, 'I think you're making a serious mistake at just the wrong age,' but Miles could see the envy in his cowardly eyes. When the head of department added, 'In two years' time you could be Director of Teaching and Learning', as if he was sliding a case of used banknotes across a desk, Miles burst out laughing. Four weeks after leaving Bangor, Miles was sitting in The Ivy in Covent Garden with his agent drinking champagne. Deborah talked him through how she was going to make him 'a lot of money'. And she did. The fact that the source of Miles's wealth was his own wit and imagination, that he had turned the contents of his head into cash which had become a three-bedroom house in St Albans, felt like a miracle, the conversion of airy prospect into bricks and mortar. 'All that energy you have, darling, it was going in the wrong direction. You were walking down the same dead end, over and over, for twenty years. But now you're free!' How could he ever repay Deborah? He had got out just in time, before he was too old to make the break.

His satisfaction with this new life is compounded, Miles recognises, by coming to Hawton, to Lawrence, as a confirmed success. Through all Miles's years of self-disappointment, Lawrence's star had steadily risen, from a coveted research fellowship to his first book, widely lauded as 'brilliant' and 'transformative', and the security and prestige of what had seemed Lawrence's inevitable destination all along, life as a Cambridge don. Lawrence's marriage to Claudia, his acquisition of a wife who was beautiful and talented and kind, and who clearly adored him, had brought Lawrence a stability that Miles had envied as much as his professional success. And it had also brought him Hawton, this rural idyll where Lawrence was almost literally lord of the manor. Their friendship had endured the disparities between them but over the years, Miles knew, it had stretched and warped into something very different from the easiness and genuine pleasure in one another that had formed its foundation in their college days. Lawrence had not been able to contain his satisfaction at how life had turned out any more than Miles could contain his disappointment. But now Miles feels himself to be Lawrence's equal, his competitor once again, and there is even a pleasure to be had in the incapacity of Lawrence, who disavows competition and hierarchy when he is winning and on top, to hide his jealousy of his old friend's transformation. Miles puts the last dish in the drying rack, hangs the towel on the oven door handle, and heads back to his room, leaving the dishwasher humming.

On her last visit to Hawton, Deborah had asked Lawrence why the doors to the house, front and back, were always unlocked. He had told her that it was because someone was usually at home: Claudia, or Tristan and the au pair, or their then-lodger, a Bulgarian doctoral student from the School of Archaeology who joined them for dinner, making flatbreads with Claudia in the warm kitchen. The back door, Deborah notices now as she closes it quietly behind her, doesn't even seem to have a key with which it can be locked. To someone with Deborah's practical mind, and with her decades of living in central London, this habit seems incautious, even performatively so: Lawrence has always prided himself on his reputation for hospitality. Returning now from an early morning walk round the grounds and not wishing to rouse anyone sleeping inside, the unlocked back door is a welcome convenience.

Deborah slips off her sandals, which are damp from the grass, and crosses to the sink to fill the kettle. It is warm to the touch. An earthenware teapot and half-empty mug stand waiting on the dining table. Deborah prefers to have the first coffee of her day in solitude, and she hopes that she will be able to pull this off. Leaving the kettle to boil, she pads through the kitchen into the hallway, which is still and silent in the early morning light.

The entrance hall at Hawton is a pleasing clutter: the family's outdoor clothes, discarded shoes and bags, and other scattered possessions spilling across the assorted kilim rugs which cover the stone floor. The back wall is lined with bookcases, crammed not only with books but the paraphernalia of family life: small constructions in Lego, postcards, a mug missing its handle, a pair of homemade clay tealight-holders. Deborah scans the shelves. There is an assortment of fiction – she's pleased to see one of her authors among the piles of familiar names – but most of the contents relate to the outside world: an atlas, collections of travel writing and city guides, books on star-gazing, anthologies of nature poetry, whole shelves devoted to books about trees and rivers and birds and to old Ordnance Survey maps of Cambridgeshire, Kent, and North Yorkshire. At the top of one bookcase Lawrence has propped a series of printed sheets of paper which look as though they have been produced on the old printing press he keeps in an outhouse: the first shows a single line of text, indistinct at this distance;

the second sheet has two lines, the third three, and so on, the type set so that each line is an identical length.

Deborah crosses the hall into the corridor on its opposite side. Entering this darker, more enclosed space, she feels a sense of intrusion which isn't entirely comfortable, as though she is encroaching on the family's private territory without permission. Against the wall ahead of her stands Claudia's piano, which on her last visit Deborah heard but did not see Claudia play. Deborah once, many years ago, saw Claudia in concert, before she had known her or even Lawrence well. It had been Bach's 'Mass in B Minor' and Deborah, not much of a fan of classical music, had nonetheless been entranced by Claudia's performance and her transformation from Lawrence's latest girlfriend to the source of such richness and beauty. Claudia has remained remarkable to Deborah ever since. Deborah reaches out and with one finger strokes the piano's cool, smooth surface. As she does so she hears voices above her, Lawrence coming down the stairs talking to someone, and that same feeling of trespassing causes her to turn quickly and retrace her steps to the kitchen, where the kettle has just boiled.

Josh takes his wireless headphones out of his ears and puts them in his pocket, bending forward, hands braced on his thighs. He breathes out steadily to calm his nausea and stands up slowly. Ahead of him, the golden stone of the church is already warming in the sun, the morning promising another sweltering day. Josh walks along the sloping path towards the gate, keeping an eye open, as he always does in a churchyard, for a gravestone with his name on it, but there are none to be seen. He's weighing up whether this is an augury of healthy longevity, or of eternal obscurity – eternal obscurity would be far worse: he couldn't endure that – when his eyes fall on a grave in the shape of a cross with two names, the dates 1842 and 1843, and a sentence cut into the stone in italic letters: 'We are what you will be, we were what you are.' Josh stops in his tracks – held by some force. He shakes his head to be free, and latches the gate behind him, and walks the last stretch back to the house. For a moment he feels as if there are tendrils pulling him back to the grave. He quickens his walk.

He is pleased when the gate creaks loudly: Josh hopes that someone will be around to notice that, despite the amount of alcohol he shipped last night, he's been for an early run.

❦

As she wakes, Lucy reaches for her phone and checks the screen: notifications from Instagram, but nothing from WhatsApp. She quickly types a message to Neil – *How is John this morning? Everything okay?* – and falls back onto the pillow. Unbelievable to have slept so late. She will be in trouble with Lawrence if she misses the allotted hour for breakfast on the timetable. She needs water, a shower, and coffee, in that order. Last night's Instagram post on the pool and gardens has several likes. Before she gets up, she takes a quick snap of the view of the sky through her window and adds it to her stories. It's going to be a beautiful day.

By the time Josh gets down to the kitchen after his shower, Claudia, Lawrence and Ash are all sitting around the table among the remnants of breakfast. Lawrence is pouring a second cup of coffee and Ash is slicing a banana onto muesli.

'Morning. Coffee? There's a drop left.' Lawrence brandishes the cafetière.

'Yes, please – just black, thanks.' Josh takes a place at the end of the table.

'Thanks,' Josh says again, taking the cup.

'Keep calm and what?' says Josh, gesturing at Lawrence's mug.

'I'm sorry?' Lawrence raises his eyebrows.

'Your mug: "Keep calm and . . ."?'

'Ah yes.' Lawrence turns the mug to show the text in full. '"Keep calm and read Wyatt." It was a gift from a student.' He takes another sip. 'Pre-pandemic.'

'How was it in that tiny bed? Josh is in Tristan's room,' Claudia explains to Ash as she smiles sympathetically at Josh.

Josh had had to hold a hunched position all night in order to remain within the confines of the hateful little bed. 'Super comfortable,' he says now. 'I love your son's room. I got up early, as it happens, to go for a run. Beautiful countryside round here.'

'Gosh, well done, you!' I sound like his bloody mother, Claudia thinks, and he must be less than ten years younger than I am. Is he making me behave like this or is it me? 'Well, there's toast or various cereals, mushrooms, eggs, if you want to cook them . . . I think that's it. It's help yourself at breakfast.' I don't like him, Claudia thinks. I don't trust him.

Josh stands to slice the loaf. 'Where is everyone?'

'Deborah's been and gone. She only came for a cup of coffee. She likes to start early. And Miles I think must have started early too, because I saw him in the lower living room when I came down, hard at it. Lucy, I haven't seen yet. And some angel came and cleaned up in here while I was swimming. Frankly miraculous. Was it you?'

Josh considers for a second claiming it was, but, weighing the risk, decides not to.

'No, I went straight out when I got up. Lucy?'

'Perhaps, although Deborah thought she was still asleep. Well, who knows. Maybe it was Mabel.'

'It's almost eight-thirty,' Lawrence checks his watch, 'and I did suggest we try to get working by nine. I hope Lucy won't be running late.'

'Lawrence, she's solo-parenting twins, this is the first night she's had away in weeks, and we all had a fair bit to drink last night. Let the poor woman have a lie-in.' Claudia gets up and starts clearing the table. Josh is finishing his toast as Claudia says, 'If everyone is done with breakfast, I'm going to go and get started myself.'

Ash says, rather suddenly, 'How's work going?', and the question, it seems to Lawrence, and also to Josh, has the intention of pausing Claudia's departure.

'Oh, it's all right,' Claudia replies.

A pause.

Ash says, 'Go on.'

'Well, there's a fairly steady flow at the moment. A trickle, anyway. I've got a piece in the *BBC Music Magazine* next month. But it's all just reviews. It's not really . . .'

Lawrence cuts in: 'Nothing wrong with reviews, darling.'

Ash says, 'It's not really . . .?'

Claudia shrugs. 'It's okay.' And then she adds: 'But it's just okay.'

Lawrence says, 'I always tell my students: cut your teeth on reviews.'

Ash says, 'I saw your one on the Bach biography in the *TLS*. Very good. The review I mean. The book sounded a bit . . . superfluous.'

'It's a decent biography. It slogs its way through. But why write a biography of Bach? If you want to understand the music, I mean. Biography is the wrong form for that. You don't understand a thing about the Brandenburg Concertos by knowing Bach had twenty children, but this book kept banging on about it.'

Ash drains his coffee. 'Yes, that must be true.'

Claudia says, 'I see your comment pieces all the time. I always read them.'

'That's nice of you.'

'Yes, me too,' says Lawrence.

'I like doing them. My academic writing is so slow. It always has been. In fact, I like that it's slow. The journalism is the opposite. I get asked to submit it the next day. I write it in an afternoon. Then there it is.'

Lawrence says, 'Is it always about race?'

'Not always.' Ash pauses to register his irritation at Lawrence's question. 'But often. I'm actually writing a longer think piece at the moment on a somewhat different issue . . .'

Lawrence speaks over these last words. 'Race and exams, race and university admissions, race and precarity, that kind of thing.'

Claudia says, 'What's the longer piece?'

'Oh . . .' Ash hesitates for a second, stumbling on his words, 'power, really. In academia. Abuses of power, I suppose you'd say.'

Lawrence says, 'Terrific topic', and then, turning to Claudia and taking her hand in a gesture that mixes affection with command, 'darling, if you see Miles, could you remind him that dinner needs to be fairly prompt this evening? I'd like to do the printing press demonstration while it's still light, if possible.'

'Yes, absolutely, I'll mention it to him if I see him,' Claudia says, thinking that this will be unlikely, as she plans to sit in the garden, but not especially wanting Lawrence to pass on this reminder himself. Ash catches the placatory tone to Claudia's voice. *She manages him*, Ash thinks, and he doesn't realise, as Lawrence scoops up toast crumbs with a crust, then pops them into his mouth, standing up from the table. Claudia takes Lawrence's plate and puts it in the dishwasher.

As Lawrence is leaving the room, his phone buzzes. 'Ah, it's Inês. She got delayed . . . she's coming this morning, should be here late lunchtime or early afternoon. Excellent. Splendid. She's extraordinarily talented, you know.' Lawrence is addressing this to the room in general. 'It would be nice to offer her a lift from the station.' He looks up at Claudia. 'Darling?'

When Claudia doesn't reply – her back is turned to the dishwasher – Lawrence adds, 'I thought if you're just finishing a review . . .'

Claudia says, 'Can you ask her to get a taxi? Otherwise I won't have much time, what with getting lunch ready too.'

'Yes, of course.' Lawrence looks down at the screen and starts typing. 'So, we'll all be here for lunch! Wonderful.'

Lawrence leaves, with Claudia behind him.

Ash slots his bowl and cup into the dishwasher. He is thinking about the way selfishness so often takes the form of hospitality. His ex-girlfriend Kate, different from Lawrence in almost every respect, was like him in this way: always making plans for visitors, guests and friends that relied on other people to carry them out. But Ash decides to let go of this resentment, and turns instead to wondering where he should work this morning. Miles is apparently in the lower living room, and Deborah had said she was planning to work in the dining room. Perhaps he should start in the kitchen, and then he will see Lucy when she comes in to breakfast. Ash cancels that thought. Ridiculous. What is he thinking will happen? He will go and work in the folly, as far from the house as he can.

Lucy had moved smoothly from her PhD with Lawrence to a three-year junior research fellowship at a Cambridge college, by the end of which she had received offers of a book contract from a prestigious academic press who had read her examiners' reports, and of marriage, from Neil, both of which she had come by easily and accepted without hesitation. This flurry of events – her friend James called it Lucy's 'imperial phase' – concluded with a permanent fellowship and faculty lectureship. Lucy's first book *Epistolary Culture and Separation in Late Medieval England* had been like completing a jigsaw puzzle: complicated, perhaps, but assembled with the certainty that a solution would be found. The reviews were excellent. The book was nominated for two prizes.

Lucy's current project – senior colleagues have a habit of referring to it knowingly as 'the all-important second monograph', as if actively wishing anxiety on Lucy – is about memorial culture: tombs, poems that describe the recently deceased, the prayers that keep the dead alive in the fifteenth and sixteenth centuries, before the Reformation stripped away those ways of remembering. The book had flickered and then caught light in Lucy's imagination after she had spent a day reading through burial records in the London Metropolitan Archives. She had come away with lists of names and places, but one brief record in particular had locked in her mind: a note, from the parish register of St John at Hackney from 1538: '12 March was buryed a woman that dyed in ye streate her name was Mary.' On the train back to Cambridge, Lucy stared out of the window as the fields flashed past and she realised that she was going to write a book about Mary.

Lucy had started with enthusiasm and clarity and the opening chapter had shifted vividly between an account of the funeral of Elizabeth of York, Queen to King Henry VII, in February 1503, and a description of the kind of burial performed for the poorest of the same parish in the same month, for someone like Mary. Lucy had been looking forward to a precious term's research leave to develop this contrast when the pandemic began. For twelve full months, with lockdowns and school closures and home-schooling and Neil's work in the lab (which expanded from nine to five to eight to seven, and which, as 'science', became non-negotiable), Lucy had not done a single day's research. In the following year, as life ground back to a version of normal and she returned to working on campus, the days and half-days that she had spent in the library had not got her much further, and then, as her relationship with Neil had broken down, her capacity to work seemed to have dissolved altogether. If the first book had been a jigsaw puzzle, this new one was a crossword with no clues. She could feel her project slipping away: what had been alive and exciting had atrophied and died.

Lucy started to wake in the night in panic, flung out of dreams of dark rooms and wrong paths. Though she has yet to articulate it to anyone, even fully to herself, Lucy is beginning to believe that her ability to write, even to think with the level of skill and intensity needed for academic work, has fallen away unnoticed in the maelstrom of the last two years. She is starting to see that recovering that capacity could be beyond her, and that dawning sense of loss, even though Lucy only perceives it at the edge of her vision, is terrifying. It is one of the reasons she has grown to hate Neil: truly, to hate him. She has come to see with clarity how love has turned into its bitter opposite. She needs to get away from him.

But Lucy is not thinking about this as she walks towards the churchyard at Hawton, two hundred yards from the gates of the manor, down the silent lane that runs through, and in fact constitutes, the village. Lucy enters the churchyard. She feels like she is drifting, as if she is gently directed by forces from the past, and she is enjoying the lightness, the lack of volition. She is remembering the effigy of Alice de la Pole, granddaughter of Geoffrey Chaucer, which lies in St Mary's church at Ewelme, near her family's home in that part of Oxfordshire; she is picturing Alice's long, sensitive fingers, held in everlasting prayer, the alabaster folds of her skirt and coif, the blank gaze of her eyes. Lucy wants to write about the tomb that remembers Alice in such extraordinary ways, the effigy of Alice as she had been in life above and, visible through elaborately carved arches, her skeletal corpse lying below. The tomb, with its double vision of life preserved and everlasting death, has become a fixation for Lucy, an image to which she returns when wandering or daydreaming, both of which she is doing now around the shady graves, out of the heat of the sun.

Alice's stone body is so much in Lucy's mind as she walks that, when she sees standing ahead of her a white figure, she starts, thinking of that alabaster Alice come to life. Lucy has come to the edge of the churchyard, where the mown grass, yellow and brittle in the heat, gives way to a thicker undergrowth, brambles snaking towards the high wall that separates the church from the old rectory. At the edge of the brambles is a set of iron railings, and within them a statue of a child – no, two children, Lucy realises as she edges around the railings, a boy and a girl. The first figure, the boy, stands, face half-raised to the sky, one arm extended upwards as though reaching to grasp some invisible object, the other hand resting on the shoulder of a female figure whose arms encircle his waist and whose face looks directly out to the viewer. The figures are not white at all, Lucy sees now, but a greyish marble, their weathered faces smoothed by time and the elements. They are standing on a plinth which is partly obscured by the ivy which grows from the statue's base and curls over the girl's limbs. The plinth has writing carved into it, but Lucy can't read it; she squats and presses her face to the railings to get a better look. 'SACRED TO THE MEMORY OF', the first line reads, but the text directly below, presumably names, is too weathered to make out. The following line reads 'OF HAWTON MANOR' and then words which might be 'IN THIS PARISH'; any further writing is obscured by the thick foliage. Lucy stands and takes a step backwards. She stares at the younger figure, her blank face a smaller, smoother version of Alice's, the chin raised, the lips just parted as if eternally about to speak. Lucy circles the railings again and stands for a moment, before retracing her steps towards the road and the house.

When Lucy has clanged the gate shut, the churchyard and the woods beyond it are for a long moment as still as the marble effigy. Then, like a breath being released, the smallest of movements return, as creatures stir in the undergrowth and a few high leaves catch the breeze. At the edge of the woods, where the trees are in shadow, a lone figure remains unmoving, watching and waiting until Lucy is out of sight.

Chapter Five

Tuesday afternoon

'I don't want to be a dick about this but I don't think people should be posting about the retreat on social media.'

Lawrence is arranging two extra chairs from the kitchen around the long wooden table by the pool. He is wearing a white T-shirt that says: *This Is What A Feminist Looks Like*, the letters printed to look spikily handwritten. Claudia moves around him, taking plates and cutlery and napkins from the tray. The sun is approaching its prime and out of the shade the heat is already uncomfortable.

'She's even put a hashtag.'

'Does it really matter, Lawrence?'

'Yes, I think it does. It threatens the sense of community and detachment that is the whole point of this week. This isn't . . . *Love Island*. Whatever the fuck that is.'

Claudia pulls the damp strap of her bikini top away from her shoulder and readjusts it. She looks at her husband, weighing the cost of pushing back against a desire for an enjoyable lunch.

'I don't understand it,' Lawrence continues, crouching

beside the table to adjust its balance, 'why she even bothers with all that stuff. It's such a waste of time and intellect.'

'Well, she must find some purpose in it,' Claudia says, 'and this is Lucy we're talking about. Ash always says she's the cleverest person in the Faculty.'

'Oh come on!' Lawrence looks up crossly. 'He only says that because he fancies her.'

He's heard that before, and from other people, and he cannot endure it: that his student should be declared cleverer than him.

'Come on, that's hardly fair to either of them.'

Lawrence stands up and is about to speak, but Deborah and Miles arrive, and if Lawrence has a single core social commitment it is not to air domestic tensions in public.

'I don't know why you'd ever leave this place,' Deborah says. 'Writing in the garden and then lunch by the pool. It's bloody paradise.'

Lawrence smiles and no one would know his irritation. 'Good morning's work?'

Miles says, 'Excellent. Do you know Henry VIII was only seventeen when he married Catherine of Aragon? He was a sixth former! She was a decrepit twenty-three.'

Deborah pulls out a chair to sit down. 'Spicy age gap.'

Lawrence says, 'And Deborah?'

'Oh I'm fifty-six.'

'I mean, what have you been up to?'

'Editing other people's genius, mostly.'

'Oh, who?'

'A young Scottish short story writer.'

'Would I know his name?'

'Their name.' Deborah leans back, face to the sky, so that Lawrence doesn't quite catch her words.

'*Their* name, did you say?'

'Yes, Lawrence.' Deborah looks over at him, amused. 'They're non-binary. Surely gender-neutral pronouns have arrived even in rural Cambridgeshire.'

'Yes, of course. I didn't hear you. Certainly, plenty of them at College.'

'Them and us, eh, Lawrence?' Miles is smiling.

'Oh for goodness' sake. Is they – are they a new find, Deborah?'

'Yes. They've only published one thing in a tiny literary journal in Glasgow which no one reads, except me. But I think I've found someone special.'

'You swoop in, don't you,' says Miles, 'and rescue people.'

Deborah leans into Miles and says, 'We should say,' and Miles replies, 'Okay, but in a minute.' He takes a handful of forks from Claudia and begins distributing them around the table.

Deborah says, 'Oh my God, Claudia!'

Claudia, who has just sat down, turns her head towards Deborah enquiringly.

'Is that a tattoo?' Deborah leans over the table and pulls Claudia's linen shirt down across her shoulder. Below the shoulder, a little above the fabric of her bikini, is the outline of three birds in flight.

'Yes, that's my new one. Well, nearly a year old now.' Claudia shifts so that her shirt falls back into place, partially covering the image.

'New one? Have you got several?'

'Well, just two. This is the other one.' She turns her wrist and shows her arm to Deborah and Miles.

Miles takes hold of Claudia's hand and looks closely at her arm. 'I like it. Both of them. They are very you.'

'Thank you.'

'You should get one, Lawrence.' Deborah catches Claudia's eye, correctly reading the domestic politics.

'Oh, I don't think so.'

Miles says, 'Yes! A massive anchor across your chest?'

Lawrence hands Deborah a pile of napkins. 'Pass these around, will you?'

Deborah puts them down on the table and says, 'You could get a bird as well. Oh, I know, a peacock!' She claps her hands together and grins. 'Or a quill! Yes, that's it, a quill pen made from a peacock's feather. On your bicep.'

Lawrence smiles tightly and says nothing.

Claudia is about to say 'Lawrence doesn't approve' but Deborah speaks before she can: 'What's the problem with tattoos, Lawrence? By which I mean, Claudia's tattoos?'

But before Lawrence can engage, Ash and Josh arrive at the table.

Ash says, 'Where should we sit?'

Lawrence waves his hand, super casual. 'Oh, there are no seating plans for lunch,' he says as though Ash has asked a misguidedly formal question. Ash takes a seat at the end of the table and Josh moves a little further along, next to Lawrence.

Plates are filled with bread and cheese and salad. Lawrence pours the elderflower cordial from a jug with ice and mint. He'd made it last spring. He tastes a sip: good; the citric acid makes all the difference.

'Has everyone got everything they need?' Claudia asks, and there are general noises of assent and thanks.

'I'm thinking,' she adds, 'of swimming again before dinner, if anyone wants to?'

'I will,' Josh says and reaches for the salad dressing. 'Certainly the weather for it.'

'Claudia swims every day without fail.' Lawrence smiles at his wife.

'Well,' she replies, 'it's the only means of survival this far from the sea, especially in this weather. I'll come down to the pool about half past five, if anyone wants to join.' She hopes there will be more people than only Josh.

Silence follows as people start to eat and Deborah says, her tone indicating a public announcement, 'So I had some good news today. We had some good news today.' She smiles at Miles who waves his hand as if to say *stop it*.

Lawrence puts the jug down and says, 'What's that?'

'I had an email this morning from Rebecca who does TV rights at the agency.'

Josh leans forward: he'd been intending to bring up Rebecca's name with Deborah later.

Lawrence can feel his heart sinking. The sunny optimism in his voice increases. 'Oh exciting. Go on.'

'They've sold the rights to *A History of Marriage in 12 Divorces* to Netflix.'

'You're fucking joking.' Lawrence's reply is immediate, the tone that of someone who has just received news that his son has been expelled from Year 9.

'Six episodes.'

'For that divorce book?'

Deborah says, 'Some people have to earn a living, Lawrence.'

'Sorry,' says Lawrence, 'that's not what I meant.'

'"That divorce book",' says Miles, laughing.

'I didn't mean to . . . I actually think it's a really important project.'

Deborah says, 'Oh fuck off, Lawrence, no you don't.'

Lawrence starts to say, 'I read every word of Miles's Stuarts book . . .' as though this was some great kindness, but Deborah's barb is not without affection and his defence dwindles away. In any case, it isn't true: he couldn't bring himself to open it.

Deborah leans back in her chair. 'When HBO wants to make a series about William Langland, I'll call you, okay?'

'I've actually not read *Piers Plowman* in years,' says Lawrence, as if he needs to rebuff the American network's advances.

Josh says, 'Bloody hell. That's amazing.' He feels that familiar sensation, a kind of dread, of being close to, but not participating in, success. 'Well done, Miles.'

Claudia says, 'Wonderful, Miles!'

Miles shrugs. 'It's all Deborah. I hardly know what it means.'

'It means money and your name on a screen and lots of emails from people you've not heard from for years.'

Josh feels he needs to say something, but he doesn't know what, so he says, 'Who will present it?'

Deborah says, 'I don't know much more than that right now. I think not Miles.'

'Someone with gravitas,' Miles suggests. 'There's quite a lot about Charlemagne. Lawrence?'

'Ha ha.' Lawrence pulls a face.

Deborah says, 'Not bad for "that divorce book"!'

'I was *joking*.'

'Forty per cent joking.'

Lucy arrives last, takes her place, says, 'Thank you, Claudia,' when the plate is placed in front of her, but her voice is barely audible and she seems detached from the present, set back and deep in thought. Lawrence puts a jar of chutney next to her plate. He turns back to Miles and says, 'Hard to believe after all those years in the wilderness that your book will be on TV.'

As Lawrence returns to his own plate, he becomes aware that Josh is waiting for his attention.

'Can I get you anything, Josh? More cordial?' Lawrence gestures towards the jug.

'No, thank you,' says Josh. 'It's all delicious.' He lowers his voice so that only Lawrence can hear. 'I wondered if I could talk to you a bit more at some point about the film. What with all this screen success in the air.'

'Ah yes, your script. Love to. As I said, I'm more than happy to read it through once you've got a draft.'

'That's enormously kind,' Josh replies. 'I have a couple of readers lined up, but obviously no one with your level of expertise.' Lawrence nods through his mouthful as the younger man continues. Josh has a sense that he needs to push this conversation forward, to keep it on track, before Lawrence's attention wanders and the moment passes.

'I actually wanted to ask,' Josh continues, 'whether you – and Claudia, of course – might be interested in coming in on the film in a more practical way, so to speak?'

'A practical way?'

'Well, as I mentioned before, there's a prospect that we could make this film with a smaller, independent production company, which would be much better creatively but also – being realistic – a better prospect than hoping to get it picked up by a major studio.'

'Yes, I can imagine it would,' says Lawrence, adding more salad to his plate. 'Not, as I said, that I know anything about that world.'

'Well, of course,' says Josh. 'But that's not a problem, you wouldn't have to.'

'Wouldn't have to . . . in order for what?'

'I'm sorry, I should make myself clear. I'm looking for funders for *Canterbury*. I need five or six backers who are prepared to put some money in initially – depending on the investment, obviously. I've prepared a document which outlines the various levels of support that could be possible. I wondered if you – and Claudia, as I say – might like to consider that opportunity. I've copies in my room which I can give to each of you.'

Lawrence puts down his fork and wipes his mouth with his napkin.

'You want us to put some money into your film?'

'Well, yes . . .' Josh pauses, 'or – to think about it?'

Lawrence looks at Claudia at the other end of the table. She is holding her glass for a refill and laughing at a joke of Miles's.

'I'll certainly think about it,' he says to Josh, 'although I should warn you, we're not exactly awash with cash. It takes just about everything we have to keep this place afloat, you know. It's not cheap.'

'Of course, of course,' Josh replies smoothly. He thinks how the very rich always seem to have a sense of themselves as financially beleaguered. 'Although you know really it might be a two-way thing. I'd see this as an investment on which you could expect a return, and potentially a very good one. This is business, not charity.'

'Well, I'll talk to Claudia.' Lawrence reaches past Josh for the breadboard, and addresses the table. 'Some more ciabatta? Baguette?'

Josh decides it's best to let it go for now, and to come back with another attempt later on. He's not giving up on this.

Josh keeps his eyes on Lawrence, who isn't looking in Josh's direction anymore. Josh tries very hard to conceal his desperation. His jaw is clenched. The desire to push Lawrence to a commitment is almost unbearable, but he forces himself to wait.

'Who are the children in the churchyard?'

Lucy's question comes suddenly, as if from elsewhere, as if Lucy was a cipher, not the origin, of the words.

She adds, 'The ones who used to live here?'

There is a pause. People look at Lucy. Claudia says, 'Do you mean the memorial?'

'Yes, with the statue.'

Claudia says, 'That memorial is so sad. They died very young.'

Lawrence is about to interrupt – this isn't a subject for lunch; there's a danger all the energy will be lost – but he realises he can't cut Lucy off.

Claudia says, 'We don't know the full story. I think partly because we didn't want to find out. Lawrence, do you want to . . .?'

'You go on. You know everything I know. Pretty much.'

Claudia puts down her knife and fork. 'In the mid-nineteenth century – it was the 1860s, I think – so a long time after Sharp . . . the family who lived here made a lot of money from the East India Company. Is that right, Lawrence?'

Lawrence nods.

'The baronet, or whatever he was . . .'

'Viscount.'

'. . . had two children, a boy and a girl, very close in age, and there was an appalling accident when they were young. They both drowned in the pond.'

'*That* pond?' asks Miles, pointing.

Claudia nods. Lucy looks at the placid water, the mass of green plants, the calm beauty of it. Her imagination starts to form the image of two children swimming, laughter and splashing but then one starting to struggle, the other moving to help, a beautiful sunny day and Francis Sharp's folly standing impassive above it all, as it does today. Lucy's mind recoils from the scene. She physically flinches, turning her head to the side, simultaneously registering and banishing what she sees in her mind's eye.

'The story my parents were told by the previous owners – who knows if it's true, they were this slightly crazy rich hippie couple – was that the family had a nurse from India, an ayah, who was devoted to them. The children spent so much time with her that they spoke her language as well as English. After their death the ayah disappeared. Most people apparently thought she went back to India. The parents . . . well, you can imagine.'

Lawrence leans forward in his chair. 'The statue is by Sir Francis Chantry.' He pauses as if the name might resonate. 'He was a big deal in the mid-nineteenth century. It must have cost a fortune. There's another one of his in alabaster to a young deceased wife in the church that is superb.'

Ash thinks, don't use words like 'superb' and 'big deal'; how can Lawrence not see what Lucy is feeling?

'What were their names?' asks Lucy.

'Agnes and John,' Claudia replies.

The names land in Lucy's heart like two stones echoing at the bottom of a well.

'There is some beautiful carving on the plinth.' Lawrence gestures in the direction of the church with his knife. 'It's terrific work.'

'Of course, we could look the thing up I'm sure quite easily,' says Claudia, 'what with archives all being online now, but I don't want to know any more than that.'

Lawrence starts to refill the glasses with elderflower. 'A chap from the Courtauld was doing his PhD on Chantry and his circle and came to look at it. He had a look at the house, too, which he thought extremely interesting. Must have been 2014, I think. I don't know what happened with the dissertation: he didn't stay in touch. He promised to send me the finished thing. I must follow up on that.'

'Et in Arcadia ego,' says Ash, who has been silent for some time.

The others turn to him.

'Oh, darling,' says Deborah, 'I never know what that means. Wasn't it a painting? Or an Evelyn Waugh book?'

'"And in Arcadia I am,"' says Ash. 'Or something like that. It's spoken by Death. Even in a pastoral idyll, death is here. There. It's a painting by Nicolas Poussin.'

A peacock squawks from somewhere in the woods.

Claudia has started to collect the plates. Lucy is half-looking at the pond, but out of the corner of her eye, as if the water is emitting a terrible high hum that only she can hear.

❈

Lawrence is seated on the bench within the restored folly that looks out onto the pond, his laptop on the low, square table in front of him. The mid-afternoon sun is strong and in order to read he has to angle the screen and turn up the brightness. This irritates him. He rubs the thumbprint on the corner of the screen, but this makes the smudge worse. The pond is thick with green, very upright plants with purple flowers that he can't identify: the garden, like the kitchen, is (he repeats the phrase often) 'very much Claudia's domain'. But he likes this view: the tree stumps covered with ivy, and the way the bank runs down to the water. Local history reports that Samuel Johnson once visited the manor in its original, eighteenth-century form, when the owner was Sharp, the eccentric university librarian who, despite a buffoonish reputation, had a knack for cultivating literary friendships. Lawrence likes the idea of writing where the founder of the English dictionary once stood, also admiring the pond. In this story Lawrence sees himself as the visiting titan of literary history, not the buffoonish host.

Lawrence is writing a book entitled *Thomas Hoccleve and the Invention of Mental Health in Fifteenth-century England*. To the college research committee, to whom he is required to write termly reports for the duration of his two-year sabbatical, Lawrence has dispatched unfailingly positive 'updates from the front line'. (He's used this phrase three times in these reports, as though he is in the Balkans in the 1990s and not seated in a restored folly in the grounds of his Cambridgeshire estate.) 'Writing continues apace and I anticipate concluding a first draft of the whole manuscript by the end of the autumn term.' In truth, Lawrence can feel his certainty slipping away. December is only four months away. For what must be the tenth time this afternoon, Lawrence clicks 'Tools' and then 'Word Count', but the total is only 23,560. He doesn't dare unclick 'Include footnotes and endnotes'. He's at least 60,000 short.

This is not going to happen, and for Lawrence this is a new sensation: his confidence, unchallenged for a lifetime, is starting to unpick itself, piece by piece. At first, he mistook this queasy feeling for something else, even for a version of excitement, but he can't now avoid the gathering sense of dread that fills him every time he turns to the book. Is this what everyone else feels? In the past, Lawrence has travelled on a cloud of unflagging optimism which, he discovered, if you don't pause to question it, seems to come true. Book one. Book two. Book three. Lawrence created an environment of positivity and expectation by the wilful assertion, repeated to himself and those around him, that things are 'super', and the realisation that if you don't *complicate* things unnecessarily, then writing comes fast. In the past he has always responded with a kind of bored bafflement to colleagues and friends who struggle to write, or feel their confidence as a researcher crumbling, or wonder why the world needs another 80,000 words on early Tudor literature.

But now Lawrence's writing mode has spiralled into a bad and self-destructive routine. It goes something like this: Lawrence writes a sentence, which he deletes, and then rewrites, exactly the same. And then, with increasing panic, he googles sentences by writers he admires to compare their sentences with what he's just written. V. S. Naipaul. W. G. Sebald. Julian Barnes. This is what he is doing now. He types his sentence for a second time. 'Hoccleve's *Compleinte* arises from his illness: the sick body produces the poetic corpus.' In past years he'd have stormed on from that to the next sentence, paragraph, page, with only a gathering sense of destiny. But now . . . 'Ten weeks before he died, Mr Mohun Biswas, a journalist of Sikkim Street, St James, Port of Spain, was sacked.' 'Hoccleve's *Compleinte* arises from his illness: the sick body produces the poetic corpus.' 'In August 1992, when the dog days were drawing to an end, I set off to walk the country of Suffolk . . .' 'Hoccleve's *Compleinte* arises from his illness: the sick body produces the poetic corpus.' 'We live in time – it holds us and moulds us . . .'

Lawrence snaps the laptop screen shut. He sits dead still for several seconds gazing ahead without seeing, and then with a jolt opens the screen again, clicks a new tab, and types 'lawrence ayres wikipedia'. The WiFi, feeding off his phone, takes a second to refresh. Still nothing – just Stuart Ayres, Rosalind Ayres, Mitchell Ayres. Who are these nonentities? He scrolls to the bottom of the page. Of course, Miles has one, although Lawrence can't bring himself to read it – just as he can't read a single word of his friends' books, their success simply too painful. He's considered writing his own Wikipedia entry, even starting a stub for someone else to fulfil. But he wants it to be written by a stranger.

'Fuck it,' he says, louder than he intended, shutting the screen again. He looks back across the lawn to the manor house to check no one has heard. Such is his commitment to productivity that this kind of self-doubt simply can't fit with his sense of self. Miles is sitting on a rug on the grass, doing something on his phone. He looks up in Lawrence's direction, then puts a tentative thumb up, the gesture suggesting a question. Lawrence waves back, and beams, and shouts, 'Super!'

❋

Last summer, on holiday in Morocco, Claudia had read *Madame Bovary* and felt a jolt of recognition. Not at Emma Bovary's affairs, or her book-fuelled fantasy life, or – thankfully – her descent into tragedy and death. No: it was Emma's deep and unending irritation with her husband Charles that made Claudia drop the book to her lap and look to the horizon. 'Even his back' – Claudia wrote the line down in her notebook, between recipes she'd gathered – 'that stolid back of his, was irritating to her.' People don't tell you about the irritation, she'd thought, sitting across from Lawrence in the bus to the airport home, watching him squinting at his phone, holding the device inches from his face, his lips tracing the shape of the words echoing in his head. But there was Emma Bovary, falling inexorably in love with beautiful young Monsieur Léon, or that version of Monsieur Léon she thought she saw, and there beside her was her husband Charles: slow and literal-minded and eternally lacking in the magical lightness she wants. And Claudia wants.

There can be a kind of pleasure in it. In a litany. Claudia is sitting in a deckchair pulled into the shade near the kitchen door, not working, almost dozing. His snoring, obviously. And the way he talks to his students, that tone of needing to be liked. His size: once so attractive, but now merely cumbersome and always in the way. The gulping – so maddening – when he drinks tea. His general clumsiness. How he doesn't hear, instead the dreadful lumbering '*What was that?*' that answers her own light asides. Once he was a scalpel, but now he is a club. The fact that—

'Hello?' Claudia looks up to see a woman walking towards

her. She is tall and slender with an abundance of curly dark hair, which, with the sun behind her, seems to glow at its edges, and she is smiling tentatively at Claudia, her eyes hidden behind sunglasses. She must have crossed the courtyard from the gate, but Claudia has not heard her approach.

'Hi!' Claudia levers herself out of the deckchair, thinking how ungainly she must look. 'Are you Inês? I'm Claudia.' She steps into the sunlight and reaches out a hand. The woman takes it, but, rather than shaking hands, she leans into Claudia and, bending slightly, kisses first her right cheek, then her left. The first kiss is given too quickly for Claudia to return it; at the second, she finds her face pressed against the stranger's hair, its texture rough against her mouth.

'Claudia! It is a pleasure to meet you.' Inês's voice is hard to place, faintly transatlantic as well as Spanish or rather, Claudia corrects herself, Portuguese. Claudia thinks: she doesn't look like an artist, she looks like a film star, and this is what people mean when they say someone is radiant. Inês's beauty is luminous, and incongruent in the dusty Cambridgeshire landscape.

'Yes, that's right. A pleasure to meet you.' Claudia takes a step backwards as Inês removes her sunglasses and props them on top of her head. She smiles. 'Lawrence will be delighted that you've made it. Come on in. I'm not sure where he is, but I can show you to your room.'

'Thank you. Excuse me for a minute, I just need to pay the driver.' Inês indicates behind her where a black cab is waiting near the gate. 'I was not sure it was the right place.'

Inês walks quickly over the cobbles, reaching into her bag as she goes. She glances back and smiles. Claudia, watching her, raises her hands to her face, pressing her fingers together and exhaling into her palms, then closes her eyes. She thinks: it must be the heat. I feel weak at the knees. But not only the heat: it is Inês. It is – Claudia takes an intake of breath as she realises the word she is reaching for – desire. Claudia had forgotten desire, or had buried it, or had placed it far down the list of qualities necessary for living, for just getting through life, and now it is filling her body and covering her skin, as if for the first time. The desire to possess, to merge, to stop time, to be consumed, to let everything else fall away.

When Claudia gets to the pool, Josh is already there, sitting on the stone edge of the deep end, legs in the water, exuding a relaxed confidence in his body.

'What are you reading?'

Josh lifts the book so that Claudia can read the cover: *Atonement* by Ian McEwan.

'Oh, I loved that,' says Claudia, 'and the film. Just beautiful.'

'I've read it before of course,' Josh says quickly, 'and I should probably be pushing on with Chaucer, but once I've reached my limit for work, I need something lighter.'

'I'm exactly the same. The Cazalet Chronicles by Elizabeth Jane Howard, have you read those? I go through them on a loop in times of need.' Josh smiles and nods though privately he thinks Howard even lower brow than McEwan.

'You match the pool beautifully,' Claudia says now, putting down the towels she is carrying on the wooden table.

'What?'

'Your shorts – that mosaic pattern goes perfectly with the tiles.'

'Oh!' Josh wonders for a second if he is being accused of deliberately choosing his clothes to fit the surroundings, but his habitual confidence in his appearance is such that the concern almost immediately falls away. He looks down at his shorts and the tiling that encircles the pool. 'The tiles are lovely.'

'We had them re-done around the same time as the folly. The idea was to recreate the swimming pool as it was when it was first built in the 1930s. We had a couple of photos and we found someone to copy the design – it's very intricate, as you can see. It takes a huge amount of upkeep actually, but I think it's worth it.'

'I suppose the pool is like the folly,' Josh replies, 'a resurrection of past beauty.' He is pleased with this observation, but Claudia laughs derisively, as though he has made a joke.

'At least the pool *is* beautiful,' she says, 'and useful, come to that.' Josh is about to ask what she means, but at this moment both he and Claudia look up to see Deborah approaching, resplendent in a billowing silk kimono and an enormous pair of sunglasses.

'You two look like an advertisement for something,' she calls as she comes into earshot, 'cigars, possibly, or Campari. From a distance, Josh, you are the absolute image of the young Hugh Grant.'

'Thank you, Deborah,' says Josh, not noting the qualifier that others would have. 'Now I can die happy.' He salutes her, throws his book towards the lawn and dives smoothly into the water.

Deborah raises an eyebrow at Claudia and, as Josh surfaces, pushing his hair from his eyes, offloads her bag onto the table. She undoes the belt of her kimono and removes it to reveal a bright blue swimming costume patterned with killer whales.

'That's fabulous,' Claudia says.

'Isn't it? The young man in the shop told me it's made from recycled plastic waste.' Deborah steps down into the water at the shallow end of the pool, drawing in her breath sharply at the cold. 'Come on, Claudia, keep me company; Hugh here is in lithe sports mode.'

Josh is doing a crawl up and down the pool, too fast for the pool's size and elegance – his quick, tidy strokes introducing competitive exercise into a place of leisure – but he comes to a stop as the women get in, the movement of the water gradually calming around him. Claudia leans forward into a slow breaststroke, but Deborah stays standing in the shallow end, submerged up to her waist.

'This will do me for now,' she says, as Josh leans back against the edge of the pool, 'and look, there's Miles.' Deborah raises an arm in a wave as Miles walks quickly across the grass.

'I've got literally five minutes,' he says, unbuttoning his shirt and stepping out of his deck shoes, 'and then I need to get back to the kitchen. I'm on a schedule. How is it?'

'Fucking freezing,' Deborah says, just as Claudia says, 'Warm!', and they laugh. Miles sits on the edge of the pool and lowers himself into the water, gasping at the cold and then swimming across the pool's width.

Lawrence and Ash have arrived together and stand at the table, removing their clothes and shoes. Josh is sitting on the edge of the pool and Claudia stops near him, halfway along the far wall. Deborah says, 'Here goes nothing,' and then, as she launches forward into the water, uttering the words with a staggered slowness, '*fuck me*'.

Miles swims to the deep end and lifts himself out of the

water in a single, smooth movement. Claudia watches the muscles of Miles's back flex as he moves, and then the taut flesh of his stomach as he turns and raises his arms for a dive.

Claudia looks over to her husband, who is adjusting the drawstring on his swimming shorts and smiling at something Ash is saying. The two men walk down the steps into the water, Ash taking a few strokes of a quick crawl, Lawrence bending forward to submerge his head in the freezing water.

'You're looking very sporty, Miles,' Lawrence says as he surfaces and wipes the water away from his face. Miles has got back out of the water and is towelling himself dry.

'Thank you,' Miles replies, ignoring the challenge in Lawrence's tone and pulling on his shirt.

'You must be in the gym every bloody day; where do you find the time?'

'You have to take care of yourself at our age,' says Miles. 'I make it a priority.'

'Clearly.'

'Anyway, you were the sporty one at college. All that rugby and rowing.'

'Only in my first year,' says Lawrence, 'before I was waylaid by wine and women.' He swims towards Claudia, who smiles distractedly and splashes water at him.

'Sorry I'm late.' Lucy is crossing the grass towards the pool. She is wearing an open shirt over her black bikini and is tying up her hair as she approaches.

'Is it freezing?' Lucy asks, squatting at the edge of the pool and putting a hand into the water. 'It was gorgeous yesterday.'

'It's perfect,' Ash replies, 'although it's getting a bit full.'

'Well, I'm off,' says Miles, 'the kitchen calls', and with a wave he heads across the grass towards the house.

'At least we almost all made it into the water at once.' Lucy slips into the shallow end and takes a few steps forward.

'Not all of us,' says Lawrence. 'Inês is here but she's not going to swim. She had a phone call to make.'

'Oh, she's here?' says Lucy. 'That's nice. What's she like?'

'Spectacular,' Lawrence replies. 'Extraordinarily talented. Of Mozambican heritage, I believe. You'll meet her at dinner.'

'Goodness. I look forward to it.' Lucy crouches a little in the water until her shoulders are slowly submerged. Ash watches the water lap against the hollow of Lucy's collarbone.

Josh lets himself slide back into the pool and looks at Lucy.

'Do you remember,' he says, 'that time we went swimming after hours at the Lido?'

'Of course I do.' Lucy is laughing. 'Skinny-dipping. Your idea, if I remember correctly. There was a whole gang of us,' she explains to the group.

'Well,' says Lawrence, 'the things students get up to.'

'A lifetime ago.' Lucy starts making for the deep end. 'Have I got time for a quick few lengths before drinks?'

'Only very quick,' Josh replies. 'I'll race you', and he sets off after Lucy at speed.

Ash walks past Lawrence up the steps and reaches for his towel.

'Hang on,' says Deborah, 'I'll come with you.' They gather their things, retracing their steps across the dry grass.

Lawrence swims up to Claudia and puts his arms around her.

'They're getting on very well all of a sudden,' he says quietly, gesturing to Lucy and Josh who have stopped swimming and are treading water together.

Claudia looks over at Lucy, her dripping face lit up in the sunshine.

'It's good to see Lucy smiling,' she says. 'She looks happy.'

Lawrence leans in and kisses Claudia.

'I can't wait for you to meet Inês,' he says. 'I think you're going to love her.'

Walking a little ahead of Ash towards the house, Deborah folds the kimono tightly around herself and enjoys the sensation of her cold swimming costume pressing closer to her skin. She feels a heaviness in her limbs which she might expect after a longer swim than the few lengths she's just taken in Lawrence's pool, the result, perhaps, of having slept badly in the unfamiliar bed in the annexe. But overlying the lethargy is a fizz of anticipation, a familiar excitement at having spent a day inside the mind of the young writer whose work she has recently found and who, she is sure, she knows in fact with absolute certainty, is going to succeed. The joy-spike of Miles's Netflix deal, and the slow-burning satisfaction of recognising her part in the transformation of his life, are gratifying aspects of Deborah's job, but the deeper thrill and fulfilment, to which Deborah knows she is addicted, comes in the slow, careful task of finding an original voice, like this new writer, and working with them, nurturing them, coaxing them into the distinct and singular talent she sees they could become. Deborah feels the sun on her face and smiles with expectation.

As they reach the point where the path through the grass

divides, one fork leading to the back door, the other around the house to the annexe, Deborah stops and turns to Ash.

'What are you going to do now?'

Ash hangs the towel that he is carrying over one shoulder.

'I'm going to do my best to get through these last difficult minutes before the ordained hour for cocktails.' He checks his watch. 'I might have a quick shower.'

As Ash moves past Deborah towards the house, she says, 'That's exactly what I'm going to do, as it happens.' Ash smiles his farewell. He has his back to her as she finishes speaking and he thinks he hears her say, 'Care to keep me company?'

Ash stands still for a moment and then turns back to where Deborah is waiting at the fork in the path. She is looking towards him, shading her eyes from the sun, and he can't read her expression. His gaze meets hers and then Deborah smiles, drops her hand from her face and gives a quick shrug as she moves away.

'See you later.'

Ash watches her leave, and then, thinking suddenly that she might turn back and catch him staring, walks on towards the house, turning over in his mind what might have happened, what Deborah might have said or what, possibly, he has entirely imagined.

Chapter Six

Tuesday evening

On the bedside table Deborah tips a small amount of white powder onto the square mirror she found in the bathroom cabinet. She chops the powder with a small knife and then uses the blade to make two thin lines. The knife is silver with Hebrew letters on the handle that spell out Deborah's name. She is amused and pleased every time she sees the letters in this context. She takes the wooden straw she keeps in her purse, places one end to her nose, and inhales deeply as she tracks the straw along the first line. She always loves the tidy way it disappears, and she always thinks the same thing: a film in reverse. She breathes out. She does the same with the second line. She breathes out. She sits still on the edge of the bed. She knows that in five minutes she will feel a new layer of confidence coursing through her, and then, after ten, that confidence will turn into a surging joy. She puts the plastic bag of powder and the straw back in her bag and looks for her shoes.

❋

In the lower living room, Miles puts out a bowl of roasted garlic and white bean dip with rosemary, and an earthenware plate with beetroot, potato and spinach crackers.

'Darling, this looks wonderful,' says Deborah.

'I assume the whole point of this week is competitive cooking. I'm channelling Lawrence. Submerged but intense rivalry played out in bourgeois forms.'

'Divine,' says Deborah.

Miles gestures at the bowl but Deborah says, 'Not for me', and then, 'God, I fucking love everything about this moment right now.'

Miles looks up at Deborah. He touches his right nostril and raises his eyebrows.

Deborah brings her finger to her lips.

Miles says, 'Don't go too wild, Debs. Don't get silly.'

'This is not a week for moderation, Miles.'

'Can I join you?' Deborah and Miles don't recognise the woman entering the living room but realise it must be the artist Lawrence couldn't stop talking about.

'Inês?' Miles stands and extends a hand. 'Please,' gesturing to the rocking chair.

Inês sits down and leans the chair back. There is a glow to her face and hair that seems incongruous in this house with its bohemian disorder and piles of old books and Persian rugs and tumbling asparagus ferns. Deborah imagines Inês in a bright white gallery in Milan.

'This place is unbelievable,' says Inês. 'As a teenager I learnt English reading Agatha Christie and this is how I imagined the whole of England.'

'We don't have a Miss Marple,' says Miles.

'That's what you think.' Inês turns to take in all the room, not looking at either of them as she speaks, as if she is talking to the house itself. She speaks and moves in a manner that suggests someone immediately at ease in new surroundings and with strangers: her tempo, her mode, is not buffeted by the people around her.

Deborah says, 'So you're an artist?'

Inês nods.

'What's your . . . *medium*? Is that the right question?'

'It is an excellent question. And the answer is glass. Engravings, mainly.'

'Windows?'

'Sometimes. Windows, sculptures, bowls, glasses. More recently it's larger pieces, mostly.'

Miles takes a sip of his drink. 'Lawrence said you're doing something at Gonville & Caius. The Donne window, is that right?'

At the same time as Inês is saying, 'Yes, that's right,' Deborah says, 'The what window?'

'The Donne window,' Miles repeats. 'You know, where John Donne is supposed to have etched his name on the glass. And then it got broken at some point – was it in the war? – and patched up.'

'That's right,' Inês says again. 'And actually the mending is very beautiful. We are going to preserve that window, the name in the glass of course, but also the mending of the glass, and then next to it we are installing this new piece. It's called *Valediction*.'

'John Donne wrote his name in the glass there?' Deborah says. 'I never knew that.'

'Actually I don't think there's any evidence it was John Donne the poet.' Inês shifts in the rocking chair so that she is leaning forward, looking up at Miles and Deborah. 'There is the name "John" scratched into the glass, quite clearly, and then a very elaborate upper-case "D". It's supposed to date from the 1580s, when Donne and his brother were students there. Though so, too, were many other boys called John. But,' she shrugs, 'it's a nice story. And I am using one of his poems. A beautiful poem. It's all ready to go in now. I think it's good.'

Miles says, 'How wonderful. But how can you do that here? What will you do this week?'

Inês puts both her hands in the air as if in defeat. 'This week I do what artists do ninety-five per cent of the time: I write grant bids. Over and over. Never ending. At the weekend I'll visit the college and talk to the bursar and the Master there. Is that the right word, Master?'

Miles says, 'Could be. I imagined you with a smock and a chisel working in the woods.'

Inês smiles and stands up. 'Is the kitchen through here? I need to say hello to Lawrence.'

Inês's exit leaves a perceptible sense of absence: her perfume, but also the sheer force of her presence moments before.

'Blimey,' says Miles. 'The group glamour quotient just went up considerably.'

'Iberian women.' Deborah circles her right hand in the air, as if conjuring a cloud. 'They are a different category.'

Miles lowers his voice. 'Do you think Lawrence is besotted?'

Deborah takes a slow, deep breath and thinks. 'I'd have thought fascinated. Being around an artist. Her success. Her commission in Cambridge. He keeps mentioning that. How talented she is. I think people who aren't artists find artists very compelling. I'd imagine Lawrence wants to be close to that, to observe it, to be in the room. But I think not more than that.'

'Yes, I think that's right. And also she's gay.'

Deborah raises her eyebrows.

'Lawrence said. But I'd have guessed.' Miles takes a scoop of the dip. 'This really is good.'

A little later Lawrence calls, 'Would we like to, let us say, move through?'

Deborah mouths '*move through*' to Miles.

In the dining room, the little vases have been replenished with new wild flowers.

Miles says, 'Grilled courgettes with garlic ricotta, raisins and capers.'

'How wonderful,' says Claudia, feeling suddenly, as Miles places the starter before her, looked after, and realising, with a shock that is unpleasant but which also has the force of truth, just how unused she is to that experience.

'You are clever.' Lawrence dips a forkful of courgettes into the cheese.

'Literally what would life be without Ottolenghi?' replies Miles. 'Sweet and sour dressing. Mint and basil, of course.'

'Of course!' says Deborah, joyfully.

Inês says, 'When I last visited Cambridge it was 2012 and there was a beautiful candlelit dinner in the college but the cooking was terrible. Black tie and wine after wine but very bad food.'

'Welcome to college dining.' Claudia raises her glass.

Lawrence, irritated but largely concealing it, says, 'Actually, things have got considerably better in recent years. At my college we've a marvellous French chef called Christophe.'

Dinner proceeds and Miles basks in everyone's approval of the food. There is conversation about the day's work: after a couple of glasses Deborah is fulsome about the short stories she's been editing that afternoon.

Before dessert Inês stands and says, 'I'll take a cigarette break if that's okay,' and Josh says, 'Oh good, I thought I was the only one', and the two of them walk out into the garden towards the pool. It's 8.35 p.m., and the sun is setting beautifully.

Standing by Inês at the edge of the pool, the water lit by a long strip of fading sun, Josh feels self-conscious and provincial. 'Wonderful sounding art,' he begins, thinking: what a stupid thing to say.

Inês ignores the comment, keeping her eyes on the sunset. 'And what about you?'

'Me?'

'You.' She waits and then adds, 'You seem . . . apart, a little.'

Josh takes in the comment and thinks for a moment before he speaks. Inês's direct style calms him and invites a similar candour.

'Well, I think that's probably true. I'm a decade or so younger than the people here, apart from Lucy. And now you. I'm Lawrence's former student. Has he mentioned that to you?'

Josh is eager to know how Lawrence frames him.

Inês nods, still looking towards the sun.

'I did a PhD with him. But then I couldn't get a job, so I left academia. So I feel I enter this world . . .' – Josh nods in the direction of the house – 'from a position of failure.'

'And now?'

'Now I'm a schoolteacher. But . . .'

'But your heart is not in it.'

'Is it obvious?'

Inês shrugs. 'You don't say anything about teaching.'

'I'm trying to make a film.'

'I see. A film about what?'

'*The Canterbury Tales*. Chaucer.'

'You have a script?'

'I'm working on it. What I don't have is . . .'

'Money.'

'Right.'

'And you hope . . .' Inês nods in the direction of the house in an echo of Josh's previous gesture.

'I've come to the crashingly obvious realisation that there aren't many medieval literature enthusiasts who have sizeable disposable incomes. The intersection between Chaucer studies and film production is . . . almost nil. I need to see if Claudia and Lawrence can be persuaded, or the thing will never get off the ground.' Josh takes a drag of his cigarette. 'They're not exactly falling over themselves so far to help . . . but they're my last roll of the dice. And the thing is – the problem is – I've managed to build up a bit of debt and I . . . I need a bit of help. The prospect of my forties and fifties being spent teaching the underwhelming offspring of affluent bankers . . .'

'What does this mean?'

'The children at my school. It's a second or third tier private school in north London.'

'So you're here to finance your film.'

'That sounds rather mercenary.'

'Not at all. I'm here to write a grant bid. If you're an artist you soon realise that focus and the . . .'

'I wouldn't really claim to be an artist.'

'. . . what is the word in English? – in Portuguese we say *mundanismo* . . . worldliness, I think. You realise creativity is a worldly thing. Despite . . .' – Inês gestures generally at the pool and the garden and the lawn leading to the pond – 'all this.'

There is a pause and then Inês says, 'Lucy was Lawrence's student too, no?'

'That's right. I was one year ahead of her.' Josh pauses, thinking about how to proceed. 'She was a star before her kids came along, and that awful husband.'

'She still may be.'

'Oh, I'm quite sure she is.'

Cigarette smoke spirals up.

Josh says, 'It's bloody hard to make a film. I hadn't fully appreciated the battle. If I don't keep pushing all the time it will never happen. It's relentless. It's exhausting. I'm trying to force something into the world but there's no space for it. No one else gives a damn.'

'I understand. Do you have children? A wife?'

'I have a girlfriend. A partner, I suppose you'd say. Gemma. And no, no children. At least not yet.'

'But maybe soon?'

Josh shrugs, as if the matter is out of his hands, but also as if the matter is incidental: a boring detail. 'That's what she'd like.'

Inês drops her finished cigarette and grinds it against the stone path under her heel. Josh finds the movement exhilarating and erotic.

'I think you are more in control than you think you are, Josh. And less of a failure. You have a good job, a PhD, a

124

creative project, a partner who loves you enough to want children with you. These are all good things.'

'Possibly.'

'Certainly. But if you compare yourself against all of this' – Inês raises both hands in an expansive movement – 'it's hard to measure up.'

There is a pause, and then Inês turns towards the house.

'Your partner. Gemma. Does she know about the debt?'

'Not exactly.'

For the first time Inês looks directly at Josh. 'Be careful there. I have experience.' Then she starts to stroll back towards the kitchen.

Josh stands still for a second, processing her words. He treads his cigarette into the stone next to hers and then catches her up. 'What's the poem on the window you're making?'

'It's John Donne. It's a poem about reflections. Very beautiful.' Inês is talking ahead, into the air, and it makes Josh feel he is overhearing, rather than participating. He feels quite sure he has barely made an impression on her consciousness – the schoolteacher in debt talking about the film he'll never make. 'In the poem, Donne cuts his name into a window and imagines his lover looking at the glass when he's away, seeing her own reflection layered over his name. "Here you see me, and I am you."'

'I know that poem.'

Josh had a chapter in his dissertation on T. S. Eliot's critical rediscovery of Donne, and Josh argued that the Elizabethan verse the modernist Eliot thought he was reading was a warped version. Josh's examiners didn't particularly like it, although it got over the line.

Josh says, 'It's a fascinating text.' He hasn't thought about it for more than ten years.

Inês doesn't react: it's not clear to Josh that she has even heard. He wishes he could quote something back, but he's not the kind of person who can quote poetry.

Approaching the kitchen door, Inês and Josh can hear the sound of laughter from inside. Viewed from the dusky garden, through the glass door, the room looks dazzlingly bright, the participants a little society cut off. The square panels of the door divide the scene into a series of sections, and this effect makes Josh think he is watching the scene as a film. Inês opens the door and for a moment Josh feels like turning round and sinking back into the deep silence outside. But he catches the door before it falls closed and makes sure to be smiling as he re-enters the raucous kitchen.

'In the nineteenth century it was used for cattle. You can see the channels in the floor.'

'You mean for cow piss?' says Deborah.

'How authentic.' Miles steps over a trough with caution.

'That's right,' Lawrence continues, unwavering. 'I'm not sure what Russell did with the place. But when we moved in, I knew immediately what I wanted. And about three years ago we finally got it up and running. As you can see.'

The barn isn't wide, so the six of them feel quite close, but the ceiling is very high. Inês isn't there: her phone rang three times and on the fourth she took the call, and is now walking round the pool speaking rapidly, switching between English and Portuguese. The space is lit with two extremely bright striplights, creating an atmosphere of focused productivity. To Miles, leaning against the wall next to the doorway, it seems at once performatively rustic and, thanks to the lighting, joylessly industrial. Against the opposite wall is a wide chest with a series of very large, flat drawers, each with a handwritten label. Garamond 12. Eaves 14. Old English 14. Times New Roman 14. Times New Roman 12. Set against the adjoining wall is a large heavy table with a black metal printing press standing triumphantly in the middle – a non-negotiable assertion. It looks extremely heavy but it's compact and not huge: the size of a small lawnmower. To the right of the press are open shelves, with stacks of paper of different sizes and quality, three tubes of ink, a box of surgical rubber gloves, a plastic bottle of white spirit, a couple of Tupperware containers with pins, pencils, toothbrushes, and rubber bands, and a wooden box with compartments containing narrow metal strips of various lengths.

'I'm just an old hack at this.' Lawrence places a loose piece of type back in the Old English 14 drawer. 'Terribly amateurish. Ash is the real scholar.'

Miles looks over at Ash, who is standing, arms folded, next to the press in a proprietorial manner. Lawrence's faux modesty doesn't appear to have made him feel awkward.

Lawrence prompts, 'I asked him to give a little lecture.'

'Not a lecture. But I can describe what we're looking at. This is a Model Press. A number 4, if I'm not mistaken.' Lawrence nods. 'A forerunner of the much better-known Adana which took over, in the UK at least, from about 1920. The Model 4 was hugely popular in the late-nineteenth century. Compact, went on forever, reliable as an ox. I'd say this is about 1880 or so. Lawrence?'

'That's right.'

'Made in . . .' Ash looks at the label at the back, 'yes, Walthamstow. It's letterpress of course, which means all those fiddly individual letters. Pressman Lawrence here will have his copy of text to follow. He'll take letters out from the tray one by one, set them in a . . .' – Ash looks around, then sees what he's after – 'a composing stick, like this. Minding his p's and q's.'

'That comes from printing?' Miles exclaims, 'I had no idea.' Despite his resistance to Lawrence's conspicuous display, Miles finds himself watching the process carefully.

'Then when a few lines are done Lawrence with *great deftness*' – Ash pauses and looks at Lawrence as if in enquiry, and Lawrence nods and says 'Absolutely!' – 'transfers the block of text to the chase – the steel frame, you can see there – and when the whole page is set in letters like this, then we get these pieces of wood – called furniture . . .'

'Like a tiny house!' says Deborah, clapping her hands.

'The whole block is tightened with quoins so that nothing moves. Sort of Allen keys. Movement is the enemy of the printer.'

Lawrence nods. 'Absolutely right.'

'And the forme – which is what it's now called – is slotted into the press. Add ink with rollers. Of course, they used to use inking balls.'

'Stop it,' says Deborah.

'Then Lawrence pulls the paper down onto the letters and if the Gods are with him . . .'

'Which of course they often aren't,' Lawrence chuckles.

'. . . then he has a page of his memoir. Or his libretto. Or his avant garde concrete poem.'

Miles says to Lawrence, 'You do realise perfectly good laser printers are available for quite reasonable prices?'

Ash has picked up a single letter and is looking at it closely. 'If you think about printing you end up thinking about inversions. About mirror images, and mirror images of mirror images. The printed words on the page are inversions of the metal letters, which are inversions of the matrices that made them, which are inversions of the original punches, which are inversions of the designer's original drawing. The line of poetry we read in a book is the product of a series of flips, back and forth, like that.'

Lawrence says, 'Ash is much more of a philosopher about these things than I am. I just pull the bloody handle!' He moves to the table. 'Actually, I set a bit of type last night to show you the process. A special retreat demonstration. If I can print six I thought you could each have a copy, as a souvenir. Can I show you?' A muttering of assent. 'Oh, and thank you, Ash, that was wonderful.'

Lawrence slots the already set forme into the press and squeezes ink onto the circular plate and then pulls the rollers back and forth to pick up the ink. He does this quickly, enjoying the fact that he has to raise his voice over the squeaking metal. 'Here we go!'

He pulls the inked rollers down over the type, up and down four or five times, and then continues pulling down so that the rollers tuck in below and the paper descends to the inked letters. He holds the pressure so that the paper presses down onto the letters. 'They call it kissing the type,' Lawrence says, grinning.

He lets the handle rise back up and the paper pulls away from the text with a little tug of stickiness.

'Now let's see.'

He takes out the four pins holding the paper in place and theatrically flourishes the page.

'Marvellous,' says Josh. 'I thought you said you were an amateur!'

'What does it say?' asks Deborah.

'Oh yes, let's see.' Lucy, who has been standing quietly at the back of the group, cranes her neck towards the sheet of paper.

Lawrence hasn't yet examined the text he is holding in his hand, enjoying as he is the waving of the page. Miles watches as Lawrence turns the sheet of paper over to read it and his face immediately drops.

'This isn't my text,' he says, all humour drained from his voice.

'What do you mean, darling?' says Claudia.

Lawrence's eyes scan the letters. 'What the fuck is this?'

'Darling?'

'This isn't anything I set. This is . . . I set a Shakespeare sonnet. 126. With the missing final couplet. I put in all these blanks to create kind of riddle. What the hell is this?'

The printing is excellent, and the letters are still glinting and clear against the thick, receptive white paper Lawrence had carefully chosen and moistened. Lawrence lowers the page and says, 'Let's forget about this,' but Ash reaches out and takes the paper from his hand.

'Come on, let me see.'

Ash begins to read out loud.

'things are not always what they seem just ask lawrence lovely house garden wife job also students but you know what's really going on lawrence do you lawrence?'

There is a pause.

Ash laughs, but then stops abruptly, feeling that he's overstepped a mark. Lawrence looks genuinely upset.

Deborah says, 'What is this, darling?'

'I have no idea.'

Everyone is silent.

Then Claudia says, 'I don't understand, Lawrence. You didn't write this?'

'Of course I didn't write this! Why would I write this? This is . . . horrible.'

There is a stillness and people seem reluctant to move.

Then Deborah asks, 'Does the barn lock?'

'What?' Then, understanding, Lawrence shakes his head.

'Local louts,' Deborah continues. 'I'm surrounded by them in Beaconsfield. They know your name, they have a few cans, they think it's funny to leave a freaky message.'

'Local louts who are trained as letterpress compositors?' Lucy asks. 'Josh and I did a printing course during our MPhil. Everyone has to do it, on a press like this. It's really difficult, not to mention slow.'

Deborah shrugs. 'I'm sure they could do one line.'

Josh adds, in a voice that suggests he doesn't believe it, 'Deborah's right. That sounds totally plausible.'

There is another pause, then Claudia says, 'Look, everyone, let's go back to the house. I think damson gin would be a good idea.'

Ash, with a sense that he's pushed things too far, says, 'Totally. Let's do it.'

Lawrence doesn't believe the local louts explanation either, but he doesn't know what else to think. Is someone trying to mess things up? He thinks, that can't be the case: I don't have enemies. Why would someone want this week to go badly? Lucy and Ash have followed Claudia back to the house. Lawrence stands still for a moment, before gathering himself, like a prime minister striding into Number 10 refusing to hear the protestors.

'Damson gin sounds perfect,' Lawrence says. And then, forcing a return of his jocular mood: 'I blame Granny Mabel for this. Only a ghost would set the whole thing in lower case.'

Josh and Miles laugh louder than Lawrence's comment merits, with a sense of relief that this obstacle is being left behind. Soon the front door has shut, the candles have been carried through to the lower living room, people have slumped into the comfortable sofas and armchairs, the damson gin has been poured, and the chatter and laughter is back.

How strange, thinks Deborah, sipping her drink, not yet quite entering back into relaxed mode, and refusing to believe the explanation she had thrown out to Lawrence as a lifeline. Something is wrong here.

Chapter Seven

Wednesday morning

The thin curtains in Tristan's room do little to keep out the sharp morning sunlight. Josh groans and rolls onto his side, burrowing his head into the space between the pillow and the wall and pulling the blanket up to cover it. Breathing slowly, he attempts to picture himself walking through a woodland. Then he tries to conjure gentle waves lapping a sandy beach. Then he goes back to the woodland, imagining passing tall trees, feeling a gentle breeze and the soft pine needles under his feet, hearing the birds sing. He senses himself sinking deeper towards sleep – a familiar doubleness, drifting off and noticing himself drifting off – and as he feels this slide Josh has a sudden and involuntary mental image of Inês, walking towards him through the woods, barefoot and wearing the white sundress she'd had on when she first arrived at the house. Then it is no longer Inês but Miles, standing next to what might be a pool, Hawton but also not Hawton, his shirt off, his hands behind his head, and now the prospect of Josh getting back to sleep has disappeared.

Claudia reaches into her wardrobe and slides out a dress, careful not to allow the clothes-hanger to knock against the wooden door. She takes her underwear from its drawer, gathers the clothes together and walks quietly out of the room. To avoid bumping into one of her guests she will shower upstairs and run the risk of waking Lawrence. In the precious first hour of the morning, the house is quiet and Claudia wants some time alone with her thoughts before she faces the day.

But as she reaches the door, the mattress creaks and Lawrence says, 'Good morning, darling.' Claudia's heart sinks. Lawrence rolls over and raises his eye mask, keeping his eyes shut against the early light. 'Been for a swim?'

'Yes, just got back.' Claudia speaks quietly; years of fearing to wake a sleeping child have built a strong habit. 'I'm just going to make some tea. Do you want some?'

'Yes please.' Lawrence's voice by contrast is loud. He props himself up on his elbows and checks his watch. 'Christ, it's early. So bloody hot already.' He pushes the sheet away from the top half of his body and looks over at Claudia. 'You look ravishing in that towel. Will you come back to bed first?'

The rubber Snore Wizard is on the floor by the door: Lawrence must have flung it there in his sleep. Claudia picks it up and puts it on his table.

'I'm just off for a shower . . . I really should get dressed and sort out the kitchen.'

'Leave that, someone else can do it. Go on.' Claudia drops her clothes onto the floor and, still wearing the towel, climbs into bed, settling against Lawrence as he lies on his back, eyes closed.

'You are freezing. I don't know how you manage to get in there at this time of day.'

'It is to be freezing that I do get in. The cold lasts.' Claudia shifts onto her side, her back to Lawrence; her damp hair seeps into the pillow and she raises her head a little to move it away from her face. Lawrence turns onto his side, too, and draws Claudia closer.

Lawrence says, 'How do you think it's going?'

'The retreat? Very well. I think everyone's enjoying themselves, getting on well, getting some work done. The weather's been amazing.'

'Good, I'm glad you think that. Me too.'

Claudia feels the scratch of Lawrence's stubble against her neck. She says, 'It was weird, that thing with the printer. The type.' They are both still for a moment. 'Don't you think?'

'Yes, totally weird. I can't understand it. It must be someone's idea of a joke. I thought maybe Ash but I can't see it's his kind of thing at all. Probably someone from the village, trespassing and thinking they'll have a bit of fun. Like Deborah said. I should get a padlock for the door.'

'It can't just be someone from the village, surely. I mean, I would barely be able to do it, and I've helped you on the press loads of times. It's too complicated. Ash would never do something like that. Or Lucy. Could Josh do it?'

'He probably could, but I don't see why he would. Well, who knows, it's a complete mystery. Inexplicable.' Lawrence says 'Inexplicable' as if it's the final word: a way to banish the topic. His hand is on Claudia's thigh, gently pulling the towel undone, as she rolls over towards him, their faces close. He smells warm and sour. She lifts a hand to push his hair back, where it has fallen across his eyes.

'Is it?' Claudia looks at Lawrence: his hairline, high forehead, thick eyebrows, every part of his face nearly as familiar as her own. His eyes, returning her gaze.

'Of course it is.' Lawrence turns away and gets out of bed, reaching for his dressing gown. At the door he turns back, about to speak, but then he doesn't say anything and heads for the bathroom.

Claudia hears the hum and hiss of the shower, and the creak of the shower door as Lawrence opens and closes it. She lies on her back and shuts her eyes.

'Anyone for a coffee?' Josh is standing at Lawrence and Claudia's gleaming bean-to-cup machine. 'If I can work out how to use this beast.'

'It probably needs more beans,' says Claudia. 'There's the cafetière if that's easier, but Lawrence prefers the machine. The beans are in that jar. Pour them into the slot at the top. Then select double espresso or whatever underneath.' She is going around the table, removing damp swimming towels from the backs of chairs and draping them over a drying rack in the corner.

Josh positions his mug under the spout and presses the button with a double cup symbol.

'I'd love a coffee, please,' says Inês, and Josh fetches a cup. Inês is standing by a dresser near the back door, which holds a collection of glassware. On the top shelf is arranged a row of tiny coloured wine glasses, the shelf illuminated by the bright morning sunlight. Inês picks up a green glass and inspects it.

'This is nice, Claudia.'

Claudia folds the last towel over the rack and goes to join Inês. 'They are Venetian glass. My anniversary present from Lawrence a few years ago.'

'He has excellent taste.' Inês turns the glass so that it flashes emerald in the light. 'There is a chemical compound in Renaissance Venetian glass which is entirely unique to Venice. It's very rich in potassium, this glass, and they have found this compound in glass fragments in Portugal that date from the early fourteenth century. Such a long way for a delicate object to travel. Almost the breadth of Europe.' She replaces the glass on its shelf. 'Were you in Venice for your anniversary?'

'No, not that time. We were there a couple of years ago; Lawrence had a conference. It's one of my favourite cities.'

'Me too,' says Inês. 'So many secrets. Ah, thank you.' She takes the cup from Josh. She notices his attentive manner, but with a spirit of detachment – she has no interest in this man, except for one thing: the curious effect he creates of imminent trouble. He is an approaching disturbance.

Lawrence enters: he stands in the doorway, observing, as if evaluating whether things are up to scratch.

The china clinks against the silver rings Inês wears on her right hand; there is one on every finger, Claudia notices, including her thumb. Her nails are short and square, unpainted. There is a scar running across the back of her hand; it is raised and pale against her brown skin.

'My war wound.' Inês notices Claudia looking at it. 'I'm covered in them.' Claudia feels a turn of excitement inside her.

Inês puts down her coffee and turns her hand over, pulling the cuff of her shirt away from her wrist to show another, newer, scar. 'A penalty of the job. I used to use metals, mostly, which is worse for injuries. There's a theory that Donne spent some time in Venice.'

'Really?' Miles sits down at the table with his tea and toast. 'When he was fighting in the Azores or whatever?'

'I think later,' Inês says. 'The early 1600s. I have a friend who is working in Venice now, reading everything he can find in the archives, trying to prove it. It was he, in fact, who gave me the idea of using a poem of Donne's in the glass piece.'

Lawrence says, 'Inês, you must tell us more about your work: perhaps before dinner one evening?'

'Certainly,' Inês replies. 'If you like.'

'Perhaps tomorrow?'

'Of course.' Inês leans against the table and sips her coffee.

Josh looks out of the kitchen window. While Inês had been talking about Donne he had a brief but intense panic about money: just a few seconds, but he felt like he was falling. He calmed himself, as he does amid these flurries of panic, by rational plotting, in this case, about how to get Lawrence and Claudia onside with the film. He says, 'Where is everyone working today?'

'Folly for me.' Lawrence is putting his plate and cup into the dishwasher. 'No pun intended.'

Josh laughs enthusiastically.

Lawrence says, 'I'm going to get started now.'

'What a lovely spot to write in,' says Josh.

'Do you have a system?' says Inês, 'or do people work anywhere?'

'Anywhere,' Lawrence replies, as if rules and systems couldn't be further from his mind. 'See where you can find a space. Lunch is at one p.m., but do help yourself to anything in the meantime. See you later, everyone.' He picks up his laptop and papers, and goes out through the back door.

'I think I'll work outside, too.' Inês picks up her coffee cup. 'It's a beautiful morning. I have to make a quick phone call before I get started, excuse me', and she goes upstairs to get her things, phone and cup still in hand.

'I'm going to work in my room,' says Josh. 'Too hot outside for me.' He looks at the window again, this time at his own reflection in the glass rather than the garden beyond. He raises his chin a little, strengthening the line of his jaw, and turns around, but everyone has gone except Miles, who is typing on his phone, his notebook wedged under one arm. Josh watches Miles for a moment in silence. This is the first time he has been alone with Miles since arriving at Hawton. He should say something, he thinks. Miles will expect him to say something. If he doesn't look away now, Miles will realise that Josh is watching him and then Miles will catch his eye and then Josh will say something. But while Josh is waiting for this moment, Miles puts his phone into his pocket and makes for the kitchen door, as though Josh wasn't even there.

The front staircase at Hawton has a half-turn, the stairs stopping before continuing upwards in the opposite direction, and this creates a wide landing, its back wall shelved, with just enough space for a low armchair in the corner. The upper shelves hold rows of novels, mostly the faded and peeling spines of orange and green Penguin classics; more recent paperbacks have been slotted between them and fitted into the gaps above the tops of the books. The tall lower shelves are crammed with photograph albums, ranging in size and vintage, their spines bearing dates either inked onto the spine or onto stickers which peel away at the edges. At the top left are two or three albums given to Claudia by her parents, with leather covers and little square pictures slotted into photograph corners, carefully protected by interspersed sheets of tissue paper, and larger group portraits, each filling a page, entire family trees held in each slim volume. Next is a neat album from Lawrence and Claudia's engagement party, and then their wedding, honeymoon, travels together in Austria and Canada and Ecuador, a collection of cuttings and pictures from Claudia's concert appearances, and then the intensely photographed years of babyhood, albums which cover only three or four months of new life, before the pace slows to a steady album a year, with occasional extras when twelve months could not be distilled into a single book: 'Ma & Pa 30th anniversary', 'Mauritius', 'Christmas 2013', 'Norfolk camping 2021'.

Lucy is sitting at the long wooden table next to the pool. No one else is outside. The garden has a stillness that is deepened by the mid-morning heat. The WiFi doesn't reach this far from the house, so Lucy has linked her laptop to her phone to access the internet. Via the catalogue page of the university library, Lucy is logged on to the *Times Digital Archive*. She types 'drowned AND Cambridge' into the advanced search screen, and narrows the date range to from 1840 to 1880. She presses the blue 'Search' bar. 178 hits: too many to track through. She changes the terms to 'drowned AND Hawton' with the same date range. One hit. She feels a surge of excitement, which is also dread. She clicks and a page from *The Times* on 17 September 1862 appears on her screen, a dense page of small black text with no breaks for pictures or advertisements, the words 'drowned' and 'Hawton' highlighted in green, part of a short paragraph under the heading 'Deaths' which Lucy enlarges to read until it fills the screen:

In the village of Hawton, Cambs, at the Manor House, on the 4th inst., between 4 and 5 in the afternoon, accidentally by drowning, John and Agnes Charsley, aged 11 and 10, the children of Sir William Charsley, the older endeavouring to save the younger, the parents and staff absent. A memorial to be held in Hawton Church.

It was 160 years ago but for a moment the event is alive in Lucy now, surging through her, spreading its awful poison. She puts her hands to her face, knowing she will never forget 'the older endeavouring to save the younger'.

Claudia has pulled a deckchair into the shade of the orchard, and is taking notes from the large hardback balanced on her thighs when she sees Deborah approaching.

'Are you distractable?' Deborah calls as she gets close. 'Tell me to go away if you're right in the middle of something.'

'Not really.' Claudia closes her book and lets it drop onto the grass. 'Distract away.'

Deborah reaches into her handbag and pulls out a small paper bag. She sits in the deckchair next to Claudia, opens the bag and passes it to her.

'Have one of these, they are absolutely divine.'

Claudia takes a macaron from the bag and presses the tip of her finger into its smooth, pistachio shell. 'Thank you. How nice.'

'I popped to Mill Road this morning for coffee and cigarettes,' says Deborah, 'and cake. Don't tell Lawrence.' She does an exaggerated wink.

Claudia smiles. 'And now you've made me an accessory after the fact.'

'My partner-in-crime. I like that.' As they eat, Deborah takes in the view back towards the house.

'It really is something, isn't it. Have you always lived here?'

'On and off,' says Claudia. 'I grew up here, really; we moved here from Cambridge proper when I was about two. It was an amazing place to be a child. I sort of left for university, although that was only just down the road, and then I moved to London, and Lawrence and I bought a flat there. And then after Dad died we came back. Tristan was born here. So it has always been home.'

'And Tristan is with Lawrence's parents?' Deborah leans forward and scratches a mosquito bite on her ankle. 'Lovely for him to have grown up here, too.'

'Yes, with his parents in France – and yes, he's very lucky indeed, although to hear him sometimes you'd think it was nothing short of torture to be raised in the country. I felt the same at his age, I think. And he's rather isolated as an only. But it changes when you get older.'

'And are you working on anything at the moment? Musical stuff?'

'Not really.' Claudia wipes her mouth with her fingers. 'The usual bits of journalism, a review here and there. Actually, I'm sort of researching a family history.'

Claudia lifts the hardback so that Deborah can read the cover.

'*The English Nabobs*. Christ, that sounds like a laugh a minute.'

'It is a little dry,' Claudia says. 'I think if I ever write properly it will be a history of the house. The people who have lived here. Or even the house itself. Could it have a history without the people?' She looks at the wall by the orchard and the arch leading to the pool, as if to test the question. 'I don't know if I'll actually finish anything. Let alone publish it. Almost certainly not.'

'You could work up the colonial side. The links to Russell, maybe.'

'Maybe.' Claudia sits back in her armchair.

Deborah says, 'I can see that working,' but she can tell Claudia's interest doesn't lie there.

Claudia watches as Inês walks back across the lawn and goes into the house through the back door.

Deborah sees Claudia's gaze and says, 'She's something, isn't she?'

Claudia doesn't reply but glances away quickly. Deborah shifts around a little so that she is looking directly at the other woman. She feels a twist of frustration, an urge to break through Claudia's placid surface, and to do it now, this moment, while she has her on her own.

'What do you want, Claudia?'

Claudia looks back at Deborah, confused by the question.

'What do you mean?'

'For yourself. Now. In the future.'

'What do I want?' Claudia pauses to think. For a few seconds she can't think of anything to say – her mind goes blank – and she feels panic. Then she says, not entirely believing her own words, or at least knowing they can't be everything, 'Oh you know, the obvious things. I want to enjoy the rest of the summer . . .'

'Okay.'

'. . . and for Tristan to do some work at school – for his GCSEs. I want to get the attic sorted out before the autumn. The sun to keep shining—'

'Very nice,' Deborah interrupts, 'but none of those things are really for you, are they? For the family, for Tristan, the house. What about for you? What do *you* want?'

'What do I want?' Claudia repeats again, as though it is a strange question.

'For yourself. It can't be that hard. You have a life, you know, you have an identity that is separate from being a mother and a wife and a whatever else.'

'You say that with such confidence, Deborah, but I'm not sure I do.' Claudia pauses again. She feels as though she is on the edge of something, balancing, precarious. She looks down, her gaze on the grass in front of them, her mind turned within. 'Some days I feel as though I could fade quietly out of my life, and as long as someone else faded back in, to get the laundry done and pick up all the stuff and cook the food and drive people around and so on, I don't think anyone would actually notice. My family love me, I know that, but I think they would love anyone in my position, if that makes sense. That's it, really.' Claudia leans forward, as if seizing this idea, and she turns to Deborah. It suddenly seems of vital importance that the other woman should understand what she is trying to say. 'I occupy a position, do you see? I'm a product of a set of relations. I have built my life, my *identity*, if you want to call it that, whatever that means exactly, on what I mean to other people. To Lawrence and Tristan and my parents, and now just my mother, my friends, the food bank people. And as for the implication of your question . . .'

'I didn't . . .'

'The true implication of your question is that I'm going to be fifty this year and I have no idea what I mean to myself. I don't think I even know what it is that you're asking. And I know this seems ridiculous to you, Deborah, because you're this amazing powerhouse of energy and achievement and you're just completely on top of everything, but I don't *want* anything. Not in the sense you mean it. Or if I do, I just want some peace, I want to take comfort in the things that give me pleasure, like swimming and sleeping and cooking and eating and being on my own. I just want to be left alone to do those things and for everyone to be all right and to just let me get on with it, and I'm fine with that, I'm really fine with it. That's what I want. Okay?' Claudia's voice has grown strained with the last few statements. She looks away from Deborah.

'I hear you.' Deborah stands up and brushes the crumbs off her trousers.

Claudia, still looking away, says, 'I don't need . . . "sorting out".'

'It's all right, Claudia,' Deborah says with kindness, but conscious that her questions suggest a crisis which Claudia perhaps thinks she does not feel. 'If you ever do want to talk, I'm here.'

Claudia sits and waits for her nauseous discomfort at this conversation to subside. It is a relief to be by herself. She watches Deborah find a path back through the trees and across the lawn towards the house. As she does so, a peacock emerges from behind the trampoline and follows Deborah for a few steps before stopping quite still. Claudia sees his tail, dragging luxuriantly across the grass. She remembers suddenly the scent of Inês's hair, the warmth of her touch on her arm. She cannot understand the strength of her response to this woman, a complete stranger for whom she feels: what? An unexpected affinity. A desire for closeness. For touch. There is a comfort in knowing that Inês is here, out of sight but present on the estate, that Claudia will see her later. I told Deborah that I want to be alone, Claudia thinks, and now I am holding the knowledge of Inês's presence to me like a jewel. That really makes no sense at all.

Josh is reclining on the child's bed in his allocated bedroom, which belongs to Claudia and Lawrence's son. His laptop is propped against his thighs and the bed is a tangle of sheets. Josh resents the Arsenal posters and the overflowing chest of drawers and the small aeroplanes made from card which hang on threads from the ceiling and turn gently in the air whenever Josh stands or moves – all of which seems to confirm his sense of not quite belonging. They wouldn't put Inês in here in a child's bed – not in a million years. If Josh is locked in an eternally infantilised state as student to Lawrence as supervisor, despite the fact he is now in his forties, it feels like the bedroom choice was designed expressly to compound this. It's all the more striking when understood in contrast to the seemingly innumerable large rooms downstairs, each decked out with a bohemian informality that belies its curation: stacks of books on the floors, worn rugs on the sofas, large old volumes of the *OED* with a magnifying glass on a string to read the tiny type, home-made collages of postcards and old dust-jackets, candle holders on tables surrounded by hardened pools of wax, a tall twisting stick in a heavy brass vase with origami birds hanging by threads from its branches. Josh has been thinking about the planning required to produce this effect of effortlessness. Last night he'd looked at a pile of books by the sofa in the 'lower living room' – the very phrase! – and realised, despite the flung-together appearance, that they were all collections of short essays: Montaigne, J. B. Priestley's *Delight*, Joan Didion, Virginia Woolf's *The Common Reader*, four or five others.

Of course, Josh would mention none of this to anyone, least of all to Claudia and Lawrence, and part of his disquiet stems from the recognition that he is disappointed in himself for noticing with cynicism (and a curl of the lip when alone) the care with which they shape and inhabit their home. How much better if Josh could simply enjoy the effect, or even one day actually live like that, and not concern himself with unpicking the process; but his noticing makes a genuine pleasure in his surroundings all the harder to achieve. Why can't he just *live*? Recently Josh has been feeling that the only legacy of the critical thinking that his PhD taught him is a kind of continual cynicism: a distrust of any nice thing, a need to expose its workings, an inability to simply enjoy.

If once Josh had looked to Lawrence as leading a life that he himself might one day choose to emulate, he now feels that the gap between them has widened immeasurably or, rather, that it had been impossibly wide all along, but that he had not been able to perceive it. In Lawrence's home, it would always have been obvious. And now here he is, skulking on his small bed rather than claiming one of the prize spots in the house or grounds like a grown-up. He will go downstairs, right now, and make a coffee and find somewhere else to work.

Josh is in the act of closing his laptop as Claudia enters the room without knocking. Startled, he sits up sharply and hits his forehead hard on the corner cupboard.

'Fuck!' Josh ducks and rubs his head.

'Oh gosh, I am so sorry,' says Claudia, 'I just came in to get some clean towels, I didn't realise you were here. The boiler's just here so we keep them in this cupboard.' She opens one of the long fitted doors which cover the side wall of the bedroom and pulls a pile of towels towards her. Josh notices that she is blushing a little and not meeting his eye, clearly embarrassed to have found him hiding in his room like a child.

'Not at all,' he says, 'actually I was just about to come downstairs and make a coffee.'

'No, no,' says Claudia incongruously, backing out of the room, 'I'll leave you to it.'

When Claudia has gone, Josh slides cautiously off his bed and straightens his back, before reaching to pick up his laptop and phone. It is then he realises: his position lounging on his unmade bed, his evident shock at Claudia coming into the room, the hastily closed laptop. Claudia clearly thinks she has walked in on him watching porn. Her phrase 'leave you to it' rings hideous. Josh closes his eyes at the mortifying pain this thought causes him. How can such a situation possibly be rescued? Within minutes Claudia will be whispering this to Lawrence, or Deborah, or *Jesus Christ* Lucy, what she thinks she has seen, a jokey tone but also a sense that Josh has somehow failed to respond to the generosity and dignity of the retreat. Not his PhD but a film script; and now not his film script, but . . . wanking. Josh braces himself to leave the room; probably to stay upstairs would be worse. As he closes the door behind him, another thought strikes him: the sorry encounter can have done little to improve the chances of Claudia's funding his film.

The printing shed has its own particular smell, not altogether pleasant. Deborah approaches the press with some hesitancy and sees with relief that she will not have to touch it in order to release the paper trapped within; there is no sign of any paper at all, anywhere in the shed. Lawrence has clearly taken away not only the text that the press had mysteriously produced the night before, but all the paper kept there, as though removing the raw materials of its production could prevent the renewed expression of the anonymous spite. Deborah stops for a moment in front of the press, which stands inert and yet latently animate, poised to spring into action. Her eye caught by movement, she looks quickly up to the rafters, but there is nothing to be seen. A pigeon, Deborah thinks, or, more likely, a rat, scuttling back to its nest in the eaves.

Deborah thinks of Lawrence, of his face the night before as he held up the piece of paper with that peculiar message, all confusion and anger. Who could want to hurt Lawrence so badly? To spoil his elaborate and harmless production? Lawrence has many grating characteristics – most of them worn on or near the surface – but Deborah finds it hard to imagine that any would provoke such a response. Her mind turns to Claudia and her speech just now under the apple trees, the strained voice saying, 'I just want to be left alone.' An anonymous prank is not in Claudia's nature. How tiresome it is, Deborah thinks, distracted from the printing for a moment, to know exactly what Claudia should do, how she should set about finding what she wants, and not to be able simply to tell her how to go about it. Her thoughts return to Lawrence. The message, its claim to Lawrence that 'you know what's really going on', suggests a secret, a subterfuge, threatening to come to light. Somebody, she realises, really wants to hurt Lawrence, to make him suffer in fearing this revelation. What can a man like Lawrence have done to engender such hatred?

Chapter Eight

Wednesday afternoon

The little downstairs bathroom has no lock, and Claudia has attached to the outside of the door a 'No Entry' sign on a piece of string so that guests can signal when it is in use. By attaching the loose end of the string to a pin in the door frame, the entrance is barred. Josh has found himself incapable of trusting the efficacy of this informal system. He has also found something maddening about the pin and the limp string, the quiet discretion of it, the assumption of shared etiquettes, and he knows this to be a failing. He reflects once again on why he can't simply accept what is placed before him without the sourness that increasingly seems to fill him. Whenever he has needed to use this bathroom he has stood silently on the threshold, one hand on the doorknob, inclining his head towards the closed door in an awkward effort to hear whether there is anyone inside. What is he afraid of? he asks himself. To be discovered by a third party in such a position would be bad, but the prospect of walking in on a fellow guest is his real fear. Because Josh fears that he is at heart bad, he has a horror of catching other people off-guard, because he feels (even as he tries to rationalise himself out of it) that he will see their bad true selves. So Josh has spent a lot of time hovering outside this door over the last three days, weighing the prospect of embarrassment against his need to pee.

On this occasion, Josh sees as he approaches that although the door is closed, the sign hangs loose. Surely he is capable, he tells himself, of managing this with confidence. He walks up to the door without pausing and in one fluid movement opens it, stepping into the room.

Lucy is hunched on the floor with her back against the radiator, her head bowed and her face covered by her hands. On hearing the door open her head jerks up, her face red and eyes unfocused.

'Shit. I'm so sorry. The sign . . .' Josh starts backing awkwardly out of the door – this is his worst bathroom door nightmare come true – but Lucy stands up and he stops.

'No, no, it's fine. I'm okay. Come in.' Lucy waves a hand in front of her in a gesture of dismissal and then moves to straighten her skirt, caught around her thighs.

'Are you . . .? Is everything all right? Is it . . . Neil?'

'No, for once it's not Neil.' Lucy takes a few sheets of loo roll and blows her nose loudly. She drops the paper into the lavatory and pulls the flush, then turns to Josh and smiles. 'Sorry. Awkward. I know you don't like awkward.'

'No need to apologise.' (In his head he says, no need to make me feel small even as you say sorry.) The pair stand in silence for a moment until Josh realises that Lucy is waiting to leave the room, and he steps sharply aside, banging his leg against the sink. Lucy slides past, almost but not quite touching, and he registers the proximity of her body and the faint scent of perfume. Josh puts a hand on Lucy's arm and she stops, turning back to him.

'Look, you're clearly upset,' Josh says. Lucy glances quickly to his hand, still resting on her upper arm, and he drops it. 'Is it anything I can help with? Has something happened?'

'No,' Lucy replies, and then, 'yes. But years ago. It's nothing you could imagine. It's just seeing that memorial, and those poor children who drowned here, brought it back. I'm feeling a bit vulnerable.'

Josh nods and says, 'Go on. It might help.'

Lucy looks away from him and draws an arm across her body, cupping her hand around the back of her neck.

'A friend of mine drowned. Here. Not here, I mean: in Cambridge. When we were at college.'

'Oh my God. When? While you were doing your PhD? I never heard—'

'No, no, before then, when we were freshers. It was at a May ball. It was unbelievably awful. I was there when it happened. I almost didn't come back.' Lucy looks up at Josh and tries to smile.

'Oh my God,' he says again, wondering at the meaning of that phrase 'I almost didn't come back.'

'That's horrendous. I'm so sorry. I can't believe I never knew.'

'And I was reading about the drowning here, and then being in the city, I couldn't stop thinking about it.'

'Of course. Bloody hell. You poor thing.'

Lucy sighs heavily. 'It just catches up with me sometimes. I'll be fine in a minute. It was a long time ago.' She checks her watch. 'God, it's nearly lunchtime. I'd better go and wash my face.'

'Did you want . . .?' Josh gestures awkwardly at the sink behind him.

'No, no, you go for it. I'll go upstairs. I want to get my swimming costume, anyway.' Lucy turns to leave and then looks back. 'Thanks, Josh.'

'Not at all.' Josh gives Lucy a little wave and then watches her retreat along the corridor, past the tall bookcase and the odd portrait of the distant family relative and Claudia's piano. He stands for a moment after she has gone, and then he steps back through the door, remembering the sign, which he pins up carefully.

At lunchtime everyone carries plates, glasses, bottles and food down to the table by the pool. It is soon crowded with bread, cheese, a tomato salad, and leftovers from the past two nights' dinners, which Claudia starts dividing between the plates as people sit.

Lawrence looks round with satisfaction. 'Finally we are all here together. Hang on a minute, where's Lucy?'

'She went to phone home, I think.' Claudia hands him a plate.

'Again?' Lawrence begins, but then Lucy is hurrying towards them from the terrace, her face flushed. The heat from the sun is intense.

'Sorry,' she says, 'lost track of time. Oh, thank you,' to Claudia as she passes her a plate of food, 'this looks delicious.' Lucy sits at one end of the table, next to Deborah, who fills up her wine glass.

'Oh, *shit*,' says Lawrence, 'did I forget the truffle oil?'

Claudia, ignoring him, says, 'So what's everyone been up to this morning?'

Lawrence decides it's not worth making a trip back to the house.

'I seem to have spent most of it on emails.' Deborah is picking at a pool of wax left on the table by long-ago candles. 'Which – I know, Lawrence, *mea culpa* – is not what this time is meant for, but unlike most of you – excepting you, Inês, I'm sure you know how it is – I'm self-employed. I can't just let the business go under while I'm sipping Picpoul in the sunshine. "Thinking." We don't all get August off, you know.' She brushes the flakes of wax from her hands.

'It's a complete myth that academics get the holidays off,' Lawrence begins, then catches sight of Deborah's smile, 'as you very well know, and you're teasing. Actually, August is when we have to get all the bloody work done.'

Deborah looks towards the pool. 'Yes, it's like a Dickensian factory, here, isn't it? The sense of toil.'

'Ha ha.'

'Where *do* you keep your lathe?'

Lawrence says, 'Don't be a self-hating intellectual, Deborah.'

'I'm not an intellectual.'

'Of course you are. And anyway, I was getting on with my book,' he says firmly. 'How about you, Ash?'

'Just reading. It's good to have space to do that.'

'I fell asleep.' Inês fills a glass from the jug. 'I always fall asleep if I try working outside. I'm going to go somewhere indoors this afternoon.'

'You can use Lawrence's study,' Ash offers. 'I'm going to read here by the pool. I might go for a swim first though.' He looks over at Lucy, who is talking to Deborah in an undertone.

'Thank you,' Inês says, just as Lawrence begins tapping his wineglass with the edge of his fork.

'Now that we are all here . . .' Lawrence clears his throat as the conversation stills. 'A toast. Thank you very much for coming, and welcome, Inês, to Hawton and to Cambridge. We are delighted to have you.' He raises his glass. 'To Inês!'

'To Inês!' they echo, and everyone drinks. There is silence for a moment.

'And,' Lawrence continues, 'we – I – have a gift for you.' He passes Inês one of the handmade notebooks, then, leaning forward, opens it and says, pointing, 'I made the endpapers.'

Inês takes the book and turns it over. 'My goodness, this is very nice, Lawrence. Thank you for including me. I am very pleased to be here.' She looks around the table. 'Isn't there still someone missing, though? The young woman?'

'Young woman?' Lawrence looks towards Lucy at the far end of the table.

'Yes – no, I don't mean Lucy – younger still, and with blonde hair. Like this . . .' – Inês holds a hand close to her head – 'I saw her in the woods. I'm sorry, I just presumed she was one of your guests. Or perhaps anyone can walk there?'

'No,' Claudia replies, 'the woods here are private to the manor. There is a big patch of woodland which anyone in the village can access, nearer the church, but our woods are separate.'

'What did she look like, this woman?' Miles, on Inês's other side, has been listening, and, catching the end of the question, Deborah asks, 'What woman?'

'Inês saw some strange woman in the woods,' Miles tells her.

'Well, I don't know, I thought I did.' Inês turns to them. 'What did she look like? I didn't see her face, she was walking ahead of me with her back to me. Blonde hair. She was quite short, shorter than me. I thought it was a child at first in fact.

And she was wearing – I don't know the word – like a coat, but long. More loose.'

'A gown?' Lawrence suggests, and at the same time, Lucy says, 'A cloak?'

'*Sim*, yes, a cloak,' Inês nods, 'that's it. A black cloak.'

Everyone is listening now. Lucy asks, 'Where did you see her?'

'Ah, I'm not sure, quite far in, I had been walking for a while. I had no phone reception, I remember that. I turned left, away from the house, I think.'

'Near the pond?' says Lucy.

'I'm not sure,' Inês shrugs. 'Somewhere near there, I guess. I did call to her, to say hello, because, as I say, I thought she must be one of your guests, but she didn't reply to me. She didn't turn around.' Inês turns her attention back to her plate, and the tomato salad.

'Seems a bit odd,' Deborah says to her end of the table, 'someone all the way out here.'

'It will be one of the villagers,' Lawrence says with authority, leaning forward to inspect the cheese board. He looks around the table and smiles. 'Probably a dog walker. Nothing to worry about.'

'It's spooky.' Lucy folds her arms over her chest. 'I don't like it.'

'She probably didn't see anything,' says Josh quietly. 'It's dark when you come into the woods after the sunshine. It's just her eyes playing tricks.' But if Josh is trying to reassure anyone, it's himself. He is thinking of Gemma, who is short and fair-haired, and for one wild moment wonders if she has made good on her threat to come and visit him. Gemma hiding out in the woods, waiting for an opportunity to pounce. Josh is shocked by the degree to which he doesn't want Gemma to be here. The prospect literally leaves a nasty taste in his mouth. He takes a large gulp of his wine, then chokes on it. Ash thumps him on the back.

'You all right?'

'Yes, yes. Sorry, I don't know what happened there.' Josh looks over at Lucy, who is rolling the stem of her wineglass between her fingers. 'And are you all right, Luce? Not too spooked?'

'Oh, no,' says Lucy, 'of course not. That would be ridiculous.' She gives him a small smile, but Josh notices her glancing over his shoulder towards the woodland, which stands dark and shadowed in the bright sunshine.

In his mental timetable of the week – although not in the version he circulated in advance – Lawrence had allowed space for at least one post-lunch walk. A stroll across the fields seemed apt for the version of a writers' retreat he imagined – pastoral, reflective, slow-paced, communal – and he had the route planned: left from the manor gate, up the narrow strip of almost always carless road, diagonally across the wheat field, beautiful at this time of year with wild flowers Claudia could identify but he can't, through the woods that once used to be Jacobean royal hunting grounds, and out across the two big wide-open fields. This was not strictly allowed, but on the few occasions he'd met the farmer there, the farmer had said, 'Morning, sir', and waved Lawrence through in a manner that suggested Lawrence's special status as resident of the manor. Lawrence had been embarrassed by the deference, and of course politically he found it problematic, precisely the kind of hierarchy he tries to subvert in his teaching, but it was very convenient: the long way round would take an age, and is mostly road. They'd end up at the tiny village of Wiston where there is a Norman church. People will love it, Lawrence thought, as he lay in bed the week before the retreat, imagining the walk, and the days around it.

In the event only Ash takes Lawrence up on the offer and the two of them have just now crossed the final field and are entering the small graveyard in front of the church. There is one particular grave, of a professor of Japanese at the university who died in 1982, that always seems to stand out in its placement and the burnished quality of its stone and the deeply cut gold text, and sure enough Ash is kneeling down now, taking a closer look, noticing the quality of the letters, feeling the depth of the engraving with his fingertips. Lawrence is pleased Ash is appreciating things the way he had anticipated.

As if to prove Lawrence's point, Ash says, 'This place is beautiful,' and Lawrence nods. Lawrence loves to share beautiful things with his friends, in part because he loves to have his judgement confirmed: his judgements in things, and in his friends.

From the graveyard there is a clear view of the fields they've just crossed. They can see the high top of Hawton Manor.

Ash stands up, looks out and says, '"Man comes and tills the field and lies beneath".'

Lawrence, who is trying to unbolt the church door, says, 'Blake?'

'Tennyson.'

'Of course.' Lawrence feels a flush of foolishness. 'Not quite my period!'

'Are you going to live here for good?' says Ash. 'At Hawton?'

'I think so. There's a part of me that dies at the sense that I won't move again. That there isn't another chapter. But I love it and I can't imagine we'll move.'

'People died so young in the nineteenth century.' Ash is walking between the graves. 'Thirty-six. Twenty-four. Forty. We'd be old men.' He carries on picking his way through the graveyard, carefully avoiding stepping on any of the graves, or disturbing the bunches of flowers that lie next to a few of the headstones. 'Maybe we are old men.'

'We are not old!' says Lawrence immediately and with a vehemence that, after a second, causes both of them to laugh.

Ash says, 'It's confusing, isn't it?'

'At my 50th someone said to me that forty-nine is the last birthday at which you can plausibly lay any claim to be in touch with your youth.'

'That's not what you want to hear.'

'I think I don't mind being in my fifties,' Lawrence says, 'but the imminence of sixty is . . . completely unacceptable. I can remember being twenty-five so vividly. Living in Elephant and Castle. Working at the British Library when it was still in the British Museum. But that was *twenty-eight years ago* and if I vault forward a similar gap then I'm in my bloody eighties. And I am not prepared to engage with that prospect.'

'The students stay the same age. They are nineteen, twenty, twenty-one, forever.'

'That's the magic trick. Esme, Isaac, Izzy, Molly, Tom. Fifteen years ago they were Laura, Sam, Gemma. Twenty-five years ago they were Tim and James and Sarah.'

'Do you have any Ashanes?'

Lawrence smiles and faintly nods but isn't quite sure what Ash means, so he just carries on.

'Five years ago I realised I felt definitively out of touch with them. I understood I was of a completely different generation. It was a relief as much as anything. Clarity after that awful late-thirties blur when you don't know where you stand in relation to them. It's so much easier to be distant.'

Ash has his back to Lawrence. He's looking at the graves. 'You haven't been crossing lines, again, have you?'

'For goodness' sake, Ash, of course not. That was once . . .'

'Twice.'

'Twice, twenty years ago. Before Claudia.'

'Sort of before Claudia.'

'Before things were really . . . let us say . . . established.'

'And that business with the student's work?'

Lawrence doesn't say anything. Ash waits, refusing to fill the gap.

Lawrence crumbles first. 'That was an absurd misunderstanding.' And then, when Ash says nothing, in quicker tones: 'The whole thing built on a staggeringly naive conception of what writing actually is.'

'Not plagiarism? You can say, if it was.'

'Absolutely not.' Lawrence is trying to open the church door. 'And it was all years ago.' He is about to add, 'Do you know how easy it is to go after senior Fellows?' but he stops himself. He snaps the bolt open: pleased that this decisive movement can serve to signal a change of conversational direction.

The church inside is small, and smells musty, and is cooler and darker than the hot, bright early afternoon outside. It's impossible to imagine this space ever warming up. The dark wooden box pews look very old. Lawrence says, 'Fifteenth century,' as he sees Ash examining them. There is a pulpit which looks a little later: Ash guesses, correctly, eighteenth century. High to the left is an organ, obviously Victorian. Apart from the dust particles illuminated by light falling at an angle through the windows, the church has a near total stillness. They could be standing here at any point in the last millennium.

Ash's gaze falls on the large but fragmentary wall painting facing the entrance: a haloed man, about eight feet tall, holding a child, the man standing in water with fish and other creatures faintly visible. A scroll of text in the wall painting unfolds from a stick the man is holding like a narrow flag. Ash is almost certain that Lawrence is going to use the word 'banderole'. Ash looks closely at the scroll to encourage him.

'Lovely banderole, don't you think?' says Lawrence, articulating the word with particular and self-conscious clarity.

Ash stands back. 'Is that an . . . *octopus*?'

'Wonderful, isn't it? St Christopher wading through the water holding the baby Christ. They uncovered it about ten years ago. It's fourteenth-century. We gave some money towards the restoration. Quite a sum, in fact. But well worth it.'

'His trousers are knotted at the knee.'

'I always thought it's odd that we're miles from the sea and yet here is Christopher walking past an octopus. I suppose the artist copied it from a bestiary.'

Both of them look at the painting in silence.

Lawrence says, 'You know I've never seen a single person in here.'

'You sound like Philip Larkin.'

And then Lawrence says, as if reaching for something, 'My worry, Ash, is that I always think things are all right.'

'That might be a virtue.'

'It isn't always. I know I turn away from difficulties.'

'Are you doing that now?'

'Well, the irony is that things now really are terrific. Work. Teaching. The family. The book.'

Ash knows that isn't true, and that Lawrence knows that Ash knows that it isn't true, but both of them are used to existence as a persisting in the face of half-felt contradictions.

Ash opens one of the box pews and sits down: the effect is odd, as if he is a tiny one-man congregation waiting for the vicar to arrive.

Lawrence climbs the steps to the pulpit and faces out. He is wearing a brown T-shirt with 'the revolution will not be televised' printed across the front, and his army cap.

Ash says, 'The eighteenth-century version of you would have been lord of all these villages, wouldn't he, Lawrence? Things are good for you now, but life would have been resplendent in 1780.'

'I'd have been a minor clergyman.'

Ash smiles. 'Yes, that's the trick, isn't it?: power that you can frame as decline.'

Lawrence doesn't quite understand Ash's last comment, but it is delivered with an edge so Lawrence ignores it, keeping going with the story of his effacement. 'I'd have been the sort of obscurity that got edited out of the last edition of the *Oxford Dictionary of National Biography*.'

'The eighteenth-century me would have been living in Jaffna, pushed around by Dutch and British officers like you.'

There is a long pause and Ash's comment hangs in the air.

Ash says, 'You know I really hate that you live in a house built on colonial wealth.'

'I understand.'

'That was also owned by an author whose primary aim in writing was to celebrate Empire.'

'Yes.'

'For whom you maintain a blue plaque.'

'We don't have anything to do with the blue plaque. It's a council initiative. I'd be delighted to take it down.'

'I really, really don't like that.'

'I know.'

'Do you? Do you really know?'

'Of course I do. I feel that . . . deeply.'

'Deeply?'

'Although I actually think that's a rather cartoonish reading of Russell who's a lot more complicated than that. *Striding to Cairo* doesn't hold up terribly well but there's a range in the other works . . .' Lawrence's voice falls away. 'I do hear what you're saying.'

Both men can feel things shifting, the new terrain both familiar (they have had this conversation before) but also exposed.

Ash says, 'I don't think you have any idea.'

'Ash, the very fact that you're here shows . . .' Lawrence grinds to a halt, conscious that he's started down a bad track.

Ash leans forward. 'Shows what?'

'Ash, you're an old friend.'

'Shows what?'

Lawrence raises a hand and shakes his head as if to signal his remark was a mistake, that he withdraws it.

There is a pause. Ash can feel his next comment coming from a long way off, outside himself.

'Is that my role? To add a bit of colour?'

'Ash that's completely ridiculous. Anyway, you're not the only' – Lawrence pauses, almost imperceptibly – 'person of colour here.'

'Me and Inês. Not too much colour. Just enough to make you feel better.'

'That's insulting and ridiculous. We've been friends for thirty years and you think I'm strategising your presence to . . . to what?'

'This isn't about strategy. This is about complacency.'

'How am I complacent? I think about these things.'

'What are "these things"?'

'You know what I mean.'

'I really don't.'

'About the past. Its wrongs. How comfort today rests on suffering in history. For goodness' sake I teach a course on . . .'

'Constructing whiteness in pre-modern literature. Yes, I know. You've told me literally dozens of times. It was nominated for a teaching initiative award. I'm sure you have the trophy on display prominently in your office.'

Lawrence shifts awkwardly in the pulpit.

Ash, watching him, says, 'Ha! You actually do. And how much work has that done in your promotion letter?'

Lawrence shakes his head but doesn't say anything.

'The past of this place' – Ash raises a hand, gesturing up the hill – 'isn't an anecdote you can shake your head at with mock pity. It's not "interesting". It's not a prompt for a course that ticks a box. It's real.' Ash thinks for a moment then says, 'Have you any idea of the privilege of your life?'

Lawrence snaps back, 'I earned everything I have. I worked fucking hard. I didn't stop working in my twenties and thirties. Every evening. Every weekend. None of this came easily.'

'You did literally inherit a manor house from your very rich wife.'

'Please don't bring Claudia into this.'

'You slid easily and inevitably from prep school to Winchester to Cambridge.'

'There wasn't anything inevitable about it.'

'Have you ever been inside a comprehensive school? Have you ever been inside an educational establishment that was built later than the thirteenth century?'

'I've been on the college outreach committee for four years. I've spent hours on widening access documentation.'

'While Tristan went to Kimbolton.'

'What the fuck has Tristan got to do with anything? What has wanting the best for my own child got to do with anything? You're being simplistic and you're being disingenuous. I can still do fucking good in the world while having a large garden!'

Ash pauses for a second. Probably he was wrong to mention Lawrence's son. He is still sitting in a pew and Lawrence is still standing at the lectern in the pulpit, which both adds a surreal quality to the conversation, and seems entirely right.

Ash says, 'Why have you organised this week?'

'What the fuck, Ash? If you don't want to be here, just piss off.'

'Why have you done it?'

'Isn't it obvious?'

'Not to me.'

'To be with friends.'

'Friends.'

'Friends I've not seen for a long time. Including, I thought, you. To write. To help my friends write. To share the beautiful space of Hawton. To eat and drink together. I suppose you think there's something terribly sinister in all that.'

'You don't think it's about displaying the splendour of your life? You don't think it's about the vanity of hospitality?'

Lawrence looks at St Christopher wading through the water holding the baby Christ, and for a second Lawrence conjures the thousands of conversations over the centuries that must have taken place in this church, St Christopher all the time standing impassively above.

'What am I supposed to do with the fact that things have turned out well? I'd have thought sharing whatever I have with friends is a good thing to do.'

As he speaks, Lawrence is thinking, how can I get this back? How can I restore a sense of equilibrium by the time we return to Hawton?

Their encounter in the bathroom has heightened Josh's awareness that he's been steering clear of Lucy out of a lingering sense of shame – his failure as an academic in contrast to her success – but as he stands by the kettle waiting for it to boil, Lucy comes into the kitchen from the garden door. She seems calm and composed, and Josh wonders if he should re-open their earlier conversation or, as Lucy seems ready to, pretend it never happened.

'Tea?' he asks, pointing at the kettle.

'Yes, please.'

Josh puts another teabag in the pot.

The two of them stand in silence for a moment, the awkwardness mutual. They both start to speak at the same time. Lucy says, 'You first.'

'No. I was just going to ask, how's the writing?'

'Ugh.' Lucy waves her hand. 'I'm a hundred years from writing. I got as far as thinking about reading. Maybe on Friday I'll start some reading.'

'I'm sorry about Neil. The divorce.'

'Thank you. There are so many ways he has made things very bad for me, but robbing me of the capacity to think is maybe the worst. I can't . . . reach things, in my head, like I used to. You know?' The water is boiling now. 'And then on the rare moments I can, I can't join one thought to another.'

Josh pours the water. He feels conversationally on the back foot: as if his difficulties are trivial by comparison, are being trivialised by Lucy right now, and even in failure he has been beaten by Lucy.

Lucy continues, 'Everyone keeps saying they always thought he was an arsehole. Why didn't people say that at the time? Or before I married him?'

Josh thinks (but doesn't say out loud), *Have you any idea how fruitless it would be to try to dissuade you from anything?*

Instead, he says, 'How are the children?'

'I don't want them to grow up hating their father, but I don't know how I can't hand on that hate.'

'Kids are very adaptable.'

The complacency irritates Lucy. 'Do you think so? I know people say that, but do you think so really?'

Josh pulls a cigarette packet from his pocket. He feels

exposed. He has no idea if children are adaptable, and certainly no sense of what it would be like for a ten-year-old to have their parents separate. He leaves the question unanswered.

Lucy opens the fridge, takes out the milk and pours it into the waiting mugs. Josh sees that she remembers how he likes his tea with only a very little milk, a legacy from writing breaks and library lunches fifteen years ago. Lucy says, 'Let's stand outside,' and opens the door to the garden. There's a small, tiled area with plants in pots and jasmine climbing over a window frame and then up the sides of wooden steps that rise to the deck. Lucy balances her tea on a step, takes her phone from her pocket and squats to capture the jasmine-framed window from below, the sky beyond.

Through the window Josh can see Miles in the lower living room, or at least the top of his head, nodding repeatedly in a way that suggests he's writing, fast.

Josh takes a cigarette from the packet, says, 'Do you mind?' and, when Lucy gestures *fine*, flicks open his silver lighter.

He takes a long drag and exhales slowly. 'What are you going to start reading, when you do?'

Lucy reaches for her tea and takes a sip. 'There's an effigy in Ewelme, in Oxfordshire. Alice de la Pole. Granddaughter of Chaucer. Fascinating, important, but lost in her grandfather's shadow. Until now, that is. I want to write about her. Partly. About her and memory: how the tomb remembers her. How the tomb . . . keeps failing to bring her back to life.'

'You mean a biography?'

Lucy looks ahead, her gaze steady, Josh's question only glancing the thought she is trying to follow through.

'Sort of. I don't know. More inside her than a biography.

What I want to know is what it was like for her to walk down a street in 1450. What it felt like to be her. The voices in her head. The taste in her mouth. What did it mean for her in 1450 to lie in bed, unable to sleep?'

'Maybe it felt like it does today.'

Lucy shrugs. 'Maybe not.'

There were times, early in their graduate work with Lawrence, Lucy in the year below but already talked about by everyone, when Josh felt they were both fighting for Lawrence's love: that there was only enough of Lawrence for one of them. Josh had wondered why he found himself hoping Lucy and Lawrence were having an affair; it was only later he realised that a sexual connection would have been far easier for him to tolerate than the intellectual sympathy Lawrence and Lucy clearly shared.

Josh can feel the old familiar resentment rise inside him but he presses it down. Offhand, he says, 'You always were the chosen one.'

'Where did that come from?' Lucy looks Josh in the eye, smiling.

'It's true.'

'Is that a compliment or an accusation?'

Josh didn't mean for it to sound bitter. 'Just an observation.'

'It sounds impossible, doesn't it, imagining someone that far in the past? Naive.'

'I don't know. It's not the kind of work I ever did.'

'The younger me would have plunged ahead with Alice.'

'You can still plunge ahead.'

Lucy feels a familiar sense of irritation. She's got used to men (it seems always to be men) saying things they think are supportive that serve only to trivialise what she's just described.

Men who say 'I understand' but mean 'Stop talking about it.' Lucy wants to turn to Josh, to everyone, and to say, 'Didn't you *listen* to what I've just said?'

Josh says, 'Is Lawrence helping you?'

'He's been very kind during this last most recent awful period. He's offered to use his college research fund to pay for a research assistant to do some initial grunt work in the libraries. There's been so much stuff about memory and lives and the fifteenth century in the last five years and I'm miles off the pace. I don't know if I can work this book out.'

Josh is quiet for a moment as he considers not Lucy's sense of being unprepared but her ease in passing over the luxury of an assistant. He repeats to himself her phrase: 'grunt work'.

Josh says, 'I've not seen Lawrence in ages. We're not in regular contact.'

'But he invited you here.'

'I sort of pushed.'

'Why?'

'Work things.'

'You mean teaching?'

'No.' Josh feels a flush of annoyance, at Lucy and more generally: was anyone listening to him at dinner? 'I'm trying to make a film.'

'Oh yes.'

'I'd like Lawrence and Claudia to be involved.'

Lucy takes a sip of tea. If she is thinking that the chance of Lawrence and Claudia putting any money into Josh's film is vanishingly remote, then it doesn't show on her face. 'How does Lawrence seem to you?'

'Generous. Pompous. Vain. Kind. Ever Lawrence.'

Lucy smiles. 'Yes, all of that. But he saved me more than once, you know. In ways that were genuine: that were about me, not him. Once, when the twins were tiny and I could hardly stand up, let alone write an article about late medieval poetry, he covered for me with the journal. He explained away my absences at conferences when I said I'd be there. And then when I told him about Neil, he said I could bring the kids and stay with him and Claudia here until I got settled.'

From the deck there is a sudden loud noise of clambering and a long squawk. A peacock has flustered its way down from a tree and is standing on the table. It looks down at the two of them, or through them. Lucy is seized suddenly by the conviction – it flashes through her like a revelation – that the peacock sees the house from a century ago. That when it looks at Josh and her it sees people from the past, standing in the spaces they occupy now. She quickly pulls out her phone to capture the bird's gaze but as she takes the photo, it lowers its head. The moment is gone.

Josh says, 'Back to the books, I think,' a phrase they used to repeat on coffee breaks outside the library fifteen years ago.

Lawrence and Phoebe are standing either side of the back wooden gate: Phoebe just outside the grounds, Lawrence just within. It's a corner of the property which is obscured by the large oil tank that heats Hawton Manor, the tank itself shaded by trees, the corner invisible from the house except for a view from its topmost window. A peacock feather is sticking out of the oil tank – the gauge is broken and Lawrence uses the feather to check the level, an aristocratic workaround that had at first seemed comical but which is now just what Lawrence does. Phoebe seems tiny next to the gate, her head only just higher than its top, and Lawrence towers over her. He is speaking in an urgent whisper.

'Phoebe, you need to calm down. You need to be reasonable. This is a misunderstanding.'

Phoebe lifts the metal latch so that it falls back into place with a clang that causes Lawrence to flinch. She pushes open the gate. 'Shall we do this inside at the kitchen table, or out here?'

'Please lower your voice and come away from the gate.'

Phoebe says, at the same volume, exaggerating her accent, 'Loud Americans, huh?'

Lawrence is acutely conscious of the house, his guests, Claudia, aware all the time that someone could stride round the corner and see them.

Phoebe pulls two stapled stacks of papers from her rucksack. Lawrence recognises the first as his own article 'What was mental health in medieval England?' published this month in *Post-Anachronism: The Journal of Medieval Studies Today*. The other is a typed chapter – the first chapter of Phoebe's dissertation written nearly two years ago, with Lawrence's handwritten notes scrawled over it in green. The typed header on each page reads, 'Phoebe Armstrong, "(Un)healthy bodies: an eco-critical reading of fifteenth-century conceptions of sickness and health"'.

Phoebe says, 'I've highlighted the relevant passages.'

Lawrence turns the pages of his article. On many of them, sentences are marked out in yellow. On page five, an entire paragraph is highlighted. Ditto the final page: the penultimate paragraph is all yellow.

'Phoebe, what is this?'

'You need me to say it out loud?'

'Look, Phoebe. You've written a terrific chapter here.'

Phoebe says nothing.

'And of course it's . . . it's your work.'

'I know.'

'But . . .' Lawrence looks quickly in the direction of the house, then back to the pages, which he turns mechanically, not reading any more. He speaks in a half-whisper. 'Look, we all know authorship is a slippery concept. That originality is a romantic fiction and . . .'

Phoebe opens her mouth to speak but closes it in silence.

Lawrence's voice stutters on. 'That texts are tissues of . . . that influence is everywhere.'

Phoebe is unused to Lawrence being so obviously rattled, and she realises how even in this moment of astonishing betrayal – which is what it surely is – she wants him to be in control.

'Are you seriously theorising your way out of literary theft?'

'Phoebe, let's not be individualists about thought. Not now. Not in 2022. Leave that to the Right. This isn't . . .'

'Isn't what?'

'This isn't . . . At most it's a kind of homage.'

'Oh, fuck you, Lawrence.'

'I thought we were thinking together. And that was a wonderful thing.'

'What do you think I should do, Lawrence? When I find my supervisor plagiarising my work?'

'This is absolutely not plagiarism.'

Phoebe says nothing.

Lawrence looks down at the pages of his article. 'Phoebe, I'm under a lot of pressure. There are so many demands on my time. At work. At home. You have no idea.'

'You're not under pressure, Lawrence.' Phoebe nods in the direction of the house in a manner which suggests Lawrence's entire being. 'I could tell you about being under pressure. I have a thesis to finish. My funding is about to run out. I'm in a foreign country. I work three evenings a week in that horrible bar. I'm leaving for the States on Saturday. There are no jobs. You're my supervisor and I'm just starting out and you've published an article which takes not only my ideas but in thirteen sentences, and two whole paragraphs, my literal words.'

Lawrence's tone shifts suddenly: he speaks fast. 'Those were *my* fucking ideas! *I* gave you those ideas. Everything in that chapter is mine!'

'What?'

Lawrence runs his hand through his hair. He breathes deeply. He closes his eyes for several seconds.

'I withdraw that. That was inappropriate. I'm sorry.'

'That's seriously problematic, Lawrence, and you know it.'

After another pause, Lawrence says, 'I've got a house full of friends, Phoebe. I'm hosting them for a whole week. There's . . . I'm spinning a lot of plates here. I've got so much going on. I'm under . . . it's a different pressure from yours, I acknowledge that. But it's real.'

'Fuck your friends. How did you think this wouldn't be found out?'

Lawrence shakes his head. She's right: what was he thinking? For a moment, something like self-reflection rises up within him. The deadline he couldn't meet; the real sense that Phoebe's chapter *was* his work, his thoughts handed down to her, for her to hold for a while; the evasion, the looking away from a thing he knew was wrong, but this wrongness was distant compared to much more immediate approbations (the editors' delight, the readers' reports, the sense of something finished, the fulfilment of a Research Committee requirement which would trigger another term's leave). Lawrence shakes his head to shut down this brief illumination.

'It's inappropriate for you to come to my house like this. I told you last time: you can't just turn up without an invitation. It isn't done.'

'That's not what we're discussing.'

Phoebe's voice is strained and her face rigid with anger. Lawrence thinks, how young she looks: her taut skin, the delicacy of her nose and chin.

He swallows. 'Did you do that printing?'

'What do you mean?'

'Someone set some type on the press here.'

Phoebe stares back.

'There can only have been a handful of people who've been anywhere near that machine who know how to use it, and you're one of them. Christ, you were in there only last week.'

Phoebe continues to hold his gaze for two, three seconds. 'I don't know what you're talking about.'

'What . . .' There is a pleading aspect in Lawrence's eyes that Phoebe finds unnerving. 'What are you going to do?'

Phoebe puts the papers back in her bag.

'I have no idea. I have to work this out all on my own, don't

I? I mean, in a moment of crisis a graduate student should turn to their supervisor, but when the supervisor is the source of the crisis that becomes a problem, doesn't it?'

'I think . . . this isn't the time for doing anything in haste.'

'That's easy for you to say.' Phoebe pauses. 'I'm seeing Angela this week, before I go. Maybe she can give me some informal advice. I won't mention names, not yet.'

'Angela Olson?'

'Yes. You know her, right? She was my advisor at Penn. I can hardly ask for advice from the faculty, can I?'

Lawrence says suddenly, 'We could co-edit my book together. You can be co-author. Your name on the cover.'

'You're actually bargaining?'

'I'm not bargaining. It's a . . . reflection of the way we came to so many of these ideas together.'

Lawrence is thinking about how the journal editors will certainly pull his article if they get the faintest whiff of this. Lawrence knows one of the editors – his age, they get on, nice bloke, they had drinks after a conference in Austin in 2018 – and considers emailing to warn him what might be coming. 'Slightly unhinged female grad student with a personal grudge' – that sort of thing. He looks carefully at Phoebe: her tattoos and bleached hair and the silver ring through her nostril. Lawrence is pretty confident he can calm things down with the editorial board. But with Angela?

Phoebe zips up her rucksack and opens the gate. 'You know the terrible thing is that the other PhD students in my year group said I shouldn't say anything.'

'You told them about this?'

'Not the details. Just that something had happened. And

they said I'd be worse off for raising it. That I should just take it. Bad things happen. What does that say, Lawrence?'

'I've spent my career fighting hierarchy, Phoebe.'

'That's laughable. Everything you have is because of hierarchy.'

Lawrence looks over her head towards the house, thinking how he can get her away.

From the small high bedroom window, Claudia watches Lawrence and the young woman standing in the shade by the fence. So this is Angela. She looks tiny, almost child-like from this vantage, and especially because she is wearing a long black leather coat, so completely out of keeping with the weather that Claudia feels a sympathetic discomfort. Claudia had imagined her older, more confident, had assumed from the tone of the message that she was a professor like Lawrence. The young woman keeps her arms folded, takes a step forward. Is the girl crying? It's hard to tell. She seems angry. Lawrence has his back to Claudia; he gestures with one hand, wildly. He runs his hand through his hair.

Last Easter, Lawrence had called from his office on the landline: he'd left his phone at home and needed the code to log on to his email. As Claudia relayed to her husband the six-digit number, still in her dressing gown, clearing the breakfast things away, thinking about the garden, about the dogwoods and willows she needed to prune back, a text message arrived from 'Angela'. Bad timing – or good timing. Either way, a message not intended for a wife's eyes. Lawrence chattered on: 'Thanks, darling – I'll be done here by five, six at the latest.' Claudia didn't look for more messages and marked the one she'd seen as 'unread'. She said nothing. The fact was established, and that was sufficient. It changed the landscape, for a while, tilting everything to the left by a degree or two, but mainly Claudia was struck by her own ability to accommodate the news and to cope. She has always had such a clear-eyed sense of Lawrence as flawed, clumsy, error-prone, that this news soon seemed not aberrant but consistent with the man she loved. And still loves. Plus there was the prospect of change. To learn that he had been unfaithful was to Claudia almost exciting – or at least there was excitement mixed up with the other emotions: now, Claudia thought, something must happen. But nothing had.

And so here is Angela. Claudia has never told Lawrence that she knows and she sometimes considers this explosive secret knowledge her own betrayal: there are, she reflects, other forms of alienation than infidelity.

The girl has turned and is walking through the gate. Out into the road. Half a minute later Claudia sees the long black coat pass the main black iron gate. She is walking back towards Cambridge.

Chapter Nine

Wednesday evening

The walls and ceiling of Inês's bedroom are painted white, and the room contains so little furniture that, lying on the bed after her shower, Inês has the impression of being suspended in a box of light. On the wall opposite is a watercolour of Hawton Manor, which Lawrence had told her yesterday afternoon, as he put her suitcase down next to her bed and opened the window and generally buzzed attentively around her, was painted by Claudia's mother. 'I'm sure naively realist to an artist like yourself but within the long history of amateur domestic art I think not uncreditable.' There is a group of trees to the left of the composition, one of them standing at an improbable angle. Inês imagines reaching out and nudging the tree straight with a fingertip. She has been looking at the painting for some time when she becomes aware of the sound of a piano being played somewhere in the house. Inês checks her phone; it's 6 p.m., Lawrence's time for what he'd called (looking at Inês as he spoke) 'terrace drinks'. She pulls a pair of silk trousers and a shirt from the drawer, puts them on, then returns to the little en-suite bathroom, hooking silver hoops into her ears and easing her rings back onto her fingers before leaning towards the mirror to apply lipstick. Inês looks at her reflection once, with a clinical detachment, and turns to find the source of the music.

The 52,000 photos in the 'Recents' folder on Lucy's phone date almost entirely from the past decade, and the faces most often picked out by its recognition software are those of her twins, as babies, infants, toddlers, and now older children. The earliest album predates the 'Recents' by two decades: it is a collection of forty images that Lucy's parents had digitised for her as a birthday gift – they had the physical photographs converted on the scanner at the computer shop in town, and the images on her phone often retain the borders or frayed edges of the tangible originals. These images seem to dip backwards and pick up the ageing process where her own children's photos leave off, recording her teenage years, and then her move to university at Cambridge. It is this last group of pictures that Lucy is scrolling through now, sitting on her bedroom floor, her knees tight against her chin.

Here is Lucy in the college bar with its low barrel ceiling; lying by the river with friends with empty bottles on their sides; waving from a bridge; rowing stroke, stern-faced and determined, for the ladies' first eight in the Lent Bumps. There are lots of photos of Lucy in groups, laughing friends leaning in with arms round each other. Here she is with her college boyfriend, Michael, both of them impossibly young, the edges of their faces so delicate and defined, their eyes bright, in the bar at the ADC theatre, where he had been directing a daring production of *Edward II*. Lucy's first year at Cambridge had been a vaulting series of such photo-worthy moments. She felt validated by conforming to this series of generic expectations of a freshers' year, and felt an obligation to gather images of each event, as if to prove she was doing it properly – and they should have culminated in pictures from her first May ball, with Lucy dazzling in a floor-length gown she'd bought from the secondhand stall in the market, slugging from a bottle of champagne, crowded on the lawn with the other survivors. But here is the final picture from that year, the one Lucy has been looking for: it is a close-up of two faces, hers and Zara's, eyes nearly closed against the sun. It was taken on the grass outside the pub by the river on the last day of exams, a spot traditionally favoured by students celebrating the end of a long year's work. Zara's bleached-blonde hair. They had been lying on the grass together when Michael had taken a series of snaphots, most of which Lucy had discarded, but this one she kept, and now it is the only photo of Zara that she has. When Lucy pictures Zara, it is this image that she sees: Zara's half-shut eyes and wide mouth, open in laughter, her bright hair, the silver ring through her nose. It is the summer of 1999. Their time at university was the last gasp of a pre-internet age, when there was not yet the assumption that everything would somehow be digitally preserved, that nothing could ever really be lost. Despite frequent late-night searches, Lucy has never found an image of Zara online.

Zara's death had been a seismic occurrence in Lucy's life, not just the event itself, which is now so fractured and worn in her memory as to be almost – not quite, but almost – irretrievable, but its excruciating aftermath, with everyone at college, and then at home, so desperately sorry for her, poor Lucy who had suffered the death by drowning of her best friend, Lucy whose goodness was heightened by proximity to her best friend's loss. Lucy had felt that her own life had been arrested, then, that she had been definitively forced into a straitjacket of virtue, a virtue that seemed to others to shine (but, to Lucy, snapped tight around her) because it persisted through adversity. It was, she knew, a virtue monstrously unearned. For a while she thought it would be the end of her studies. Everyone had thought her paralysis was because she mourned Zara so deeply, had loved her so well. Nobody knew why Zara, apparently trying to leave the ball alone at three in the morning, had climbed the railings above the dark river rather than go round by the gate to the road, why she had tried to edge over the iron bar that marked the boundary between colleges above the deep water flowing beneath, leaving a smear of blood on the greasy metal. Many people had asked Lucy these questions – the police, her tutors, their friends, even, hideously, Zara's parents – and to all she had said the same thing: 'I don't know. I'm sorry. I wasn't there. I wish I had been there to help.' But repeating these words, even when they became smooth and worn over time, had not made them true, had not lessened Lucy's knowledge that she was a liar, and worse: a killer. Now, wedged tightly in the space between her bed and the wall, Lucy looks Zara in the face and braces herself against the memory of her own betrayal.

'Luce?' Deborah's voice calls from the other side of the bathroom that joins their bedrooms. 'I'm going down for drinks now. Are you coming?'

'Yes. No. I'll be a minute.' Lucy quickly puts her phone

face down on the floor, as though Deborah can see over her shoulder, and then covers it with a pillow. 'Go on without me. I'll catch you up.'

'Okay – see you there!' Lucy listens to Deborah walk down the stairs, and then the door of the annexe closing behind her with a click, and then silence.

The corridor where the piano lives is always dark, and always cool, even on very hot days like this one. The darkness is one of the things Claudia likes about the piano. When they had moved into the manor with this upright piano, which was Claudia's own, and which she much preferred playing to the grander instrument her mother had kept on display, everyone – the removals man, her mother, Lawrence – had told Claudia that this was the wrong location for it. In a house so large and with so many light-filled rooms, to keep her piano in a dark passageway seemed perverse, but Claudia was insistent. This corridor, with its wooden panelling and its windows set high into the wall, felt to Claudia like an enclave, an enclosure to which she could retreat in her spare moments. She likes passing the piano on her way to other places. Now she sits at it, the keys warm beneath her fingers, and slowly plays the opening bars of the final duet from Monteverdi's last opera, *L'incoronazione di Poppea*. Each time she plays it, Claudia stops at the point where the first singer's voice would begin, pauses, and then starts again.

On the fourth iteration, Claudia becomes aware of someone watching her, and this time she continues playing until she has finished the piece. As the last notes fade, she turns to see Inês silhouetted in the doorway. Inês is leaning against the stone wall, her eyes on the patterned kilim rug in front of her, and she is still for a moment before looking at Claudia.

'Thank you,' she says. 'What a piece of music. Did you write it?'

'Me? No!' Claudia laughs. 'I wish I had. It's from an opera by Monteverdi called *Poppea*. She was the mistress of Nero, the Roman emperor. It's the piano arrangement of a love song.'

'By Monteverdi?'

'Yes, although, actually, this specific aria is probably not by him. It's more likely that one of his apprentices wrote it.'

'So he stole it?'

'Not exactly. It's more that the opera itself was written collaboratively. Some younger men working under his supervision. Lots of things were written like that then. In the seventeenth century.'

'It has words as well, in the original?'

'Yes. Words and a story.' She plays the opening chord again, holding it.

Inês says, 'It can't be good, being the mistress of Nero.'

Claudia shifts to the second chord.

'She does get crowned empress at the end. And she's declared goddess of earthly beauty. As she is being crowned,' Claudia changes chord, 'she and Nero gaze at each other, and they sing this duet.'

Claudia picks out the melody with her right hand.

'And what happens to Nero's wife?'

'Good question. Octavia. Nero thinks that she can't have children. Hence Poppea. Then Octavia tries to have Poppea killed, but the man she asks to do it, who's a former lover of

Poppea, as it happens, can't go through with it. So she gets banished from Rome.'

'Poor Octavia,' Inês says.

'The wife,' says Claudia, looking at her fingers on the keys. 'Hard to accept that your expulsion is the cause of such beautiful music.' She stands up from the piano stool. 'Come through here.' Claudia leads Inês to the lower living room and picks up her phone from the coffee table. 'Listen.'

She and Inês sit on the low sofa, and Claudia puts her phone on the table between them. There is a brief silence and then the music begins, the slow notes of the piano now picked out in the strings of what sounds to Inês like a harp, and something else she can't identify, maybe a cello, and then the singers' voices, first one and then the other, following and merging with one another until Inês can't tell them apart.

The phone screen shows a picture of an album cover: a collection of Italian duets called 'Amore e morte dell'amore'. When the music finishes, the two women sit in silence.

'My God,' Inês says. She has tears in her eyes.

'Do you speak Italian?'

'No,' Inês replies. 'I didn't understand a word.'

'*Pur ti miro*,' Claudia replies. 'I gaze upon you, or I desire you, or I admire you; *pur ti godo*, I delight in you; *pur ti stringo*, I hold you tight . . . and more in that vein.'

'Is it you singing? In the recording?'

'Oh no,' Claudia replies. 'I do have a recording of me somewhere but it's definitely not on Spotify. I've never performed in the opera. I just woke up with it this morning. Those voices have been chasing each other around my head all day.'

186

'And do you sing, still? For your job?'

'Not any more. I stopped after Tristan was born. That's nearly fifteen years ago, but actually towards the end I was hardly getting any work anyway.'

'Do you miss it?'

'I miss making music. I sing in the choir here and very occasionally in Cambridge, but not professionally. I miss the feeling of contributing to something beautiful, necessary. I miss getting nervous. Being preoccupied by it. I do some bits of reviewing now, so I'm still sort of in the world, but writing about superfluous biographies is not the same. The lifestyle is just not compatible with children. Late nights, last-minute travelling, having to practise. I can't see how we would have made that work, especially with Lawrence's job.'

'Being a professor?'

'Well, yes.'

'That always seemed to me the easiest job in the world.'

'Don't let Lawrence hear you say that. He calls it "labour unending". He needs support, and it makes sense for someone to be here for Tristan, the house . . .' Claudia looks around her.

'Your son won't need you forever, Claudia.'

'Do you have children?'

'Me? No. I had a stepson, for a while, but his mother and I aren't together any more. I still see him but of course it's different to having my own child.'

'Why did you break up?' Claudia is surprised at her own question: the sort of intrusion she would normally carefully avoid.

Inês doesn't seem to mind; she turns to Claudia as if appreciating the intimacy.

'We were no longer compatible. Our lives. It had gone.' Inês touches her palm to her chest. 'No children, no wife. I am lucky I can do whatever I like. For work, for travelling, for fun. Being here.'

'Claudia!' Lawrence's shout booms out from the kitchen. 'Are you coming? And do you know where Inês is?'

Claudia is almost certain Lawrence will be saying 'For goodness' sake' under his breath right now.

Inês says, 'Caught,' and Claudia feels a thrill pass across her at the sense of transgression Inês's word implies. She slips her phone into her pocket and follows Inês out into the dark hallway.

'Oh please don't tell me we are out of ice.' Lawrence is staring into the open top drawer of the freezer, where the two trays are usually kept. One has already been emptied for the first round of cocktails; the second is nowhere to be seen.

If Claudia wonders why Lawrence expects her to have superior knowledge of the contents of the freezer, or why he expects her to be the one to take responsibility for the minutiae of domestic life, or indeed why he turns to her with this expectation as a son turns to his mother, she says only, 'Is the tray not in the drawer?'

'No.' Lawrence's reply is curt. 'Obviously.' He pushes the top drawer shut and grapples with the one below, which is overfull and will not easily slide open. 'How am I supposed to make a gin and tonic with no ice?' He says this as much to himself as to Claudia. 'It's the Camerons' visit all over again. Guests sitting on the deck and the Ocado order delivered to the cottage in Hay.' He tugs at the drawer again. 'Complete bloody farce.'

Finally, with an aggressive pull he succeeds, and an open bag of peas springs forward, spilling its contents on the floor.

'For fuck's sake.' Lawrence scoops up some but not all of the peas and puts them back into the freezer drawer in the vicinity of the bag. Several fall through and back onto the tiles.

'I'll check the deep freeze,' says Claudia, but Lawrence looks up from his crouched position in front of the freezer, gives a quick check behind him, and says, 'Hang on a sec.'

'Yes?'

'Could you have a word with Lucy for me?' Lawrence shuts the freezer and stands up, brushing his hands against his trousers.

'Lucy? What about?'

Lawrence lowers his voice and brings his mouth close to Claudia's ear.

'About the Instagram stuff. Posting pictures of the house. I checked today and there's one of *Harold*.'

'Lawrence,' says Claudia, turning her head to look him in the eye. 'Harold is your peacock. Not your child. If you don't want pictures of him on social media, fine, but you ask Lucy about it. Don't make me your go-between.'

Lawrence sighs crossly through his nose. 'I should have put it in the email. No social media. It cheapens everything.'

'So ask her not to.'

'I don't feel I can,' Lawrence whispers rapidly, biting the skin at the side of his thumbnail.

'Well, I'm not going to. I honestly don't give a shit what she puts up there. No one will see it. What are you worried about? I'll go and get more ice. If you don't like the social media stuff, just don't look.'

Lawrence watches his wife leave the kitchen. Claudia seems out of sorts. Perhaps she's right, he thinks, and he is being too officious about Lucy's postings. Lawrence takes his phone from his pocket and opens Instagram: nothing new from Lucy since the picture of the peacock. He scrolls down his feed and holds a sudden intake of breath. Phoebe has posted a photo of Russell's blue plaque on the wall of his house, with a tendril of ivy curling beside it. In the caption, she has written 'Catching up with some English country houses and their deep dark secrets #colonialism #horatiorussell #Hawtonmanor #Hawton #englishcountryhouses', followed by three skull emojis. The picture has 23 likes. Lawrence clicks on Phoebe's profile. The next post on her grid has 61 likes: a photo of Bob Dylan standing on a podium holding a sheaf of papers. The caption reads: '"Bob is not authentic at all. He's a plagiarist, and his name and voice are fake. Everything about Bob is a deception" – Joni Mitchell #JonahLehrer #IanMcEwan #plagiarism #power #speakingtruthtopower.'

Swallowing hard against a rising wave of nausea, Lawrence closes the app and stares at the blank phone which now only reflects back his own face. As if summoned by his nervous attention, a WhatsApp notification from Phoebe flashes onto the screen – the letters displacing his reflection. Lawrence swipes it open.

Hi, glad we cd talk earlier. Think I dropped my bracelet outside yr house, not this time but last time? Its my mom's & I need it back, can you look & let me know asap, its urgent. & we'll be in touch about other thing. Thx P.

Lawrence looks at the phone for a long time before putting it face down on the kitchen counter. He hasn't technically opened the message, so Phoebe won't be able to see that he's read it. She can hardly expect him to go hunting about in the garden for her when he's busy, anyway. Lawrence pushes the phone away from him and goes to join his friends.

When Claudia returns to the kitchen, it is hot and noisy, with most of the group milling round the table, everyone on the second round of Miles's champagne cocktails. Lawrence, Phoebe's Instagram post and WhatsApp message forgotten, is playing his vinyl of *Hunky Dory* and he and Miles are singing along.Inês is watching and laughs as Miles wraps an arm around Lawrence's neck and throws back his head for the final words. Claudia catches her eye and smiles as she squeezes past them with the bag of ice, enjoying their shared feeling of being grown-ups watching the children play.

'Claud, have you seen Lucy?' Lawrence untangles himself from Miles and turns to follow his wife. 'It's time to go through but no sign of her at all, and she's on the rota, but behold!' Lawrence flings wide his arms theatrically. 'No food!'

'I presume she's still in the bath.' Claudia shuts the freezer door and stands up, brushing off her hands. 'She went up to run it earlier. Actually ages ago.' Claudia glances back to see Inês moving towards the turntable, reaching for the records Miles is handing to her from a stack on the floor.

'A bath?'

'I said just use the main bathroom.' Claudia reaches for a

191

glass from the cupboard and offers it to Lawrence. 'Didn't you want a gin and tonic?'

'What?' Lawrence looks in confusion as Claudia gives the glass a little shake. 'Oh, no, thank you.' He raises his empty tumbler. 'Miles made me one of these instead.'

'Claudia?' Miles comes up behind Lawrence. His face is flushed and happy.

'Yes, please.'

'Time for round three, then.' Miles turns to the kitchen counter and starts reassembling his ingredients. He calls back over his shoulder. 'Inês? Deborah?'

Deborah is sitting at the table recounting an elaborate story to Ash, their chairs turned to face one another. She leans in towards Ash, her back to Claudia, and Ash laughs across at her, hands resting on his knees. Claudia watches as Deborah suddenly stands up, raising a hand above her head as if to indicate great height, then stumbles a little on the flagstones. Ash puts out a hand to steady her, laughing, and Deborah leans back against the table, her leg resting against Ash's as she reaches behind her for her glass, enjoying the contact.

'Debs?' Miles is counting sugar cubes into glasses. 'Ash? Do you want another?'

They look towards him, but as Deborah opens her mouth to answer, Lawrence says, suddenly speaking louder, 'Shouldn't we find Lucy and get dinner started? It will be midnight before we eat at this rate.'

'Let the poor woman finish her bath.' Miles pours a small measure of cognac into each glass, pleased at the way the liquid soaks into the waiting sugar.

'Bath?' Deborah says, 'She's not in the bath. She was still in the annexe when I left. On her phone.' She checks her watch. 'That was over an hour ago now. Unless she came back through?'

'I don't think so,' Lawrence says, looking to Claudia. 'Claud? Could you go and check?'

Claudia has taken a champagne flute from Miles and is raising it to him in a little toast. She turns back to her husband. 'Check on Lucy? Over in the annexe, you mean? Can't you go?'

'No.' Lawrence crosses to her and lowers his voice a little, 'I mean upstairs.' He gestures with his head towards the ceiling, raising his eyebrows. 'In the *bath*.'

'Oh, all right.' Claudia puts down her drink on the counter before she's had a chance to take a sip. 'Just be a minute.'

'It's okay, I'll go. Have your drink.' Inês puts down the record sleeve she has been reading and heads for the kitchen door.

There is silence for a moment in her absence, a quietness as the room adjusts, and then Miles hands round the drinks, and he and Lawrence put on the next record. When Inês returns, Lawrence looks up and asks, 'Any luck?'

'I don't know, sorry.' Inês sits down at the table next to Ash and takes the drink he offers her. 'I knocked but I don't think she heard me. Someone is in the bathroom, though, I could hear them moving about.'

'I'm sure she'll be down in a minute.' Claudia is standing at the fridge, rooting through the vegetable drawer. 'But let's eat or Miles will have us all steaming drunk. There's some rocket left, I'll make a salad, and there's plenty of fresh pasta, we can have it with the pesto Lucy bought from the deli.' She puts the bags of pasta and lettuce and the tub of pesto onto the work surface. 'I know there's some Parmesan somewhere.'

'Pasta and pesto?' Lawrence's tone is disappointed.

'Gourmet pasta and fresh pesto. It will be fine.'

Lawrence lowers his voice so that only Claudia can hear. 'Not exactly restaurant quality, is it? Which is what we've been hitting pretty consistently thus far.'

Claudia locates the cheese and hands it to Lawrence. 'Grate, please.'

Ash stands and says, 'I'll lay the table', and Miles starts clearing glasses and newspapers and books to make space.

'Wonderful, thank you. We may as well just eat in here.' Claudia reaches into a drawer for the largest saucepan. 'It won't take long.'

Conversation and music resume as the meal comes together, and no one notices as Lawrence slips out of the room. Upstairs, he walks softly down the corridor towards the family bathroom. As he pauses outside the door and leans to listen, the door suddenly opens to reveal Lucy, face scarlet and apparently, or so it seems to Lawrence in that moment, having just got out of the bath, clutching a large pile of soaking wet towels to her body.

'Lawrence!'

'God, I do apologise.' Lawrence takes a step backwards. 'I'm so sorry. I was just popping back to check on you, the cooking. I didn't realise—'

'Oh, Lawrence, thank God.' Lucy moves towards him and Lawrence notices with relief that she is in fact still dressed in the vest and shorts she has been wearing all day, though her legs and arms are wet. Lucy stretches awkwardly to open the bathroom door more fully and Lawrence sees that the floor, which, like most of the upper floors at Hawton is made of old oak floorboards, is awash with water.

'What happened? Here, let me take those.'

'It's a fucking nightmare.' Lucy offloads the towels onto Lawrence and he registers the discomfort of their warm, sodden weight. 'I completely forgot about the bath. I went over to the annexe to get my stuff and I forgot about it, I don't know, I just got distracted. And then I came straight back and there's water fucking everywhere and I couldn't get the plug out for ages.' Lucy runs a wet arm over her face and looks back at Lawrence, stricken. 'And I think it's leaking through the floor, look.' She gestures towards the far wall, where the bath, now empty, stands directly below the open window and its view over the fields. Water is pooling a little against the skirting boards.

'Please don't tell Claudia!' Lucy is almost crying. 'Or anyone else.'

'It's all right. Don't worry. I'll just get rid of these and find some dry ones.'

'I can't even run a fucking bath.'

'Lucy, stop. Look at me. It's not a big deal. I've done this kind of thing a thousand times.'

When Lawrence returns, Lucy is standing in the same spot, one hand over her eyes. She looks up as he approaches.

'I'm so, so sorry.'

'It's fine!' Lawrence replies, with a little more levity than he feels, and he says again, 'Don't worry. Here, stick a couple of these down here, and I'll do by the window.'

On his hands and knees, Lawrence presses towels into the remaining water. Lucy watches as he gradually works his way across the floor, laying more towels under the bath, before stopping to sit back on his heels and pull the damp linen of his shirt away from his skin.

She is thinking about the time when, as a graduate student, she had organised a symposium, with five speakers over the course of a day, and the keynote speaker, an eminent professor, who was supposed to open proceedings, had phoned at the last minute to say he'd missed his train and that there wasn't another for three hours. Lucy found herself almost sick with terror, standing on the threshold of a hall full of people she wanted to impress, the most junior person in the room, tasked with explaining that the person they had all come to hear wasn't going to be there. Lawrence had come over to her then to find out what was wrong, and had then calmly set about fixing it, offering to give an extended version of his own paper ahead of schedule, and then to chair the following panel in place of the absent professor. No one had even seemed to notice. Full of gratitude at this memory, Lucy watches Lawrence throw a towel into the bath and then leans forward to squeeze his arm. 'Thank you,' she says again, 'I thought I'd ruined everything. You're a lifesaver.'

Miles and Josh fall back into the two deep armchairs.

'To have a "lower living room" suggests . . . what?' says Miles.

'An upper living room,' says Josh.

'Certainly. But also . . . a long gallery. A stables. A family ostler.' Miles looks round the room, as if capturing the spirit of the place. '*Aristocracy.*'

Josh says, 'I'm very far from possessing an upper living room.'

'And I have no ostler. We each have our struggles.'

Lawrence comes in carrying two bottles of wine. 'I did a playlist.' He taps at his phone. 'Why is it not coming out of the speakers? There.' Elvis Costello starts to sing 'Alison' but the volume is far too loud, so Lawrence quickly turns it down. 'Sorry.'

Deborah and Lucy arrive with glasses. Then Ash and Claudia, each carrying a candle which they put on the round glass table in the centre of the room.

Deborah says, 'This takes me back.'

'This place is such a bubble.' Lucy holds out a glass for Lawrence to fill. 'It could be the 1930s. A true golden age.'

'*Golden?*' says Miles, incredulous, and although he is smiling his tone is sharp. 'Who for? The ostler?'

'Oh, you know what I mean,' Lucy replies, smiling back at him, 'the glamour, the wealth. Houses like this. Before things fell apart.' Miles is working out how to respond to this as Deborah turns to Josh. 'What about you, Josh? Do you want to stay here forever in 1930?' The question sounds more aggressive than she'd meant it. 'Or are you looking forward to getting home – to Gemma, isn't it?'

Josh feels his face flush. 'That's right. Of course, I've missed Gem. But I could certainly do with a few more days writing.'

Deborah thinks how neither sounds true: both the missing of Gemma, and the desire to stay here longer.

'Tell us about her,' Lucy takes a sip of her wine, 'I can't believe I've never met her. Is she a teacher, too?'

But before Josh can speak, Miles says, 'It's weird, isn't it, that no one has asked about my husband.'

Lawrence, who is pouring wine into Miles's glass, stops. 'What do you mean?'

'Just that. I've been here three days and he's not been mentioned.'

Lawrence continues pouring. 'I don't think that can be right.'

'Do you all know what his name is?' Miles waits a second. He lifts his glass but puts it back down without drinking. 'Do you know what he does for work?'

Claudia says, 'Of course we do!'

Lucy says, 'He works in TV. He's called Chris.'

'Craig.'

'Sorry.'

'And he works in radio.'

Lucy says, 'I knew that. I'm really sorry.'

'Why do I know about Neil and your kids and . . .'

Lawrence turns to his friend. 'Oh, come on, Miles, Lucy's in the middle of a terrible break-up and . . . in any case, we haven't talked about Josh's partner.'

'We just did. Gemma. But you're right. Forget it. Sorry. I'm a bit drunk. Three cocktails in. It was just a stray thought.'

'What was the thought?' says Lucy.

'Oh, just about what counts.'

Lucy keeps looking at Miles, her not moving or even blinking indicating *go on*.

Miles says, 'Oh you know, what gets *seen*' – he does air quotes as he says the word – 'and what doesn't.' His tone is caught between making and trivialising a point. 'Nothing. It doesn't matter.'

Lawrence says, 'I'd certainly love to hear more about Craig whom I very much enjoyed meeting at the *TLS* party last summer. I thought he was a charming chap.' But Lawrence is anxious to shift the mood away from this odd place that it's landed. Miles is trying to find the words to say just why 'charming chap' is so maddening, but he's had too much to drink for clarity and remains locked in a clumsy boldness that makes it impossible to be precise. Lawrence, sensing Miles's thought, speaks before Miles can. 'But shall we play a game, now?' No one says yes but Lawrence wants to keep the momentum moving. 'Does everyone know the name game?'

'Oh, darling, we always do that.' Claudia leans forward to balance her glass amid the books on the low table. 'There must be something else.'

Deborah looks at Miles, tilting her head to suggest an enquiry, but Miles shakes his head a little back at her, the movement indicating *it's fine*, and *it's nothing*, but also *it's not worth it*, and *they won't understand*.

Lucy thinks: he's right. No one did ask.

'The name game is all I know,' Lawrence shrugs. 'I'm not a great games host. Any suggestions?'

Inês comes in from the other door – she ducked out of the end of dinner when her phone rang for the third time. 'You English and your games,' she says, sitting down neatly on the edge of the low sofa. 'You are obsessed. It's a distraction, isn't it? From the big questions.'

Josh says, 'I've got one. But I need a book. Ideally a not very good book. A sort of Jeffrey Archer kind of book.'

Lucy grins. 'You think Lawrence and Claudia have Jeffrey Archers in this place?'

Ash is looking at the shelves on the stage. 'You've got masses of Russell. Three copies of *Striding to Cairo*! If you want me to read my undergraduate dissertation on *Striding to Cairo*, I'd be more than happy.'

'Oh, Russell is perfect,' says Josh. 'Good old Horatio. Throw me over one. And we need paper each, and a pen.'

Josh explains the rules: he'll read out the first line of Russell's novel – the front cover has a sombre-looking Russell, dressed in lord-of-the-manor tweed, staring out as if reckoning on behalf of his generation with his moment – and everyone makes up a second line. Josh will gather them in, read out all the made-up lines, plus the real line which he'll copy out too so he's not obviously reading from the book, and everyone guesses which is Russell's. Points if you guess right, and points if people guess yours.

Inês says, 'But I'm not a writer.'

'We can't very well each etch a window, can we?' says Miles.

Inês laughs. 'Okay, okay, I'll try.'

Deborah says, 'I love it. I think this sounds fabulous.' She refills her glass, and then Claudia's, and then Lucy's.

Lucy says, 'I'm really quite drunk,' taking another sip.

Ash tries not to watch her but he is drunk too, and Lucy seems more intoxicating than ever. He fetches a jam jar full of pens and a notebook from a desk and sits next to her at the end of the sofa; Lucy shifts along a little towards Deborah on her other side. Ash starts tearing pages from the notebook and passing them round.

Josh says, 'Okay, here it is.' He looks at the book cover. 'The *Daily Mail* said this was "A total joy, and a reminder of how great a stylist Russell was."' Josh turns to the first page. 'Here's the opening line. "In his dreams Frederick was haunted by Mr James's face, which seemed like an unmoving sun in that strange landscape."'

'What utter nonsense,' says Miles.

'Read it again, will you?' Lawrence starts to laugh.

'"In his *dreams* . . ."' Josh is giggling too now, putting on a very posh accent and slurring a little . . . '"Frederick was *haunted* by Mr James's *face*, which *seemed*" – stop it, you bastards, I'll never get through it at this rate – "seemed like an unmoving sun in that strange landscape."' By the time he finishes the sentence, everyone is laughing, and Josh is pleased by the effect.

'"His unmoving son"?' says Miles, 'what does that mean? Why is his son immobile?'

Josh says, 'Not his son, a *sun*. "Unmoving sun", as in a star which stays still.'

'Is this science fiction?' says Deborah. 'I make a point of never reading science fiction. I won't be able to do it if—'

'*Striding to Cairo* is three hundred pages of advocacy for colonial rule dressed up as jolly good fun. It's not science fiction,' says Ash, 'which I think is unfortunate,' but he is smiling, passing around the pens. 'Don't you, Lawrence?'

Lawrence doesn't look up from the line he is writing but half smiles and says, 'I think we have different views on this one, Ash.'

'So now you have to write the next line,' Josh continues. 'So stop pissing around and focus. Everyone writes one down and then I read them out.'

Lawrence says, 'Done mine.'

Miles says, 'I can imagine you as a teacher now. I bet you're fierce with your Year 8s.'

'My Year 8s are total shits.'

'I don't doubt it.'

There is a moment of silence as everyone thinks and writes.

Lawrence looks round the room, as if checking on each of his guests.

'If there's swearing I'll know it's you, Debs,' says Miles.

Deborah pulls a face of mock anger.

There is grumbling, more laughter and then brief silence. People fold up their pieces of paper and pass them to Josh who shuffles them together into a pile. Josh reads the first sentence and Lucy says, 'That is *so you*, Lawrence.'

'I don't know what you are talking about,' Lawrence replies, as if in outrage. 'That's clearly the right one.'

Lucy says, '"*Trajectories of despair*"?', and Lawrence just shakes his head and says, 'Vintage Russell.'

Josh reads the second slip, but he is hesitant and the handwriting is evidently a problem.

'"Frederick would . . . keep lute"?'

Deborah says, 'What does "keep lute" mean?'

'Sorry, I mean "sleep late". Can't read my own handwriting! "Frederick would sleep late and . . . and . . . upon making up . . ."'

'"*Waking* up"!' Miles shouts. 'For goodness' sake it's not Elizabethan secretary hand. "Frederick would sleep late and upon *waking up* felt uncertain as to where he was."'

'Oh, that's so colourful, darling,' says Deborah, 'but I think do stick with the non-fiction.'

Almost everyone votes for the last line which Josh reads, thinking it the real one, which turns out to be Ash's.

'The satisfaction of having out-Russelled Russell,' says Ash. 'I'm not sure I like that. At least my dissertation from thirty years ago has served a purpose. It may not have brought down British imperial self-regard but at least it helped me win a parlour game!'

'Didn't you get the top mark in the year for that dissertation?' Lawrence asks, knowing that Ash did (Lawrence remembers things like that, not least because he didn't: twelfth in the year – not even top ten – still stings), but Ash ignores him.

As the game progresses the whole group seems captured by a contagious hilarity; Lawrence is laughing so hard at a joke of Josh's that he is crying, unable to speak, and he has to put down his wine glass, pressing the heels of his hands to his eyes.

'Oh God, I haven't laughed like this in ages, my stomach hurts,' Lucy says and puts a hand on Ash's knee to lever herself up from the sofa; she wobbles a little as she stands and he catches her arm. 'Whoops. Back in a minute.'

Most of the rest of the group get up and begin scanning Claudia and Lawrence's shelves for the next book for round two. Deborah and Ash stay on their sofa; she looks over at Ash as he reaches for his drink.

'Still smitten, I see.'

Ash turns to her, not sure he's heard properly, 'Sorry, what?'

'With young Dr Jeffrey?' She nods in the direction of the door.

Ash drains his glass. 'Is it that obvious?'

'Only to me, darling, don't worry. Not to her. What are you going to do about it?'

'Do about it? Can't you guess?' Ash grins. 'Absolutely nothing.'

'Ah, that would be a shame. She needs a bit of a lark after that prick Neil. Right, I need some water.'

As Deborah leaves the room, Lucy returns, carrying a bottle of wine from the kitchen. She sits down on the sofa and attacks the foil neck of the bottle with the opener.

'Give it to me, you'll stab yourself.' Ash takes the bottle, removes the foil and uncorks it, pouring wine into both their glasses. Lucy clinks hers against his, takes a swig and then shifts back into the corner of the sofa so that she is half-lying, with her legs along the seat and her feet in Ash's lap.

'Cheers. That's comfy.' Lucy rests her head on a cushion and closes her eyes.

'What's this?' Deborah comes back in and pulls over a stool to sit at Lucy's end of the sofa. Ash goes to stand and make space for her, but she ushers him back down. 'No, I'm fine here, thank you, darling.' Deborah nudges Lucy with her elbow. 'Don't go to sleep, please, it's nearly time for round two.'

Claudia and Inês are laughing together at the window; Inês is miming something elaborately, her face animated. As Josh passes around more bits of paper and Lawrence and Miles bicker over who is going to read the next first line, Ash settles back in his seat. Lucy's legs are crossed at the ankles, her left heel balanced on his thigh. Her toenails are a metallic blue, the nails chipped, her skin brown from the sun. He moves her right foot so that her feet lie more comfortably, side by side. Lucy flexes her toes, and Ash gently closes his hand over them. He looks over at Lucy, but her head is tipped back to face the ceiling, eyes still closed. And then Josh is asking him to pass round the paper, and Lucy sits up, as if waking, and withdraws her feet. She smiles at Ash, and reaches for a pen.

In the kitchen, Miles is loading the dishwasher with a mix of drunkenness and care. Claudia is tidying up the lower living room, collecting scattered corks and wine bottle foil, and the dozens of paper slips littering the floor with made-up lines from novels. *Rufus steadied himself in the saddle, looked to the horizon, and trotted on.* Claudia smiles, then goes on collecting the other slips. From outside she hears a gradual glassy crash which is shocking for a fraction of a second before she realises it's Lawrence emptying the bottles into the recycling. Lawrence does everything loudly when he's drunk. Josh, Ash and Inês have gone to their respective rooms. Claudia left the kitchen door open for Lucy who looked unsteady on her feet and said she needed some 'country air' before going to bed.

Lucy has come outside into the garden to clear her head: she's not used to drinking like this. The closing two years of her marriage to Neil saw her retreat into a kind of survival mode in which anything that wasn't either looking after John and Isobel, or simply getting through the minutes, then hours, then days, of sharing a house with Neil, was jettisoned. Lucy didn't drink. She hardly ate. She lost weight. She went to bed by 10 p.m., the small box room on the other side of the landing a sanctuary. She stopped writing and, apart from practical questions of organising the children – the playdates, the after-school clubs, the homework, the snacks, questions which Lucy continued to answer with absolute order, pouring everything she had left into these tasks – she stopped thinking, too, at least in the creative, brilliant sense that had characterised her twenties and thirties. She lost touch with her friends. She had a sense of her own body, her presence in space, receding: as if her mark on the world was growing dimmer and dimmer, and even – it sounds strange to say – that her skin and hair and face were somehow growing back inwards. Tonight is the first time she has properly laughed for two years.

Lucy is standing in the area Lawrence referred to as 'the

orchard'. It's very dark – there's no moonlight – and she can see only the outlines of the fruit trees around her: she remembers apples, plums and pears, but she couldn't identify them now. She is thinking about Ash's glances, her feet in his lap, the way he held her feet: she is happy to turn over these moments in her mind as she walks slowly back to the house. Lucy is used to men holding her gaze just long enough to pose the question – it seems to happen now more than ever, and she has wondered whether these men can intuit her domestic situation, perceiving it as a kind of opening or weakness, or whether she is in fact sending a signal without realising it – but it's such a release to perceive interest from someone she likes and respects. She notices and enjoys Ash's careful kindness, the feeling of being held in his attention. Lucy is approaching the back door now but instead of entering the house she walks carefully around its outside, past the annexe and into the cobbled courtyard. She stands looking at the railings which separate the manor from the road beyond. In the gloom she can just pick out the gate, standing ajar, its angle breaking the smooth line of the metal railings against the dark sky. Lucy approaches the gate and pulls it towards her. Is she attracted to Ash? She has no idea: it's another register of the bleak battleground of Lucy's domestic life that she doesn't even know whether she can extend herself beyond the essentials of survival into feeling for someone else.

She looks back towards the house, which is in darkness except for the ground floor hall where the portraits of Mabel and other family figures hang. Claudia had said earlier she leaves a low light on there all night. Lucy imagines the whole retreat group held protectively by this beautiful old house – the house like arms, older than them all, gathering them up, telling them it will be okay. She feels a surge of energy and a sudden desire to keep moving, to turn her back on Hawton and the city and to walk deeper into the countryside, into the black field lying beyond the far hedge and the woods behind it. For a moment she weighs this possibility as though she might actually do such a thing. Instead, she slips through the gate and turns right, following the road the short distance to the churchyard where the wooden gate, too, stands open.

The churchyard is almost completely dark, but Lucy's eyes are adjusting to the dimness and she can pick out the shapes of the gravestones, the lighter gravel of the path around the church, the outline of a bench against its pale stone. She follows the sloping path downwards. Then, suddenly, she stops sharply and gasps, turning her head quickly towards an urgent scrabbling sound in the brambles, barely visible at the churchyard's outer edge. Lucy feels her heart beat thickly in her chest and takes a breath to calm herself. It will be a cat, or a fox, or a hedgehog, she tells herself, making its way home. Then she remembers Lawrence's misprinted message, its obvious malice, and the possibility of an intruder that was never resolved. The silence rushes back, filling space, as though no sound had been made at all.

As Lucy turns to retrace her steps her gaze falls on the pallid contour of the memorial to John and Agnes Charsley, perhaps ten yards away from where she is standing. From this angle the statue has its back to her, and Lucy can see the dull gleam of John's stone body and the outline of his head against the sky. Despite the dark, the stone statue can clearly be distinguished from its surroundings, and she can perceive very faintly the darker outline of its base, surrounded by foliage. And then in a lurching, sickening moment of clarity she sees that there is a figure, a small, black figure, slumped at the base of the statue, leaning back against its side. As she watches, the figure seems to give out a brief flash of orange light, and then another. It is the spark of a lighter, Lucy realises, and she can hear the tinny rasp as the lighter is struck again and fails to flame. At the next try, the lighter catches and its faint light illuminates the figure's face in profile, leaning in to hold a cigarette to the fire. Lucy gasps again, louder this time, and the face turns towards her, bright now in the glow of the lighter held in front of it. In the surrounding darkness, this face is all that Lucy sees. Looking back at Lucy, the outline of her head covered by a hood, her eyes shadowed and unseeing, her mouth open, lips parted to speak, is Zara. Her face from 1999; the fine line of her nose and chin; the silver nose ring. Lucy opens her mouth too, to call Zara's name or to scream, she can't tell, but before she can make any sort of noise the lighter goes out, and Zara's face disappears back into the dark mass of the churchyard.

Chapter Ten

Thursday morning

Even in his sleep Ash feels his heart racing, and as he wakes he registers the soreness in his body before knowing its cause. He is lying spreadeagled on his front, his head thrust upwards against the pillow, arms outstretched, and because he would never normally sleep in this position Ash feels a sense of physical confusion which adds to his discomfort. He lies still, eyes closed, as the pain concentrates itself in his head and neck, and then intensifies as he begins to move.

With pantomime cautiousness Ash raises himself onto his elbows and gradually turns onto his side. The morning is already glowing against the thin curtains of Lawrence's study and Ash becomes aware of his dry mouth and the comforting smell of his own sweat, the damp sheets cooling on his back. He feels on the bookshelf for his phone and slips it off the charging cable, squinting at the screen. There is a notification for a new email and Ash swipes it open with his thumb.

Although the subject line reads 'Your enquiry' it's from an address Ash doesn't recognise, random letters and numbers

@yahoo.com. Just spam, Ash thinks, but as he scans the message he realises that this is a reply to his own email of several months ago, which he'd almost given up hope of receiving. He shifts onto his back and reads the email again, more carefully this time, already pulling out the quotations he will use for his article: 'I never even thought plagiarism was a risk – I was just a student'; 'I trusted Lawrence completely but I soon realised how naive I'd been'; 'so after that I couldn't get out fast enough. It was the single worst thing that's ever happened to me'. Ash drops the phone on the bed and leans to retrieve his laptop from his bag. He arranges his pillows so that he can sit against them and as he types his password into the computer he thinks, how funny that it should come today, right at this moment, when he is in Lawrence's house, in his study of all places, has been sleeping surrounded by his books.

'It's early for a run,' Claudia says. 'And hot. Very impressive.' Josh is sitting on the bottom step of the back staircase, tying the laces on his trainers, as Claudia turns the corner to come up the stairs.

'If I leave it any later it will be really warm.' Josh stands up to let her pass and takes his headphones from his pocket, opening the white case. He doesn't move back but holds his position – an instinct – so Claudia's body has to brush against his. 'And I can't start the day without a jog. I'm just going round the grounds.'

'Well done, you,' says Claudia as she continues up the stairs. The trace of sarcasm in her voice – and the more cynical version of Claudia from which it springs – is discernible only to herself. 'See you later on.'

Josh sees the opportunity: he needs to have another go.

'Actually, Claudia?' Josh calls after her retreating form. Claudia comes to a stop near the top of the stairs and looks back over her shoulder. She doesn't turn fully round, and inside – but not perceptibly – she sighs. Claudia doesn't want to talk to Josh: she doesn't like his pushiness, and if she wasn't the host, she'd make her irritation clearer.

'Mmm?'

'Did you have a chance to think about my film at all?'

'About your film?'

'Yes – the Chaucer film.' Josh feels hope – it hangs in the air for a second – then feels it falling away. After a pause, he says, 'I wondered if Lawrence mentioned anything? About the funding thing?'

'No, no, he didn't,' says Claudia, 'was he supposed to? He is rather preoccupied at the moment.'

'Of course,' Josh replies. He feels sick. 'It doesn't matter.' *Fuck it.* 'I'll catch up with him about it.'

'Okay, see you later.' Claudia continues up the stairs. Josh looks down at the white earbuds in his palm: a little blue light is flashing on the side of each one, out of synch. He makes a fist around them and raises it, and for a moment he thinks he will throw them against wooden floor, hard, to break them, but he stops and lets his fist fall. Josh closes his eyes and waits for the flood of adrenaline to pass. Time to refocus. This is a setback, but not an insurmountable one. At least Lawrence hasn't said to Claudia that he definitely won't support the film – unless Claudia was lying just now, and Josh thinks Claudia lacks the ability (he thinks of it as an ability) to dissemble. He will just have to think of some other way of getting Lawrence on board. Josh finds his running playlist on his phone and puts in his earbuds. As the opening bars of Kanye West's 'Power' drum and chant, he strides down the hallway and breaks into a jog when he reaches the door.

No one else is down for breakfast yet and Lawrence is eating toast with jam while he checks his email. He's irritated with himself for logging on. He made a promise to keep the week of the retreat clear from emails, and made sure he told all the guests in advance to only contact him, if they couldn't reach him in person, on the WhatsApp group he'd set up. But Phoebe's visit has rattled him and now he's checking his inbox for the fifth time this morning, partly out of a concern that Phoebe will have written, but more fundamentally because in a state of anxiety Lawrence turns to email as a potential source of consolation, as if some kind of Platonic message might arrive that will put everything right, and for good. Which of course it never does.

He scrolls through the stream of new mail. Even though early August is by far the quietest time of the year, there are still about forty new messages since Monday morning. Esme, a second-year undergraduate, is asking for more reading for her dissertation on Thomas Wyatt, Henry Howard, and the circulation of poetry in manuscript. A new office has become available on staircase fourteen and fellows are invited to apply. *The Journal of Tudor Court Studies* is seeking a book reviews editor. Next term's Visiting Scholars at the University Library are listed: Lawrence knows three of the nine, all from America – in fact he'd written a reference for two of them – and makes a mental note to drop them a line before they arrive. The college kitchen is closed until 10 September. A long message from the head of Diversity and Inclusivity: 'Action required: updated Bystander Training Online Course'. Lawrence deletes all of these messages apart from Esme's.

But at the top of the inbox, sent this morning at 5.28 a.m., is an email from Phoebe, as there had been a text from her at 6.11 a.m., and two missed calls at 6.51 and 6.54. She needs to see Lawrence in town today at 10.30 a.m. at a café near Great St Mary's. The café is less than ten minutes' walk from the Hotel Metropole, where Angela said she was staying last night. Lawrence thinks for a second of Angela, and the world away from everything she offers him. He thinks of his repeated insistence to the others that they should stay within the Hawton estate for the duration of the week, and of the proximity of the city beyond its walls.

Lawrence realises he has no option and he says 'Fuck' out loud. When Lucy enters the kitchen Lawrence can't tell if she heard him or not, and Lawrence, hating any public display of unease or indeed of anything that falls short of social mastery, and doubly so in the presence of his former student, feels immediately off-kilter. His response to feeling rattled is to assert immediately and unequivocally the opposite: to declare things good, calm, great, super.

'What a beautiful morning, Lucy.'

Lucy sits down at the table as though she hasn't heard him, taking a mug and pouring coffee from the cafetière.

Lawrence says, 'Don't you think?'

Lucy takes a sip. 'Can I ask you something strange?'

He feels unease at her tone.

She continues, 'I saw something I don't understand.'

Lawrence feels panic begin to spread through his stomach and quickly up to his neck, a creeping sensation just under his skin, and he thinks – suddenly, and with conviction – she knows. She knows about Phoebe. The plagiarism. She saw. She heard. She may even have discussed it with the others. This is the very worst possible catastrophe.

'Of course,' he says, smiling and sitting back.

'Yesterday I . . .'

Lawrence feels his pulse pounding in his neck. Lucy pauses and looks towards the courtyard. He says, 'Go on.'

'After the book game.'

After the book game, Lawrence thinks. Then this isn't . . . He swallows and says, 'Yes?'

'You're going to think me insane. Everyone had gone to bed, and I was feeling like I'd had too much to drink.'

'I think we all felt like we'd had too much to drink,' says Lawrence, smiling, relief flushing through him, suddenly feeling warm pleasure for this conversation now that it isn't the crash he was expecting.

'I went to have a look at the church. It was beautiful. Pitch-black. Incredibly quiet. And then I saw something, by the statue.'

Lawrence is listening closely now, interested, not concerned for himself but unclear where this is going.

'It was a person, Lawrence, a woman. Sitting by the statue, smoking a cigarette. I saw her face as she turned towards me.'

'You mean one of the women here? Claudia, or Deborah, or Inês?'

'Definitely not. I thought – I thought it was someone else. Someone I used to know.'

'I don't understand what you're saying, Lucy.'

Lucy takes another mouthful of coffee, swallows, focuses on the handle of the mug.

'Lawrence, it was someone who couldn't possibly be here. But I am almost certain it was her.'

'How do you mean?'

Lucy pauses and looks out of the window, then back at Lawrence.

'I've never seen a ghost before.'

Lawrence smiles and is about to laugh but holds it, trying to read Lucy's response. 'Oh, come on, Lucy, isn't that pushing it a bit? A ghost smoking a cigarette in the churchyard?' He paces his next sentences to ensure the tone isn't dismissive or mocking, although that, in essence, is what they are. 'You were drunk. It was pitch-black. We'd been playing games. The moon reflected off the church windows. Or something like that.'

'There wasn't a moon.'

'You're . . .' Lawrence thinks how to put this carefully. 'You're going through a lot right now.'

'I'm not delusional, Lawrence.'

'Of course. But there are no such things as ghosts.'

'Then what did I see?'

He looks at Lucy and says, 'Things are as they seem, Lucy. There are no strange events going on beneath.'

She looks up at him as he says this. There is something wrong, something excessive and out of place and discordant, about that statement. She looks directly into his eyes. Lucy knows Lawrence's habits of speech so well after hundreds of hours of conversations. There is something off in what he just said: an assertive desire to make something true that isn't.

Lawrence – who, after all those supervisions and talks on walks in the botanical gardens, knows Lucy's acuity so well, knows the way Lucy's intelligence moves instinctively to separate off something aberrant from what should be the case – sees Lucy's insight flash across her eyes.

Claudia is reading in the lower living room when the landline rings. In all probability, she thinks, the call is for Lawrence, and if she leaves it, he will emerge from wherever he's working and take it. After three more rings, Claudia remembers that Lawrence is most likely out of earshot in the folly, and gets up resignedly to answer. It is Lawrence's sister Helena, with a complex update regarding their parents' 55th wedding anniversary to which Claudia half-listens, eventually suggesting she fetch Lawrence so that he and Helena can discuss the various decisions in person.

'Okay, I'll go and get him. It might take a minute, he's in the garden.' Claudia rests the phone on the hall table and crosses through the kitchen into the garden, making her way towards the pond.

As Claudia approaches the folly she sees that the figure at the desk is not Lawrence, but Inês. Inês is reading something intently on her laptop, her hair falling over her eyes, and she has not seen Claudia approach. As Claudia watches, Inês pulls her hair off her face and neck, arching her back and closing her eyes. It is a curiously intimate gesture and Claudia stands for a moment, not moving forward or backward, before turning and retracing her steps to the hallway. When she picks up the phone, Helena has rung off.

✳

'Anything else I can get for you?' The waitress picks up Josh's plate and adds it to the stack she has left at the next table. 'Another coffee?'

'No thanks, I'm fine.' Josh watches the young woman's retreating back, then calls after her, 'Just the bill, please!' The waitress gives no sign of having heard and for a moment Josh contemplates standing up and leaving, jogging back across Parker's Piece and out of sight. No one would stop him. Instead, he angles his chair towards the large square of grass, moving it a little more into the shade. At this time of the morning there is a steady stream of traffic tracing a line across the field from each corner, cyclists and parents with buggies and couples walking and a small tourist group gathered around a woman holding an umbrella aloft and pointing in the direction of the police station. Josh enjoys how their movement and activity enhances his sense of relaxation and stillness. It is a pleasure, too, to be somewhere anonymous, without the effort of constantly having to undertake complex social interactions within the enclosed space of one house and garden. Josh has found the week so far at Hawton exhausting: a continual, finely calibrated performance that may at any point spool off into disaster. The relief that he feels at leaving the retreat – the word could not be less apt – easily compensates for his anxiety at having broken the rules and left Hawton.

A moment later the waitress puts the folded bill down on the table. She smiles at him in a way he's used to, tilting her head, but he's not on this occasion interested. She can't be more than twenty-five; perceiving his dismissal, she takes the empty cup and glass briskly away. Josh stands up to fish his phone from his shorts pocket and as he does so the sun catches a glass door to his left, about forty yards away, as it's pushed open. Josh's eye is drawn by the momentarily dazzling light and he turns towards it, shading his eyes. The door gives onto a set of stone steps leading down to the pathway beside the grass; it is a side entrance, Josh realises, to the large hotel – the Metropole – that sprawls across that side of the green. It rests open for a moment and then a man steps out of the building and Josh realises – it takes him a second or two – that it is Lawrence. Definitely. His face is angled downwards, looking at his phone, and there is something immediately covert about him; but it is unmistakably Lawrence, framed in the open doorway.

Josh feels a clutch of nausea and a powerful desire to run, not to sidle away from an unpaid bill but to sprint, to fly from the horror of being found by Lawrence consuming a full English breakfast at 10 a.m. in a Wetherspoons – a *Wetherspoons*! – in the middle of the city when he shouldn't be in Cambridge at all. But almost at once, the fear subsides. Lawrence hasn't seen him; is probably too far away for discovery to be possible. Nonetheless Josh pushes his chair a little further into the shade as he resumes his seat and waits for the waitress to return. Lawrence is still standing at the open door, phone in hand, and now he is turning to talk to someone behind him, out of Josh's view. Josh watches Lawrence's back for a moment and is about to get up again in search of the card machine when he sees a woman's hand curl around the back of Lawrence's neck and then, as Lawrence takes a step backwards, the woman herself, moving through the doorway as she pulls Lawrence's head towards her and kisses him hard on the mouth. Lawrence turns as they kiss so that Josh can see the length of the woman's back as Lawrence slides a hand under the waistband of her denim skirt. Josh sits for a moment. He is appalled, then thrilled, then captivated. He senses, instinctively, before it is legible to him as a rational thought, that this is knowledge that can be put to use.

'Earl Grey for one. Anything else?' The barista slides a cup and saucer on the tray.

'Just the tea, please.' Lawrence pays, then carries the tray to the cluster of tables which are arranged outside the café. In the hot weather, the outside tables are in high demand, and Lawrence scans the street before finding a vacant table for two. He settles his tray and looks around. He would be less visible inside, but the café itself is almost empty, so that two people sitting in the window would be more conspicuous than anyone lost in the crowd outdoors. He sits down with his back to the road and pulls his cap further down over his face.

Lawrence sees Phoebe approaching before she sees him, walking briskly along the pavement from the direction of King's Parade, a stack of books in her arms. She adjusts one of her earbuds and crosses the road, glancing behind her and then ahead. With this gesture he sees her notice him and raise a hand in greeting. Lawrence looks quickly down. As she reaches the table, he begins to stand up, the metal feet of his chair grating against the paving stone ground.

'Hi.' Phoebe unloads the books onto the table and hangs her bag over the back of a chair.

'Hi, Phoebe. Can I get you anything?' Lawrence offers, hovering over his own chair.

'It's cool, I'll get it.' Phoebe turns and heads into the café, where Lawrence can hear her being vociferously greeted by the barista, followed by laughter and conversation he can't quite catch. He sits back down. He's older than everyone here by at least twenty years. Probably twenty-five. Phoebe's pile of books is like a series of bricks forming a tower, getting progressively smaller: *The Riverside Chaucer*; *The Penguin Book of Renaissance Verse*; *An Anthology of Elizabethan Prose Fiction*; and finally, on top, a slim edition of *The Poems of Henry Howard, Earl of Surrey*. Phoebe seems a different person from the furious girl who confronted him only yesterday, and this is unsettling. He had steeled himself to be met with anger, or distress, but this Phoebe moves with energy, is smiling and laughing in the café, looks happy. She is feeling better, Lawrence tells himself, and that should be a good sign. Maybe the whole thing is already forgotten?

Phoebe sits down opposite Lawrence and puts a large glass of iced coffee on the table. Most of the table is taken up with Lawrence's tray holding a jug of milk and an egg-timer as well as the pot of tea, cup and saucer.

'Your timer's run out,' she says, and Lawrence hears: Your time has run out.

'I'm sorry?' he says.

'Your timer,' Phoebe repeats, gesturing at the tray. 'The sand has all gone through.' Realising Lawrence's confusion, and enjoying her contrasting quickness, she says, 'It's not a metaphor. Your tea is ready.'

'Right. Sorry.' Lawrence reaches for the pot, pours tea, adds milk. He tries to drink it but it is scalding hot and he quickly replaces the cup in the saucer. 'So. You wanted to see me. To talk.'

'I've had some time to think about your offer.'

'My offer,' Lawrence repeats. The word sounds more contractual than he would like. He thinks for a moment – what did he say in the heat of yesterday's exchange? – and then remembers the book. He is struck by the realisation that Phoebe has been thinking about what he said yesterday continually, while he hasn't given it a second's thought once the moment had passed.

'Yes,' Phoebe says again, 'and I want us to be clear about it before I accept.' She leans forward and takes a long sip of coffee through the straw.

'Of course. Go on.'

'You offered me co-authorship on the monograph.'

'Yes.'

'Fifty–fifty.'

'I mean, I can't promise fifty–fifty. I have the press to answer to; I can't just change the whole thing without their say-so.'

'I would have thought that's exactly what you could do.'

'I can also help with your book, obviously. The book of your thesis. I can be quite influential in helping you place it with CUP.'

'Wouldn't you have done that for me anyway?' Phoebe sits back in her chair and Lawrence can't read her expression.

'Yes, of course I would. But I'd be prepared to . . . to really exert an influence.'

'OK. So: I want my name attached to your monograph. It can be Lawrence Ayres *with* Phoebe Armstrong, I don't mind, and then I want you to "exert an influence", whatever that means exactly, as hard as you possibly can with CUP for my book, when the time comes.'

'All right.' Lawrence picks up a sachet of sugar from the bowl and rolls it between his fingers. 'You want me to do both of those things. And in return?'

'Just a minute,' Phoebe says, 'I haven't finished. I also want you to put in a good word for me for the Pembroke Junior Fellowship. More than a good word. I want you to make it clear to Professor Smith that you want me to get it.'

'I don't have any influence over that, Phoebe. It's nothing to do with me or the faculty.'

'Come on, Lawrence. She likes you. It will make a difference. I want to stay in the UK and I need a job lined up for next year or my visa is toast.'

Lawrence is silent for a moment, then he says, 'Look, Phoebe, I can't work miracles for you. I need time to think.'

'All right, you can have time to think. It's Thursday. I'm flying the day after tomorrow. I need to know by Monday. I need an answer then. I have to be able to see a way forward. We work on your Hoccleve book together, while I finish writing up, and I get credit, and then you get me this JRF, and then you help me get my book ready for CUP and you help me get it published. That's the deal. That's your offer.'

Lawrence shifts in his seat. He has a sudden image of Angela, just that morning, astride him in a hotel bed he'd occupied for less than an hour and which had cost him £218; he'd spent the night that money had paid for in his own home sleeping next to Claudia. He is struck by the injustice of his situation: surrounded by these women with demands and expectations and a total lack of care for him.

'And what if it's not my offer? If I can't offer you that?'

'Then I will have to go to the faculty about it. I have to, Lawrence, because if I don't, what's going to happen if examiners read my thesis and they've also read your article, which they will have done? What will they think? It will derail my whole viva. I'll probably fail. And there'll be an investigation then anyway. If you do what I'm asking, I can rewrite the first chapter so they won't know, no one will be able to tell. I mean, you can help me do that. And I think this whole thing works pretty well for you. I can work on the new book, Lawrence, I'll earn my name on the cover, I don't want it for free. I've got lots of good ideas. As you know.'

Lawrence takes another sip of his tea and looks away from Phoebe. He watches a man cross the end of the street at a fast pace, his long black gown streaming behind him, one hand holding his square cap on his head. He thinks of his monograph, stalled, and of Phoebe's quickness, her energy, her capacity for work. This could be a solution.

'I can't – I can't make any decisions now. I'm not even supposed to be here now.' He rubs his brow with his index finger. 'I need time to think,' he says again, and Phoebe nods.

'Like I said, you have till Monday. I think we can work this out. I like having you as my supervisor, Lawrence. I don't want to have to talk to anyone about this.'

Lawrence sits back in his chair.

He says, 'We'd have to have some rules. You can't come to the house again like that. Obviously, we can put nothing about this in writing but I'd need your guarantee this goes no further, not a single soul, otherwise—'

'Don't threaten me. You're not the one in control here.'

Phoebe drains the last of her coffee and stands up to go.

'Phoebe, wait a minute. Look, I will give you a definite answer by Monday, I promise. But in the meantime – and afterwards – it is extremely important that what's happened stays between us. Our secret.' Lawrence regrets the word as he says it.

'That depends on you, doesn't it?' Phoebe picks up her bag and the pile of books. *The Poems of Henry Howard* slides as she lifts them and falls on the ground at Lawrence's feet.

'You can keep that one,' Phoebe says, smiling at her supervisor. 'See how you get on with it.'

Chapter Eleven

Thursday afternoon

Lawrence arrives in the kitchen as Claudia is loading up a tray to carry down to the pool.

'Oh, there you are! I was wondering where you'd got to.'

'I completely lost track of time,' Lawrence says. 'I'm sorry not to have been here to help.' He leans down and kisses her, holding the back of her head with his hand. 'You look beautiful.'

'Thank you. I think I'm melting in the heat. And it doesn't matter, there was nothing to do, really.'

'Here, let me carry that. Can you get the door?' He lifts the tray from the worktop as Claudia opens the back door, then follows him into the garden.

'Tasked with the job of cleaning the pool, our two young heroes fall at the first hurdle.' Miles says this in a kind of Pathé News voice as he walks slowly along the edge of the swimming pool, hands in the pockets of his blue linen shorts.

On the other side of the pool, Ash is lying flat on the ground, stretching out one long metal pole with a brush on the end which he is using to reach and lift up another long pole with a net that he had a minute before let slip into the water. That pole is now lying at the bottom of the pool.

Ash says, 'Got it . . . nearly . . . shit.' The pole with the net falls back to the bottom.

'The water seems to me entirely immaculate.' Miles peers into the deep end. 'I don't really know what Lawrence is talking about.'

'He used the word "skimming" a lot, didn't he, at lunch?'

'Classic Lawrentian discourse. He likes that kind of technical precision. I'm surprised he didn't talk about Ph levels. A mastery that he can calmly explain. It's like the printing. The "furniture" – all that chatter. It's actually why Lawrence is a good teacher. He loves being the one who knows, and also the one who conveys. Teaching is the perfect dynamic for Lawrence. His students are lucky to have him. I mean that.'

There is a pause while Ash precariously raises the pole with the net from the bottom. 'I think egoism and generosity are pretty much the same thing,' says Ash. 'For Lawrence. And maybe always.' He grasps the pole.

'Magnificent. Well done. Here, you "*skim*", as we must call it, and I'll do the filters.' Miles lifts the square white cover by the edge of the pool and pulls out a plastic basket that is full of leaves.

Ash starts near the steps and drags the pole and net round the perimeter of the pool, tracing an invisible path. Every so often he raises the net to see how much he has collected. It's almost nothing each time.

'I want to know about the book,' says Miles. 'How's it going?'

'Oh, I don't know. I never know the answer to that question. Sometimes I think the book is just a fiction I need to justify simply reading and thinking. I definitely prefer reading and thinking. I'm deep in Eaves's world right now. Eighteenth-century typography. The invention of British typography as a tradition, in fact. William Wise in 1720, then Eaves. Before those two there wasn't anyone making type with any kind of skill and printers just used Dutch founts.' Ash slightly changes the sound of his voice to indicate quotation. '"Having been an early admirer of the beauty of Letters, I became insensibly desirous of contributing to the perfection of them."'

'Is that Eaves?'

'In the preface to his wonderful edition of *Paradise Lost*. 1758. Printed in York. The paper is polished so smooth it seems to shine, even today, three hundred years later. It's the only time he talks in one of his books about his intentions. He gives a kind of autobiography through letter-making. And you know he didn't start working properly as a printer until he was fifty. I should tell Lawrence that, in fact.'

'Are his books amazing?' Miles pulls the last of the leaves from the filter and flicks them into the flowerbed.

'Macaulay said that they went forth "to astonish all the librarians of Europe".'

'Perhaps your book will do the same.'

'I had an annual royalty cheque for my 2010 edited collection on regional printing earlier this year.'

'Tell me.'

'£4.23.'

'Oh God, don't mention that to Deborah.'

'Actually, I don't mind. You know about academic print runs. It's a different model of readership.'

'I'll say.' Miles runs the filter under the tap by the shed and then returns it to its compartment by the pool.

'My Eaves book will sell for £65. It will get three reviews in academic journals. Two hundred university libraries will buy it in the UK and the States, five individuals will buy it, of whom you and Lawrence will be two, and Eaves's eccentric and slightly creepy 85-year-old distant descendant who keeps inviting me to visit him in Winchester will be a third. It's never going to be on the three-for-two table at Waterstone's.'

'Don't you want readers?'

'I'll have readers.'

'You've listed three. One of whom by your own description seems to be mad.'

'He's not mad. Just . . . eager. I'll have readers through time. That's the difference between our book worlds, Miles. You have an explosion: a launch, reviews, radio, TV. I'll have a little flurry when it's published. Maybe the book will be set on some graduate courses. Libraries will gradually acquire it. But then it will persist. And I love that idea. I cling to it. The consolation of a book that quietly endures, read by people far into the future. Maybe thirty new readers a year. But in a hundred years, that's a lot of readers.'

'But you'll be dead.'

Ash shrugs his shoulders. 'Doesn't matter.'

'Surely it does a bit.'

'I don't think so. *Ars longa, vita brevis.*'

'Too bloody *brevis* for my liking.'

Ash leans the pole and net against the wooden shed. 'Well, I'm playing a longer game.' He pauses. 'That said, I'm thinking about trying something different at some point. Fiction.'

'A novel?'

'Possibly a novel.'

'About typography?'

'No. Even I have to admit that's not a runner. It would be political.'

'As in . . .?

Ash walks round the edge of the pool, looking at the water.

'Don't you think it's remarkable how little has changed?'

Ash waits and when he says nothing, Miles says, 'Go on.'

'I mean with all the talk about diversity, inclusivity. All of that. The sheer volume of all that banging on about changing the demographics of businesses, universities, publishing, the film industry – opening everything up. But nothing at all has changed. It's still the same people ruling the same world.'

'Is that really right?'

'Yes, it is. I've come to the conclusion that the actual *point* of conversations about widening access schemes and non-white voices and women on boards and all of that . . . the *actual point* of all that is to keep mediocre upper middle class white men in power. It's the literal opposite of what it seems. And it's worse than no one talking about it because it gives total cover to people like . . .'

'Like . . .?'

Ash smiles. 'It's not about individuals. It's about a system.'

'If you're going to write a novel then it is about individuals.'

Ash pauses in his walk round the edge of the pool. He says,

'Yes,' and then resumes. 'But I'm not sure anyone would want to read it.'

'You must care about readers for the journalism. That's not the long game.'

'I don't pay much attention to that,' says Ash. 'It's not like I go looking for it. They ask me to write something, usually at short notice on a specific issue. There's a ready-made readership for that, obviously. And then sometimes I get to do something with a bit more meat to it. I'm drafting a piece at the moment on abuses of power in higher education – I've been working on it for months now, on and off – and that won't be out till the autumn. I'm gathering new examples all the time.'

'But don't you get a bit – well, a bit tired of it?'

'Tired in what sense?'

'Being, I don't know, a face for hire, all those opinion pieces, and the rubbish on Twitter afterwards. All that noise.'

'A face for hire? A brown face for hire, you mean?'

'No, that's not what I mean,' says Miles evenly. 'Just always having to stoke the flames, have an opinion.'

'I *do* have an opinion on the issues I write on,' Ash replies. 'It's not noise – it's public debate, Miles. It matters.'

'Yes, of course it does.' The two men are leaning now against the wooden picnic table: the surface is covered in a silver-green lichen that suggests it has stood at this point for years. The midday sun flashes bright on the immaculate smoothness of the pool: almost too bright to look at.

There is a pause, and then Miles says, 'I don't mean to be a dick.'

'You're not.'

'One of those still holding the reins, despite the chatter.'

'I was thinking yesterday at lunch when your whole Netflix triumph came up, about those miserable years when you failed to write anything. What was that awful article you spent three years on?'

'Oh, Christ, how could I forget. "Edward Poynings (1459– 1521) and the Warden of the Cinque Ports: New Evidence from Sandwich Record Office."'

'"New evidence"!'

'Yes, it has a pleasing hold-the-front-page quality, doesn't it? Edward Fucking Poynings. Literally, who gives a shit? I'd rather have thumbscrews fitted, permanently, than go back to that world. I never did finish it. What was I doing, Ash? I was at the bottom of a well and couldn't get myself out.'

'Well, you are out now. Out, and flourishing.' Ash stands up, stretching. 'I've been trying to work out if I'm jealous or not of your TV triumph. The odd thing is I don't think I am. If it had happened to Lawrence, I know I'd find it intolerable.'

'Because you doubt his ways.'

Ash looks at Miles and doesn't say anything but slowly nods.

Ash gets to the end of the chapter and closes his book. He checks the time on his laptop; he has been working intently for nearly three hours and has a satisfying file of notes to show for it. The prolonged concentration has left him feeling foggy, as though he is at the limits of his capacity for organised thought and would struggle to remember basic facts about current affairs, or the weather. Not the weather, actually; the unfailing heat has made the sunshine and cloudless skies an ever-present fact, lodged in his consciousness like the continual hum of a background noise.

Ten minutes later, Ash is climbing the footpath which runs alongside Hawton churchyard. The best way to shake off the fog, in his experience, is to change his physical circumstances – exercise, a shower, or loud music all work – so he's wearing his swimming shorts and carrying a rolled-up towel, planning to walk around the churchyard, and come back to the house via the pool in time for 6 p.m. drinks. This will also give him the chance to see the memorial to the drowned children, with which Lucy seems to have become preoccupied.

Ash lets himself into the churchyard through the gate at the top of the lane and looks down across the gently sloping grass and the stones jutting out at various angles. He can't see anything that looks like the statue Lucy has described. Turning to his left, he follows the stone wall which curves downwards towards the driveway of what must once have been the vicarage, stopping halfway to lean against the wall and take in the view before him: the church ahead and road beyond, and to the right the path he took a moment ago. To his left the grass is shaded by trees and beyond them the ground becomes rougher and untended; there, Ash now sees, is the statue on its plinth, surrounded by high railings which look from this vantage as though they are sinking into the ground under the weight of brambles and ivy. Ash is staring fixedly at these railings when a movement catches his eye just beyond them, where the ground levels out before the vicarage wall and the brambles rise into bushes.

A woman is standing with her back to him, one arm raised, as though mimicking the elder girl in the statue. As she lowers her hand, Ash realises that it is Claudia, her hair tied up in a patterned scarf, reaching into the bramble bushes for blackberries. He is wondering whether to retrace his steps without speaking to her when Claudia turns and looks towards him.

'Ash! Hello!' As Claudia waves, Ash pushes himself off the wall and walks to meet her. The ground is hard and dusty beneath his feet, but the grass is greener at the edge of the churchyard, where the shade deepens.

'Have you been for a walk?' Claudia asks as he approaches.

'Not really. I finished work and thought I'd wander over here then go for a swim. I'm too hot to think any more.'

'Me too. A swim sounds like a great idea. I thought I'd make a blackberry fool and these are the best ones for miles. I think they must be fed by an underground spring or something. Here, try one.' She selects a berry from the Tupperware box she is carrying and holds it out to him.

Ash takes the blackberry, blows the dust off it and puts it in his mouth. It is sharp and juicy and unusually sweet.

'That's very good.'

'Isn't it? They have to be really good ones to make a fool or it just tastes of cream and sugar. I need a few more, though.'

Claudia puts the box on the ground, turns back to the bush and pulls down a cluster of the fruit, quickly stripping them away. Ash moves to join her, reaching above her to a knot of berries which he removes from the brambles and places in the Tupperware.

'I used to come here with Tristan when he was younger,' Claudia bends down and then straightens up, returning to her task, 'but he ate more than he picked, mostly.' There is a pause. 'Did you come to look at the memorial?'

'Sort of,' says Ash. 'Lucy seems rather upset by it.'

'It's a very sad story. And the children close to her own in age. It must resonate with her. Especially when she's away from them.'

'I guess so.' Ash transfers another handful of berries to the container. There is another pause while they work side by side.

'I was sorry to hear about Kate,' Claudia says, moving a little away from him to her left. 'Lawrence mentioned you broke up.'

'She called off the wedding. Although it was a long time ago. Two years. More than that.'

'I'm sorry,' Claudia repeats.

'It was the right thing to happen,' Ash says and reaches upwards again. 'I had rather . . . messed everything up. Just bad timing, with lockdown, still in the flat together. We were locked in a break-up that couldn't stop happening. But people went through much worse.'

'Yes, but that doesn't make it any easier.' Claudia looks down at the Tupperware. 'I think we've got enough. Shall we head back? Or did you want to look again at the statue?'

'Not particularly,' says Ash. 'Not now.' He checks his watch. 'I might need to hurry if I'm going to get a swim in before six.'

'Ah, Lawrence will survive if we are late. It might do him good,' says Claudia, as Ash picks up his discarded towel and they start along the path towards the road, and something in her tone makes Ash look at her directly. She glances towards him and smiles. 'We can't follow the rules all the time, can we?'

Ash smiles back and holds the gate open for Claudia before closing it behind them.

'Lawrence is masterminding all of this, but you are doing most of the work.'

'Possibly. It's not that much work really. Everyone is chipping in with meals.'

'What do you get out of it, though? To have Lawrence fill the house with his friends for a week?'

'Come on, I knew you before I knew Lawrence. You're my friends, too,' Claudia says, and as Ash starts to protest she continues, 'it's all right, I know what you mean. I like it when the house is busy. I like the contrast between having time to work and be by myself and also to be sociable. Last year Tristan was away for a week and it was such an empty time. We were looking forward to having the week free but when it came we just sort of sat around, a bit lost. Time slowed to almost nothing. Nothing in the house moved. Lawrence got the idea that when Tristan was away this year, we would hold a retreat instead. He kept on saying the word: "the retreat". He got obsessed with the planning. Timetables and all the things everyone might do. It matters to him, doing this sort of thing; and it keeps him occupied. He's impossible without a project. You should see him on holiday: he doesn't know how to be at all.'

'You make him sound like a child.' They have nearly reached the manor; Claudia is holding the container of fruit in front, and Ash reaches past her to push the gate.

Because of the gate opening, there is a little pause in the conversation and in the gap, Ash is conscious that his last comment could be taken either as affectionate and trivial, or as damning.

'Ha! Maybe. You know Lawrence,' Claudia says, her tone indicating she has taken, mostly but not entirely, the former connotation. They are crossing the courtyard now. 'He's always got a scheme on the go.' There is something in Claudia's tone – in the way 'project' has become 'scheme' – which snags on the easiness of the conversation, but Claudia glances away when Ash offers his gaze. 'He likes to be occupied,' says Claudia. 'But then so do I.' She turns towards Ash and gestures to the archway which leads directly to the garden behind the house. 'You should get straight in the pool. I'm going to pop these in the fridge and grab a towel and then I'll be right there.'

'Okay. See you in a minute.' Ash watches as Claudia opens the back door, the taste of blackberry on his tongue.

'What did people drink in the fifteenth century?' Deborah is trying a first sip from the heavy glass. 'Was it barrels of mead all the time?'

Lucy is inspecting hers through the glass. 'Lots of ale. Ale was safer than drinking water. Everyone drank it. You had it at breakfast.' She takes a sip.

'Sounds like my sister in the nineties before she got cleaned up. I've always imagined Georgian England as essentially drunk for a hundred years. A century of gin. The whole country one vast lolling Hogarth print. Maybe medieval England was the same.'

Lucy shook her head. 'The ale was very weak. Unlike this.'

Deborah says, '*The Tipsy Middle Ages.* You should write that.'

'More Miles than me.' Lucy takes a second sip. '*Fuck.*' And then: 'Sorry. I shouldn't say that about Miles. I don't mean to be disrespectful.'

'You can let your guard down, you know.'

Deborah looks at the high trees at the edge of the estate: poplars, so high that even the gentlest wind makes them sway. 'Sugar, bourbon, Angostura bitters, a dash of water and burnt orange peel. I don't know why they call it an Old Fashioned.'

'You actually burnt orange peel?'

'Over the hob. I was hoping Lawrence would walk in and feel trumped by my mastery. But he didn't.'

'I've sort of got out of the drinking habit but I'm making up for it this week.'

'I don't know how you can not drink in a crumbling marriage. Christ, I was completely wild after Ben and I split. I was out every night for at least six months. Drink. And men. What's that in Latin?'

'*Vinum et viri!*'

'There we go. Put that in embossed lettering on my grave. It was definitely quantity over quality but it was a lot of fun. Pile them high. Almost literally on one occasion. I did calm down, though. And of course my boys were a bit older than your two. I couldn't have kept that pace up forever.' She shifts her position on the bench so that she is a little more out of the sun and rubs a mosquito bite on her thigh. 'Bloody mozzies. And how about you? Are you seeing anyone since Neil?'

'Oh no, no,' says Lucy, and then feels she has been a little too vehement. 'I mean, I just don't have the time for all that, or the energy. To be honest it takes everything I've got just to look after the kids and manage work. I'm in bed by nine most nights – I *am*,' she insists, in response to Deborah's snort, 'and, anyway, where am I going to meet someone new? At work? All the half-decent men are married by now.'

'Did you and Josh never . . .' Deborah lets the sentence drift away.

'Josh?' Lucy thinks for a moment. 'No, that was never on the cards.'

'Because you were rivals?'

'We weren't rivals. Or at least we didn't have to be. I think Josh still feels it, though. I never did.'

'That's because you were always winning.'

Lucy feels the edge in Deborah's comment.

'Josh had flocks of younger women after him.'

'He's a very attractive man.' Deborah takes a sip. 'I would.'

Lucy looks quizzically across at Deborah who shrugs her shoulders as if to say, *why not*, or, *why are you surprised*, or even, *Jesus, Lucy, you're so boxed in*. Deborah is drawn to Lucy, was immediately, on meeting her at the launch of one of Lawrence's books, five years ago, loved right away her quick and unusual intelligence. And she feels the pain of Lucy inching through divorce. But she feels just as strongly irritated by Lucy's sense that – what? Not quite that this has never happened to anyone else, because she is sure Lucy doesn't think that. But that this is the first real adversity Lucy has faced. She's using it as a trump card for just checking out.

'I'm forty-two, Deborah. I don't want to get back out there and do what, online dating – can you imagine?'

'Get a grip, Lucy. You're talking like you're eighty-five. It's not as bad as all that.'

If Deborah had been a man, Lucy would have felt a spike of anger at the apparent complacency of that comment, that easy trivialising of what she's going through. But it's different coming from Deborah.

Lucy feels pushed into a kind of candour by Deborah's impatience.

'You do online dating?'

'From time to time. I've got a fleet of apps. Subscriptions I should keep better track of. It's quite convenient in some ways. You have to spend a fair bit of time sorting through the dross but it's worth it, by and large, especially if you're not looking for a relationship. It's transactional, and if you take it like that, it works.'

'You make it sound easy.'

'Well, like most things in life, it's easy if you want it to be. You just have to live without apology.' Deborah takes a sip of her drink. 'With lightness. I'd go and make another of these, particularly if I thought Lawrence would see me, but I shouldn't get totally hammered this early.'

'Lightness,' says Lucy, thinking about the word. 'I don't think I've ever had much of that.'

'It's not incompatible with being clever. If that's what you mean.'

Lucy can't quite read the tone of Deborah's last comment. Is she being supportive, or accusing her of vanity? She makes a mental note to return to the exchange, later on, to think it through. For now, she carries on. 'The other day, I was in a bakery talking to the guy who runs it. By any standard he's . . .' Lucy suddenly feels an odd coyness.

'Insanely hot?'

'I suppose so, yes.'

'My God, you're blushing, Lucy.'

'Well. We were chatting and there was a definite spark and then afterwards I realised, he must be in his *twenties*.

Obviously, he was just humouring me, being nice. I do realise men still fancy me and some of them even proposition me but, honestly, how long is that going to last?'

'Oh, for fuck's sake.'

'It's true.'

'You once told me at a book launch that your work is all about criticising misogyny.'

Lucy is stung by the comment: flung back. She re-gathers her thoughts. 'All I mean is that at some point I'm going to become unfuckable and in ten years I'll be menopausal and then it will all be over anyway.'

Deborah puts down her drink on one of the low wooden drinks tables that Lawrence had placed next to each deckchair. She says, 'You know I . . .' but then stops. She was about to talk about breast cancer, about being in your fifties and having a doctor talk to you about percentages, and sitting in the car park and having a crashing realisation that all we are are bodies, flesh that occupies space for a time – and that yes, enduring one bad husband is grim, but it's also everywhere so stop . . .

'It sounds ridiculous,' says Deborah. '"Unfuckable", for goodness' sake. I'm fifty-six, for what it's worth. I am coming out of the other side of what you're facing and believe me, as far as I'm concerned, the good times are just getting going. I can't tell you the *relief* of being freed from all that bullshit. Okay, the menopause is no walk in the park, you may have to go through pain and indignity, but it is absolutely worth it for the freedom from all of the reproductive hassle, marketing yourself for other people, and at the end of it you're still *you*, and you think about where you want to put all your energy. By the time you're where I am, your kids will be grown up and all of that effort, all of that love, can go into yourself. I spent *years* ploughing all my energy into my kids, Ben, the agency when they wouldn't even make me a partner, looking after my parents – without stopping to ask what I wanted or needed for myself. I see Claudia doing the same thing. Although, thank God, she's finally starting to turn round and realise that she needs her own fucking life! God, I was raging at everyone.' Deborah finishes her drink and looks at Lucy. 'Look, I don't mean to be patronising, but stop . . . stop staring into space all the time. Nothing is done and dusted at forty-two. And you know what my mother always used to say about ageing? It's better than the alternative. Lucy, you are alive, you have to go out there and live for yourself. Everything else will take care of itself. I don't know if your baker is metaphorical or literal, but either way, go and fuck him. Or don't. Just . . .'

Deborah waves her hand as if the gesture concludes her sentence. She picks up the two empty glasses. 'There endeth the sermon.' She stands up. 'God, I do feel a bit pissed actually.'

Chapter Twelve

Thursday evening

With each door that he opens Josh feels increasingly panicked. He has hunted through the kitchen twice already. There are cupboards filled with china and glasses, deep drawers with stacked cast-iron casserole dishes and every sort of kitchen paraphernalia and even one entirely devoted to what appear to be baskets for making bread. Nowhere can Josh find his target: powder to make gravy, nor indeed any sort of sauce or seasoning. He mutters, 'Why is there nothing normal in here that a fucking normal kitchen would have?' He is opening the cutlery drawer again when he hears footsteps behind him, and closes it rapidly.

'Hi, Josh!' Claudia enters through the back door, still wearing her swimming costume, a towel wrapped around the lower half of her body, carrying a selection of mugs gathered from the garden. 'I meant to ask earlier – do you have everything you need for cooking tonight?'

'Yes, absolutely,' Josh replies, 'although, now you come to mention it – perhaps seasoning? Only if you have it. I need to make a gravy. And mustard, maybe? I couldn't find either of those.' He gestures to the half-open cupboard doors which line the walls.

'Oh, we don't keep that sort of thing in a cupboard,' says Claudia, setting down the mugs and crossing the room briskly. 'Those are all in the pantry. Here: help yourself.' She opens a narrow door set into the far wall, which reveals a large walk-in cupboard with deep shelving. Claudia pulls the cord for the light and a fluorescent strip flickers on.

'Super,' says Josh, waiting for her to move away from the pantry door. 'That's great. Thanks so much.'

'No problem. Right, I'm going to go and find some clothes and then I'll be back down for drinks. And unless you have plans for pudding, I thought I might make a blackberry fool? Ash and I picked some earlier.'

'Super,' Josh says again, and Claudia smiles at him as she leaves the room.

Left alone, Josh cautiously enters the pantry. Its ceiling is much lower than the rest of the kitchen and this combined with the closeness of the stocked shelves makes Josh feel suddenly claustrophobic. He looks helplessly at the vast array of jars, tins and packets that press in on him from all sides. Heritage bread flour. Pomegranate molasses. Za'atar. A bottle of hot sauce labelled 'Homemade in New Orleans'. Mustard he locates quite quickly, and salt and pepper – but what are the chances that any of these objects is a tub of gravy granules? They can do without gravy, he thinks to himself, trying not to knock anything over as he backs out of the pantry, imagining with a growing satisfaction the look on Claudia's face were he to tell her what he'd seen Lawrence doing. Who he'd seen

Lawrence *with*. The pleasure he feels at this thought is like a rush of saliva to the mouth: a physical anticipation of an appetite soon to be satisfied.

'It's entirely typical of you two that you have what is basically a home cinema, but you put it in a shed.' Miles shifts his position on the old, sagging sofa, trying to get comfortable. 'The seating, however, is deplorable.'

'This is not a shed, Miles,' Claudia retorts in mock severity. 'It is my *studio*, and you can only stay if you play nicely.'

'"Please behave with decorum in my *atelier*",' says Miles, already quite drunk. 'Quite right.'

'No fucking around in the *studiolo*,' says Deborah, also on her third drink.

Claudia balances on the arm of the sofa, feeling it give a little under her weight, and takes a sip.

'Buffoonery aside, Miles, this is very nice. It tastes . . .'

'Like sin?' says Deborah.

Claudia smiles. 'Like Eden, after the apple.'

'It's the drink of knowledge. A negroni *sbagliato*,' Miles says, shifting to make room for Claudia. 'Champagne instead of gin. *Sbagliato* means bungled, or mistaken, or generally messed up.'

Claudia takes another sip. 'Perhaps I should get generally messed up.'

'Do it,' says Deborah.

Lawrence is standing on a wooden chair in the middle of the studio, adjusting a dial on the projector. He gets down and turns it back on at the wall switch.

'Ah, there we go,' he says as the machine comes to life. 'That should be fine now, Inês. If you just open whatever document on the laptop, it will connect.'

Inês is crouched in front of her MacBook on Claudia's desk. She stands and turns to the side wall of the studio, which runs parallel to the house beyond it. Onto the wall is projected a white rectangle of light, and in its centre a muddle of writing which is not quite clear enough to read.

'Hang on.' Lawrence replaces his chair under the projector and climbs back up. He rotates another dial and the text on the wall comes into focus.

'*Perfeito*. Thank you.' Inês turns to the group assembled on the other side of the room. There are Claudia, Miles and Deborah on the little sofa, and Lucy, Josh and Ash on wooden chairs brought in from the garden, each holding a glass and looking at Inês with an air of expectation. She laughs.

'I feel like a teacher now.' Inês comes to stand next to the sofa by Claudia, leaning back on the wall. 'Lawrence, will you read the poem? You will do it better than I will.'

'Certainly.' Lawrence, pleased to be asked, has just sat down next to Ash, but stands up again at once. 'It's just the first bit, not all eleven stanzas, is that right?'

'Yes,' Inês replies. 'The bit in bold. There's a limit to what one can fit in a window.'

Lawrence clears his throat, faces the projected image on the wall, and begins to read:

'My name engraved herein
Doth contribute my firmness to this glass,
Which ever since that charm hath been

As hard, as that which graved it was;
Thine eye will give it price enough, to mock
The diamonds of either rock.
'Tis much that glass should be
As all-confessing, and through-shine as I;
'Tis more that it shows thee to thee,
And clear reflects thee to thine eye.
But all such rules love's magic can undo;
Here you see me, and I am you.
As no one point, nor dash,
Which are but accessories to this name,
The showers and tempests can outwash
So shall all times find me the same;
You this entireness better may fulfill,
Who have the pattern with you still.'

'I can't believe you're going to engrave all of that,' Lucy says. 'It must take an age.'

'I'm afraid I've basically no idea what you just said,' said Deborah. 'Someone's name engraved?'

'It did take forever,' Inês says to Lucy. 'The engraving is already done, we just have to put the glass into the window now. Which is as hard as it sounds.'

'And reflections,' Miles interrupts, 'I got reflections.'

Josh says, 'I wrote about this poem in my long-ago dissertation. You remember, Lawrence?'

Lawrence doesn't answer: he's absorbed with rereading the words.

Josh feels a familiar surge of anger at Lawrence's indifference, at the sensation of waiting, disregarded, for Lawrence to respond, mixed with self-disgust at his craven need for recognition from his former supervisor. How many times has he stood by, like this, asking for Lawrence's approval while Lawrence looks the other way? Josh keeps his eyes on Lawrence, but Lawrence doesn't notice him.

'Here is my name engraved in glass.' Ash speaks in a calm voice as if it comes from elsewhere, his words slicing through the chatter. 'Cut by diamonds. But it's only valuable when you look at it. And then this is the good bit – the Donnean bit. The woman looks at the glass and sees her reflection, but also his name, layered on top. "Here you see me, and I am you." And the rain can fall and the storms blow, but "So shall all times find me the same."'

'You are clever, Ash,' says Deborah. 'I honestly didn't get any of that.'

'The promises of constancy are bollocks, of course,' adds Miles. 'He was a total shagger.'

'Donne?' asks Claudia.

'Tried to bury his youthful pornographic verse when he became Dean of St Paul's. It's very funny.'

'So why did you choose this poem, Inês?' says Claudia, captivated by it, and ignoring Miles.

'It's for a window. It's about glass. It's about someone being there, and not there. It's about love. We will place it next to the glass where Donne may or may not have carved his own name. All these things.'

'It's beautiful.' Lucy's voice is quiet.

'I hope it will be beautiful,' Inês says, 'and that it will last. The window itself is made from different pieces of glass. Some of them are coloured. One of the pieces is from a church near Sortelha. It's very old. Maybe as old as the poem.'

'I published an article on Donne,' Josh feels determined to finish his point, 'or rather on T. S. Eliot on Donne. He was obsessed with Donne's body imagery. The contrasts. The bracelet of hair round the bone, that sort of thing.'

Lawrence breaks in, talking across Josh's last words. 'It's an act of extraordinary *control*, really, this poem. An exercise is maintaining a hold.'

'Of control?' Deborah asks.

'Yes, absolutely. I mean, Donne is playing, of course, with the conventional image of the beloved object being possessed by the lover, an act of ownership through writing.'

Deborah snorts. 'Of course!'

'But really,' Lawrence carries on, probably not even hearing Deborah, 'that "I am you" deprives her of any selfhood at all. Don't you think?'

'I didn't read it like that,' says Lucy. 'But I can see your point.'

Miles can feel an idea half-emerging about what Lawrence just said – something about how describing a silent woman becomes a way of wanting a woman to be silent – but he can't bring it into focus.

'Ha! That's it exactly.' Lawrence is warming to his subject. 'The *firmness* of the point that he uses to penetrate the glass is an extension of himself as lover. After he marks the glass with his diamond it becomes his, do you see? The glass is his, and so is the woman – and he wants that to be permanent. It's really a desire for control, let us say, both of literary form and the figure of the woman in the poem. And that's the ethical problem of the poem. It's beautiful. But where is her voice? It's what I say to my undergrads. How can we listen for these other voices?'

There is silence as the group digests this analysis, but the effect is not of the light of explication, but of a bruising, of the listeners having been pushed back away from the object.

Miles is the first to speak. 'I taught "The Flea" once to a group of first-years and it was the single worst teaching experience of my life. It was so bad that by the end of the hour I had no idea what the poem was about. I had undone the poem – pun very much intended. I think in a real way I killed "The Flea".'

Deborah says, 'So who is the woman he's writing to?'

'Squashed it,' Miles laughs.

'Well,' Lawrence replies, 'there's probably no actual *woman* involved at all, Deborah.' The original event of Inês showing this poem has now been displaced, almost entirely, by Lawrence's exegesis. 'It's just a conceit. A clever idea.'

'I know what a conceit is, Lawrence.'

'Most love poetry from this period is not about real people. I mean he went on to marry Anne More. But I don't think it matters.'

Claudia says, 'It does matter, surely? It must matter whether it's about a real person or not? To the meaning of the poem?'

'"The meaning of the poem"? That's a lovely sentiment but rather naive, darling,' Lawrence replies, patting her leg. There is a moment of silence.

Deborah can't quite tell if Claudia is hurt, or if she's simply so used to this that it doesn't register. Deborah levers herself up from the sofa.

'If love poetry is not about love, then I can't see the point of it,' Deborah says, collecting her glass from the floor. 'But Renaissance love poems always turn out to be about politics or astrology or gardening or something like that. Not what you expect. I've never understood why. Thank you for that, Inês. Fascinating. Come on, Lawrence, come and find me a good old-fashioned glass of wine.'

Taking his arm, Deborah draws Lawrence out of the studio and they cross the lawn back to the house.

Lucy asks, 'Who's cooking tonight?'

'Me.' Josh looks at his watch. 'Christ, I'd better get on with it. Not that it's proper cooking. I'm afraid I've taken a few short cuts.'

'Deliveroo?' says Ash.

'Not quite. But not hand-caught trout, either.'

'I'll help,' Ash offers, as they leave the studio. 'I can operate a microwave.'

Lucy, Josh and Ash drift back to the house.

Miles sits for a moment, looking at the poetry on the wall. He is aware of Claudia sitting to his left and Inês beyond her, both silent, and has a sudden sense of being a third wheel, of words unspoken. 'Right,' he says, extricating himself from his seat, 'time for another of these,' and he retrieves his glass from beside Claudia's foot. 'See you in a bit.'

Claudia feels the restfulness of being in a room that has been filled with people and has quickly emptied. The sofa arm is growing uncomfortable and she shifts her weight so that both feet are on the floor. She reads through the text on the wall again.

'Do you like it? You didn't say.'

'I like it very much,' says Claudia. 'Their two reflections, melding together like that. I can't believe he didn't write it for a real woman. Don't you think? How could he write like that without real longing?'

'I'm sure you're right.'

'It's like *Poppea*. The characters are made up, but the feeling is real, or it wouldn't work. Whoever wrote the words of "Pur ti miro" felt true passion.'

'I desire you.'

Claudia freezes for a moment, and then, understanding, says, 'Or "I embrace you." It can mean either.'

They sit in silence for a moment, facing the words on the wall. Claudia feels stirred up, as she sometimes does after an argument with Lawrence, when she knows that her equilibrium has been unbalanced and will take some time to settle. Inês stands and turns the projector off at the wall.

'We should go in,' she says. 'Join the others.'

'Yes. I told Josh I'd make pudding.'

Neither of them move for a moment.

Claudia's eyes are on the wall where the words used to be; for an instant, she can still see their outline, and then it fades to white.

It is Miles who proposes a midnight swim, and the suggestion has a last-night-of-the-retreat quality that makes it irresistible to most of the guests. They are sitting amid the after-dinner clutter at the long table by the pool, faces brightly animated in the soft spotlights thrown by the candles against the blackening night. Gradually the table is cleared of clutter and then of people as the remnants of the meal are carried back to the house and the group scatters to tidy up or gather swimming things, until just Miles and Lucy remain in the still garden. Lucy has turned her chair to face the dark surface of the pool, so that Miles, clearing the table of bottles, steps out of its candle-lit aura to refill her glass. The air is still very warm.

'Just a drop, please.' Lucy hovers her hand near its rim. 'I should slow down if I'm going to swim.'

'Oh, come on.' Lucy smiles faintly as Miles sloshes wine into her glass. 'The risk of drowning adds piquancy.' He looks back to the table for his own and, not finding it, upends a tumbler of water and fills that instead.

'You look very serious.' Miles turns the chair next to Lucy so that it faces away from the table and sits down. 'What were you thinking about?'

'Just now?' says Lucy. 'I was thinking about Inês's poem, the one she told us about before dinner.'

'Oh yes, her reflections.' Miles settles himself and takes a swig from his glass.

'I thought it was beautiful,' Lucy continues, 'but I was just thinking, really, how much of a fantasy it is. You know, "all such rules love's magic can undo", as though love is a sort of superpower.'

'Donne's magic wand?'

'Exactly. Not the case in my experience. He can't mean it. And his promising not to change, to stay the same – that makes it meaningless too in a way, don't you think? Because everything changes. It's just . . . words.'

Miles bites back the witty response he is tempted to deliver and decides to take Lucy seriously. He turns towards her a little and says, 'Maybe it's more hopeful than destructive, that promise to stay the same.'

'Maybe.' Lucy is holding the wine glass in front of her, slowly twisting its stem between her fingers. 'I think the trouble is I still want to believe it very much, the existence of that kind of love. But clearly, it's not for me. Neil and I promised to love each other forever but that becomes impossible when one of you changes, or when you both do. Maybe marriage vows are premised on non-development. On non-growth. On you having finished growing by the day of your wedding. Maybe their purpose is to keep you frozen at a certain point.'

'I say that in my book. Why do we think constancy is a virtue? I think it's actually anti-human.'

'My mum and dad never changed. That's what drove me mad as a teenager. The same attitudes, over and over. The same stories. I could see them coming three sentences away. But that's why they were so happy together.'

'Growth and change is life.'

'But it's also the problem with life. Neil changed so much I couldn't recognise the person I fell in love with. It was exhausting, trying to love whoever he had become. Trying to convince myself in my own head every hour of the day. It was like doing one of those impossible tasks in a dream, some awful taxing calculation, that I had to restart over and over and could never be finished.' She looks around the table. 'I wish I smoked.' She takes a drink. 'What about you and Craig? Do you love each other no matter what? Is it like that?'

'God, I don't know. It's like I said in the studio about Donne: he might have written love poetry about constancy, but he can hardly have lived that way when he wrote it. I don't intend on changing so much that Craig can't love me any more, no. But I want to live and grow. Maybe he'll be the one who changes into something else. You just have to live it in the present, don't you?'

Lucy takes a sip from her glass and savours the wine before speaking. 'Neil said I was unfeeling, at the end. That I had lost the ability to feel. The worst thing was, I thought he might be right. I did feel sort of dead. And it made me think, maybe I lack some sort of *capacity*.'

'Capacity for what? For feeling? You seem perfectly normal in that regard to me.'

Lucy turns towards him as though captured by this idea. 'Do I? But how would you know?'

'Oh, come on, Lucy.' Smiling, Miles leans backwards in his chair, so that its front legs tip off the ground. 'You're an empathetic person. It's in everything you do.'

'But I mean it!' Lucy pulls at his arm so that the chair is suddenly righted. 'I'm fine in most ways. With my kids for example. But in others ... There are people I love, people I used to love – but I can't feel what I should for them. Something's missing. I think I've broken it.'

Miles says gently, 'All right, now you've lost me.'

Lucy is looking at him intently. He can see the outline of her face and her eyes shining in the darkness. He thinks: she is very beautiful.

'Miles, if I tell you something, will you keep it to yourself?'

'Sure. I mean, that's an abstract promise until you tell me. But yes, I'll try.'

Lucy pauses for a few seconds and then speaks quickly and directly, as if the lines have been rehearsed. 'I had a best friend at college. Zara. We were inseparable. People used to call us the twins. And then, at the end of our first year, she died. She was nineteen.'

'Lucy, that's awful. I'm so sorry.'

Lucy looks behind her, to the table, still deserted. It's impossible to see past the dancing candlelight but sound carries in this still air. She is sure they are alone.

'It's worse than that, Miles. She died because of me. It was the end of the summer term and we were leaving a ball. 1998. It was the middle of the night. I wanted to go home. I made her climb these railings over the river. She slipped and fell. I made her do it.'

Lucy has recalled these events often enough that without effort now she can hear her own voice, urging Zara on, telling her to climb the railings, not to be a coward, laughing at Zara's hesitations and her nervous look back. As if the calm dark surface of the pool in front of her were the river itself, Lucy can see the scene before her, the sudden shock of Zara's fall into the river, what it was like to watch her slip, then drop, fast, but not so fast that Lucy could not see the surprise on Zara's face as she spun onto her back, her last look at Lucy as Lucy stood stock still, Lucy not leaping forward into the water as she might have done to save her friend, as surely any normal person would have done, but in fact doing the very opposite, backing away, seeking immediately to refuse what had happened by retreating slowly over the dampening grass.

'She hit her head on the way down and she went right under the water and she didn't come up. It was awful. I saw the whole thing.'

'Christ, Lucy. What a terrible thing to witness.'

'Witness is right. I watched her die, Miles. I must have done: she was under there for so long. I couldn't see her. I didn't go into the water. I didn't even think about it. Why didn't I act?'

Miles shrugs his shoulders as if not acting was the thing anybody would have done. 'It would have been dangerous. I'm sure you went to get help, that's the only thing you could have done.' Miles takes Lucy's hand where it's resting on his arm and holds it in his own.

'I didn't do that, though.' Lucy is speaking quietly but purposefully, as though she can't stop. 'I watched the river for a long time and then I went back to the party. I had another drink. I watched people dance the last dance. And when no one could find her I said she'd gone, that she had planned to climb out over the river. But I didn't say I was there. And then they found her body, the next day, and her blood on the railings where she fell.'

'Jesus Christ.' Miles lets go of Lucy's hand, or perhaps she pulls it away as she continues talking.

'Now do you see? Because maybe she was alive when I was watching, Miles. Maybe I killed her. I don't know. It was a test, of sorts, just two or three seconds, when I needed to act, to really risk something, the test of my life, but something in me, I don't know if it was self-preservation, or fear, or plain weakness, made me just stand there while she was dying. I failed her, and then I lied about it. No one ever knew I was there.' Lucy stops and there is a profound silence as she and Miles sit by the water. Miles is about to speak, not knowing what he is going to say, but then Lucy continues, her voice dry and quiet.

'Then afterwards, everyone said it was the shock, but I felt kind of absent from it, you know? I felt sad but at the same time I didn't really feel anything. Certainly nothing commensurate with what had happened. Everything became like I was watching things happen to someone else. And ever since, every time someone talks about something good I've done, the PhD or the book or whatever – even the twins, having the children – that's the first thing I think about. I killed someone, I killed my best friend, that's a fact at my core, and I didn't tell anyone, and I don't even know how much I cared.'

Miles exhales loudly. 'Fucking hell, Lucy. That's quite a story. Poor you.'

Lucy attempts a smile. 'I'm sorry. I'm a bit of a downer. I bet you wish you hadn't asked, now.'

'No.' Miles smiles too, although it takes an effort. 'It's just a lot to process.'

Lucy is looking out again towards the pool and the dark outline of the trees beyond it. 'It's sort of monstrous though, isn't it? And I don't know: did I do that because I lack something, because there's something wrong with me? Or is there something wrong with me because I did that?'

'Lucy, I don't mean to trivialise what you're talking about. And I think you *should* talk to someone about it, properly I mean. But also, I think you might be overplaying it. Your marriage has failed, okay. Half of marriages fail. It doesn't make you an unfeeling monster. And also, you married a twat.' Miles is relieved when Lucy laughs. 'And that sense of responsibility you're feeling, that kind of paralysis around your friend's death, that's not unique either.'

'Oh, come on.' Lucy reaches for her wine glass. 'I'll accept that fifty per cent of marriages end in divorce, but not that half the population has – has done what I did.'

'You didn't murder anyone.'

'Letting them die, then. That's what I did, and it comes to the same thing.'

257

'You were very young. And if you look closely enough, you'll find lots of people have a version of that, I bet.'

Lucy replies quickly, 'No, they don't. That's simply not true, Miles. You don't. Lawrence doesn't. Claudia doesn't.'

Miles drains the tumbler and lets it drop onto the grass at his feet.

'I do, in a way. I had a friend who died. Nothing like your friend's death, but I did, in a way, watch her die and did nothing.'

Lucy is looking straight ahead but Miles can feel her concentrating on what he is saying.

'She'd been ill for a long time, actually, although I don't think any of us realised how ill. We'd lived together, we were housemates, when I was in London, but I didn't see much of her when I moved away. You know how it is. And this was twenty-five years ago, no internet, I didn't even have a mobile phone. Late nineties. I'd just started teaching at Bangor. Every now and again I'd go back to London and see her and she'd be a bit worse, things would be going badly for her.'

'What was her name?'

'Sarah. She was an actress. Or she was trying to be one.'

'What was wrong with her?'

'She was depressed, she had depression, although it took a long time before I realised that's what it was. Before she realised, I think. The last time I saw her she told me she'd been to the GP and she'd started antidepressants but she hated the way they made her feel. She couldn't work – she said she couldn't learn her lines. She came off them in the end, although I didn't know that.'

'What happened?'

'Well, it was a bad time for me too, in a way, although nothing like as bad as it was for her. I'd started my job and was realising I hated it. I stopped coming back to London as much, it was too painful. And then one Christmas – it would have been the same year, 1998 – I had a series of missed calls from her over a couple of days. I didn't answer because I was holed up with a vat of cognac and I just couldn't face talking to her. I didn't have any resources. I couldn't . . . I thought I'd call her back. I was planning to call her back. But it was too late. She killed herself. I didn't know until a few days later. Her sister found her body.'

'Oh, Miles.' Lucy turns to him and Miles can see tears glinting in her eyes.

'I kept her voicemail messages for years.'

'I'm so sorry.'

'I've come to terms with it now. It was a long time ago. She was desperate and maybe there's nothing I could have done, even if I had spoken to her. And there can be' – and Miles looks across to Lucy at this point as if to watch her reaction – 'a narcissism in the kind of guilt we both felt. The flip-side of feeling you failed is feeling you should be the saviour. I can sense my heroism in its absence. But it's not about us. After she died, I felt all sorts of things: guilt, yes, but also a sort of absence of feeling of the kind you're describing. It's a weird thing, grief. It can be cruel and self-serving and contradictory and desperately incorrect.'

'It wasn't your fault, though. That's the difference.'

Miles shrugs. 'There's a version of this story where it's all about my failed responsibility. It's quite plausible. And there's a version of your story that isn't about you at all. You can decide.'

Lucy doesn't answer, although she is thinking it can't be as easy or as arbitrary as that: simply changing one story for another. They sit still and quiet for a long time, until Miles stands up and reaches for Lucy's hand.

'Come on. Let's go and get changed. I need to find Deborah and make sure she's in a fit state.'

Lucy allows herself to be pulled out of the chair until she is standing by the pool. They start walking back towards the house, slow steps, picking their path carefully through the dark garden, Lucy ahead, and Miles close behind her.

Lawrence has declined to join the midnight swim, not having planned it himself, but he urges Claudia to go, and is pleased with her evident delight as she heads upstairs to grab a pile of towels for everyone from the cupboard in Josh's bedroom. He is standing at the sink, rinsing the plates before stacking them in the dishwasher, as Josh brings in the last of the glasses from the dining room.

'You're not swimming, then?' Josh asks.

'Not tonight. Too bloody cold. Also, I thought I should tidy up a bit, let Claudia go swimming – very much her sort of thing.'

'Very much not mine.' Josh in fact wouldn't normally be averse to jumping in cold water at midnight with friends, particularly after the wine and the cocktails, and particularly knowing the admiring glances he would receive, but by staying behind he has an opportunity to get Lawrence on his own. He's conscious that the days are ticking by. He's running out of time.

'Those pies were very good,' Lawrence is saying, 'especially the steak and kidney. Nice to have some meat after all the veggie stuff.'

'Good,' Josh replies. 'I didn't know if I'd have time to cook so I picked them up from the butcher.'

'Oh, the one in the village? Sullivan? I hope you told him you were our guest. He's completely devoted to Claudia.' Lawrence slots a handful of forks into the cutlery rack and digs in a cupboard for the dishwasher tablets.

'No, no,' says Josh. 'I went into Cambridge. On my run this morning. Had a quick look round the market.' Lawrence pauses in his search, then continues.

Josh goes on, 'I know it's not strictly sanctioned but I didn't think I'd find anything in the village – I should have asked you or Claudia, saved myself the journey – although it was nice to see the city again. I had a little wander round. I worked out that until this week I've not been to Cambridge for seven years.'

'Cambridge will always be pleased to see you.' He puts the dishwasher tablet in and presses the 'eco' setting. 'You were a good student, Josh.' The machine starts to hum. 'And as for going into town: I'm fairly sure more than one of our guests has broken that rule.'

'And not just the guests, hey?' Josh is conspiratorial, leaning against the wooden table and turning to fill a glass from the open bottle waiting there. 'I'm sorry?'

Josh pauses. He feels himself to be on the brink of something, that there is still time to turn away, to step back. Until there isn't.

'Didn't I see you, Lawrence? With your . . . friend? Coming out of the hotel?'

Lawrence doesn't say anything. Standing over the dishwasher, his back to Josh, he catches sight of his own face in the black glass of the window. Strange that the moment of reckoning should finally have come, he thinks, not from Claudia or Lucy, but from this pushy little failure.

'I mean, no judgement,' Josh continues. 'I can imagine what it's like, especially when you've been married for . . . well. And there must be temptation all over the place, in your job.' He stops as Lawrence turns to face him. Lawrence's face is ashen.

'Sorry,' says Josh. 'I shouldn't have mentioned it. I just meant, who would blame you? You must have women throwing themselves at you. It's the cliché, isn't it? Doesn't apply to school teaching, I'm sorry to say, not in my school anyway.'

'It isn't like that.'

'No, no. I'm sure. My mistake, anyway.' He tops up his glass and offers the bottle to Lawrence, who gestures *no* with a minimal movement of his fingers.

'As it happens,' Josh continues, 'I was hoping we could have a bit of a chat. I think perhaps it was too big an ask, expecting you and Claudia to make a financial commitment without seeing anything, but I thought maybe now that the script is nearly done, you'd like to reconsider? Especially given that the situation has changed somewhat?'

'The situation?' Lawrence turns to face Josh and the younger man is aware of Lawrence's size.

'Well, given that you – that Claudia – that you wouldn't want Claudia to . . .' Although he'd thought carefully about the speech on the journey back from Cambridge, even saying it out loud as the taxi took him back to Hawton, Josh is still shocked to find himself actually speaking the words. 'I'm sure it's the kind of information you would want to keep . . .' Josh's voice trails away.

'If you breathe a word of what you saw, or what you think you saw, to my wife, you little shit,' Lawrence says in a low tone, taking a step closer so that Josh is forced to move backwards, 'I will ruin you. I will come for your job, if that's what it takes. I will tell your shitty little school things that will make them want you nowhere near their pupils. I warn you, Josh, you don't want to make an enemy of me. Do not fucking try to blackmail me.'

'I'm just trying to finance my film. You can't stop me,' Josh retorts, but the words sound more pleading than any kind of threat.

'Your "film"?' Lawrence spits the word.

Josh thinks, Lawrence has had this anger in him, always, coiled and ready to launch: it was there, latent, beneath anything he ever smilingly said to me.

Lawrence says, 'I don't need to try to stop you making your film, Josh, and you know why, don't you? Because no one, *no one*, is ever going to consider funding it or making it or doing anything else with it other than laughing at it behind your back. "The situation has changed", has it? Fuck off. Fuck off and leave. You are a failure. You are a failure once more. I never want to see you again.'

Still holding the bottle, Josh watches as Lawrence walks past him through the door to the hallway, a plunging sense in his stomach. This is a mistake from which there is surely no return.

❀

Miles and Deborah head off to the pool first, whooping with excited delight.

'Watch out for the nettles,' Miles says. 'To the right.'

Deborah calls, 'I can't see a bloody thing. Wait for me.'

'Here. Follow. Straight down.'

Deborah can see the outline of the old climbing frame and, beyond that, a shape that must be the trampoline. She extends her hands in front of her as she walks. There's almost no moonlight. 'Oh my God, are we expected to take our clothes off?' says Deborah. 'Is this the sort of thing academics do in August?'

Miles says, 'Strictly optional,' but he is unbuttoning his trousers as he walks briskly through the orchard, and by the time he leaps into the pool – spreading his arms and legs joyfully in the air and letting out a shriek – he has nothing on at all.

Miles is under water for a second and then bursts back up. 'Oh, Jesus Christ, it's fucking freezing!'

A second splash, and Deborah is in, whooping with delight.

'Marvellous!' she gasps. 'I can't see the edges of anything!'

The darkness changes the effect of swimming: the pool is endless. Things are transformed into unknowns – everything is heightened, but also harder to perceive. The noise of the water is different, too: it seems louder than if they were swimming in the day.

Deborah says, 'I think I can do about two minutes before I turn blue and then die.'

'Yes, me too, but keep going. Let's stay in until the others arrive.'

Ash and Lucy appear now, not with Miles and Deborah's clothes-shedding exuberance, but both wearing swimming costumes, having changed in their rooms. They now edge down the pool steps into the water.

'This is still wet from my last swim,' Lucy pulls her bikini strap away from the back of her neck, 'it's so strange to feel chilly. I'd forgotten what being cold even feels like.'

'Jump!' Miles shouts.

'I'm not jumping.' Ash is knee-deep now in the dark water.

'It's not often one has the chance for a literal leap into the dark,' says Miles.

Lucy pushes slowly off from the steps, turns over and swims on her back, her arms straight, her eyes on the sky above. Ash's front crawl is an elegant glide, most of his body staying still as he moves through the water, his face not rising for air until he reaches the end of the pool.

Miles is treading water in the deep end. 'Who's next?' he says in response to the blindingly bright light that moves towards the pool.

Inês turns off her phone light and stands in the shallow water of the top step.

'I don't have a costume.'

'Me neither,' says Deborah.

Miles says, '*Sin ropa!* Is that what you say?'

'*Sem roupas.*' Inês surveys the pool for a second and then starts to take her clothes off.

Claudia picks her way cautiously through the orchard, still wearing her swimming costume under her dress, and carrying a pile of towels and her son's goggles. There are raucous shouts and laughs: she can see bodies in the water, some splashing around, some tracking up and down more methodically, although it's not clear who's who. There is a form by the side of the pool. It takes a few seconds for her eyes to grow used to the darkness. She realises she is looking at the back of a naked Inês, standing on the edge of the pool, her clothes in a scattered pile beside her. Inês leans forward and dives elegantly in: the water makes almost no splash.

For a moment Claudia feels as if she can't breathe and she starts to turn back to the house, but Deborah has seen her and calls, 'Claudia, come in, it's wonderful, swim for ten seconds and then we can all go inside.' Then, when Claudia doesn't answer, Deborah yells, 'Put the towels down and join us!'

Claudia places the pile of towels on the wooden table. She realises she can't look in Inês's direction. She lifts her dress over her head and, clutching it against her body, heads to the edge of the pool.

Deborah calls, 'You *must* jump, Claudia,' and there is something about the certainty with which Deborah says it that makes Claudia think yes, I must, for once, and she tosses her dress to the floor, stands for a second on the edge of the pool, and then jumps in.

'Hooray!' shouts Miles.

None of them can last more than a few minutes in the water. Miles and Deborah head back into the house first, shrieking as they scamper across the grass half-dressed, and then Lucy followed by Ash. Claudia, in the deep end, turns away as Inês skips across the grass to a towel and her pile of clothes. As Inês puts her clothes on, Claudia swims one final length, but she raises her head every second stroke and looks across at Inês knowing as she feels the push of the water against her body and the chill of the air on her skin that she will relive these moments in her mind.

After dressing, Inês comes to the pool steps and reaches out a hand. 'Come, Claudia, you'll freeze in there.'

Claudia starts to climb out.

'You are shivering.'

Claudia is shivering, but she doesn't feel the cold. This moment, right now, is pressing in on her. There is a humming in her ears.

Inês says, 'Everyone has gone.'

Claudia reaches the top step still holding Inês's hand. The momentum keeps her moving towards her and she doesn't stop until her lips touch Inês's.

Claudia can feel Inês's shock – a flinch – and then her stillness, for a second or two – and then she feels Inês kissing her back.

'Do you want to go back to the house?' Inês's voice is a whisper in Claudia's ear, her hair falling against Claudia's shoulder.

'Not unless you do.' As Inês steps back to look at her, Claudia runs her fingers along the side of the other woman's face, still a little wet from the pool. She traces the line of Inês's jaw with a fingertip. The skin is warm and smooth to her touch.

'You're very cold.' Inês's arms encircle Claudia as she kisses her again and Claudia feels Inês's warmth through the damp fabric of her dress, her hands on Claudia's naked back, the unfamiliarity of another woman's body pressing against her own.

'I don't feel cold. And it's okay, no one can hear us here,' Claudia says in a low tone. 'You don't need to whisper.'

'Is there somewhere else we could go?'

Claudia thinks for a moment. 'How about the folly, where you were working? Just there, past the trees.' She reaches for a towel and wraps it around herself. Inês follows her as she walks over the warm grass and catches hold of her hand, squeezing her fingers. Claudia finds herself tiptoeing as if she is the one scared of making a sound, and then she and Inês are laughing and running towards the stone folly. They are breathless when they reach it and as Claudia leans with her back against the wall and catches Inês's eye, she is overtaken by a wave of uncontrollable laughter. The absurdity of bringing this extraordinary woman to Lawrence's absurd folly, to do something – what? – something which Lawrence would never think her capable of, seems ridiculous and joyful and impossible to believe.

Inês is laughing too, and she leans in towards Claudia, her hand resting on the wall of the folly. Very gently she kisses the base of Claudia's neck where it curves into her shoulder and runs the tip of her tongue along the ridge of Claudia's collarbone. Claudia feels a vertiginous lightness and weakness and she pushes the palms of her hands into the stone wall behind her until it hurts. Inês kisses her again, then raises her head, looking past Claudia through the arched doorway of the little building.

'I don't think it will work,' Inês says.

'What?'

'In the folly, it's too small,' Inês replies, 'unless you want to sit side by side on that little bench. Which I do not.' She reaches for Claudia's towel and loosens it so that it falls to Claudia's waist, then lifts her dress over her head and drops it onto the grass. The two women face each other, and this time it is Claudia who pulls Inês towards her for another kiss. Inês's mouth is warm and tastes faintly of cigarettes and chlorine. It is shockingly unfamiliar. The world shrinks to what she can feel right at this moment: the push of Inês's thigh on her own; the perception of muscle, bone, flesh beneath the skin; the soft pressure of Inês's breast against her hand.

Then Inês's head dips and she kisses Claudia's breasts before taking a nipple into her mouth. As if in reflex, Claudia arches her back and feels a long shudder run through her body. Inês rests her weight on her left arm and draws her other hand down the side of Claudia's ribs before easing the towel from her hips, bringing her hand to rest on the soft flesh above Claudia's hipbone.

'You are so surprising.' Inês kneels in front of Claudia and runs both hands down the length of Claudia's thighs so that Claudia shivers again.

'I don't think I can stand,' Claudia says, or perhaps it is, 'I don't think I can stand it.' She allows herself to slide down the wall, the stones rough on her back in a way that ought to hurt her but doesn't, until she is kneeling opposite Inês and then Inês is leaning into Claudia and they are lying together on the grass. The ground is dry and hard beneath Claudia and she shifts a little as Inês moves against her and lets out the breath she has been holding. She feels the weight of Inês's body on hers, the pressure of Inês's hand and then the exquisite sensation of Inês's fingers inside her. Holding tight to Inês's back Claudia looks up at the trees and the moon and the sky full of stars and then, closing her eyes, at nothing.

Chapter Thirteen

Friday, 12 a.m.

This midnight, the air holds a heat that could, in another August, be that of a midday sun. The closeness, so strong in the day, hasn't entirely dissipated. Sitting on the wooden bench by the back door, Miles leans forward to refill his glass from the bottle of cognac on the table. One last drink, and he will go to bed. He thinks with satisfaction of the amount of work he's managed to do at Hawton, and that tomorrow he has earned a lie-in, and a late breakfast. Afterwards he will go for a stroll and maybe a spot of lunch with Deborah to talk about the filming, and then home to Craig. He enjoys the thought of telling Craig about the midnight swim – all his own idea. It's the sort of story that will delight him. Miles will embellish it a little in the telling. He has a surging longing to see Craig. He swirls the amber liquid in his glass and closes his eyes, resting his head on the back of the bench.

So it is that, his eyes closed, Miles hears rather than sees Josh approach, registering the irregular slap of his flip-flops on the stone steps and the shift in the still night air. Even from several yards away Miles can smell his sweat. Josh holds on to Miles's bench to steady himself, raising a whisky glass in his other hand. Miles can tell that Josh is very drunk.

'Miles! What a coincidence! Come to drown your sorrows?' Josh slides onto the bench opposite Miles and grins. 'Mi. My Mi. That's funny.' A brownish liquid has splashed a stain on the front of his white shirt. 'Do people call you Mi?'

'No,' says Miles. 'No one does.'

'They should.'

'I was just about to go in, as it happens.' He leans forward and takes a sip of his drink.

'Ah no, stay out with me for a bit,' Josh replies. 'I need someone to cheer me up.'

Miles doesn't answer but Josh's lumbering conversational progress needs no prompting.

'Put my foot in it with Lawrence.' He takes another drink. 'Completely fucked it up. Fucked. It. Up.' Josh drains his glass and gestures at the cognac. 'Mind if I help myself?'

'Be my guest.' Miles pushes the bottle towards Josh, who pours a very large measure into his glass. He takes a mouthful, and then another.

'Fucking hell, that's good.' Josh prises his cigarettes from one pocket and his lighter from the other. Miles is possessed of a very strong desire not to know what Josh did with Lawrence, but he suspects he can do nothing to stop Josh talking. At the second attempt, Josh lights up and pulls deeply at the cigarette. There is a moment of stillness, and then the smooth hiss of Josh exhaling the smoke.

'Aren't you going to ask what I did?'

Miles says nothing.

'Well, the ultimate sin,' Josh continues. 'As far as Lawrence is concerned.' He removes a piece of tobacco from his teeth. 'I let on that I can see through him. His pretence. His perfect marriage. All that . . . bullshit. All this perfect *Brideshead Revisited* charade but it's a total sham, isn't it, the lord of the manor act. You know that, Mi. He's more like a benevolent dictator, nice as pie as long as you don't cross him and a *complete cunt* if you do.'

'Josh,' Miles says in a warning tone. 'Come on now.'

'Oh, don't pretend you don't think the same. It's obvious you do.' There is a reckless bitterness in Josh's voice that Miles finds alarming: a desire to bring things crashing to the ground. 'And you know he's fucking someone on the side, don't you? I saw her, she's fucking gorgeous. Christ, what do they see in him? Making a complete fool out of Claudia.'

'Claudia's not a fool,' Miles replies carefully. He doesn't think Josh is in control of himself. 'And who knows what goes on inside someone else's marriage?'

'Fair enough, Mi. I have no idea what goes on inside yours. Are you happy?' Josh doesn't pause for Miles to answer. 'You were right, you know, when you said we didn't talk about your husband. I'm afraid I've forgotten his name for the moment.'

'Craig.'

'Craig. Here's to Craig.' Josh drinks, and there is a pause. Miles readies himself for whatever is coming next, but Josh seems to have lost the thread of the conversation. The two men sit in silence for a minute, and then Miles starts to stand up, pushing the table back a little as he does so. Josh also gets to his feet, leaning unsteadily on the table so that Miles can't move it further.

Miles says, 'I should go.'

'Stay and finish your drink, man. For fuck's sake. Don't walk off.'

Miles sits back down, saying nothing. Josh pours brandy into both glasses in aggressively large quantities.

Josh said, 'I always thought you're all right.'

Instead of returning to his bench, Josh moves around to Miles's, the extra weight causing the bench to rock a little and the lack of space forcing Miles to shift towards its other side.

'You remember that night Lawrence hosted a dinner for me? To celebrate my PhD?' Josh turns to face Miles and Miles leans back, avoiding the smell of Josh's breath and cigarettes and sweat, nauseated too by what he knows Josh is about to say.

'Of course you do,' says Josh. 'Lucy was there, Miss Fucking Perfect . . . Claudia didn't come, but you came. Don't tell me you don't remember, because I know you do. It was very hot then, too, not a proper heatwave like this, but still hot. That was a fun night.'

'It must be over a decade ago, Josh.'

'Twelve years. Funny isn't it, twelve years but I feel just the same person now as I was then. Nothing's changed.' Josh leans forward and puts a hand on Miles's thigh.

Miles tries to shift his leg away, but Josh holds his leg hard.

Miles says, 'Let go, please. Josh: let go.'

Josh doesn't let go and pushes his mouth to Miles's ear and whispers, 'Let me suck you off.'

Miles stands up forcefully, pushing the table back. The cognac bottle falls to its side, rolls, then smashes on the ground.

Josh says, 'Don't be a cunt, Mi. Sit down,' and he grabs Miles's arm.

'I want to leave and you're in the way. Get off my arm.'

Josh leans forward and lowers his voice and says, 'You can fuck me. Just do it.'

Miles feels a violent surge of panic and disgust and he pulls away from Josh.

'Get off my arm. I'm married. It's not 2010. Get the fuck out of my way.'

'Jesus Christ, don't be so uptight. You should be flattered.'

'I'm really not flattered.'

Josh reaches for Miles's belt buckle and pulls him hard but as Miles lurches he swings his arm and his fist connects square, and very hard, with Josh's nose and cheek. The sound is half slap, half crunch. Josh is knocked back: the bench falls over and Josh sprawls on his back on the floor. He doesn't move.

There are a few seconds of complete stillness.

Then Miles says, 'Fuck.'

He moves round the table and kneels by Josh's side. 'Fucking hell.' Blood is running out of Josh's nose. He's out cold. Miles slaps his cheek but no response. Josh's hand is still holding his glass.

Lawrence is usually a heavy sleeper in the mornings, but today he wakes early and with a jolt. Raising a corner of his eye mask and opening one eye a fraction, he checks the time on his watch and then slumps back onto his pillow. Just as Lawrence feels himself relaxing towards sleep, there is a ping from his phone. Lawrence reaches for it from beside the bed and lifts his eye mask again. There is a WhatsApp message from Phoebe. It reads:

Just to say I appreciated our conversation yesterday &
I have some thoughts already about the book. Let's talk
soon. Also no sweat about the bracelet, I found it in the
end. Phoebe.

Lawrence drops the phone onto the bed and raises a hand to
his face, covering his eyes. He turns over towards Claudia's
back and its reassuring warmth, but Claudia isn't there.

On Friday morning, Claudia does not swim.

When she gets to her studio at seven o'clock, a patch of
sunlight has already begun to work its way over the floor,
picking out the oranges and blues in the Persian rug. One wall
of the studio, facing away from the house, is taken up with
folding glass doors, which overlook the slope of the garden
towards the woods. Claudia usually leaves these open but
today she slides the doors closed and crosses to the stereo which
stands against the back wall of the room. Beside it is a towering
rack of CDs, relics of a former age which Claudia can't quite
bear to part with. Claudia finds the one she is looking for,
clicks the disc out of its case and slots it into the machine. As
it whirs into position, she lies down on the rug in the dusty
sunshine and closes her eyes against the light. The silence fades
into the first quiet bars of the music, and Claudia catches,
barely discernible, her own recorded intake of breath before
she starts to sing.

Claudia has never been able to recapture the intensity of
feeling that she experienced the first time she heard 'Pur ti
miro', has never, in explaining it to someone else, succeeded in

275

expressing how it moved her. For all that she has inhabited this piece of music, has grown to know it, to possess it, nothing has matched that first, overwhelming night in Venice when she had felt the aria swell in and around her until she could feel and think of nothing else. Now she lies on the floor and allows the exquisite sound to wash over her. When she weeps, it is not only for the beauty of the music but for the pure happiness and exultation and for the relief of being herself in that moment.

'Darling, do you know where my hydrating balm is? Darling?'

Lawrence is looking in the direction of Claudia as he speaks. She is filling the kettle at the sink and humming to herself.

When Claudia doesn't reply – she seems not even to have noticed Lawrence's arrival in the kitchen – he adds, 'Claudia?'

'Oh, hello. Morning.'

Lawrence rests his hands on Claudia's waist and kisses the side of her head.

'My Aesop moisturiser. Do you know where it is?'

'Afraid not.'

'I *hate* starting the day without it.'

Claudia doesn't turn.

Lawrence says, 'You must have barely got any sleep, poor thing. When did you come to bed? And I presume you were out in the pool again at dawn. Did you dry off at all in between?'

'Hmm, not sure,' says Claudia vaguely, pouring tea into two mugs.

'Oh, look, darling, you've hurt your back.'

Claudia is wearing a linen sleeveless top and her hair is tied up, leaving her neck bare. Just below the top vertebrae of her spine is a deep graze. Lawrence can see where the blood is beginning to clot, just reddening the pale linen.

Claudia reaches a hand to the back of her neck and touches the graze gently, almost reverently.

'What? Oh, it's nothing. I went brambling with Ash.'

'Pretty full-on brambling by the look of it. How was the midnight swim?'

Claudia pours the milk and considers Lawrence's question. 'Remarkable.'

'I imagine it was freezing.'

'It warmed up, after a while.'

'Oh, I am pleased. Got the blood running? The pulse? Thank you.' Lawrence takes the mug and wraps his hands around it. 'I do think it's marvellous the way you keep at the swimming. I don't know how you do it. Vaguely chilly this morning, despite the sunshine. A presentiment of autumn, perhaps.'

Claudia joins him at the table and indicates the vase of sunflowers in its middle. 'I found this propped against those just now.' She shows Lawrence a folded sheet of paper, with 'Claudia' written in large letters across one side.

Lawrence looks at Claudia and raises his eyebrows.

She says, 'It's from Josh, actually.'

Lawrence gets up from the table and goes to fetch a plate from the dresser. 'What is he writing in a note that he can't say in person?' he asks, his back to Claudia.

'Well, just that he's had to go home,' Claudia says. 'His girlfriend is ill and called him in the middle of the night, apparently. I do hope she's okay. He must have left very quietly. What was her name?'

'Jenny,' says Lawrence. 'Or Gemma. Something like that.'

277

And then he says, speaking a fraction slower, 'I rather suspect she'll be all right.'

Claudia looks up at Lawrence, catching the tone.

Lawrence shrugs slightly, as if to indicate, *nothing's there*, or, *hardly anything's there*. 'Just a feeling.' He carries the plates back over to the table and checks his watch. 'A shame he has to miss the last day.'

Ten years ago, Claudia would have pulled at this thread. Now she is content to leave it. Not everything needs to be unpicked.

Lawrence says, 'I think I might make pancakes. I fancy something celebratory, don't you?'

'Yes,' says Claudia. 'I do.'

Josh is driving extremely fast. His phone had suggested a cut-through off the M11, and the winding village lanes took him past boarded up country pubs and empty playgrounds and rows of new-build cottages until he reached the M25 with none of the rush-hour torment he'd feared. Right now, he's approaching the exit for the A10. The speedometer ticks up to 95. So anxious was Josh to leave Hawton Manor before anyone was up that he sacrificed breakfast, writing the goodbye note in his room – he'd made something up about Gemma's flu symptoms – and leaving it propped against the vase without pausing on his way out of the house. Josh shut the front door quietly, and briskly walked to his car parked on the road by the iron gates.

As he started the engine, the peacock, making its jerky way out from the courtyard, through the gate and onto the road, had raised its head and looked up and for a second Josh felt sure it was going to squawk. But just at the moment when it seemed it would wake everyone up, a second peacock appeared through the gateway. Josh said, 'There's bloody *two* of you,' somehow feeling that this belated comprehension marked him out, yet again, for ridicule. The two birds walked out into the road and stopped dead in the centre, five yards in front of his car. Each of them looked up at Josh, or through him. He said, 'Get the hell out of the way,' waving his hands frantically, but the birds stood immobile, despite the running engine and his animated gestures. Josh felt a sudden irrational panic that he would never be able to get away – that the house was waking and he was about to be trapped – and seized with this fear, said out loud, 'Well fuck you', and slammed his foot on the accelerator, the gravel crunching. As the car pulled out into the road it hit the bird on the left whose body caught under the front bumper and was pulled along for several yards. Josh could feel its object-ness beneath the car, its tail feathers trailing to the side, before it fell inert on the road, a lump, left behind by the back of his rapidly exiting car whose brake lights blinked briefly as it rounded the corner and was gone. The other peacock remained stock still, its head looking the other way.

Right now, Josh is following the signs for 'Services'. As he drives, he tries to assess the scale of what has happened in the last twenty-four hours. He looks at his face in the mirror. The area around his eye is tender and dark red and very swollen. When he touches the bridge of his nose there is a sharp pain: he thinks it's broken. He'd woken up lying on his bed with his clothes on. There was dried blood across his top lip and a throbbing pain down the left side of his face. God knows how he got there but he wasn't going to ask around to find out. The last thing he can remember is Miles standing up and then everything went black. Did he make a pass at Miles? He can't remember, but he knows it's possible. And with Lawrence: he's screwed up definitively. Whatever relationship the two of them had is now, Josh feels sure, permanently broken. Not even broken: just despatched, into nothingness, in the way Josh had observed Lawrence as a supervisor despatching lazy graduate students into oblivion by refusing to work with them any more. In the cold light of day, Josh can't think what made him imagine that his intimations of blackmail – he has to admit that that's what it was – would be anything other than a disaster. As he had spoken the rehearsed words about 'the kind of information you would want to keep . . .' and felt his voice trailing away, he'd been flooded with all the weakness and insecurity of his worst student days. In retrospect, the idea of getting Claudia and Lawrence to invest in the film had been a complete non-starter, but even in his darkest moments Josh hadn't anticipated quite how badly things would go wrong. He knows he will never forget Lawrence's parting words – quite possibly, Josh thinks, the last words Lawrence will ever say to him, after all these years. 'You are a failure once more. I never want to see you again.' And then he was knocked out by Lawrence's oldest friend.

He parks the car in front of the Starbucks. He takes a guilty look at the bumper but it looks okay. The man behind the till clearly notices Josh's battered face and for a moment Josh feels something like a sense of pride: he's briefly the kind of man who gets into fights. He thinks about saying, 'You should see the other bloke,' but as he's about to speak his phone buzzes.

Gemma. Josh doesn't read the message but pushes his phone deeper back into his pocket. It dawns on him that, apart from the lie about her having flu, he hasn't thought of her for a single moment in the last twenty-four hours.

He takes the coffee and the bacon roll in a silver foil sleeve. On the cup, the barista has written 'Gosh'. He gets into the car and fastens his seat belt. He checks his phone: the drive home should take thirty-seven minutes. But he can't go home. Can he? How can he possibly explain what happened? He looks at his face again in the mirror. What the hell is he going to say to Gem? That he was mugged? In the grounds of a country house? On a writing retreat? He closes his eyes and for a moment has an image of himself scrambling desperately at a volcano's edge. Then he slams the steering wheel hard with his fist: once, twice. On the third time he screams '*Fuck!*' at the top of his voice, the word extended over three or four seconds.

'There you go!' Lawrence slides the stack of pancakes carefully onto Lucy's plate and stands back, waving his spatula with a little flourish.

Lucy reaches for the maple syrup. 'It's been a while since anyone made me a breakfast like this.'

Lawrence is replacing the pan on the stove and dripping the last of the batter into the remaining fat. 'Pancakes are very easy,' he says self-deprecatingly.

'Deborah says everything is easy,' Claudia is setting out cutlery, 'but I can't remember how she arrived at that conclusion.'

'Did you hear Josh has left us?' Lawrence asks Lucy, joining her and Claudia at the table.

'No, really? Why?'

'His girlfriend has the flu or something like that. It's a pity, really, I hoped we'd all make it to the end of the last day.'

'Everyone else is staying until evening, I think.'

'Well so they should,' Lawrence says quickly. 'That was the plan. Final group chat. We can't all just . . . wander off. It's got to finish properly. With a bang, let's say.'

'How about you, Lucy? Can you still stay tonight?'

'Yes, I'll head home first thing tomorrow, if that's all right?'

'Of course. The twins will be thrilled to see you.'

'I can't wait to see them.' Lucy cuts into the stack of pancakes in front of her. 'We Facetimed and Isobel showed me this countdown she'd made, crossing off the days. It feels like it's been ages.' With her fork she pushes a slice of pancake around in the syrup on her plate. 'What are Inês's plans?'

'I don't know,' says Claudia, and at the same time Lawrence says, 'She's here until early evening. Then she's going into College for a few days. They are installing her piece this week.'

'So exciting,' says Lucy. 'I can't wait for the unveiling. Is that the term? Will you be there?'

'Absolutely,' says Lawrence, 'wouldn't miss it,' and Claudia gets up from the table and starts to put some plates into the dishwasher.

'It's great how well she fitted in,' Lucy continues through a mouthful. 'It's incredible really, that none of us even knew her a week ago, or at least only you knew her a bit, Lawrence. I feel like I've known her forever now, don't you?'

'Didn't she? I was a bit worried she might feel left out, but I don't think she did at all. Less than Josh, actually.'

'He seemed out of sorts.' Lucy centres her cutlery on her plate and looks at Lawrence.

'You know, I found the notebook I made for him on the desk in his room? I don't think he'd even opened it.'

�֍

Ash and Lucy are in the deep end of the pool, side by side, arms folded over the stone edge. Having set a target of a hundred lengths, eventually losing count and agreeing that they have probably reached it, they are both a little out of breath from the fast swim.

Lucy turns to face Ash, resting on one forearm, and pushes her hair out of her eyes. 'I honestly don't think I've slept this much or this well since the kids were born. I feel drunk on it. It's felt like this perfect bubble of time: the beauty of this place, the weather, spending all of this time with people and talking, really talking, you know?'

'What about work stuff? Any progress?'

'Well – a bit,' says Lucy. 'I did start some reading. And some thinking, that's the real progress. I should be doing something bigger or getting started on a grant – and this summer is like every other summer, I always have a huge long list of things I'm going to achieve and end up doing less than half of it. You'd think I'd learn.'

'You needed a break more than you did an intensive research week.'

'True,' Lucy replies, 'and the best thing has been all the adult company and only having to look after myself for a bit. Just to focus on what I want to do: what do I want to eat, when do I want to do things. Going for a swim. It's been revelatory. God, it's been awful existing in that . . . poisonous fog.' She turns back to face the pool's edge and heaves herself out of the pool until she is sitting on the side, legs in the water.

'You're staying till tonight?'

'Yes, the kids will be at Neil's parents' house in London till lunchtime tomorrow so I don't need to rush back.' Lucy stands up. 'I should get dry now, though, actually get some work done before lunch.'

'Yeah, me too,' says Ash, though he doesn't move.

'I'm so sorry,' says Lucy. 'I didn't ask – have you had a good time? Did you get much done?'

'Some work on this chapter. Some time with Eaves. The drinks and the games have been a lot of fun.' Ash lifts himself out of the pool and walks to find his towel, draped on some shrubs at the other end of the pool. Lucy follows, tucks her towel around her, and starts gathering up her things.

Ash watches her do this, observes how she is intent on the task, moving quickly, her face flushed from exercise and sun, wet hair pushed back behind her ears. The hours and minutes until they part are gradually ticking away; twice already today he has been on the verge of saying something more definite, to let her see something of what he feels for her, so that today's goodbye is said with the confidence of a future meeting. Earlier, before their swim, he had watched her picking leaves out of the pool and had been so close to doing it, right on the brink of speaking, but then she had started talking about something else and the moment was lost. *Now*, he thinks to himself. *Do it now.*

'It's been lovely to see you, Lucy.'

'You too.' Lucy is distracted, bending down to examine the sole of her foot. 'I've trodden on something . . . No, just a thorn, that's all right.' She stands up and smiles at him. 'Shall we go in?'

They start to walk towards the house, but as they get to the trees, Ash stops and puts a hand on Lucy's arm.

'Just – wait a minute. Just a minute. I can't go without telling you that it has been really, really good to spend so much time with you this week.' He pauses. 'Really good. I know things are difficult for you at the moment, but I want you to know that if at some point . . . if at some point you feel ready to . . .' The sentence lies unfinished between them.

'You mean . . .?'

'Yes.'

Lucy thinks for a moment and then says, 'Ash, I've enjoyed being with you a lot . . . I have.'

Ash thinks, *oh no.*

'But I'm not ready for anything at the moment. I am still . . . I am processing so much with the divorce, you know?'

'Yes, yes, of course. Forget I said anything. I'm sorry. It was crass.'

'No, it was lovely. It's me who should be sorry.'

They walk on in silence to the house, when Lucy turns aside to go to the annexe. 'I'll see you in a bit,' she says, 'for lunch, yes?'

'Definitely.' Ash calls after her, raising a hand to wave, aiming for a light-hearted tone. He goes through the kitchen and into the hallway. A line from a poem learnt long ago flickers up into his memory: 'A joyous shot at how things ought to be, / Long fallen wide.' The house is dark and cool after the intense brightness of the garden, and when he stubs his toe on the leg of the hall table, Ash says loudly and distinctly, '*Fuck.*'

Chapter Fourteen

Friday afternoon

Whoever designed the swimming pool at Hawton, Lucy reflects, seems to have placed it deliberately near to the natural body of water, as if to make a point of contrast between its manicured beauty and the brackish, murky depths of the pond, which has banks barely discernible among the weeds and long grass.

When Agnes and John Charsley had lived at Hawton, the pond would have been the only source of respite from the summer's heat, a temptation too strong for children to resist. Lucy pictures them on the other side of the water from where she is now, sitting at the base of the tree, her back resting against the trunk, her toes just at the water's edge. Who stepped in first, John or Agnes? Did they both want to swim, or was one the reluctant accomplice of the other? Lucy imagines their hushed laughter, all those years ago, and cries of shock at the cold grasp of the pond, their fragile limbs in translucent linen and hair floating in the dark water like weeds. She thinks of how her own children love to swim, in the summer at Grantchester, leaping wildly into the water in a state of complete joy. All at once the yearning to enfold their warm, familiar bodies in her arms, to feel the weight of them against her, is unbearable, and Lucy stands up, to free herself of it in movement. She extends one foot into the water, thinks for a moment how easy it would be to step forward and let it sink into the mud below, and then withdraws it. She gives a last look at the pond and then turns back towards the house. Her love for her children brings with it, as a shadow or terrible opposite, an awareness of the extent of her possible loss: her love is an opening up which admits that possibility. How wonderful it is that she should have these two children to come home to; and how precious, the last few hours of solitude.

Some things aren't designed for phone screens, and seventeenth-century metaphysical poetry is one of them. Claudia's screen is cracked in two places and, sitting in her deckchair, she tries to find an angle where the sun's reflection does not further obscure the text. Shortly after leaving Cambridge – it feels a lifetime ago – Claudia had been booked to perform one of the nine songs in Benjamin Britten's cycle *The Holy Sonnets of John Donne* somewhere deep in Suffolk. The song had been a fierce imagining of the Judgement Day, a plea for repentance and mercy from the poet to his God: a prayer, not a love poem. Inês's poem (as Claudia has come to think of it) about glass and reflections, was not one of those that Britten put to music, but she would like to sing it if she could. Claudia imagines standing at the window after Inês has engraved it, singing back to it the lines immortalised in its glass, and then smiles at the thought of a surprised College trying to go about its business as a middle-aged soprano bursts forth. She thinks of herself and Inês standing in the dark garden last night, Inês's eyes, Inês's mouth, level with hers: 'Here you see me, and I am you.'

As if conjured by her imaginings, here is Inês, crossing the lawn towards the orchard. Claudia puts her phone down and stands up from the deckchair, as though replaying their first meeting; Inês is wearing the same sundress, the same scarf tucked into the strap of her handbag, but this time the sun is full in her eyes, and she raises a hand to shield them as she approaches.

'Hello,' says Claudia, and then, 'are you leaving?' Inês stands a couple of feet away from Claudia, who stops herself from scanning the house to see if anybody is watching.

'Not quite yet. Not till tonight. I was planning to leave this afternoon, but Lawrence spoke several times about a "final group chat". He made it clear he wanted me there very much. I can get a cab later on. I need to be at the college at 7.30. Or Lawrence said he might give me a lift.'

'He's showing off to you that he has negotiated a college parking space,' says Claudia, smiling. 'They are like hen's teeth in Cambridge.'

'Hen's . . .?'

'Sorry. It's a funny saying. Hen's teeth. It means they're very rare. Lawrence is always going on about his parking space.'

'I will make sure to be very impressed.' Inês takes a step closer to Claudia and briefly rests a hand on her upper arm in a gesture that is only half a caress. 'Look, I won't stay long now, but this might be our last chance to talk alone. I'll be at the college until Wednesday to oversee the installation, and then back in Lisbon till the end of September when my fellowship starts. I think I'll be in Cambridge from the first of October.'

'That's my birthday,' says Claudia automatically, and then blushes.

'Really? That is very auspicious.' Inês smiles. Claudia thinks, her smile is the most familiar thing in the world, and yet I hardly know her. 'On October the seventh is the unveiling and the dinner at Caius. Lawrence is invited to that, and you, too.'

'I don't usually go to college things,' Claudia says. 'It might be a bit strange.'

'It might be very strange. Let's see, okay?'

They are standing close together now and Claudia looks directly into the other woman's eyes. They have, she thinks, so little and so much to say to one another.

'Let's see,' she echoes, and she steps forward and kisses Inês, not on the cheek as she had meant to but on her mouth, a soft warm sensation of coffee and a trace of cigarettes, and then Inês responds and Claudia is overwhelmed at the thought that she is kissing this extraordinary woman in full view of the house and feeling such a sense of abandon and weightlessness. As they break apart, Inês smiles and adjusts the bag on her shoulder.

'What do the English say? Thank you for having me. Is that it?'

'That's right,' says Claudia. 'And you're very welcome. Thank you for coming.' She is rewarded with Inês's laughter and a moment of conspiracy between them.

Inês raises her hand, a half wave, as she turns away.

Claudia mirrors the gesture, and then moves her hand to her mouth. She runs a fingertip over her lower lip as she watches Inês retrace her steps towards the house.

❋

From the raised position of the field Deborah and Miles can see across a series of other fields hemmed in, far away, by a road to the left and, closer, by woods to the right. Pointing from the manor gate, Lawrence had said to cut through the woods to the Red Lion, but otherwise his description of the route had been uncertain: Miles sensed that Lawrence didn't want them to leave the estate and, rather than clearly stating that resistance, his ambivalence came out in the form of purposeful vagueness.

The field has been very recently ploughed and the footpath cut back to a narrow strip studded with loose chalk. Lawrence had said, 'I think it's the third or fourth stile that you want.' Miles stumbles over a stone and swears under his breath.

'Deborah, this is a fool's errand. I think we should go back.'

'Oh come on,' says Deborah, 'it's just a walk in the fields. This isn't *Fitzcarraldo*. Anyway, I've got to get out of the house. Lawrence moping about how everyone's leaving earlier than planned is getting on my tits. I loathe waiting around for journeys to begin.'

'You could sit in the garden with a cocktail like a normal person would, instead of turning our last afternoon into an orienteering exercise.'

'Turn down your metropolitan impatience, Miles. We've got this far,' Deborah replies, hoisting herself onto the first step of the stile and looking back at her friend, 'and it can't be more than a mile further on. It will be worth it. A country pub and a drink that isn't fucking damson gin.'

'Well, yes, I have rather had enough of that stuff. Very viscous, isn't it?'

'I've come to hate it.'

Tomorrow evening, Miles thinks, he will be back home,

with Craig, relating it all to him, making stories and jokes from the week's events, exaggerating some details and leaving others out. The six o'clock damson gin will play its part in the list of Lawrence's foibles. Already Miles is beginning to see the retreat as a past event, the subject of anecdotes and shared jokes and do-you-remembers. He thinks, for the first time: I wonder if Lawrence will do this again next year? And then, do I want to come if he does?

As she steps over the fence, Deborah's phone pings with a message and Miles says, 'Coverage. A miracle.' Deborah's foot slips a little as she carries on over the stile and she grabs at the fence to save herself from falling.

'You see?' Miles gestures at the cracked plank at the base of the stile. 'It's treacherous. We'll both get broken ankles and die out here of exposure.'

Miles's yellow silk scarf catches on a thorn and tightens uncomfortably around his neck. Deborah snorts as he carefully works the fabric away from the brambles.

Miles says, 'Hawton is paradise itself, but I do find myself yearning for roads and pavements and shops, don't you? Not to mention a pub in walking distance. I don't count this', and he takes Deborah's arm as they walk along the field-edge towards the trees. With her other hand, Deborah is fishing in her bag for her phone.

She holds the phone close to her face. 'Bloody sun. I can't see the screen.' She squints. 'My stepmother. Hang on.' Deborah stops walking and cups her right hand around her phone. 'She says give her a call as soon as possible.'

'Well, we can do that from the pub,' says Miles, moving forward, 'can't we?'

Deborah stands still, holding the phone in both hands against her chest. She looks at Miles.

'My father is dead.'

'Your father? What do you mean? Is that what she says?'

'No, not yet,' says Deborah. 'She says to call at once. I know what it means though.'

He looks at her and wonders for a moment if she is joking, but her face is serious and pale in the sunshine.

'I don't understand,' he replies, walking a few steps back to Deborah's side. 'Is he ill? Is he in hospital or something?'

'No, he's fine. Was fine. At home. But I know that's what this is.'

Deborah's eye has been drawn towards the line of trees a little ahead of them. A green woodpecker dips and swoops into the high branches of an oak tree and is lost in the canopy.

Miles gently takes his friend's arm. 'Debs, do you want to go on to the pub, and give her a call, or back to the house?'

Deborah looks up at him, but before she can speak, her phone rings. Deborah presses the screen and holds it to her ear.

'Hello? Janey? Yes, it's me. Are you all right?' There is silence as Deborah listens to the distant voice, her head lowered. Miles takes a few steps and looks away, back towards Hawton. It feels awkward to be listening to this private phone call, but he can't do anything about it. He takes his own phone from his pocket and swipes it open, scrolling through his photos. He looks back through the most recent images: the square window in the lower living room, framed by the clematis outside; Lawrence and Ash clinking cocktail glasses, heads together, faces mock-serious; Lucy lighting candles on the garden table in the dusk, the half-light blurring the flames so that her hands seem surrounded by fire.

After a moment Deborah nods, and raises a hand to her mouth, running her fingertips across her lips. 'I'm so sorry, Janey. I'm so sorry. Yes.' Another pause. Miles catches Deborah's eye and points back towards the fence; she nods again and, gently taking her arm, he leads her towards it and she sits down on the stile.

'Of course. Of course you did. I know you did. Please don't worry.' There is a catch in Deborah's voice and she is quiet for a moment; then she says, 'Look, I'm in the middle of a field at the moment but I'm coming. I'll come this afternoon. Yes, a field. No, of course I will, it's fine. All right. Yes, the coverage is awful. I know you did. I know. I'll text you from the train. OK? All right? Take care now, Janey. Speak soon. Bye.'

Deborah returns the phone to her pocket.

'Debs, I'm so sorry.' Miles crouches down so that he is on her level and takes her hands in his. 'You poor thing. Your dad?'

'Yes. He fell. At home. It was so strange how I knew that's what it was.'

'What do you want to do? Shall we go back to the house?'

For a moment Miles thinks she hasn't heard him, but then she stands up and brushes down her trousers.

'Yes. I suppose we should.'

'Okay,' Miles says, 'that's what we'll do. Come on, now.' He helps her over the stile. She moves slowly and deliberately, holding tight to the top of the fence.

As they walk, Miles finds himself wondering about what this means for their plans to meet with the film people next week in London, then feels guilty for having allowed such a thought to enter his mind.

'Where does – did – your dad live?' he asks.

'West Midlands. Droitwich Spa,' says Deborah. 'That's where I'm from.'

'Really?' says Miles in surprise. 'I never knew that.'

'But don't worry, I'll still be around next week. I'll spend a couple of days with my stepmother but not long. The TV talks go ahead.'

'Obviously I didn't mean that,' Miles says, embarrassed, but not so much that he isn't also reassured. 'And you should take your time, I wouldn't dream of . . .'

'Miles, it's all right,' says Deborah, 'I will be back at work. It's what I do. I am sure there will be a lot to see to, but it won't stop me working.'

By the time they reach the gate that leads into the churchyard, the afternoon sun is just behind the church so that the whole building seems illuminated from within. To Miles Deborah seems older, compared to just a few moments' ago; diminished, as though without the costume of her joyful energy and caustic chatter, Deborah's real frailty can be seen. As she passes the church door, she stops.

'Miles, I can't bear to go into the house and have to tell everyone. My bags are all packed. I'm going to slip into my room discreetly, but can you possibly cover for me? Lawrence kept banging on about this "final chat", as though we were all about to kick the bucket. Ironically enough. But I don't want to do that now. I'll call a taxi and wait in my room and then go.'

Miles opens the gate and stands back to let Deborah go ahead.

❈

With the kitchen windows and the back door wide open, Claudia's voice, and the recording it accompanies, carry through the still air of the garden, as far as the trees beyond the terrace. Miles, sitting in a deckchair in the shade of the back wall, lifts his head from his phone to listen. He can't quite catch the words but recognises the melody, a Puccini aria he associates with *A Room with a View*. Miles closes his eyes and pictures Florence, which he last saw on a day as hot as today, its wide river and streets, its golden stone the same colour as the church at Hawton.

Lucy enters the kitchen through the back door, three earthenware mugs in each hand and a plate under her arm. She is surrounded by the music coming from the speakers and by the rich sound of Claudia's voice. Claudia is scrubbing a large saucepan in time to the recording, her arm moving at double speed as she sings. Lucy unloads the crockery onto the work surface and Claudia turns towards her.

'I'm so sorry, what a racket.' Claudia drops the pan into the sink and, drying her hands on a tea towel, turns off the stereo on the dresser behind her.

'It was beautiful,' says Lucy. 'Your voice is lovely.'

'That was at least half Renée Fleming,' Claudia smiles. 'But thank you.'

'I seem to have been stockpiling cups in my room like a teenager. It's been an age since I had tea in bed in the mornings.' Lucy opens the dishwasher and begins to make space on the top rack.

'In a couple of years maybe the kids will bring you tea in bed,' Claudia says. 'Although I must say mine never has. One or twice on birthdays, but he usually got it wrong and I had to make it again, out of sight.'

'I don't think I ever made tea for my mum at Tristan's age.' Lucy tries to slot the plate into the lower half of the dishwasher. 'I think this is full.' She picks up a tea towel and starts on the row of glasses on the drying rack. 'In our house my father used to bring my mother tea and breakfast in bed every single Sunday. He still does, I think.'

'A rare bird.'

'He's just completely devoted to her. They are to each other. But you're right: it's rare. Growing up I didn't realise just how unusual they were. I mean I didn't realise how unusual that kind of devotion was in a marriage. Which is wonderful but also . . .' – Lucy thinks for a moment – 'a totally skewed image of married life to grow up with as natural.'

'That's true.'

'I've worried so much what the divorce will do to the kids, but I think I was messed up by my parents' happy marriage. There was a sort of . . . toxic perfectionism to it. I just thought I'd marry someone who adored me. I'm surrounded by these perfect marriages: my parents', my sister's – her husband is a lot like Dad. And yours and Lawrence's. And then I married Neil.'

Claudia rinses the pan.

'Lawrence is not devoted to me.'

'No, well, not in the breakfast-in-bed sense, I suppose. But you know what I mean. Fundamentally, all these strong marriages. I thought I had that, but actually I don't think I ever did. You're very lucky.'

Another pause.

'I am lucky in some ways,' Claudia says. 'Lawrence is a good father. He loves Tristan very much and he'll do anything for him. Hours of Lego-building, making dens, playing cricket, all that stuff. But you know, Lucy, not every marriage that endures is perfect. It doesn't need to be perfect to endure. There's a big tract of land between your parents' devotion and the kind of hell you're enduring with Neil, and that's where most marriages play out.'

'Of course. I understand that. Everyone has their flaws. I bet Lawrence leaves wet towels on the floor and doesn't notice when the bins need taking out.' Lucy finishes drying the glasses and carries them over to their cupboard to put away.

Claudia stands with her hands resting on the edge of the sink. Through the window she can see the gentlest of breezes lifting the edges of the willow tree. She says, 'Lawrence is a serial adulterer.'

At first Lucy doesn't say anything: she opens her mouth but she doesn't speak. She is still holding a glass in her right hand.

'What do you . . .?' Her voice slows, then trails off.

Claudia turns to face Lucy.

Lucy says, 'He has affairs? With other women?'

'With other women.' Claudia picks up the tea towel again and leans back against the work surface, turning the cloth slowly in her hands. 'There's something going on right now, with one of his students. At least, that's what I think. If it's who I think it is, she's young enough to be his daughter. Young enough to be my daughter, come to that.'

'Oh my God, Claudia. I'm so sorry. How did you . . .?'

'Find out?'

'Yes.'

Claudia glances at the open door and lowers her voice. 'I saw a text she'd sent. Although looking back I can see that signs were there already. I just didn't spot them. Usual thing, I imagine.'

'And you think he's done it before?' Lucy crosses the room and closes the back door softly. She sits down at the big table and pulls her feet onto the chair, hugging her knees to her chest.

'He tried it on with a friend of mine once, at a party, years ago. I mean before I had Tristan. I was still singing then and she was a singer too, very beautiful, she was quite famous at the time. She told me about it and I confronted him but he dismissed it and I believed him. But now, looking back . . . yes, I think he's done it before. Many times.'

'My God.'

'I'm sorry to tell you. I know you look up to him. I know looking up to him is important for you.'

'Maybe, but I don't want to be deluded. Does he know you know?'

'Not sure. I think he does. There's something . . . there, between us. Our marriage has become full of these known unspoken things.'

'What are you going to do?'

'What am I going to do?' Claudia looks at Lucy directly for the first time since her disclosure. 'That's such a good question. I don't know.'

A pause, then Claudia says, 'How did you find out? About Neil?'

'Oh, he told me. I think he was proud of it, secretly, although he made out he was very sad – said he'd been forced into it, not that he'd had sex with someone else. We went to couples therapy and he told her that he had to have an affair because

I was so emotionally cut off.' Lucy reaches for some fallen petals on the table and rolls them between her fingers. 'I think she even started to believe him, that's the weird thing. Then I began thinking maybe he was right, maybe there is something broken in me, unfeeling. But I had to get out, anyway. We were horrible to each other. He was horrible to me. By the end I couldn't bear to be anywhere near him. In the last few months, I was afraid of him.'

Claudia sits down at the head of the table. 'There's nothing broken in you, Lucy. You must believe that.'

'I can feel things, now, for other people. But it's so hard – to re-enter real life. I feel like I'm on the edge of it, somehow. *Fuck*, I can't believe that about Lawrence.'

'It's the most predictable thing in the world.'

'I can't believe he would do that to you.'

'He's a good man in many ways but – well, now I have to work out what I can live with.'

'That's a good way of putting it. That's a good question to pose.'

Claudia stands up and starts stacking the clean crockery on the draining board. 'Like for example now. Am I cleaning plates? Or is everything collapsing? I just need to decide. Do you know what I mean?'

'Yes. It feels like I have to make that choice most days. Choose how to perceive it, and then live that way. But even if you decide you're cleaning plates – it doesn't mean things don't collapse anyway, sometimes.'

Chapter Fifteen

Friday evening

The door to Lawrence's study stands ajar and Lucy pauses before going in, one hand on its wooden panel. She listens for noise from within, but the only sound is the faint Monteverdi which Claudia is playing on a loop in the kitchen. Lucy pushes the door gently and leans a little way into the room. Standing at the large bay window, his back almost completely turned to her, is Lawrence, one hand holding his mobile phone to his ear, the other in his pocket, his head angled downwards as though looking at his feet. Lucy is about to withdraw from the room when Lawrence moves to sit on the edge of the sofa, still pulled out into a bed, but stripped of sheets and blankets. His back turned to Lucy, he switches the phone to his other hand and laughs softly and says, 'I know you do. I know.'

There is something in Lawrence's tone and his demeanour which holds Lucy there, standing in the doorway, half in and half out of the room. That he is speaking to someone whom he knows intimately is evident. Now is the moment when she should retreat, but Lucy stands watching Lawrence as he leans backwards onto his elbows so that he is half-lying on the sofa bed, phone propped against his ear. Lucy thinks of all the kindness he has shown her over the years. It's true that she considers her former supervisor morally expedient; she has seen him cut enough corners in his dealings with colleagues to know that he is not a man with strong principles. But it is nonetheless a struggle to transform the generous, flawed but essentially benign person whom she has for so many years considered a mentor into a habitual liar.

Lucy thinks, too, of the fact that Lawrence has never, in all the time that she has known him, made sexual advances to her, has never once even suggested, during one of the many coffees and meetings they have shared, or one of the parties or dinners that they have attended, that he is interested in anything other than collegiality and friendship. Several memories chase through Lucy's mind. She remembers starting her PhD with Lawrence, her friends teasing her about her good-looking supervisor with his glamorous lifestyle – but also, of course, there was his glamorous wife, whom Lucy had met and liked at once. Lucy recalls walking across the market with Lawrence on a warm spring day when a man had called out to him from the flower stall, 'How about a bunch of beautiful flowers for your beautiful girlfriend?' and they had laughed about it, and Lawrence had corrected the man politely and been almost apologetic that anyone should make such a mistake.

Then, unbidden, comes a memory of being at a faculty event with Lawrence and several others during the second year of her PhD. Lucy had been coming down the stairs on the other side of the hall from him when she had seen Lawrence approach two junior colleagues who were talking together, the woman with her back to him. When he got close to them, Lucy had watched Lawrence run a swift, proprietorial hand down the length of the woman's spine in her green silk dress, resting it briefly against the small of her back before leaning in to shake the man's hand. A moment later, he had taken a glass from a nearby tray and was laughing with them both and clapping the man on the back. Lucy had registered then the curious intimacy of that quick, secretive touch and had decided that she had probably been mistaken in what she thought she had seen – but had known, too, that she had not been mistaken. How long, she wonders, has she been aware that Lawrence had this side to him, and chosen not to see it, because it suited her not to?

Lucy thinks of all this while watching Lawrence lounge on the sofa. It's time for them to gather in the lower living room. Lawrence had been insistent that they should all be there promptly. Lucy has come to retrieve some books but also because she feels an inclination, which she can't really understand, to see Lawrence on his own before leaving. She retreats behind the door, then knocks loudly and opens it slowly. By the time she is fully in the room, Lawrence is sitting upright, hair and shirt rumpled. He turns to her, raises a hand in greeting and mouths, 'Sorry!'

'Just getting my books,' Lucy points at the volumes she's left on Lawrence's desk as she goes to pick them up. In reply, Lawrence pantomimes intense boredom at whatever he is having to listen to from the person on the phone, then pretends to shoot himself in the temple. He holds up a finger: one minute. Lucy nods and turns to go. She closes the study door behind her and pauses for a moment, listening to Lawrence say loudly and clearly, 'I'm terribly sorry but I'm going to have to stop you there – yes, yes, that's it exactly,' and then end the call, but by the time he's put the phone down, Lucy has left.

The fireplace is the centrepiece of the lower living room, with the furniture oriented around it, even when, as now, the fire has only a few blackened, half-burnt logs which have lain dormant since January. Lawrence has a rule about no fires after 28 January (the date Charles I was executed) passed down from his grandparents, and their grandparents before them, although no one, including Lawrence, can remember the exact logic of the proscription.

There is an exhausted quality to the room: its inhabitants are already exited, mentally, and no one got much sleep last night. Lawrence had issued a reminder via WhatsApp – 'Final group chat!' – early this morning. He'd written 'Retreat reflection' at first, then deleted it as it sounded too away-day. But 'chat' isn't right, either: not quite formal enough. Lawrence had initially planned that everyone should present for five minutes on what they'd written during the week, but his attempt at something similar on Tuesday evening really hadn't taken off, so he's changed it to 'the one big thing you've learnt on the retreat'.

Ash is squeezed into the corner of a sofa, flicking through an old copy of the *TLS*. Inês is next to him, looking out of place on the battered brown leather, and then Lucy next to her. Miles is in the facing, collapsed old armchair, the one with burn marks from the fire – all the furniture in the lower living room, Lawrence has told them more than once, is 'straight from the homeless charity shop in Landbeach'. Miles flexes his right hand, then gently makes a fist; the hand is still aching although there aren't any visible marks. Josh of course isn't there and there's an unvoiced but felt sense that no one should

303

mention him: Lawrence naturally has told no one about Josh's attempted blackmail and his decisive despatch, and no one knows about Miles knocking Josh out except Miles. But Josh's absence is a marker of the group's incompleteness, and his exit – uncommented-on yet discordant – means everyone feels something is slightly awry.

Claudia has just finished pouring tea, and sits back on the low footstool.

Lawrence is standing in the centre of the room, hands in his pockets.

'Where's Deborah?'

Miles says, 'She's in her bedroom. Waiting for the cab.'

'Well, she should come through. She shouldn't sit on her own.'

'I think she wants to be alone.'

'But it's the last time before you all leave.'

'It's really not the moment, Lawrence.'

'Everyone knew about this in advance.'

Ash says, 'Evidently her father didn't,' not looking up from the *TLS*, and then adding, 'inconvenient'.

Lawrence doesn't respond. He digs his hands deeper into the pockets of his shorts. Part of his driving rationale is that he really doesn't want the week to be in effect four days: that isn't a full retreat. It needs to stretch across the full five if he can tick the whole thing off as a proper success.

Miles says, 'Let's just leave her to it. Her father just died.'

'But should she be alone? And the taxi won't be here for an hour. She said.' He lowers his voice as if the pragmatics shouldn't be overheard. 'She can sit here with everyone else. She doesn't need to present.'

'"To present"!' Miles exclaims. 'Jesus, Lawrence.'

Miles looks at Lawrence: is this what he is? Self-absorbed to the point where he won't let a family death intrude on his parlour games.

Then Deborah appears in the doorway. 'I can sit. I don't need to wait in my room alone. Lawrence is right. I'd rather be among all of you. But I'm not going to make a speech.'

The piano stool creaks a little as she sits down.

Lawrence gestures a hand at the rocking chair, but Deborah is already checking the Royal Cars app.

Lawrence says, 'It's great to have you here, Deborah. We're all here for you.'

Deborah looks up from her phone, as if momentarily confused. Then she says, 'Thank you, Lawrence.'

'I know our minds have probably begun to turn to journeys home and to the rest of life, but I wanted us to gather one last time—'

'It's been *four days*, Lawrence.'

'Five days, Ash. This is the fifth. Which means a week.'

Ash raises the palm of his right hand as if conceding a point which, legalistically correct, in fact strengthens his position.

'And I thought it would be valuable to think about what we've learnt this week.'

Miles says, 'Can't we just have one last drink?'

Lawrence says, 'So let's start. What have you learnt this week, Lucy?'

A mobile rings.

Lucy says, 'Sorry – that's me.' She looks at the screen. 'I need to take this.'

Lucy shuts the door to the hall and then there's the sound of the front door opening and shutting.

Lawrence, feeling like he's losing momentum, says, 'Inês. What about you?'

'I don't understand quite what you want, Lawrence.'

Claudia looks up at Inês and then at Lawrence.

Lawrence says, 'You didn't know any of us at the start of the week. We'd only met briefly on one occasion. But you came. What have you discovered here – among the dusty corridors of Hawton, as it were?'

Inês turns the rings on the fingers of her left hand.

Ash says, in a tone that is largely jovial, 'He means, how has he transformed your life? How has he let light in?'

Inês smiles. Lawrence ignores Ash, and when he says 'What's the thing you'll remember?' it's not clear if this is a restatement of Ash's comment, or a corrective to his sarcasm.

Inês says, 'It was a generous risk for you to ask me. And . . . I will remember this week.' She reaches forward and picks up a cup of tea. 'That is all I've got to say.'

'Thank you. I somehow knew you'd fit in. Felt that immediately as a certainty. More than fit in. Add so much.'

'I passed the exam?'

'That's not what I meant. But yes, of course. A top first. Just like Ash's.'

Ash is about to say something about the way in which a compliment to Inês has become a compliment to Lawrence, but Claudia cuts in.

'Who knows what will happen, Inês. But thank you for spending this week with us.'

'Well put, darling,' says Lawrence, although actually he found 'who knows what will happen' a little misjudged, tonally.

Lucy returns. Claudia catches her gaze and raises her

306

eyebrows to denote all okay? and Lucy gives a quick nod and says, in a half-whisper, 'I need to start packing.'

Lawrence says, 'Just sit, Lucy, for a few minutes.' And then, when she complies: 'How about you, Ash?'

Ash shakes his head. 'I'm all talked out, Lawrence.'

'I know you've been writing masses.'

Ash's eyes remain on the paper although it's clear he isn't reading.

Lawrence says, 'The little typography book and whatever the latest column is.'

Ash turns a page and sighs, a conscious deep breathing out.

Lawrence tries again: 'So what you will you take from the retreat?'

Ash puts down the paper. 'I'm sorry, Lawrence, you've been in many ways very generous this week, the food and the garden and the writing and everything, but I can't take any more.'

'Any more what?'

'Any more of your . . .' Ash pauses, wondering whether to cross the line. Then he says, 'Vanity.'

'My *vanity*?'

Lucy says, 'Ash, hang on, that's a bit strong.'

Ash says, 'I can't stomach the . . . utter hypocrisy of how you live, Lawrence.'

Deborah is looking at Ash and she raises her palms as if to say what are you doing? but Ash is standing now and he turns in a way that suggests he is addressing everyone. 'Have you any idea who Lawrence really is?'

Claudia says, 'Ash, please,' and he turns his head to look at her.

Lawrence's strong instinct is to shut this down as quickly as possible, to quash this public acrimony and to get back to the reflections on the week. He'd even give up the reflections if it would mean a return to quiet order. But he's too shocked to react with his normal swift and total control. He just stands looking at Ash.

Ash continues, 'What happened with Josh? What happened there? Because something did.'

Lucy says, 'Ash, I think now isn't the occasion for this discussion.'

Ash says, 'I'd have thought a feedback session on lessons learnt was precisely the occasion.'

'This isn't the time or the place.'

Deborah looks up and before she's conscious of what she's doing, says, 'Lucy, for fuck's sake: just stop it.'

Lucy says, 'Stop what?'

'This ceaseless head-girl performance. This being eternally in control. Sometimes you have to actually live, which may mean saying things that aren't perhaps aptly and perfectly curated.'

Lucy thinks for a moment. 'Deborah, I understand what you're going through.'

Deborah snaps back, 'What would someone have to do to snap you out of your perfect shape? You're such a fucking people-pleaser.'

'I don't – no I'm not.' Lucy glances at Claudia, who is looking at her sympathetically. Claudia stands up and crouches next to Deborah, taking one of her hands. She leans forward to speak quietly to her and Deborah closes her eyes.

Lawrence says, slowly, and a little weakly, 'His girlfriend was ill.'

Ash holds his gaze and Lawrence's words seem to wither.

Miles suddenly says, 'That wasn't anything to do with Lawrence. Josh and I had an argument. We had a fight.'

Claudia turns quickly towards him. 'A *fight*?'

Lawrence, uncertain whether he's on the rack or mercifully released, says, 'When?'

Miles says, 'Last night. Very late. Outside. He was very drunk. He made a pass at me. More than a pass. He . . . I hit him.'

Lawrence says, 'I don't understand. Josh is engaged to Gemma.'

Claudia says, 'Oh, Miles.'

Ash says, 'But there's something else here, isn't there, Lawrence? I don't know what, exactly, but I know it.'

Lawrence says, 'What's happening, Ash? There's nothing "here", whatever you mean by that. Miles has just explained everything.'

Ash says, 'It's more lying, Lawrence. You're a fraud. No one here believes a word you say, and after what you've done, why should they?'

Miles says, 'Ash, it did happen.'

Ash looks hard at Lawrence, as if waiting for something to crack, as if the intensity of his stare will open things up, but nothing happens.

Ash says, 'You'll never let truth in.'

Lawrence's expression is locked in injury and victimhood.

Ash says, 'I have to go. I'll call a taxi. I'm sorry, Claudia. All of you.' He tries to look at Lucy, seeking a glance that will produce some sense of complicity or shared understanding or just the prospect of repair, but she is gazing away from him, towards the window, sensing but avoiding his look. Ash walks down the hall in the direction of his room.

After the sound of Ash's door closing, Lawrence looks at Claudia, who has returned to her seat. 'I don't understand what that was about. Do you? What did he mean, my vanity?'

Claudia catches Deborah's eye and the two of them suppress a laugh.

Lawrence says, 'Why are you laughing? Literally, what are you laughing at?'

Miles says, 'I'm sorry about things with Josh. I'm not sorry I hit him. He's a creep. Actually worse. He's bad news. But I'm sorry I derailed your plans, Lawrence. And Claudia.'

Claudia says, 'It's okay. I thought he was a snake the first time I met him.'

Lawrence says, 'You did?'

'Miles, I can't believe you punched him.' Deborah starts to laugh.

Lucy looks at Lawrence and for the first time in the twenty years she's known him she has a sense of him that is at first hard to identify, just beyond reach, but which she then comprehends: he's a ridiculous figure. He is laughable. Is it just now, or was it always so?

Deborah says, 'Fucking drama, darlings,' and then, 'I'm sorry, Lucy. That was uncalled-for, what I said,' although part of her is glad she said it, and she realises, in retrospect, that she has been waiting for the right moment for the last couple of days.

Lucy gives a little wave as if to say, it doesn't matter, but it does: Deborah's words have knocked her back, not least because Lucy felt at once the truth of them.

Lawrence looks round the room, trying to see if there is anything redeemable here, if he can turn things around, but there isn't, and with a promptness that looks like decisiveness,

310

but is in fact panic, he walks out of the room, striding fast out through the hall, opening and slamming the front door, across the courtyard, and onto the long lawn. Claudia slowly stands to follow him.

Deborah says, 'Why not leave him, C?'

Claudia says, 'I need to go.'

Lawrence is walking across the long lawn and when he reaches the furthest point, beyond the pond and the folly at the edge of the estate, he continues to walk, but in circles. In any kind of crisis Lawrence has to move: standing still is intolerable. Claudia has just passed through the doorway from the courtyard. She walks past the deckchairs. Six white metal hoops are leaning against the tree stump, and on the ground there are four coloured balls and four mallets. Lawrence had placed them there at the start of the week, but no one has taken the invitation.

Lawrence looks at Claudia with an expression of utter bafflement. He says, 'I mean what the literal fuck? What's the matter with that man?'

Claudia looks at him but she doesn't give him back the sympathy, and confirmation of his victimhood, that he wants.

Lawrence looks at the ground as if in deep thought, then back to Claudia. He says, 'But if we ignore Ash's extraordinary attack, it's still a success overall, isn't it? The week as a whole has still been good, don't you think?'

'You mean if we ignore Ash storming off and Miles assaulting Josh and Deborah laying into Lucy?'

'That's a very partial way to put it.'

As he walks round and round, Lawrence is trying to revive that sense of the week.

'Lawrence can you just stand still for a second?'

'There were masses of great things that happened. The book game was hilarious, wasn't it? And your midnight swim. You loved that, didn't you?'

Claudia's stillness is striking in contrast to Lawrence's continual movement. She is looking across the lawn, towards the pool, at the beginnings of a sunset. The high poplars are positioned in such a way to frame the view to the west as if the sun is being held delicately between two hands.

Lawrence says, 'And the notebooks.'

'Lawrence, there's something I need to tell you.'

'Yes?' Lawrence is only half listening, his mind lifting elements of the week that he can redeem.

Claudia says, 'Can you sit, please?'

Lawrence looks at Claudia, noticing a change of tone. She gestures towards the garden furniture. On the white table there is a bowl containing cashew nuts. Lawrence sits down.

Claudia speaks hesitantly. 'Lawrence, I need to talk to you about Inês.'

Lawrence is thinking he should have made a point about the garden furniture. He's fairly sure it belonged to Russell. The curling table legs and the lattice work on the back of the chairs have the right 1930s feel.

'Lawrence?'

'Sorry. Yes, totally listening.'

'I said I need to talk to you about Inês.'

'Well, she certainly *is* a positive thing in the week. We can cling to that. She alone means it's been a success. Isn't she a total smash?' Lawrence runs a hand through his hair. 'I'm so delighted she was part of it. I have to admit it was a bit of a risk – I'd only met her a couple of times. And what with everyone else knowing each other. But she's added something unique. There's a quality to artists, isn't there? A capacity to cut through. To deal only in what's significant. No waffle. No trivialities. Wonderful. I'm so pleased I asked her. In lots of ways she might have not worked if—'

'Lawrence, please stop talking and listen to me.'

'I am listening. Absolutely. Go ahead.'

Claudia looks away. 'I need to tell you that . . . Inês is a very special person. And a very beautiful woman.'

'Absolutely. Couldn't agree more. She's extraordinarily talented.'

'And . . . and it's been an intense kind of week, hasn't it? A close atmosphere.' She risks a glance directly at her husband, who is smiling expectantly.

'Certainly.'

'And the night of the swimming . . .' Claudia drops her eyes and trails off, doubting herself, or perhaps reconsidering the virtues of speaking candidly to Lawrence.

'Last night, you mean?'

Claudia thinks for a moment but when she continues, she can only repeat what she's already said, as if she's stuck on a precipice. 'She's a very beautiful woman, and it's been an intense week.'

'You said that. Darling are you quite all right? Why don't you sit down, too? I feel exhausted, I must say. Sort of pulled in different directions.'

Lawrence looks back at the lawn in the lowering light. 'What a place this is.' Then, conscious that his wife hasn't spoken, he turns to look at Claudia, trying to read her thoughts. After three or four seconds his face falls to seriousness. His tone shifts. He says quietly, 'Oh I see.'

'What?'

'I see.' And then: 'I understand what it is you are trying to say.'

Claudia sits completely still.

Lawrence's face warms with a sympathetic smile. He reaches to take her hand in his and strokes it with his thumb. 'Claudia, I understand what has happened here.'

For a second Claudia feels a euphoric wave wash through her – to be understood, so quickly! She realises how she has missed that sense of quick comprehension which she felt in the earliest days with Lawrence, lost amid a sea of hints not taken and questions misunderstood.

'I understand and I think it's entirely reasonable that you want to speak to me about it.'

'Reasonable?'

'For you to worry that Inês would . . .'

'Would?'

'Well, that I might be attracted to her. Or she to me.'

'What?' Claudia pulls her hand free of Lawrence's grasp.

'But, darling, there's absolutely nothing there. I mean of course I can't control what Inês feels – and there's something predictable about . . .'

'Lawrence. I slept with Inês.'

'What?'

'I slept with Inês. Last night. After the swimming. This morning.'

'Darling, what are you talking about? Slept as in . . .?'

'Jesus Christ, Lawrence.' Claudia shifts her position so that she is looking straight at him. His face is a study in incomprehension. 'Inês and I had sex with each other, at about half past midnight this morning. By the folly. Will that do?'

'By the *folly*? But you're not . . . Inês is gay.'

'Yes, I know.'

'That's a restored eighteenth-century building.'

'Lawrence. I've been . . . sort of transfixed by her since she arrived. We went swimming. I kissed her. And then . . .'

Lawrence looks in the direction of the pool, as if the evidence of the kiss might still somehow survive.

'Darling, this is a joke.'

'Stop saying that.'

'But it's not possible.'

'Stop saying that. Why is it not possible?'

'You're not a lesbian is why it's not possible!'

'But it happened, Lawrence. You may think it's not possible that it happened, but it did.'

'Oh, come on, Claudia. Inês is a beautiful woman! And she's what – ten years younger than you? If not more!'

'What are you saying, Lawrence?'

'I'm saying it's fucking ridiculous! You're very nearly fifty years old, you're married, you're a *mother*, Claudia, please don't forget that—'

'None of those things, Lawrence, none of those things have anything to do with what I felt for Inês. What I feel for her. Or she for me.'

'But how can she . . .? I mean, are you sure that she really . . .'

'That she what, Lawrence? That she really wants me?' Claudia is standing now, speaking loudly and quickly. 'Someone as old, and motherly, and beyond desire as you apparently think I am?'

Lawrence casts an anguished glance behind them towards the low fence. 'Claudia, please. Keep your voice down. The Bradburys are back from Spain today.'

'Lawrence, look at me.' Claudia comes closer to Lawrence's chair, standing directly in front of him. Lawrence is hunched in his seat, diminished. For once Claudia seems to tower over him. He looks up.

'You don't think it's possible that someone like Inês could desire me, is that it?'

'I didn't mean that.'

'I think you did.'

'Look, Claudia . . .'

Claudia walks back to her chair and sits down, brushing her hair back from her face. 'Lawrence, I can endure you fucking your students.'

He looks baffled in a way that surprises Claudia. She had expected a crumbling, or a defensive denial, not an expression of total shock.

But Claudia says, 'Don't lie any more. I know. About Angela. Your student. I saw her by the gate.'

Lawrence's face creases as his scrambling brain tries to separate out the several strands.

'I don't have a student called Angela.'

'The girl with the long black leather coat. She came to the house.'

'No one . . . That was Phoebe. You know, my PhD student.

316

She . . . for goodness' sake, I am not having an affair with Phoebe.'

Claudia looks deep into Lawrence's face and sees that this statement is true.

'So tell me who Angela is.'

'I don't know anyone called Angela.'

'Lawrence. I read her text. You fucked her in your office. She was very clear on what you did together. There was no ambiguity.'

'You looked through my phone?'

Claudia shakes her head. 'That's irrelevant, Lawrence.'

Lawrence looks to the ground.

'Who is Angela?'

'She's the Danby Visiting Fellow in Medieval Studies.'

'Oh, for fuck's sake . . .' Claudia is almost laughing. 'This fucking university. So you know her from work? For how long?'

'I don't know.'

'A long time? Years?'

Lawrence is silent.

Claudia says, 'All right. So now I know about Angela and about God knows who else.'

'Claudia, I can say with absolute certainty that there has never been anyone else.'

'"Anyone else" apart from me, or "anyone else" apart from Angela?'

'Of course, *you*, darling,' he says but even Lawrence can't make this lie seem truthful. His words are exhausted; he speaks them pitifully into the grass at his feet.

'The problem for us, Lawrence, is that I know you are lying.'

He looks up sharply. 'But for Christ's sake, you've just told me you've been unfaithful!'

'Once. And I told you today, the next day. That is not the same as serial adultery, over *years*.'

'I'm not a serial adulterer!'

'Lawrence, I know that you are. But you know what? You know the brutal irony amid all this? I could put up with Angela and the certainty of others about whom I just don't want to know. I could in time work out a way to deal with that. I was beginning to do that. What is intolerable is not your tedious, predictable infidelity, but your . . . sense of me.'

'But, darling, I think you're—'

'Your contempt for me.'

'You'll always be, let us say . . .'

'Don't fucking say "let us say". You coward. You equivocating coward. Why can't you look at life in the eye? I won't be the person you think I am, Lawrence. I won't reduce myself to that. How dare you. How *dare* you! You used to be so proud of me. God knows neither of us is twenty-five any more but I am not going to spend the next twenty-five years surviving on the crumbs of what you have left over for me, Lawrence. It's not enough.'

'Claudia. Please listen. I am sorry – about Angela. I hope you know that it's over with her. I told her last week that it was finished. She accepted that. I can reconfirm that next week.'

'*Reconfirm?*'

'I could do it today. I can text her. In any case, she's going back to America. And we can – we can talk about it all. If you want to. But this – this *thing* with Inês. You must see that you are making a fool of yourself. It's just ridiculous. I mean, come on, middle-aged housewife has lesbian affair as some perverse expression of her mid-life crisis, it's such a cliché—'

'A cliché, is it? A *cliché*?' Claudia gets up from her chair. She is speaking loudly now and as she takes a breath she feels her heart miss a beat and then thump hard, out of time, as though her anger might simply be too much for her body to carry; but to feel this rage and to express it directly at its object is such a rare occurrence for Claudia that she feels drunk on it, drunk and elated and utterly lucid and dizzyingly powerful.

'I'll tell you what's a fucking cliché, Lawrence, and it's not a woman reaching for the one bit of pleasure within her grasp. Reaching for her last chance at happiness. It's a middle-aged male academic who professes every progressive cause in the world and behaves like a selfish cunt.'

Lawrence has got to his feet while Claudia is talking, and she is looking up at him now.

He takes hold of Claudia's upper arms, bringing his face close to hers so that she can feel his breath against her when he speaks.

'You fucking bitch.' His words are quiet but exact: they have the quality of precise aggression. 'Have you any idea what it feels like after years of . . .' Lawrence stops suddenly. He drops Claudia's arms and she stumbles backwards.

'Go on, Lawrence. Please do go on. After years of what?'

Lawrence moves to the wrought-iron bench and pushes it over, but it is heavier than he anticipated and only tips backwards gradually: the gesture is one of impotence, not power. He turns back to Claudia.

'You want me to say it? All right then, after years of feeling like fucking me is another of your weekly chores, something you do to keep the peace at home. Bins out. Dishwasher on. Bed. Is it any wonder I need to look elsewhere for a bit of

319

excitement? For passion? Is it too much to ask? It's not me who made the decision to be unfaithful. It's the last thing I wanted. You forced me into it.'

'Fuck you, Lawrence.' Claudia takes another step backwards, more steadily this time. 'Don't make this about me. This isn't about me, it's about you and your narcissism and that's it, really, isn't it – the person you have always loved most is yourself. It wouldn't even occur to you to think about what this would be like for me. I bet you've had her here in my house.'

'Your house, is it? Your house?'

Lawrence's voice is raised now but Claudia's is louder when she says to him, 'Yes, Lawrence, in my house. My house, *mine*. Our home. Where we live with our child, our family.'

Claudia goes over to the bowl on the table, lifts it, then smashes it down. The bowl breaks; cashew nuts fall everywhere.

Lawrence says, 'Jesus Christ, Claudia.' And then, assessing the damage, 'That's from the pottery in Burnham Market.'

It takes several seconds for blood to appear.

Claudia says, 'Oh fuck,' and presses her handkerchief to the wound at the base of her thumb.

Lawrence moves closer and starts to say something, but Claudia says, 'It's fine. It's not deep. I'll sort it out. Just . . . stay away from me. Don't touch me.'

There is a long pause while they hold each other's gaze, and it is Lawrence who looks away first. He goes to the table and leans on it as though in need of support.

'Claudia, I love you. I am sorry, truly sorry, for what I have done. I don't want to lose you.'

'Lawrence . . .' Claudia thinks, I will always remember this conversation, every time I am here at this spot, looking at this view, I will remember what he said and how he spoke, I will not be able to forget. '. . . I think we've reached a point of no return, don't you? I think we've reached a point of clarity.'

'What does that mean?'

But at that moment Claudia is conscious of a figure by the wall where the door leads from the lawn to the courtyard. Lawrence, catching Claudia's gaze, turns in that direction, and both of them see Ash, standing in the doorway. There is a long moment's silence in which no one moves, and then Ash steps forward onto the grass.

'Ash!' Lawrence and Claudia speak at the same time and alongside her surprise Claudia feels a rising tide of laughter at the turn the conversation has taken, as though they are all three actors on a stage, performing an opera in a stately home.

Lawrence stands and walks across the lawn at speed. Claudia thinks he is going to embrace his friend, but by the time Lawrence reaches Ash he is shouting.

'Christ, what the fuck is this, a group intervention? You've come back to hammer me for another round about what a morally defunct person I am, is that it? Are you two going to undertake a joint attack on me now? My wife, and my oldest friend? After everything – was that the plan, Ash, eh? She does her bit and then you do yours?' By this point Lawrence is standing opposite Ash, who can see tears in his eyes. Ash reaches out to his friend, but Lawrence pushes past him.

'I'm not staying for this. You can go fuck yourself.'

Lawrence's footsteps across the courtyard die away, and at the sound of the front door slamming, Ash and Claudia stare at one another and then Claudia drops her head and clasps her injured hand with the other. Ash sees the handkerchief is red.

'Jesus, what happened, Claudia? Your hand.'

Claudia opens her palm. Two streaks of blood trickle down her wrist.

'I broke a bowl.'

Ash's silence feels like doubt.

Claudia looks at him. 'He didn't do this, Ash. I smashed a bowl in anger.'

'Do you need A&E?'

'No. I just need to clean it and put on a plaster. Maybe a bandage. That's all.'

'Let me help. Come on.'

Ash puts his arm round Claudia's shoulder; she draws her injured arm towards her body, and they follow the route back to the house that Lawrence took moments before.

'I'm sorry to have interrupted you. I meant to apologise – to you and to Lawrence.'

'It doesn't matter. Thank you.'

For the first time in a decade Ash feels a strong desire for a cigarette.

'I couldn't help but overhear,' he begins. 'Are you sure you're okay? Not just your hand, I mean – everything.'

Two bright streaks of blood are running from Claudia's wrist to her elbow.

'I'll be fine. It's been . . . it's been quite a week.'

'Claudia, I didn't know about this affair. He didn't tell me about it.'

She turns to face him. 'Lawrence likes to keep his life compartmentalised. I think part of his moral outrage is because the person he is with me – the person he is with you too, perhaps – simply does not have affairs. That person is a

322

family man who loves his wife and son. It's as though *I'm* the one threatening that, not him. You see?'

Ash nods. 'For what it's worth, I know he loves you very much.'

'If it's love, it has so much other stuff inside it, I don't know what the fuck it means any more.'

There is a pause and Claudia looks beyond Ash to the apple trees. A book is lying on the grass next to a deckchair; broken pieces of a bowl on a white table. She hears the words again in her head: *I know he loves you very much.*

'I think what I have to do now,' she says, 'is to answer that question: how much is it worth?' She looks back at Ash. 'Did you call a cab?'

'Yes, it should be here in a minute.' Ash checks his watch. 'Five minutes.'

'And the others?'

'Deborah and Miles just left for the station. She said to say goodbye and she'll call you. He got a lift with her. I need to get going too or I'll miss my train. Lucy went to pack. I'm not sure about Inês.'

'Right. Look, I must sort this out, I'm sorry not to see you off. Have a good journey home.'

Ash says, 'Let me help you back inside.' The two of them walk across the courtyard, his arm around her, as if her injuries were more serious than the cut to her hand.

Outside the house, Claudia raises her uninjured hand to Ash's face, her fingers just touching his hair. They smile at one another. Claudia leans up and kisses Ash's cheek as he draws her in for a hug. She smells his cologne, like sandalwood, and beneath it a hint of chewing gum and sweat. She closes her eyes and for a fraction of a second Claudia thinks: what if I had wanted this man, instead of that one? What if I had married Ash, and not Lawrence?

Claudia pushes opens the heavy front door and Ash crosses to the tree near the gate, where he's left his bags. He stands for a moment, turning things over in his mind, thinking of the piece he's been working on this summer: 'Et In Arcadia Ego: Power Abuse in the Academy'. He had thought of opening with an anonymised case study of Lawrence's affair with a junior colleague from 1999. Ash had met the woman at the time and it hadn't been hard to track her down, even all these years later. Lawrence had not only had a sexual relationship with the woman but had also co-written a book of essays with her during the course of which, she has recently alleged to Ash, he'd taken her work and passed it off as his own. The woman involved had left Cambridge, and then academia entirely, soon afterwards. Ash thinks about the disturbing fragments he just heard from Claudia and Lawrence, screamed across the lawn of this eighteenth-century manor. He is convinced there are other bad things going on, too: that there is a pattern of behaviour, and not just a series of incidents. He can find this out. He feels suddenly certain that everything that Lawrence has – the achievements which Ash feels, he admits, as stinging opposites to his own merely moderate success – is built on deceit.

Ash pulls his phone from his pocket and is about to start a new voice note when he pauses and lowers his hand. He looks around the courtyard. The house and its history. The door to the garden. Above everything, the swaying high trees. He has a sudden conviction that he needs to join things up. He thinks, there is a bigger project here. For a year or more he's had the idea of writing a novel, but he kept this covert, even to himself. His mention of it to Miles at the pool on Thursday was the first time he spoke the thought out loud. But now, in a flash of revelation that is as sudden as it is decisive, Ash is sure: the story of what he's seen. Ash thinks of Lawrence's words: *what have you learnt this week?*

In his bedroom, Lawrence looks around the room and at its comfortable disordered clutter of clothes and books and papers, empty mugs by his side of the bed and, by Claudia's, a picture of him and Tristan in cricket whites, arms around one another. He sits down on the bed. He remembers the day they bought it: Claudia had insisted when they moved into her parents' bedroom that she would not inherit their bed, and had found this one at a local auction house. They had driven out to the middle of nowhere to bid for it and had come back victorious and with a Victorian umbrella stand, a portable writing desk, and a pair of vases shaped like fish, all of which Claudia had fallen in love with and he had bought for her, enjoying the impulsive extravagance. Until the bed was delivered a week later, they had slept on a mattress on the floor, wearied every day by the effort of moving but still, he remembers, reaching for each other every night, and such desire he had felt for her then, and she for him. Suddenly exhausted, Lawrence pulls back the covers from the bed and lies down, face into Claudia's pillows, seeking the familiar scent of her perfume and her body and, finding it, he closes his eyes.

'You don't have to wait with me. It'll be here in a minute.' Ash stands at the main gate and scans the road for his taxi.

'I don't mind. I'd rather be out here than in there.' Lucy glances back towards the house. 'I can't face packing anyway.' She traces the ironwork of the gate with her hand.

'Not looking forward to going home?'

'No, I am, really. It's just the transition, I think. Being here has been a lovely kind of unreality. Until this evening.' She pauses, then gives an effortful smile. 'And I'm dreadful for scattering my possessions everywhere. I always hate packing.'

'Here it is.' A black Toyota Prius turns the corner; Lucy watches as the car approaches with its near silent glide and Ash shoulders his rucksack. 'Bye, Lucy. It's been lovely to see you. Don't – don't pay too much attention to what Deborah said. She's all over the place. People say weird things when they're in shock.'

Lucy makes a dismissive gesture as if to say it doesn't matter.

Ash raises his hand to the driver and the Prius pulls to a halt beside them. The driver gets out and opens the boot, and Ash lifts his bag in. As the man returns to the driver's seat, Ash opens the back door and moves to get into the car.

'Ash, wait.' Lucy steps towards the car and places a hand on the open door.

'Hang on a minute – be right with you,' Ash says to the driver and then closes the car door carefully.

'Is everything all right?'

'What is it the princess says at the end of *Love's Labour's Lost*?' Lucy speaks quickly.

'I'm sorry, what?'

'You know, at the end, when the king and all his men say

they will be faithful to the women, but the women aren't sure, and the princess says something like, wait a year, wait a year, and then come back to me? Do you remember?'

'I remember how the play ends,' says Ash, a little tersely. 'The princess tells Ferdinand she doesn't trust his oath and all the men have to wait a year to prove their love. Ferdinand has to go and live in a monastery. I'm not sure I see your point.'

'Right, well, that's not exactly how I remembered it,' says Lucy. 'I just remembered the bit about waiting a year and then coming back.'

'Lucy, I'm still not sure I . . .' Ash lets the sentence fall away. 'You want me to wait a year and then . . .?'

'Oh, God.' Lucy covers her face with her hands so that her voice is muffled: 'I am doing this badly. I'm sorry.' She drops her hands and takes a step closer to Ash.

'Don't wait a year. Just wait a bit. Just give me a bit of time to get my head straight and the summer holidays out of the way, and then . . . come back.'

Ash takes Lucy in his arms and kisses her lips. He can feel Lucy's body close against him and her hand on the back of his neck. When he opens his eyes, she is smiling widely back at him.

'You should go.' Lucy gives Ash a little push towards the car and clasps her hands in front of her. 'You'll miss your train.'

For a moment Ash looks above her head and has a far-away expression and Lucy, puzzled for a second, realises he is trying to remember something. Then he looks back at her, and says, 'You that way: we this way.'

'For now.'

Ash gets into the back seat of the car and slams the door

shut. As the car pulls away, he can see Lucy in the rear-view mirror, leaning against the railings and watching him leave.

The invitation had said 'Informal dress: no gowns', and because Inês had appreciated receiving a handwritten card in her new, temporary pigeon-hole at Gonville & Caius, she'd made the decision to attend, even though she hadn't known about it before and had planned only to drop off her bags in her bedroom. It's a Caius tradition on Friday evening to have drinks for visiting fellows and graduate students. The idea is that the graduate students can meet the artists, musicians, poets and minor media stars who are offered short-term affiliation with the college in return for giving something back: a series of lectures open to all students; a piano recital; a creative writing workshop; or, in Inês's case, the engraved glass installation.

Inês had chatted for a while to a tiny man who introduced himself as the bursar. He'd made a series of what Inês understood to be jokes, or at least comic observations – that was what his tone had suggested – but since they all seemed to concern the relative age, history and standing of other Cambridge colleges, Inês had no idea what he was saying. The tiny bursar was called away by a flick of the hand from a tall man with a very red face and sweeping white hair who had the affect of significance. For a few pleasant moments, Inês enjoyed standing alone, the solitude, even amid a busy room, a welcome relief after the week of the retreat. This is Inês now: this is where we see her. She looks out of the glass wall at a large square of grass that provides the architectural focus of the college. The square is enclosed by a brick walkway, and then, just beyond, four glass walls that open out onto four different rooms. Inês is thinking about transparency – this college seems to be built from it, all glass and chrome, with the consequence that it feels as if everything can be seen from everywhere. Inês is formulating in her head something about the way transparency gives way to surveillance when she is suddenly conscious of a person beside her who wasn't there a moment before.

'Hello.' A young woman, smiling, bright blonde hair, tattoos on her arm, a glass of wine in her hand.

'Hello,' says Inês, extending her hand. 'I'm Inês.'

'Phoebe.'

'Hello, Phoebe.' Inês takes a wine glass from the silver tray offered by a waiter. 'And who are you?'

'I'm a student. I'm just finishing my PhD. Trying to.'

'Well, let's drink to that. The finishing, more than the trying to.'

They clink glasses.

'Actually,' says Phoebe, 'I came over because I saw you earlier.'

'Here? At the drinks?'

'No, I just got here. It was an hour or so ago. You were getting out of a car by the porter's lodge.'

'That's possible.'

Inês notices how fast the young woman is drinking. She thinks, maybe this is just an English thing.

Phoebe says, 'Sorry. I don't mean to be all stalkery. I noticed your beautiful dress. And then I was planning to come to this drinks thing anyway, and then there you were.'

'Here I am.'

There is a pause and then Inês says, 'I was just thinking

329

about the transparency of this place. The way you can see into all different parts of the building. All the light and glass.'

'Light and glass.' Phoebe takes another sip. 'What is it with power, and light and glass? I always feel like I'm being watched in this part of College. Like a panopticon.'

'Yes, I was thinking that too.' The women look together through the glass wall, which shows the blur of their reflection against the green space beyond.

'Cambridge isn't all that big on transparency.' Phoebe takes a large mouthful of her drink. 'I should know.' She takes another. 'I think we have a friend in common. Lawrence. Lawrence Ayres. You've been staying with him? On that retreat?'

Inês looks at Phoebe. 'How do you know that?'

'I heard – overheard – one of the porters mention you'd come from Hawton. And I know it was the retreat this week. Lawrence has been talking about it for ages. So I just thought – that must be it.'

Inês takes a sip of white wine and waits before speaking.

Phoebe says, 'Do you know a man called Ashane?'

Inês thinks briefly, then shakes her head. 'I don't think so. No. Should I?'

'I think he might have been on the retreat.'

Inês looks blank for a second and then says, 'Oh, you mean Ash. Yes, I do. Well, I mean he was there and I got to know him a bit this week.' She wonders why Phoebe would ask about Ash and suddenly recalls something Miles said about Ash dating younger women. Not as young as this girl, surely? 'May I ask why? Is he a friend of yours?'

'No. I've not met him. I don't know anything about him, really. It's just that he emailed me this morning and introduced himself as a colleague of Lawrence. He said he was staying with him this week, and he was writing an article about academic supervisors. He asked if I knew of any instances of supervisors plagiarising their student's work.'

Inês lowers her glass. There is something happening here which she does not understand.

'Why did he email you?'

Phoebe shrugs.

Inês says, 'And what did you say?'

'I've not replied yet. I only got the message this morning.'

Phoebe takes a sip.

Inês says, 'But do you?'

Phoebe opens her mouth to reply but before she can say anything there is a shout from behind them – 'Phoebe!' – and both women turn to its source.

Walking towards them is a tall woman in a fitted black dress and high heels which click rapidly as she crosses the room. Inês's first impression is of a jumble of different features: red lipstick and straight white teeth, bare tanned shoulders, one manicured hand holding a wine glass. In Cambridge the invitation to informal clothing has been taken at its word and the approaching woman is by far the most smartly dressed person in the room. Inês notices that several of the older men have turned a little to watch as she makes her way swiftly to where Inês and Phoebe are standing. One of the men is the bursar: his lip curls a little in what Inês takes to be contempt. As the woman gets closer, Inês feels the atmosphere shift and resists the involuntary urge to take a step backwards.

The woman draws Phoebe into an embrace and kisses her cheek.

'Phoebe, I'm so glad you're still here.'

'Oh, me too,' Phoebe says, 'I got here late. I was starting to think I must have missed you. I'd had rather a lot of this.' Phoebe raises her glass.

The woman turns a little towards Inês and smiles.

'This is Inês,' Phoebe continues, 'we literally just met.'

Inês reaches forward to shake the stranger's hand.

'Inês Corval Moreno.'

'Inês, it's a pleasure to meet you. Are you a fellow of the college?'

'Ah no – I'm an interloper. I'm installing a window here next term.'

'You're installing a window?'

'I'm an artist.'

'Oh I see – in that sense.' And then: 'Oh my God, you're *Inês*!' The newcomer stands back and looks Inês up and down in a manner that a less confident woman might find intimidating. 'Well, you are exactly how I would have pictured you. I can't believe I didn't realise.'

'I'm sorry?' Inês's smile is interrogative and the stranger steps closer and pats her reassuringly on the arm.

'Oh no, I'm sorry, that must have sounded impolite. I've heard about you, is all.'

'Heard about me from . . .?'

'From Lawrence Ayres. Lawrence and I go way back.'

Phoebe also steps a little closer and turns to Inês.

'Inês, this is Angela Olson, she was my Masters thesis advisor at the University of Pennsylvania and she's a visiting fellow here. She was the only person I knew in Cambridge when I started.' Phoebe turns to Angela. 'Although in fact you immediately left to go home!'

Angela laughs, 'I come back often enough.'

'I see. A pleasure to meet you, Angela.' Inês takes the final mouthful of tepid wine.

'But it's a coincidence,' Phoebe continues, 'because I was about to tell Inês about Lawrence.'

'About Lawrence?' Angela repeats, looking from one woman's face to the other.

'Just that I know him too. Because Inês has been staying at Hawton, isn't that right?'

'Of course,' says Angela, 'you must have come straight from the retreat.'

'That's right.'

'"The retreat",' Angela repeats the phrase with mock import.

'He's my supervisor,' Phoebe says, 'on my doctorate.'

Inês says, 'And what were you going to tell me, Phoebe? About Ash's question? How are you going to reply to his email?'

Phoebe looks at Inês and then at Angela and then behind them, at the whole room, the dons in gowns and the graduate students and the serving staff in black waistcoats and white shirts, and then Phoebe starts – surprisingly herself with the sudden conviction that this is necessary – to tell both women calmly what Lawrence did to her work.

Chapter Sixteen

Saturday morning

It is a bright sunny late morning. Light pours through the large kitchen window above the sink piled high with pans. Everyone has left – the house is standing empty – and the beautiful sunlight falls unseen across the kitchen floor, the drying rack, the oven, reaching the long wooden table stained with wine glass rings, and half-covering the vase of sunflowers standing in its middle.

Claudia had tidied quickly before she drove to the train station to meet Tristan who is returning from France this morning. He had texted to say the Eurostar had got into London six minutes early, at 10.24 a.m. Tristan had felt so far from them all during the week, but suddenly Claudia feels a deep longing to see her son.

Hawton Manor is an old house. The rafters click and the walls breathe as the building shifts slightly in its skin. In the hall, a messy pile of shoes and boots stands beneath a row of pegs from which hang jackets, hoodies and three bike helmets. Two battered straw hats rest on the windowsill which looks out onto the courtyard, across which, right now, the peacock picks a path in the direction of the garden. The dark wooden bench, which was once a seventeenth-century chest, stands against the wall facing the front door; the lozenge-shaped engraving cut into its seat is obscured by a tangle of white wires, plugs, chargers and adapters. The door off the hall is open and leads to a long, darker, cooler corridor: the piano and stool; an old typewriter on a small table illuminated by the window light; the portrait of Mabel and various bits of art made throughout the course of Tristan's childhood; and, at the end, the foot of the stairs.

It would be tempting to say the house is waiting for Claudia and Lawrence and Tristan to return, but the kind of deep patience in its near stillness is indifferent to any human timetable. An hour passes. A century passes. Another hour. Owners come and go. It's 1865. It's 2022. It's 1726. The rafters click and the walls breathe and sunlight pours in through the window. The house makes its tiny accommodations and time vaults past generations. At the station, the train from London pulls in and Claudia clasps her hands tight as the doors open.

Epilogue

Eve looks through the neat metal twists of the iron gate, across the courtyard overgrown with weeds taller than her, towards the high window in the main building. The sun reflects brightly off the glass.

The heat is intense. The winding lane behind her is deserted. Mid-summer silence.

'It's a total wreck, Dad.'

Tristan is standing next to her, calculating. 'Twenty-nine years ago. That's when I last saw it. 2028. That's what – exactly twice your lifetime? Christ. It's so different. But also the same.'

'2028.' Eve says the number tentatively, under her breath, as if trying to identify something only half glimpsed.

Tristan says, 'I went to university that year. And then we sold Hawton while I was there – the following Christmas. It was a long time ago. Long before you were born.'

'So no one has lived here since?'

'The people who bought it lived here for years. I don't know what's happened. Maybe they died. Maybe they sold up.'

Tristan looks up at the house and points to a window on the top floor. 'That was my bedroom, there.' Eve pushes her face against the gate, trying to see. 'Mum and Dad's overlooked the garden. The swimming pool. It feels like another world.'

There is a clunking metal sound and then a high squeak.

'Dad! What are you doing?'

'Come on! If I can get through, you can.' Tristan forces the gate as wide as it will go and starts to squeeze his body through the gap. He pushes the tall weeds and grass to each side to create a path across the courtyard – or what once was a courtyard – but it's so overgrown, and the weeds spring back so quickly, that after five steps only the top of his head is visible.

'Dad! I can't see you! Wait for me.'

They reach an archway cut into a wall and, passing through, come to the edge of a long lawn. The grass hasn't been cut for an age but it's not as overgrown as the courtyard. The lawn runs away towards a large pond which has a small grey stone building next to it, perched on the bank. There is a sense of deep calm: of the garden standing as it has done for hundreds of years.

'Dad, look!'

A peacock emerges from the far woods, followed by a second. Because of the state of the grass, the two birds pick their way along the low brick wall which runs down the edge of the lawn.

Tristan gives a shout of laughter. 'The peacocks are still here! Or their distant descendants. I don't know how long they live for. Look, that's the folly your grandpa had restored.'

'What's a folly?'

He points at the little building. 'There's a plaque in there with his name on it. I bet it's still there.'

'Your family were obsessed with labelling things. Is that the swimming pool? It looks . . . disgusting.'

'No, that's the pond. I used to swim there sometimes but Mum and Dad didn't like it. The pool is that way. Let's go and have a look.'

Fighting their way through the undergrowth, the pair cross the lawn towards the terrace. Its stone steps are no longer visible, consumed entirely by greenery. Beyond them is the pool, mostly covered by a large piece of tarpaulin which is held in place with house bricks and is sagging and tattered with age. Surrounding the pool is an elaborate mosaic of tiles, some chipped away, flashes of colour just visible among the moss and leaves.

Tristan bends to pick up a leaf from the grass – turns it over – then lets it fall back to the ground.

After a moment he says, '"Then a cloud passed, and the pool was empty."'

Eve looks the sky, and then at her father.

'It's a quotation,' says Tristan. 'Eliot. Your grandmother loved that poem.'

'Well,' says Eve, practical, 'I can't imagine anyone wanting to swim in there.'

'It used to be very beautiful.' Tristan leads the way back across the lawn until they are standing near the water's edge. 'How about the pond instead?'

'You've got to be joking. It stinks.' Eve wrinkles her nose and turns away. When she looks back, her father is unbuttoning his shirt.

'*Dad.* No. You can't. This is so embarrassing.'

'No one is here. It can't be embarrassing.'

Tristan takes off his shirt and starts to unlace his shoes.

'*Dad.*' Eve covers her face with her hands and makes retching noises.

'It's all right. I'm perfectly decent.' Still wearing his shorts, Tristan picks his way through the rough foliage that clings to the edge of the pond. The ground feels damp and cool beneath his feet. He edges nearer, holding on to a tree stump as he gets to the point where the bank slopes into the water.

'Dad, I don't think you should.'

'I'll never get this chance again,' Tristan calls back over his shoulder, and before his daughter can reply he is in the water.

'God it's so warm. And it feels like ink. Or silk.'

He wades deeper and then swims towards the middle of the pond.

Eve laughs. 'You're insane.'

As Tristan swims towards the centre he can feel what might be weeds or even fish against his legs. In the middle of the pond he stretches his feet down as far as they can go with his head above water but they don't reach the bottom. 'It's deep,' he says, and then, 'Eve! Look!', and he raises his body up before ducking completely under water, forcing himself down head first.

Eve watches from the bank.

She half laughs.

His feet disappear last and then the choppy water settles into a flat surface.

There is silence, and stillness, and heat.

Eve waits. Seconds pass. Eve says, 'Dad! That's enough', and she reaches for a branch to help her move to the edge of the water.

She calls, 'Dad!', louder now, her laughter gone.

And then there's a splash, two or three metres from where

he went under, and Tristan thrusts up suddenly through the water, like something being born.

'It's pitch-black under there. My God. It's another world.'

Tristan climbs out of the water, his legs and soon his arms covered with mud, rubbing the back of his hand across his face.

Eve says, 'I can't believe you just did that.'

'Eve, this place. I can't tell you what it's like to be back.'

'Is it nice? I mean, is it nice to be here?'

'Nice? No. Deeply strange. Sad. Joyful. I'm glad you can see it.'

There is a chair and a table inside the folly and Eve sits down. Tristan stands directly in the sun to dry himself off, using his shirt as a towel.

'Are you just going to go to the party covered in mud?'

Tristan looks at his legs and shrugs.

'It'll dry off.' He checks his watch, which he never takes off. 'God, we are going to be late.'

A few minutes later, the lane, silent in the midday heat, is suddenly filled with the sound of Tristan's car starting up.

Tristan says, 'Thanks for tolerating that, Eve.'

A brief smile flickers across Eve's face. She pulls her seat belt across but pauses before clicking it into place.

'Dad – wait. Give me one second.'

Eve gets out, walks to the gates, back through the courtyard and the entrance to the lawn. She stands on the grass, looking towards the pond and the folly. She closes her eyes for a moment. She concentrates hard. She tries to imagine her grandmother walking across the lawn, all the happy scenes this garden must have seen, then tries to bring her dad, or a fourteen-year-old version of him, into her mind. She focuses

340

hard and holds her breath and tries to make it – she works out the years – 2022. She tries, but she can't: it is gone. She opens her eyes and looks at the high trees and hears a woodpecker tapping and smells the air. She feels the heat on her neck and her scalp. She takes her camera from her pocket and frames a shot of the lawn, the pond, the little building clinging to the bank. The camera clicks, and Eve runs back to the car.

A week later, Eve prints out the picture. She puts it in a frame which sits on her bedroom desk for four years and then, when she's away at university in France, her mother tidies Eve's room and the photo is moved with a stack of papers of uncertain significance to a suitcase which is placed in the attic. Around this time, Hawton Manor is acquired by an upmarket hotel chain and renovations to turn it into a country spa hotel are begun but abandoned after its foundations are found to be damaged. Ten years later, after Tristan's death, the case in the attic is moved, along with various other junk, to Eve's home in Norwich, where it is never opened but sits at the back of a cupboard in a cellar. It is a hard winter and the roof at Hawton falls in during a storm as the Cam rises and the city floods. Ivy grips the frames of the long-broken kitchen windows and mould blooms on the bedroom walls. The place resembles a ransacked monastery in the 1530s. Thirty years later, looking for something else, Eve opens the case and turning the papers from long ago sees the print and puts it on a bookshelf in her living room, liking the image but not quite knowing where it came from. Eve's daughter, visiting with her two young children, asks Eve where this place is and Eve looks close and has a memory of heat, and maybe her father, but nothing sharper. Hawton Manor is demolished that summer and its surrounding woodlands gradually cleared for building. The graveyard around the church is narrowed to make space for an access road: old gravestones are lined up against the exterior church wall, including one in the shape of a cross with italic letters: 'We are what you will be, we were what you are.' Twenty-eight years later, in the weeks after Eve's death, her Norwich house is cleared and the contents are sold and the photo ends up in a second-hand furniture shop in Ely. The frame has been lost; it's just a loose print. At around this time, a university laboratory is built on the grounds of Hawton, nothing of the original remaining except the gradual curve of the land (now a car park) around what used to be the pond, and the memory of the manor's longest residents in the name Peacock Technology. The print sits in a box of loose images – portraits of nameless couples and groups, photographs of sunsets and cathedrals and bridges and market towns and mountains – for twelve years until the box is bought by a young woman who, looking to occupy her children during the Christmas holidays, spreads out the different pictures she has bought for almost nothing on the living-room floor, on a day in December in 2141 with the snow falling, and the children take scissors and glue and snip and paste the images to make collages. After the children have gone to bed, the mother places the two finished collages on the mantelpiece and picks up the unused pictures, including the one of a lawn and a pond and a building clinging to a bank somewhere deep in the past, and drops them in the fire.